THE
TREASURE OF THE
SIERRA MADRE

B. TRAVEN

ISHI PRESS
INTERNATIONAL

The Treasure of the Sierra Madre

by B. Traven

First Published in 1927 in Germany
as Der Schatz der Sierra Madre

First Published in English in 1935
by Alfred A. Knopf, Inc.

This Printing in June, 2011
by Ishi Press in New York and Tokyo
with a new foreword by Sam Sloan

ISBN 4-87187-896-1
978-4-87187-896-8

Ishi Press International
1664 Davidson Avenue, Suite 1B
Bronx NY 10453-7877
1-917-507-7226

Printed in the United States of America

The Treasure of the Sierra Madre

Foreword by Sam Sloan

The Treasure of the Sierra Madre is regarded as one of the greatest books ever written. Then, it was made into a movie by the same name, which in turn is regarded as one of the greatest movies ever made.

It is also the source of one of the most often repeated lines ever in movie history. Different versions of this line are repeated so often that it has become part of the English language. In both the book and the movie, it is spoken by the villain, known as "Gold Hat", who is played by Mexican actor Alfonso Bedoya. The line, like most of the lines in the movie, comes directly from the book. It can be found on page 193 of the book, where the bandit says, "We don't need badges. I don't have to show you any stinking badges."

[In this scene, actor Alfonso Bedoya speaks those immortal words, "I don't have to show you any stinking badges."]

Although the movie closely follows the book, there are differences. In the train robbery scene, the bandits led by "Gold Hat" attack the train on horseback, but are fought off by the passengers, including Dobbs, Curtin and Howard. In the book, Dobbs, Howard and Curtin never meet Gold Hat except in the scene where Gold Hat says, "I don't have to show you any stinking badges."

In the book, the train robbery takes place in Chapter 12, on pages 163-169. Dobbs, Curtin and Howard are not on the train. They later learn about the train robbery incident because Cody has read about the incident in the newspapers. The bandits had gotten on the train as passengers and then, after the train had reached the country-side, the bandits had pulled out their guns and had killed most of the adult male passengers.

[Here Gold Hat, one of many bandits, is riding a horse and attempting to rob a train. In the book, the bandits board the train as passengers and, once the train is out in the countryside, they shoot and kill the soldiers there to guard the passengers, rob the passengers and then jump off the train with their loot.]

[One of the most important scenes in the movie. Here, Dobbs throws a glass of water in the face of a young Mexican boy who is pestering him to buy a lottery ticket. Even after having the water thrown in his face, the boy persists and Dobbs finally buys a ticket. The ticket later proves to be a winner, giving the prospectors enough money to go up into the mountains and prospect for gold.

[This scene was shot over and over again to get the right splash of water into the boy's face. It has been remarked that nowadays the director would have been arrested and charged with child abuse. However, the boy loved it and took the glass of water and the cup of coffee Dobbs is drinking from as souvenirs, (which he will probably sell on ebay some day). The boy is Robert Blake, who grew up to be an actor and the star of the TV series "*Baretta*" and was later charged with the murder of his wife.]

When Dobbs and Curtin confront McCormick, who cheated them of their wages, McCormick finally pays them without a fight, realizing they are prepared to beat him if he doesn't.

[Here, McCormick is strolling with a lovely senorita, actress Jacqueline Dalya, who has just asked McCormick to buy her a pair of shoes, showing that McCormick has money. Dobbs and Curtin confront McCormick, demanding to be paid their wages for a week of work. In the book, McCormick finally pays up after being threatened by Dobbs and Curtin. However, in the movie, a fight starts and they take the money, but only the amount owed to them, although McCormick is carrying a much larger stash which they could have taken. This proves that Dobbs and Curtin are honest men.]

In the movie, McCormick refuses to pay and a fight breaks out. The fight scene in the movie was one of the most difficult scenes ever to film and without it the movie would be different.

Here is one of the most important scenes in the movie and one of the reasons why Walter Huston won the Academy Award for Best Supporting Actor. Here Walter Huston is dancing a jig because he has just discovered gold. Huston says that Dobbs is too stupid to realize what is under his feet. Dobbs is about to smash Howard's face in with a rock.

One of the most important scenes in the movie and the subject of correspondence between the author B. Traven and the director John Huston. The mine has just caved in and Dobbs is trapped and injured in the mine. Curtin rushes to save him, but then realizes that if Dobbs dies he gets half of the gold but if Dobbs lives he only gets one-third. He stops to think about this, then turns and starts to go away, but then finally makes up his mind and rushes in to save Dobbs.

[This scene in the movie where the Mexican bandits are made to dig their own graves and then are shot and buried in the graves they have just dug, does not occur in the book. In the book, the bandits are shot while trying to escape.]

All of these changes were made with the approval of the author, B. Traven, even though nobody involved in making the movie was ever able to meet Traven. Traven kept some artistic control over the movie through his agents, who sometimes visited the movie set.

A remarkable fact about the movie is that it has no leading lady. There are only three scenes in the movie where a woman appears, and all are brief. In the first, an elegantly dressed and beautiful young woman passes Dobbs just after he has received a much needed shave and haircut. She then gives Dobbs a sideways glance as she enters the Hotel Oso Negro. After Dobbs has received a small amount of money, by panhandling the man in the white suit (Director John Huston) again, he turns to go to the hotel. It has been suggested that the woman is a prostitute and Dobbs is going into the hotel to enjoy her pleasures, However, there is nothing like this in the book.

In the second scene where a woman appears, McCormick is walking with a beautiful young woman. This is to show that McCormick has money, as beautiful women are not known to spend much time with men who have no money. So, when McCormick claims that he is broke, we know that this is not true.

In the third, Howard has been made the medicine man by a local Indian tribe and is feted by a beautiful young senorita.

As to the absence of women in their lives, when the men are counting their gold and are asking each other what they will do with their money once they reach civilization and reduce it to cash, Dobbs and Curtin stare wistfully off into space. Howard realizes that they are thinking about the women they will get with all the money they will have. Howard warns them not to think of women.

The book contains information about the history of the mine. Howard, Dobbs and Curtin were not the first to discover the mine. There were several previous discoveries of the same mine, over hundreds of years. The Aztecs had worked the mine four centuries earlier, before the first Europeans had arrived. Howard talks about this on pages 66-79 of this book. However, in all those previous cases, the miners had killed each other because of greed, or they had been killed by Indians or bandits. Bones of the dead earlier prospectors were still to be found there. As we will see, almost the same thing ultimately happens to the three prospectors in this movie.

John Huston was asked how he became such a great director when he does very little directing. He replied that the key is in the casting. If you chose the right cast, all you have to do is tell the actors to be themselves.

John Huston is credited with discovering Marilyn Monroe and many other stars. One of the great finds in this movie is the villager here, "El Presidente" played by **Arturo Soto Range**, who appears in many scenes in the movie.

Here, he is telling Gold Hat "Estos burros no son suyos", meaning "These burros are not yours." Gold Hat replies, "Why don't you believe that they are ours? Do you think that we are bandits?" "Exactly this", answers El Presidente. He knows this because he had sold the same burros to the three prospectors earlier in the movie.

He also sees that one of the bandits is wearing the boots of Dobbs. He realizes that these three bandits have killed Dobbs and are also the bandits who robbed the train. The three bandits are arrested and put in jail and later taken out and executed.

Howard teaches Curtin and Dobbs how to pan for gold.

Curtin goes into the town to buy provisions and another American in the town named Cody, who is called Lacuad in the book, sees him buying a large quantity of provisions and realizes that he must have found gold. So, he follows Curtin up into the mountains and then demands that the prospectors take him in as a partner. The prospectors decide to kill him instead. Here, just as Dobbs is about to shoot him, Cody points out the bandits who are on their way up the mountain to attack them.

In the shoot-out that follows, Cody is killed. They open his belongings and find a letter from his wife. This is one of the great ironies in the movie. They had thought that Cody was coming to steal their gold. Turns out that Cody was a good guy with a wife and small child waiting for him back in Dallas.

At the end of the movie Curtin decides to go to Dallas to visit the wife, inform her that her husband is dead, and possibly to hook up with her.

Bruce Bennett (1906-2007) who plays Cody in the movie was a legitimate athlete who won the silver medal for shotput in the 1928 Olympic Games. He lived by far the longest of any adult in the movie, dying in 2007 at the age of 101 !!!!)

This minor, insignificant scene is one of the most talked-about in the movie. The photo credits say that the girl in this scene is Ann Sheridan (1915–1967), a famous actress. However, the girl in the movie does not look like her.

Right after seeing her, Dobbs again encounters the man in the white suit (Director John Huston) and asks him for money again. The man in the white suit complains that Dobbs has asked him for money three times that day. Dobbs promises not to do it again. The man says, "Just to make sure you keep yopur promise, here's another peso". Dobbs then turns and follows the girl into Hotel Oso Negro.

Here, the girl walks past and then gives Dobbs a furtive glance while entering the Hotel Oso Negro.

Dobbs saying, "You keep your watch. I'll keep my gun". Howard then shoots the watch with his pistol. The watch was undoubtedly part of the loot stolen in the train robbery. This comes just before those famous words, "I don't have to show you any stinking badges", most often misquoted as "I don't need no stinking badges."

Here, the man in the white suit (Director John Huston) gives Dobbs money for the third time today, after Dobbs has promised not to ask him again.

The water-hole scene where Dobbs is found by the bandits

who are preparing to kill him and chop off his head, just to get his burros. This one scene which lasts only a few minutes required seven days to film, showing the painstaking detail that went into this movie to make every scene exactly right.

This is the final scene in the movie. Howard cackles outrageously and breaks into a maniacal laugh. Curtin is wondering what is so funny. Howard explains that all the gold has blown away. "The gold has gone back to where we found it." Ten months of hard work are down the drain. Curtin finally sees the humor in this and starts laughing too.

The greatest mystery of *The Treasure of the Sierra Madre* concerns the identity of the author, B. Traven. B. Traven wrote twelve novels and numerous short stories. Nobody knows who he was and great efforts have been made to find out. Life Magazine once offered a $5,000 reward to anybody who could prove the identity of B. Traven. The reward has never been claimed.

Many, perhaps even most, published authors use pen names for various reasons. Usually, their real names eventually become known or revealed as their works become popular. Authors who keep their identity a secret have a good reason to do so.

I am among those who believe that William Shakespeare was the name of a mere actor and that the plays under the Shakespeare name were written by somebody else. In that case, there was an obvious reason for his anonymity. The plays of Shakespeare often contain attacks on the monarchy and the king, and the author might have lost his head, had his identity become known.

Charles Lutwidge Dodgson may have written under the name Lewis Carroll because, in his great work, "Alice in Wonderland", The Queen of Hearts bore a clear resemblance to Queen Victoria. Dodgson must have feared that Queen Victoria would say "Off with his head" with respect to him. Fortunately, however, Queen Victoria liked Alice in Wonderland, and so Dodgson made his identity known.

The real name of George Eliot was Mary Anne Evans. She used a male name because she feared that a female author would not be taken seriously.

There are many theories about the identity of B. Traven. People who study this are known as "Travenologists". It seems certain that B. Traven was a left-winger, possibly a Communist. This is apparent from his books, although his political observations were left out of the movie.

I have a theory that nobody else has yet suggested, which that B. Traven was actually a woman. The motivation is obvious. This is a novel about three extremely macho men. One would never think that a woman would write such a work, and had it become known the work might not have been taken seriously. I find support for this theory in some stylistic factors in the book. The author spends 12 pages describing the interior of the Hotel Oso Negro, pages 4-16. Yet, the Hotel Oso Negro is not central to the plot. Women, due to their nesting instinct, pay more attention to interior design than men do.

Later, the author makes the comment that no women would want to be associated with men like these, as they are scruffy and probably smelly. This too seems to be the sort of observation that a woman, but not a man, would make.

It is also the fine structure and detail of the writing itself that makes me think that a woman wrote it. Women in general make better writers than men.

This book was first published in Germany in 1927 as "Der Schatz der Sierra Madre". This has led many to conclude that B. Traven was German. Perhaps he had even fled Germany to get away from the Nazis. Perhaps this explains the reason he kept his identity hidden. Perhaps he was a fugitive from justice or even an illegal alien and for this reason did not want his identity made known.

The book was first published in English in 1935. Thus, it seems that the original version was German and the English version was a mere translation. Traven himself however stated that he was American, not German, and the original book was in English.

There are three persons who must have known the true identity of B. Traven:

Esperanza López Mateos, sister of the man who was President of Mexico from 1958 to 1964, translated *The Treasure of the Sierra Madre* into Spanish and represented B. Traven in negotiations for the movie rights to his books during the 1940s. She must have met him. However, she committed suicide in 1951, so any information she had was lost.

After her death, her place was taken by Rosa Elena Luján, who published biographical articles about B. Traven.

During the pre-production of *The Treasure of the Sierra Madre* , director John Huston corresponded with B. Traven but his efforts to meet him in person were rebuffed. Finally, Traven agreed to meet him at Hotel Bamer in Mexico City, Mexico. John Huston traveled to Mexico to meet him, but Traven did not appear at the designated place. Later however a man who identified himself as Hal Croves appeared in Huston's hotel room, and said that he was authorized to negotiate on behalf of B. Traven. Huston assumed that Croves was Traven himself, although Croves denied it.

During the shooting of *The Treasure of the Sierra Madre* , on the Hollywood movie sound stage, Croves appeared again and was paid a salary of $500 per week. However, during the final stages of the filming, the production manager reduced the salary of Croves to $100 per week and Croves angrily disappeared and did not return.

Croves later married Rosa Elena Luján. Hal Croves died in Mexico City on 26 March 1969. On the same day, his wife announced at a press conference that her husband's real name was Traven Torsvan Croves, and that he had been born in Chicago on 3 May 1890. That seemed to end the controversy, but later she made contradictory statements, so the controversy was re-kindled.

The controversy about the identity of B. Traven seemed settled except for the fact that little was known about Hal Croves. The birth records of Chicago do not show anybody by that name being born there. Hal Croves seems to have been just another of the many fake names that B. Traven used, so concluding that B. Traven was the same person as Hal Croves leads us nowhere. Another pseudonym was Ret Marut, a German stage actor and anarchist. The real name of Ret Marut is not known either.

When I reprint a book, I make great efforts to obtain the original hard-cover first edition. There are several reasons for this. One is the first edition usually contains the best quality type-face and production. Later, as the book is reprinted in soft cover, it contains increasingly fuzzy copies of the original.

Secondly, in reprinting there are often small editorial changes. The new editors will often claim a copyright on whatever changes they have made, however small.

In this case, I have used the original hard cover 1935 edition of *The Treasure of the Sierra Madre*. This is the only one I have ever been able to find.

There have been many reprints. The most commonly available reprints are from the Time, Inc. book edition, which came out at the time of the movie in 1948. The type was reset for this edition. It has 423 pages, whereas the original had 366 pages. This is because the text in the Time version is narrower with less characters per line. The original has 56 to 60 characters to a line and 34 lines to a page. The Time Inc. version has 50 characters in a line and 29 lines in a page. Also, the type fonts are different.

None of this affects the copyright. Fonts, type-faces and color are not copyrightable. However, words are. I have not found any changes in the words of the text in the Time, Inc. version, but some might be found after a thorough search. Time Inc. did include a new preface in their version. Of course, I did not use their preface. I wrote my own (much better) preface.

Hollywood can do amazing things by getting us to believe the unbelievable. For example, the most famous Bogart performance of all is in the movie Casablanca, where Bogart does not even appear to be acting. Watching that movie, we become convinced that the nearly impossible is true. We believe that a tall, blond Swedish girl, Ingrid

Bergman, is hopelessly in love with a short, ugly man, Humphrey Bogart, who is three inches shorter and 16 years older than she is. In order to make this impossible thing seem possible, Bogart wore three inches high platform shoes when standing next to Bergman to make it appear that he is slightly taller than she is. The result is so convincing that movie goers often believe that a real affair was going on between them and they were sleeping together between takes. Even Bogart's wife, Loren Bacall, got jealous.

The reality was that they had never previously met and did not even like each other. They met for the first time on the first day of the shooting, and Bergman famously asked the director, "Which man am I supposed to be in love with -- I don't know how to play my character."

In *The Treasure of the Sierra Madre*, many viewers will doubt the probability of three Americans going to Mexico to prospect for gold. However, the story is far from impossible. As to the probability or improbability of the story, it must be recalled that when Hernán Cortés conquered Mexico in 1519, he found large quantities of gold in Moctezuma's palace.

Nowadays we think of Mexico as a poor country and the United States of America as a rich country, but Mexico was fully developed and a rich country long before the first development of North America. The first permanent colony in what became the USA was in 1607, nearly a hundred years after the conquest of Mexico. The United States of America was not crossed by land until the Lewis and Clark Expedition of 1805, amazingly three hundred years after the development of Mexico. The famous California Gold Rush of 1849 took place more than three hundred years after the discovery of gold in Mexico.

Mexican coins made of gold and silver set the standard for world currency, starting in 1497, especially the **gold**

doubloons and *"pieces of eight"* starting in the 15th century. These coins set the standard for world currency and were legal tender in the United States of America and used to back the United States dollar. Even as far away as China, Mexican coins were the standard currency. Mexico was the richest country in the world prior to the Twentieth Century.

Thus, the idea of three Americans going to Mexico to prospect for gold in 1925 is not as outlandish or improbable as it might seem nowadays. It is only in the last century that America became the richest country and Mexico became one of the poorest countries in the world.

Sam Sloan
San Rafael, California
June 19, 2011

Dobbs saying, "You keep your watch. I'll keep my gun". Howard then shoots the watch with his pistol. The watch was undoubtedly part of the loot stolen in the train robbery., This comes just before those famous words, "I don't have to show you any stinking badges", most often misquoted as "I don't need no stinking badges."

Gold Hat attempting to negotiate the sale of the burros to El Presidente. El Presidente either realizes or is about to realize that these are the same burros he sold to Dobbs, Curtin and Howard earlier in the movie and thus are stolen.

The treasure which you think not worth taking trouble and pains to find, this one alone is the real treasure you are longing for all your life. The glittering treasure you are hunting for day and night lies buried on the other side of that hill yonder.

THE
TREASURE OF THE
SIERRA MADRE

.

I

The bench on which Dobbs was sitting was not so good. One of the slats was broken; the one next to it was bent so that to have to sit on it was a sort of punishment. If Dobbs deserved punishment, or if this punishment was being inflicted upon him unjustly, as most punishments are, such a thought did not enter his head at this moment. He would have noticed that he was sitting uncomfortably only if somebody had asked him if he was comfortable. Nobody, of course, bothered to question him.

Dobbs was too much occupied with other thoughts to take any account of how he was sitting. Just then he was looking for a solution to that age-old problem which makes so many people forget all other thoughts and things. He worked his mind to answer the question: How can I get some money right now?

If you already have some money, then it is easier to make more, because you can invest the little you have in some sort of business that looks promising. Without a cent to call yours, it is difficult to make any money at all.

Dobbs had nothing. In fact, he had less than nothing, for even his clothes were neither good nor complete. Good clothes may sometimes be considered a modest fund to begin some enterprise with.

Anyone who is willing to work and is serious about it will certainly find a job. Only you must not go to the

3

man who tells you this, for he has no job to offer and doesn't know anyone who knows of a vacancy. This is exactly the reason why he gives you such generous advice, out of brotherly love, and to demonstrate how little he knows the world.

Dobbs would have carried heavy stones in a wheelbarrow ten hours a day if someone had offered him the job, but even had the job been open, he would have been the last to land it, because there already would be hundreds waiting and the natives of the country come first and a foreigner afterwards, if ever.

He shot a look at the bootblack on the plaza to see how his business was going. This bootblack owned a high iron stand with one seat. It looked rather swell, though there was no customer sitting on the comfortable seat. Competition was strong in this business, too. A dozen or more youngsters who couldn't afford to own stands were running like weasels about the plaza looking for customers. Whenever they caught one whose shoes were not perfectly polished, they were after him until, to get rid of them, he gave in and had his shoes polished once more. Usually two of these agile boys went about the job, each taking one of the customer's shoes and then dividing the pay. These boys carried small boxes with them, and a little bench, hardly bigger than a hand, to sit on while they worked. Such an outfit, Dobbs calculated, might cost three pesos. So, compared with Dobbs, they were capitalists, they had money invested. Anyway, seeing them chasing customers the way they did was proof enough that living was not so easy.

Even if Dobbs had had three pesos to buy the outfit, bootblacking was out, for he could not be a bootblack here among the natives. No white has ever tried to run around here shouting: "Shine, mister?" He would rather die. A white may sit on a bench on the plaza in rags, three-fourths starved; he may beg and humiliate himself before another white; he may even commit burglary or other crimes; for that the other whites will not loathe him; he will still be considered one of them. But should he happen to shine shoes in the street, or beg from a native anything but water, or carry around iced lemonade in buckets for sale by the glass, then he would sink below the lowest native and would die from starvation. No white would ever again give him a job, and the natives would consider him the most undesirable competitor. Native boys would kick his buckets and spill the lemonade, and should he find a pair of shoes to shine, all the native bootblacks would surround him and pester him with practical jokes and filthy language, so that the customer would leave before his shine was finished.

A man dressed in white strolled up to the bootblack's stand and sat down. The bootblack got busy on the tan shoes before him.

Dobbs rose from his bench, walked slowly over to the stand, and said a few words to the man in white, who, hardly looking up, put his hand in his pocket, brought out a peso, and handed it to Dobbs.

For a moment Dobbs stood bewildered, not trusting his eyes. Then he walked back to his bench. He had not counted on anything, or at least not on more than ten centavos. He caressed the peso in his pocket. What should he do with this treasure? One dinner and one supper? Or two dinners? Or ten packages of cigarettes Artistas? Or five cups of coffee, each with a roll, or what they called here "pan francés"?

After some heavy thinking he left the bench and walked down a few blocks to the Hotel Oso Negro, the Black Bear Hotel.

2

The Hotel Oso Negro would not have been much of a hotel back home. Even here, in the republic, where good hotels are rare, it would not be classed among the decent ones. Just a kind of a cheap lodging-house, it was.

The boom was at its peak, so good hotels were expensive. As the boom had come a thousand times quicker than good hotels could be built, there were few worthy of the name, and the owners of these could ask anywhere from ten to fifty dollars for a shabby room with a simple cot, a squeaking chair, and a shattered table as the entire furnishings. All a guest could hope for was that the cot would be well covered by a tight mosquito-netting and that the hotel could offer cold showers any time of the day or night.

On the ground floor of the Hotel Oso Negro at the left there was a store, run by an Arab, which carried shoes, boots, shirts, soap, perfumes, ladies' underwear, and all kinds of musical instruments. To the right there was another which had for sale deck-chairs, elaborate brass beds, mattresses, cameras, guns, rifles, ammunition, books on finding and drilling for oil, tennis-rackets, watches, American papers and magazines, automobile parts, and flashlights. The owner of this store was a Mexican who spoke English fairly well and who advertised this fact all over the window.

Between these two stores a long corridor led into the patio of the hotel. This corridor could be shut off from the street by a very heavy door, which was kept open day and night.

On the upper floor of the building there were four rooms looking toward the street and four rooms looking into the patio. One could hardly picture poorer hotel rooms than these, yet none could be had for less than twelve dollars for the night—without bath, of course. The hotel had only two shower-baths with cold water. Hot water was unknown. The two cold showers had to serve for all guests of the hotel. Often there was no water at all for the showers, as the water-supply was limited, most of it being bought from street venders who carried it in five-gallon gasoline-cans on the backs of burros.

Only two outside and two inside rooms on the second floor were rented to guests; the other four rooms were occupied by the owner of the hotel and his family. The owner, a Spaniard, was practically never seen; he left all work and the care of his business to his employees.

The real business of the hotel did not come from these rooms, which stood empty often for weeks, since the price, despite the boom, was considered robbery on account of the fact that the guests could not stand the bedbugs for more than two hours and then had to go to another place for the rest of the night. The owner did not lower the price, and only occasionally did he do something about the bugs. After his warfare on them ninety out of a hundred felt happier than before.

The bulk of the business for the hotel came from the patio, where the patrons did not care about bedbugs or furniture and where the only thing that counted was the price of a cot.

The whole patio was surrounded by shacks made of boards of the cheapest sort, which were weather-beaten, cracked, and rotten. The roofs were partly corrugated sheet-iron, partly roofing paper, all leaky. Most of the doors were hanging on only one hinge, and none could be closed firmly. There could be no privacy in any of these shacks. Above each door a figure was written in black paint so that each shack could be identified.

Inside of these shacks cots were set up closer than in a

field hospital during the war, damn it. On each cot a label was nailed telling its number. Every cot had two bedsheets, supposed to be white, clean, and without holes. Supposed to be. Then there was to every cot a thin blanket. Hardly one blanket could be found with more square inches of goods than square inches of holes. As the blankets were all of a dark color, it could not be seen whether they had been washed once since they had left the factory. A small, hard pillow was on every cot—hard like a chunk of wood.

All light and air entered by the doors and by the many cracks in the boards. Nevertheless the air in these rooms was always thick, smelling none too good. The wooden floor was broken through almost everywhere, and right beneath was earth, sometimes muddy, sometimes dry, but always infested with rats, scorpions, little venomous black spiders, and centipedes.

The patio was closed in by buildings on all sides, so there was no ventilation of any kind, and the sun, even when directly above the patio, could not penetrate. The privies were only slightly better than those in the trenches, damn them.

To this unpleasant atmosphere was added the thick smoke from a fire which burned in the middle of the patio all day long and until late into the night. For fuel anything under heaven that might burn was used, including old shoes and dried dung. Over this fire a Chinaman boiled his laundry in old gas-cans. He had rented a small extra shack, set up in the farthest corner of the patio, where, together with four compatriots, he ran his laundry. This, under the conditions of the boom, paid a high profit, from which the hotel-owner collected a certain cut.

The hall of the hotel, serving as the lobby, was identical with the corridor leading from the street to the patio. At the left, just before entering the patio, the manager had his office. He conducted his business through a small window in the corridor. Another window allowed him to watch all that was going on in the patio and to see that no guest took a better cot than he had paid for.

The greater part of his office was occupied by huge shelves on which, behind chicken-wire, in compartments, trunks, boxes, bags, suitcases, packages, and sacks were piled up to the ceiling. In another small room behind the office, and connected by a door never closed, there were still more shelves, all filled with guests' belongings. No guest took the risk of having his bags or boxes or trunks in the sleeping-quarters.

Here on these shelves, well guarded by the clerk, were kept belongings not only of guests, but of patrons who had not had money to pay for their lodging more than one night, and who after that one night had slept on benches or in some nook near the docks or under trees on the river-banks, where no manager asked for payments, but where it sometimes happened that they were murdered for the thirty centavos in their possession.

Having paid at least for one night, a guest considered it his right to leave his belongings in the care of the hotel. If he needed a shirt or a pair of pants or whatever it might be, he came to the hotel, asked for his bag or package, took out what he needed, and returned the bag to the care of the manager. The manager could never tell whether the man was still a guest or not, and he was too polite or too indifferent to ask. There came a day when the man needed badly a quick change of climate for some reason or other. He had no money for train or for boat, so he had to rely on the means of transportation given him free of charge when he was born. Walking, he could not carry his bag or trunk—not here in the tropics, where there is no hitchhiking. Today he is perhaps in Brazil, or in the Argentine, or in Hongkong, or his bones are bleaching in the sun somewhere near Venezuela or Ecuador. Who the devil cares? Perhaps slain, or dead of thirst, or eaten by a tiger, or bitten by a snake. His bag, regardless of what has happened to its owner, is still well taken care of by the hotel.

There came a day when the shelves could no longer hold all the bags, boxes, sacks, and grips of former guests, and there was not an inch of space left for the bags of newcomers. The owner of the hotel then ordered a general cleaning out.

Checks had never been given; such a luxury was not expected in this hotel. Some bags bore a label with the name of the owner. Others carried labels of the express companies, or a ship, or a hotel in Spain or Morocco, or Peru, by which its owner recognized it. Other bags had the name of the guest written on them in chalk or in pencil. It often happened that the owner could not get his package, which he recognized by its appearance, because he had forgotten the name he had given when he had handed his bag to the manager, having in the meantime changed his name several times for the sake of convenience.

From many suitcases and boxes the labels had dropped off or been torn off, or, if they were greasy, eaten by rats. Names written in chalk or pencil had disappeared. Often the clerk had forgotten to ask for the name of the owner, or the man had come in drunk and unable to remember his name. The clerk then wrote on the bag only the number of the cot which had been assigned to the guest, who, of course, forgot this number at once, if he ever knew it.

It was difficult to say how long certain things had been stored. The manager or the hotel-owner estimated the number of months things had been kept by the thickness of the layer of dust which covered them. They rarely made a mistake by this method of judging.

The owner of the hotel, in the presence of the manager, opened the baggage and packages, looking through them for valuables to be claimed by him in payment for the keeping. Mostly he found only rags or junk, for anyone who had something of value did not go to the Oso Negro Hotel, or if he did, he remained no longer than one night.

The rags were given away to those who were hanging around begging for them. In this world no shirt, no pair of pants, no shoes can be so shabby that some human being will not say: "Let me have it, please; look at mine. Thank you, sir!" For no man can ever be so poor but that another believes himself still poorer.

3

Dobbs had no suitcase with him, not even a pasteboard box or a paper bag. He would not have known what to put into them. All he possessed in this world he carried in his pants pockets. For months he had not owned a waistcoat, nor a coat. Such things had gone long ago. He did not need them, anyway. Nobody had a coat here except foreign tourists and men who wished to make a good impression. Here coats look as silly as a top-hat on the head of a New Yorker who cannot afford a taxi.

Dobbs stepped up before the clerk's window, where on a board there stood an earthen water-bottle. This was the community water-bottle for all guests. No water was to be had in the rooms or in the shacks. If you were thirsty, you had to leave your cot and come here to get water. Experienced patrons, especially those who frequently felt thirsty during the night, took with them a tequila-bottle filled with water when turning in.

The manager, who during the day acted also as clerk, was a very young man, hardly more than twenty-five. He was short and very lean, and he had a long, thin nose. His nose indicated that he was a born hotel-clerk. His cheeks were hollow, his eyes fallen in and set in dark rings. He was suffering from malaria, which had turned the skin of his face pale yellow, with greenish shadows. He looked as if he might die any minute. Your mistake, mister, for he could wallop any tough sailor who opened his swear-hold farther than was considered decent by the clerk. He worked from five in the morning until six in the evening, when the night-clerk relieved him. Then he would go to the plaza and walk around fifty times for exercise.

The hotel never closed, and the clerks had a busy time. There was not a half-hour day or night when there was not at least one patron to be called because he had to go to work. Few tourists stopped in this hotel, and if they did, it was mostly by mistake and they went back home telling the world what a dirty country the republic was.

The patrons here were almost exclusively working-men, with jobs or without, sailors who had been left behind by their ships or had jumped them. Occasionally an oilman or two stopped here who the week before had been million-aires, but who had gone broke because their wells had run dry or had not come in at all. In general the lodgers were bakery workers, street-pavers, watchmen, cooks and waiters in cafés, news-boys; and many had professions and jobs which cannot be easily named or explained in a few words. Many of these men could have rented a room with a family or in a private house where they would have slept better and where they would not have been permanently in com-pany with all sorts of thieves, card-sharpers, tramps, dice-loaders, vagrants, and adventurers who, as long as they paid, also lived here. The only class distinction here was indicated by the answer to the question: "Can you pay for your cot or can't you?" It was because the hotel could be trusted to call a man at the right time and see to it that he left that scores of decent working-men lived here permanently. They preferred to live here among all this scum of five continents rather than risk losing their jobs for being late to work.

Both clerks were efficient. Day after day new guests came, old ones left. Every hour, day and night, new faces were seen. All nationalities were represented here. There came and went whites, blacks, browns, yellows, and reds; old and young, tall and short. But neither of the clerks ever made a mistake. Whoever passed by the window, the clerk on duty knew instantly whether he had paid or not. If he was in doubt, he glanced at the register and then watched to see into which room the man went. Since none of the shacks had locks, no keys were needed. Anyone smart enough could have gone into any of the shacks and taken a cot. But the two clerks were so well trained that they knew at once the face of a guest, the name he had given, the number of his cot, and the payment he had made, and whether or not these details coincided.

A few rooms containing old dilapidated beds were separated by cracked boards from the other rooms. These were so small that outside of the bed only a narrow space a foot wide was left for the occupants to undress in. These little cages were rented by men who brought their women along with them. For these accommodations one peso was charged for each person.

Two huts were kept solely for women patrons. Here also doors could be neither locked nor properly shut. The women who lodged here were mostly girls employed in restaurants and hotel kitchens. In spite of the fact that anybody could easily have sneaked into the women's quarters

at night and that the rest of the hotel was full of men of
all sorts and kinds, the girls were safer here than in
many a hotel which makes a fuss about its moral standing.
The women were never molested by men coming in drunk.
By the unwritten law of the hotel and of the men who lived
here any man who tried to harm one of the girls would
have been dead at sunrise. The men never even went near
enough to the women's quarters for a peep through the
cracked clapboards. The women were the only guests in
the shacks of the patio who had mosquito-bars for their
cots. The men had to manage without.

Many of the guests had been living here two, three, even
five years. These old-timers usually occupied the corners
of the shacks in which they bunked, and so obtained a
certain privacy not enjoyed by others. They were freer
here than in a private house, for they could come and go
as they wished. No landlady ever asked them questions or
felt it her duty to pester them with her own opinions on
morals and punishment hereafter.

The shacks had no closets and no wardrobes of any kind.
Patrons whose cots were in the middle of the hut laid their
things on a broken chair or tied them to the under side of
their cots with strings. The men who occupied corners or
had their cots alongside a wall hung up their clothes on
nails. Others kept theirs in wooden boxes under their cots.
Others, again, whose belongings hung on the wall covered
them with sacking and then fastened them with strings
crosswise tight against the wall, so that it would have been
difficult for a thief to drag a pair of pants or a shirt out of
this mass of clothes.

It rarely happened that anything was stolen. Anyone
leaving with a parcel was scrutinized by the clerk in such
a way that if the man was not honest he dropped the package and ran away. A thief in this hotel was never afraid of

the police or of jail. He was only afraid—terribly afraid—
of the beating he would receive if he was found out. The
clerk had only to call into the patio, where always, day or
night, a score of guests were hanging around. They would
take the thief into one of the shacks and there preach him
a sermon which would make such an excellent impression
upon his mind and body that for the next seven days he
could not move a finger or an eyelid without moaning.
These sermons had proved so effective that the hotel could
guarantee that no theft would recur inside of two months
to come.

Only old-timers left a part of their belongings in the
shacks while they were at work. Their coats, pants, and
shirts were so well known by the clerks that it was hardly
possible for anyone to leave wearing stolen clothing without being caught.

In the room where the clerk had his little desk there was
also a safe in which the patrons' valuables were kept, such
as cash, documents, watches, rings, and instruments. Among
these were all sorts of implements used by geologists, topog-
raphers, prospectors, and miners, as well as revolvers, guns,
rifles, and fishing outfits on the wall, either checked here or
left in lieu of payment.

In corners and on narrow shelves, near at hand for the
clerk, dozens of little parcels, card-boxes, and books were
piled up. These were checked to be called for within an
hour or two. Most of them were never claimed. The owners of some of them were probably at the other end of the
world, for if a man needed a job and was at the docks just
when a ship, short a hand or two, was heaving anchor, he
hopped on and left his parcels or instruments behind. You
can't eat a theodolite and you can't sell it, not for twenty
bucks, if all second-hand dealers and pawnshops are glutted
with them. But a job means food, and a man would be a

fool not to let instruments or fishing tackle or guns go and to seize his chance to hop on a bucket where there are three square meals a day.

A shelf with little compartments was filled with letters for patrons. Bundles of letters, many of them from a mother, a wife, or a sweetheart, were piled up, covered with thick dust. The men to whom they were addressed might be dead, or working deep in the jungles clearing new oil-fields, or on a tramp in the China Sea, or helping the Bolsheviks build up a workers' empire, with no time to think that the letter-writers back home might be crying their eyes out over a lost sheep.

What the manager or the clerk called his desk was a small table, wabbly and well worn. On this were the register, a few letters and papers, an ink-bottle, and a pen. Every patron had to register, as a reminder that he was staying in a civilized country and not with an Indian tribe. Only his last name was written in, with the number of his shack and his cot and the amount of money he had paid. All other information concerning a patron, his nationality, his profession, his home town, were of no interest to the clerk or to the police, who never came to inspect the register except when looking for a criminal. The tax officials frequently looked into the register to find out if the hotel had made an incorrect declaration. The city had no surplus of officials, and only where there are more officials than are actually needed are people pestered to tell the police all about their private affairs.

4

Dobbs came to the window, banged his peso upon the table, and said: "Lobbs, for two nights."

The clerk took up the register and wrote: "Jobbs," because he had not caught the name and was too polite to ask again. His answer was: "Room seven, bed two." "Room" meant "shack," and "bed" meant "cot."

Dobbs grunted something which might have been: "Okay, brother," or perhaps: "Kiss me somewhere, you mug."

He was hungry and had to go hunting or fishing. . . . But the fish would not bite. He went after a man in a white suit and whispered a few words to him; the man, without looking at him, handed him a toston—that is, half a peso.

With these fifty centavos Dobbs hurried to a Chinese restaurant. Chinese cafés are the lowest-priced in the republic, but not the dirtiest. Lunch-time was long past, but in a Chinese café one may get dinner, called "comida corrida," at any time. If dinner is over, the meal is called "cena," meaning "supper," whatever time it is by the cathedral clock.

Dobbs, knowing he could pay for his meal, kept the Chinese running like the devil. Everything that was set before him he had changed for something else, exulting in feeling once more how pleasant it is to chase someone around without mercy.

Then he trudged again to the plaza, picking his teeth on the way, and rested on a bench until he felt hungry for coffee. He walked the streets for a good while without success, until a man in white finally gave him a silver coin, fifty centavos again.

"Geecries," Dobbs said to himself, "I'm sure lucky with gents dressed in white." He walked across the plaza to the side nearest the docks of the passenger liners and freighters. Here was a café without walls, doors, or windows, which were not needed since the café kept open twenty-four hours every day.

Dobbs ordered a glass of coffee—the greater part of it hot milk with coffee poured on the top of it—and two pieces of milk bread. He sweetened the coffee with a quarter of a pound of sugar. When the waiter put the ice-water on the table, Dobbs looked up at the price-list painted on the wall and yelled: "Haven't you bandits raised the price for that stinking coffee five cents more?"

"Well," said the waiter, chewing a toothpick, "running-expenses are getting higher. We simply can't do it any longer for fifteen fierros."

Dobbs did not really object to the price. He just wanted to complain, as any patron who can pay feels he is entitled to do.

"Go to hell! I don't buy any lottery tickets," he bellowed at a little boy who for the last five minutes had been brandishing lottery tickets right under his nose.

The little merchant, barefooted and wearing a torn shirt and ragged cotton pants, did not mind; he was used to being yelled at. "It's the Michoacán state lottery, señor," he said; "sixty thousand pesos the main premium."

"Scram, you bandit, I don't buy tickets." Dobbs soaked his bread in the coffee.

"The whole ticket is only ten pesos, señor, and it's a sure shot."

"Son of a poacher, I haven't got ten pesos."

"That's all right by me, caballero," the boy said. "Why don't you buy only a quarter of a ticket, then? That's two pesos fifty."

Dobbs, swallowing his coffee in big gulps, had scalded his lips. This made him mad, and he roared: "To hell with you and stay there! If you don't leave me to drink my coffee in peace, I'll throw this whole glass of water right in your face."

The boy did not move. He was a good salesman. He knew his patrons. Any man who could sit at the bar of a Spanish café at this time in the afternoon and drink a huge glass of coffee and eat two pieces of milk bread must have money. A man who has money always wants more and likes it to come easy. This man was the right customer for lottery tickets.

"Why don't you take one tenth of the ticket, señor? I'll sell the tenth to you for one peso silver."

Dobbs took up the glass of water and threw the contents in the boy's face. "Didn't I tell you, you little rascal, I'd do it if you didn't leave me in peace?"

The boy laughed, wiped the water off his face, and shook it off his ragged pants. The lottery makes men rich —always one in twenty thousand—but the boy knew from experience that it was safer to make a certain living by selling lottery tickets than to buy them and wait for the premium. He considered the free bath merely the first sign of opening business connections with Dobbs.

Dobbs paid for his coffee and received twenty centavos change. Catching sight of these twenty centavos, the boy said: "Señor, you ought to buy one twentieth of the Monterrey lottery. A twentieth costs you only twenty centavos. Main premium, five thousand pesos cash. There, take it. It's a plumb sure winner—an excellent number. Add the figures up and you'll get thirteen. What better number could you buy? It's bound to win."

Dobbs weighed the twenty-centavo piece in his hands. What should he do with it? More coffee? He didn't want any more. Cigarettes? He didn't want to smoke; he liked the taste of coffee on his tongue better just now, and smoke kills any fine taste. A lottery ticket, he thought, was money thrown away. Still, money comes, money goes. There was fun in waiting for the drawing. Hoping for something is always good for the soul. The drawing was only three days off.

"All right, you brown devil," he said. "Give me that

twentieth, so that I won't have to look at your dirty face and your damned tickets any longer."

The little merchant tore off the twentieth of the sheet and handed it to Dobbs. "It's un número excelente, señor. A sure winner it is."

"If it is such a sure winner, why the hell don't you play it yourself?" Dobbs asked suspiciously and jokingly at the same time.

"Me? No, sir," said the boy. "I can't afford to play the lottery. I haven't got the money." He took the silver piece, bit on it to see if it was good, and said: "Muchas gracias! A thousand thanks, sir. Come again next time. I always have the winners, all the lucky numbers. Buena suerte, good luck!" And off he hopped like a young rabbit, chasing another patron he had just glimpsed.

Dobbs put the ticket in his watch-pocket without looking at the number. Then he decided to go for a swim.

5

It was a long way to the open river. The river at this point was the meeting-place, so it seemed, of all the bums in port. When Dobbs arrived, the water was well crowded with a multitude of Mexicans, Indians, and whites who had reached the same social level as Dobbs. None of them wore bathing-suits. Farther up the river girls were in the water, also without bathing-suits of any sort, accompanied by boys to make the affair more lively.

On the high hills that formed the banks of the river to the east was the residential section of the port. Here, in beautiful modern bungalows, American style, the Americans, English, and Dutch who were employed by the oil companies lived with their families. The city was very low, only a few feet above sea-level, and suffocatingly hot, for

on the plaza, Dobbs thought it would be a good idea to have some ready change in his pocket, because you never know what may happen. This excellent idea occurred to him when he saw a man leisurely walking on the opposite side of the street—a man dressed in white.

Without any hesitation he approached the man and said his prayer. His victim burrowed in his pocket and brought forth half a peso. Dobbs reached out for the coin, but the man kept the piece between his fingers, saying dryly: "Listen, you, such insolence has never come my way as long as I can remember, and nobody on earth could make me believe that story."

Dobbs stood utterly perplexed. Never before had he encountered anyone who addressed him in this way. Usually the answer was only a few angry words. He was uncertain what to do. Should he wait or should he run away? He could see the toston, which made him sure that this coin sooner or later would land in his own hand. He let the man have the pleasure of preaching, as a small return for his money. "Well, if I get fifty centavos for listening to a sermon, it may be hard-earned money, but it is cash," he thought. So he waited.

"This afternoon you told me," the man continued, "that you had not had your dinner yet, so I gave you one peso. When I met you again, you told me you had no money for your bed, so I gave you a half peso. A couple of hours later I met you again and you said you had had no supper and you felt hungry. Once more I gave you fifty centavos. Now may I be permitted to ask you, with due politeness: What do you want the money for now?"

Without thinking, Dobbs broke out: "For tomorrow morning's breakfast, mister."

The man laughed, gave him the fifty centavos, and said: "This money is the last you'll get from me. If you want to do me a favor, go occasionally to somebody else. To tell you the truth, it's beginning to bore me."

"Excuse me, mister," Dobbs answered, "I really never realized that it was you all the time. I never looked at your face, only at your hands and at the coins you gave me. Now for the first time I've noticed your face. But I promise, sir, I won't come to you again. Beg pardon."

"That's perfectly all right. Don't shed tears. And to make sure you won't forget your promise, have another fifty so that you'll have your dinner tomorrow. But understand that from now on you are to try your best to make your living without my assistance. That's all," and the gentleman went his way.

"Seems," said Dobbs when alone, "this well has run dry now, and for good. Luck with gents dressed in white is spilled. Let's have a look in a different direction."

So he came to the conclusion it might be better to leave the port and go out into the country to learn what things looked like there.

7

That night in the hotel he met another American who wished to go down to Tuxpam, but couldn't find anybody to accompany him.

Hearing the magic word Tuxpam, Dobbs jumped at the idea of going with Moulton to visit the oil-fields, where there might be something doing.

It is not easy to go down to Tuxpam with no money. Half of the way down is a road on which occasionally you may meet a car; the other half of the way is a big lake, and the motor-boat is not accustomed to accommodating hitch-hikers. You have to pay or you stay behind.

Of course you may go 'way round the lagoon. But there

is hardly any road at all, and this route may take two weeks. You can visit a larger number of oil-fields, however, and it was this long overland route that was chosen by the two men.

First the river had to be crossed, at a charge of twenty-five centavos. They preferred to save that money for better use, so they waited for the Huasteca ferry, which takes people across the river without any charge. This ferry crosses the river only when it has enough freight to make the trip worth while. It is meant for the company's working-men and their families exclusively.

Dobbs and Moulton started out in the morning right after they had had a cup of coffee and some dry bread. On reaching the ferry they asked the boatman when he thought the ferry might cross. He said he probably would not be ready until eleven, so there was nothing to do but wait.

This part of the river-bank was a lively spot. A few dozen motor-boats and half a hundred row-boats waited for customers to be taken to the other side of the river. Speed-boats carried the big oilmen and other business men who were willing to pay special fares. Working-men and small traders and peddlers had to wait until a taxi boat had enough passengers to take them for the regular taxi fare. The place looked like a fair, for people who had to wait were buying fruit, lunch, shirts, cigarettes, guns, ammunition, hardware, leather goods.

The boats and ferries ran day and night. On the other side of the river were the hands, on this side of the river was the brain. Here on this side were the banks, the head-quarters of the oil companies, the rich stores, and the gambling-halls and cabarets. On the other side of the river was the hard work; here on this side, in the city, was the recreation from work. On the other side of the river the oil was practically without any value. All the value the oil finally had in the market was put into it on this side of the river. Oil, like gold, is worthless in its natural state. It obtains its value only by handling and being taken where it is needed.

Many millions of dollars were carried across the river; not in coins or in notes, not even in checks. These millions of dollars were carried often in short lines and figures scribbled in a notebook. A certain tract of land worth two thousand dollars yesterday is worth today five hundred thousand dollars. For this difference a geologist was responsible, one who maintained that this tract of land was a sure shot to bring in a dozen gushers. Next week the same tract may go begging for five hundred dollars, and its actual owner may not be able to buy himself a fifty-cent lunch in a Chinese café, because six other geologists have staked their reputations on finding that the tract is as dry as an old picture-frame. Two months later it may be impossible to buy the same lot for twenty-five thousand dollars in cash.

8

It was noon when Dobbs and Moulton reached the opposite bank of the river, which was crowded with tankers coming from or going to all parts of the world. Here the banks were lined with huge oil-tanks belonging to a dozen different oil companies.

The fair on this bank was even more lively than on the other side, and it was more varied, for the small merchants doing business here catered not only to the natives, but also to the officers and sailors of the ships lying at anchor. Not only parrots and monkeys were for sale, but lion- and tiger-skins, lion and tiger cubs, snakes of all sizes, young alligators, and huge lizards. Sailors could take these animals home and tell the girls how they fought and killed the tiger to catch the tiger kitten as a present for the girl back home.

The air bit into your lungs because it was filled with poisonous gas escaping from the refineries. That sting in the air which made breathing so hard and unpleasant and choked your throat constantly meant that people were making money—much money. Unskilled labor was getting fifteen pesos a day, and Americans and Mexicans alike were spending five thousand dollars a night without giving a thought to where it went. Tomorrow there will be heaps more money. No doubt this will go on for a couple of hundred years. So why worry? Let's spend it all while the spending is easy and pleasant.

Farther down the river were the saloons, the cabarets, and long rows of shacks where girls, gayly dressed and more gayly painted, were waiting for their sailor friends, officers and crew. All was love, song, and oceans of liquor wherever you cast a look. Mother cannot always go with the sailor boy to watch out for him. Certain trips are better made alone.

Seeing so many jolly sailors hanging around because their ships had hoisted the red flag which indicated that they were taking in oil, Moulton had an idea. He said: "It's noon in this part of the world. What say? Let's hop on this tanker here. Maybe there's some dinner coming. I could take it, buddy."

There were two men with no shirts or caps on standing before a fruit-seller and trying to make him understand that they wanted bananas and asking the price.

Moulton was right at them: "Hi, you mugs, what's doing? What can are you on?"

"*Norman Bridge*," came the answer, "and what of it?"

"That's good. How about some eats?" Moulton asked. "We have a damn long way to walk, and in this tropical heat, too. So you guys'd better come across with a good man-sized meal, or, hell, I'll sure tell your grandmothers back home that you meant to let two Ams starve out here, and in foreign country, too."

"Aw, gosh," said one of the sailors, "don't talk so much squabash. It makes me sick hearing you. Come up, you two beachers, and we'll stuff your bellies until they bust. We throw it away anyhow. Who the funking devil can eat a bite in this blistering heat? Gee, I wish I was back in that ol' Los An, damn it."

When they left the tanker, they couldn't walk very far. They lay down under the first tree they reached.

"That was what I call a square meal, geecries," Dobbs said. "I wouldn't walk a mile even for an elephant tooth. I'm out for the next two hours. And we better get a rest."

"Okay by me, sweety."

They snored so loudly that people passing by and not seeing them under the tree got frightened and hurried away thinking a lion had overeaten and was taking a nap.

Moulton woke up first. He pushed Dobbs in the shoulders and hollered: "Hi, you, get up! And what about us going to Tuxpam? Let's hustle before it gets dark."

With much whining and moaning over the sorrows of human life they got going.

They went up the river on the right shore. The whole road, an ugly dirt road at that, was covered with crude oil. It seemed to break through cracks and holes in the ground. There were even pools and ponds of oil. It came mostly through leaks in the pipes and from overflowing tanks which were lined up on the hills along the shore. Brooks of crude oil ran down like water into the river. Nobody seemed to care about the loss of these thousands and thousands of barrels of oil, which soaked the soil and polluted the river. So rich in oil was this part of the world then that the company managers and directors seemed not to mind when a well which brought in twenty thousand barrels a day caught fire and burned down to its last drop. Who would care about three or four hundred thousand barrels of oil running away every week and being lost owing to busted pipe lines, to filling tanks carelessly, or to not notifying the pumpman that while he has been pumping for days, sections of the pipe lines have been taken out, to be replaced by new ones. The more oil is lost, the higher the price. Three cheers, then, for broken pipes and drunken pumpmen and tank-attendants!

Even the sky appeared to be covered with oil. Thick clouds darkened the bright tropical sun. Poisonous clouds coming from the refineries wrapped the whole landscape in a mist that stung your lungs like thin needles.

After a walk of a mile the view to the left became friendlier. Set against the slopes of the high river-bank were the bungalows in which engineers and other officials of the oil companies were living with their families. They had tried to make their residences as near as possible like those they had been used to in Texas. Yet everything had been in vain. The nearness of oil prevented people from living as they wished. The outcome was exactly what it is when a Negress with the help of powder and paint tries to look like a Swedish gentlewoman.

Soon the two men reached Villa Cuauhtemoc. This little town, situated on the shores of a large lagoon, and connected with the river and the port by a picturesque channel, on which a lively traffic of boats and launches is carried on, is in fact the ancient Indian principal town of this region. The Spaniards, after they had conquered this region, preferred to build their town on the other side of the river, as more convenient for shipping. The new town, the port, became more and more important and left the old town so

far behind that the inhabitants of the port forgot its existence entirely; when they heard of it, they thought it located
in the depths of the jungle and peopled by primitive Indians.

On reaching the last huts of the town opposite the lagoon,
Dobbs and Moulton saw an Indian squatted by the road on
the top of the hill. The Indian wore rather good cotton
pants, and he had on, furthermore, a clean blue shirt, a high
pointed palm hat, and on his feet huaraches—that is, sandals.
On the ground before him was a bast bag filled with a few
things which perhaps were all he owned in this world.

The two, being in a hurry, passed by the Indian without
taking any special notice of him.

After a while Dobbs turned his head and said: "What the
devil does that Indian want of us? He's been trailing us for
the last half-hour."

"Now he's stopping," Moulton said. "Seems to be looking
for something in the bush there. Wonder what he is after."

They went on their way. Then, turning their heads, they
noticed once more that the Indian was still on their heels.

"Did he carry a gun?" Moulton asked.

"Not that I saw. I don't think he's a bandit. He looks
rather decent to me," Dobbs said. "Anyway you can never
be sure about that."

"Looks a bit screwy to me."

They marched on. Yet whenever they looked back, they
saw the Indian following them, always keeping at a distance
of about fifty feet. Whenever they stopped to catch their
breath, the Indian stopped too. They began to get nervous.

There seemed no reason for being afraid of a poor Indian, but they began to feel sure that this single native was
only the spy for a whole horde of bandits who were eager
to rob the two strangers of the little they possessed.

"If I only had a gun," Dobbs said, "I'd shoot him down.
I'm cracking up. I can't bear it any longer to have that

brown devil on our heels waiting for his chance. I wonder if we could catch him and tie him to a tree and leave him there."

"I don't quite agree." Moulton looked back at the man, trying to guess his intent. "Perhaps he's a harmless guy after all. But I admit if we could get rid of him some way, it might be safer."

"Let's go on and then stop suddenly," Dobbs suggested. "We'll let him come up and ask him straight out what he wants."

They stopped under a tree and looked up as if they saw something very interesting in its branches—a strange bird or fruit.

The Indian, however, the moment he noticed that the two Americans had halted, stopped also, watching them from a safe distance.

Dobbs played a trick to get the Indian to come near. He showed a growing excitement about what he pretended to see in the branches of the tree. He and Moulton pointed into the dense foliage and gesticulated like madmen. The Indian, as they expected, fell for it. His inborn curiosity got the better of him. Step by step he came nearer, his eyes fixed on the upper branches of the tree. When he finally stood beside the two, Dobbs made an exaggerated gesture and, pointing into the dense bush, yelled: "There, there he is, running away now." He drew Moulton close to him as if he wanted to show him clearly the spot where some strange animal had disappeared. At the same moment he turned round and held the Indian by his arm so tightly that he could not escape.

"Listen, you," he addressed him, "what do you want from us? Why are you trailing us?"

"I want to go there," the Indian answered, pointing in the direction in which Dobbs and Moulton were going.

"Where to?" Moulton asked.

"Same place where you are going, señores."

"How do you know where we are going?"

"I know where you are going," the native said quietly. "You are going out to the oil-fields to look for work. That's the same place I am going. Perhaps I can find some work there too. I have worked in the oil-camps before."

Dobbs and Moulton smiled at each other, each silently accusing the other of being the bigger jackass and coward. No doubt what the native said was true. He looked like a camp worker and might well be after honest work exactly as they two were. Looked at closely, there was not a trace in his face or anywhere about him to remind one of a bandit.

To make absolutely sure, Dobbs asked: "Why don't you go alone? Why do you follow us all the time?"

"To tell you the truth, caballeros," the Indian explained, "I had been sitting by this road already three days, from sunrise to sunset, waiting there for some white men passing by with whom I might go to the camps."

"Can't you find your way alone?" Moulton asked.

"Yes, I could. Maybe. But the trouble with me is soy un gran cobarde, I am a big coward. I am afraid of going alone through the jungle. There are huge tigers, and snakes huger still."

"We aren't afraid of anything in the world, we aren't," Dobbs said with great conviction.

"I know you aren't. That's the reason why I was waiting for whites going the same way."

"But whites may be eaten by tigers, too," Moulton said.

"No, señor, there you are mistaken. Tigers and lions of our country don't attack Americans; they attack only us, because we belong to the same country, we are sort of compatriots, and that's why our tigers and lions prefer us and never bother an American. What is more, along the road to the camps there are also sometimes a lot of bandits sitting and waiting for someone to come along to rob. The shores of the Tamihua Lagoon is infested with these murderers."

"It looks very promising," Dobbs said to Moulton.

Dobbs replied: "What's biting you now? What's the joke?"

"I was just thinking how afraid we were of this pobre hombre here, this little piece of human being, and he was a hundred times more afraid of us."

"Aw, shut up, you make me sick." Dobbs wanted to forget.

"Besides," Moulton continued, "sometimes it's a good thing not to have a gun on your hip, or this poor devil would no longer be alive and we might find ourselves in a hell of a mess, for no one on earth would believe we acted in self-defense."

From now on the Indian went along with them, hardly speaking a word, walking by their side or behind them, just as the road would permit.

Shortly before sunset they reached a little Indian village which consisted of only a few huts. The inhabitants, hospitable as they are at heart, were afraid of the strangers, owing to the many tales about bandits in the neighborhood. So with kind words and many excuses they persuaded the three men to go on and try to reach the next village, which, they stated, was bigger and had better accommodations— even a fonda, a little inn—and since the sun had not completely disappeared yet, they might reach that big village still with the last rays of daylight.

There was nothing else to do but go on. One mile they covered and there was no sign of a village. They marched another mile and there was still no village in sight.

By now it had become pitch-dark and they could no

longer see the road. If they went on, they might easily get lost in the jungle.

"Those people in the village must have lied to us about that big place we were supposed to come across soon." Moulton was angry. "We shouldn't have left the village, but stayed there with or without their consent, even if we had to sleep in the open but still near the huts."

Dobbs, not being in any better mood than his partner, said: "The Indians usually don't act this way. They let you stay with them for the night and even give you part of the little food they have. It seems to me they were too much afraid of us. There are three of us, and they may have figured we might easily overpower them if they offered us hospitality. They must have had bad experiences of this sort, and I can easily imagine a good many bums in port, whites and natives, who wouldn't mind robbing or even killing a couple of villagers if they couldn't get what they wanted otherwise. Anyway, there's no use arguing this point. Here we are now in the open road surrounded by jungle and we have to make the best of it."

"Looks to me," Moulton said, "as though we couldn't even go back to that little village, even if we wanted to."

"Right," Dobbs admitted. "We'd get lost. I can't even see a stone at my feet any longer. Nothing else to do but stop right where we are."

"I think that big village can't be far." Moulton did not like the idea of spending the night on a jungle road. "I noticed there were tracks of horses and cows on the road. We must be near. Perhaps we ought to try once more."

"I'm against it." Dobbs was determined. "That village may be near, and it may be still three miles away. I don't take any chances of being lost in the middle of the jungle. Here we are still on the road and by all means safer than inside the jungle."

With lighted matches they looked around on the ground for the best place to rest in for the night. It looked bad enough. The road was not at all clean. It was just a dirt road, rarely used, covered with small cactuses and low thorny brushes. Whole armies of huge red ants were running about, and a multitude of other insects were crawling and creeping in all directions, leaving practically not a square inch of soil uncovered in their search for food or safety or the pleasures of love.

"Didn't that Indian here say something about tigers, snakes, and lions being at large in this section?" Moulton asked with a desperate voice on seeing the ground so uninviting.

"He said something to that effect," Dobbs remembered. He turned to the native, who stood near by, seemingly without the slightest interest in what his companions were doing or saying. He was waiting for the two Americans to decide where and how to spend the night, and whatever they might decide, he would accept their decision and spend the night as near them as he could. Where an American could sleep and feel safe, an Indian could sleep still better and safer.

Dobbs said now to the Indian: "You're quite sure there are tigers hereabouts?"

"Positively, señor. Hay muchos, muchísimo tigres aquí. There are so many tigers here in this jungle that whenever an American goes out hunting for a day, he never returns at night without at least four big tigers loaded on his car. I have seen them, señores, or otherwise I would not mention it."

"Thanks for the information," Dobbs said. "Well, partner, I wouldn't be in the least surprised if you should find me in the morning between the paws of a tiger, half eaten up for breakfast."

"Better don't joke about that," Moulton answered. "We haven't even a flashlight with us to chase them off. Well, I think there's nothing left now but to pray to the Lord, who is the King of all men and beasts."

From talking and thinking and standing around they became sleepy. It was impossible to stand on their feet for the whole night, so they lay down on the ground, forgetting all about ants and beetles and reptiles.

Hardly had they settled themselves, when the Indian squeezed himself between the two like a dog. He did this very slowly, trying to disturb them as little as possible, but none the less with all the firm determination that he could muster. The two Americans might push him, kick him, try to pull him away; no sooner did they cease than he was snugly in between them once more. He felt safe only between the two. They had to give up and leave him where he wanted to sleep. He preferred their kicks and beatings to the claws of the tiger.

Moulton was awakened by a small reptile creeping over his face. He shook it off and sat up. While he was trying to realize where he was and listening to the eternal singing of the tropical jungle, he was stricken as by a shock. His breath stopped, and he could now hear very distinctly steps slowly approaching. Very soft steps they were, but heavy. No doubt they were the steps of a huge animal. Only very huge animals would make such heavy steps, and since they were at the same time very soft, they could only be those of a great cat. A tiger. A huge tiger, a tigre real, one of the biggest in those jungles he must be.

Moulton didn't want to be afraid. He wanted not to wake the others until he was sure. So he listened again. The steps had halted. The great beast was obviously feeling his way and looking for the best place from which to jump at his victim. After half a minute Moulton heard the steps again,

more slow and more cautious than before, and step by step
coming closer. They were heavier now and each time he
heard them set more firmly on the soft ground. When he
thought a suppressed growl reached his ears, he jerked
Dobbs awake.

"What is it?" Dobbs asked in a sleepy voice.

"A tiger is right behind us."

"A what?"

"That's what I said," Moulton whispered. "A tiger is
after us."

Dobbs listened into the night. Then he said: "You're
right, buddy, that sure is a huge beast. I think it must be
a tiger. A human being wouldn't sneak through the bush
this way. It can only be a tiger or a lion."

It was not clear whether the Indian had been awake for
some time already or whether he had been aroused by the
excited talk of the two. But at the same moment the two
partners stood up, he was up too, keeping as close to them
as he could.

"Es un tigre, muy cierto, por la Madre Santísima; that's
a huge tiger, so help me the Holy Virgin." His voice
trembled for fear. "He will jump at us now any minute.
There he is, hardly twenty feet away. I can see the green
glow of his eyes." He stared into the dense thicket and at
the same time embraced Dobbs's whole body. Dobbs shook
him off. Then he hid close to Moulton. The terror-stricken
Indian, who certainly knew a tiger when he smelled one,
deprived Dobbs and Moulton of the last bit of courage
they had kept so far. All three now held close together.

"We can't stay this way all night," Dobbs said after a few
minutes. "We have to do something."

"We'd better make as few moves as possible," Moulton
advised. "Somewhere I've read that these huge cats jump
at their prey only when they see it make a move."

They listened again into the darkness to find out whether the animal was still near or had disappeared. For many minutes they could hear nothing but the never ceasing singing of the jungle insects. Then they heard the steps again, very distinctly. They seemed to be at the same distance as before.

The Indian then whispered: "Best thing we can do is climb up a tree."

"Tigers climb trees just as easily as they walk on the ground," Moulton said.

Dobbs was of a different opinion. "That muchacho here is right, I think. It's the safest thing we can do. Even if that beast tries to climb the tree, if we are high enough we can defend ourselves with a stick, maybe."

Cautiously feeling around, they succeeded in finding an ebony tree. Dobbs was the first to climb up. No sooner had the Indian taken note of what Dobbs was doing than he was right after him, climbing close behind him and pushing Moulton, who wanted to be next, away from the tree. He keenly wanted not to be the last and so nearest to the ground. He considered the safest place of all exactly between the two Americans, Dobbs above him, and Moulton beneath him. He was ready to sacrifice either of them as long as he could be safe from the claws of the tiger. Anxious as he had been to climb the tree, he had nevertheless not forgotten to take along his bast bag. Not even this bag did he wish to leave to the mercy of the jungle beast.

Moulton had no choice but to climb after the Indian and be so near the ground that the tiger could easily reach his legs with one jump. He consoled himself for his precarious position by calling up to Dobbs: "That devil of an Indian has robbed me of all my chances. But bad as it looks, I am still safer here than on the ground. On the ground I could be carried away by that cat, while here I can hold on for quite a while and I may lose only one leg. Listen, Dobbs, can't you climb up a few feet higher so that I can have a better chance?"

"Nothing doing here," Dobbs said. "I'm already sitting on top of the tree."

After clinging there for a quarter of an hour, they began to feel easier. They now breathed more freely and began to think of more safety. The night had still long to go. It could hardly be ten o'clock. And hanging in the tree like untrained monkeys, they were afraid of falling asleep. Then they might let go and drop to the ground, perhaps right into the open mouth of the tiger, who would surely be waiting under the tree for such a welcome accident. To avoid this they took off their belts and fastened their bodies firmly to the trunk. This done, they felt safe enough to try how one could sleep in this position.

It was a long night; it seemed to them that it would never end. The little sleep they got was frequently interrupted by ugly dreams and by all kinds of hallucinations which tortured their minds. Whole herds of hungry tigers and armies of savage Indians seemed to be after them.

At last morning came with rosy cheeks. In the bright light of the early day everything around them looked absolutely natural—not so very different, it seemed to them, from an abandoned orchard in Alabama. Even the ground beneath them looked not at all so gruesome as at night, when the flickering light of matches gave it such a ghastly impression.

Hardly fifty feet away a green pasture was seen through the trees. It spread out under the morning sun almost like a lawn in the home town. All the imaginings and visions they had had during the night appeared ridiculous by daylight.

The three sat down and had a smoke. The Indian opened his bast bag and produced half a dozen dry tortillas, which he in brotherly fashion divided with the Americans for breakfast.

While sitting there chewing the tortillas, which under these conditions tasted none too good, the three suddenly stopped, held their breath, stiffened their bodies, and listened. Clearly, without any doubt, they heard again the curious steps and the suppressed growling or mumbling they had heard during the night. These peculiar and unmistakable noises had settled in their memory so firmly that for the rest of their lives they would never forget them; they would recognize these sounds anywhere and any time. These were the same steps and sounds they had heard during the night. It was strange that a tiger should come out of his lair in bright daylight to attack men.

On hearing the sounds again, they jumped up together. They stared between the trees in the direction from which these steps and sounds came now, as they had also come during the night.

Their glance fell upon the green pasture. And there was the tiger. The tiger was stepping lazily around and eating grass, at times letting off a sort of a grunt out of sheer content. The tiger was a very harmless one; he was a burro, in fact, an ordinary ass tied to a tree by a long lasso, the property, doubtless, of a peasant in the next village, which certainly could not be far away. Where a simple burro could pass the night and survive, there surely could be no tiger near; otherwise the peasants would not leave their animals overnight in the bush.

Dobbs looked at Moulton, and Moulton at Dobbs. Just as Moulton started to open his lips for a hearty laugh, Dobbs said to him harshly: "Listen, you, if you don't want me to sock you, don't laugh. What's more, if you ever tell anybody one word about this night and make both of us the joke of the port, I—bigawd, I'll murder you in cold blood

THE TREASURE OF THE SIERRA MADRE 41
and throw your carcass to the pigs."

"All right by me, buddy," Moulton said; "if you take it that way I'll keep quiet. But I think it's the best joke I ever heard." As could be seen from the contortion of his face he did all in his power to keep from exploding with laughter.

Dobbs looked at him and said: "Brother, you are warned. Don't play any tricks on me. Even the faintest smile will cost you a smashed nose."

It was at this moment that the Indian thought it proper to speak up. He did not accept defeat. So he said: "Por Madre Santísima and by all the saints in heaven, señores, this is not the tiger. But around us last night was un tigre real y muy grande, it was a royal tiger of the biggest sort."

"Aw, shut up!" Dobbs interrupted him.

"You, caballeros, may think what you may. But I know mi tierra, my country where I was born, and I know well what is a tiger and what is not. I can smell it. Besides I saw his glowing greenish eyes glaring at us. And they were not the eyes of a burro." The Indian sure was smarter than the two Americans; he knew how to stick to a good story and to avoid being laughed at.

The big village of which the Indians had spoken last night was hardly fifteen minutes away.

"Now, didn't I tell you last night that these Indians don't lie?" Dobbs asked when they reached the village.

"But they said it was only a short hour's distance."

"Well, that's just the matter with these people, they have no conception of time and distance. They say it is one hour away, but they don't tell you if they mean an hour run by a Tarahumare, or walked or crawled, or an hour's ride on a good horse. That's what you have to figure out when an Indian peasant tells you how far away the next town is. You can't blame those Indians of last night. They told us the truth in their own way, and that makes all the difference."

In this village the three found fine hospitality. They had breakfast, consisting of tortillas, black beans, and tea brewed from lemon leaves.

The same day they came to the first oil-camp. No work. The manager told them that they might stay there a day or two and have their meals, but more he could not do for them.

"I am afraid, boys," he added, "there is no camp around here where work may be had. Tell you a secret, believe it or not, but I'm an old-timer and I know a cat when I see one, and I tell you I've got the feeling oil is going on the rocks hereabouts, maybe in the whole God-damned republic. Guess we'll have to go back home to good old Oklahoma and grow beans once more. It's slacking down in all the camps and with all the companies. Good times are over, so it seems. The war came to its God-damned end too early, that's the trouble; that's what I think. There's more oil than the world will ever need in the next ten thousand years. Nobody wants to buy oil any more, and if anybody buys, damn knock me cold, he offers you flat two bits for the barrel, take it or go to hell. I know oil and I know when the fat is gone. All right, sit down and push your spoon between your teeth. Don't worry, the boys will stand for what you eat today, and tomorrow too, if you want to stay."

The Indian went to his own people, to the peons of the camp, where he stuffed his belly full. The peons had their own kitchen, managed by one whom they seemed to trust better than the two Chinese who were in charge of the catering for the Americans.

Next morning Dobbs and Moulton left to try another camp. The Indian was again with them. They could not shake him off. His excuse was: "I need work, señores, but

I cannot go alone through the jungles, the tigers would get me. But these terrible beasts won't do anything to me if I am with gringos. Tigers are horribly afraid of gringos, but un pobre Mexicano is eaten by them just like nothing, going alone through the jungle."

Dobbs and Moulton threw stones at him to show him that he was not welcome. It looked somewhat awkward for two Americans looking for work and a free meal to bring along an Indian with them. Rough as they might treat that poor man to induce him to stay behind, he was stoical. He followed them like a dog, not minding stones thrown at him nor the promise of a sound beating. He would even have taken the beating if he could have gained by it the right to walk behind them. The two finally let him have his way. So he was the winner after all.

They reached another camp. It was the same story there. No work, and the outlook far from promising. The field manager had also the feeling that oil was no longer easy money, only he had another explanation to offer—that the new oil laws of the republic were to blame for the dying of the business. "That hell of a government is confiscating all the oil, declaring all oil land the property of the nation. Why, for devil's sake, didn't they think of that fifty years ago when we had no money stuck in it? The whole world goes Bolshevik, and I don't care a worn-out step-in either. I'll go Bolshevik too, first thing when I see it coming; that's what I'm going to do, blaze my time. Sit down and fill up the ol' tank to the rim. I got word from H.Q. we are closing down. Likely next week I can go along with you, pushing camps for a meal."

Having made five camps and swallowed five different stories about the lack of work and the causes of the oil business breathing its last, both Moulton and Dobbs decided that it would be a waste of time and hard work to go any farther. In two camps they had already met men coming back from other camps who had lost jobs which they had held for years.

"Best thing for us to do," Moulton said, "is to go back where we came from. In town there's a better chance than here to get work and to meet somebody who is looking for men for rigging a new camp. Around here are the old established fields. There's no chance here. Better look for new fields."

"There's something in what you say," Dobbs answered. "I was told that to the north of the river, near the Altamira section, there might be something doing very soon. Guess you're right. Let's hoof back."

So one day, late in the afternoon, they arrived in the port again. Moulton said: "Here we are. Now everybody for himself once more."

With these words their partnership was broken up.

9

While they had been away, no change had taken place in town. The same fellows were hanging around the curbstones and pushing every man that came to town from the fields for a drink, a good steak, a gamble, and a girl. Not one of these curbstone-polishers had left for better places. And exactly the same boys that held the corner of the Southern Hotel and the entrance to the bank on the ground floor were doing exactly the same as they had done last week, last month, last year perhaps. That is to say, waiting to be taken to the Madrid Bar or the Louisiana to help somebody with money to get drunk. They all knew the prayers to say at the right time and in the right way and to the right gods. So they spent life, strength, and will-power.

Dobbs did not feel sorry for having gone out to the camps

to look for work. It was worth the trouble to know that out of town jobs were just as rare as in town. He had no longer to worry about having missed his chances in life or having overlooked opportunity knocking at the back door.

One morning, strolling along the freight depot, he was hailed by the manager of an American agency for agricultural machinery. They were unloading machinery and he was asked if he would like to lend a hand for a day or two. He accepted and was offered four pesos a day. The natives who worked at the same job got only two pesos.

The work was hard and his knuckles peeled off ten times a day. Anyway the four pesos were welcome money. After five days the job was finished and he had to go.

A few days later, standing at the ferry that crosses the river to the Pánuco depot and wondering if he might get a chance to go to that town for a change, five men came running along to catch the ferry that was just about to make off.

One of the men, square-shouldered and rather bulky, caught a glimpse of Dobbs, stopped, and yelled: "What you looking for? Job?"

"Yep. Got one for me?"

"Come here. Hurry, the ferry is making off. I've got a job for you if you want to go. Hard work, but good pay. Ever worked at rigging up a camp?"

"Sure."

"I've got a contract to rig a camp. The hell of it is I'm short a hand; one dirty son of a bitch has kicked out and left me flat. Maybe malaria, or what the hell do I know, or perhaps it's a God-damned skirt that's holding him. I can't wait for that guy to show up. All right, you're hired."

"What's the pay?"

"Eight bucks American a day. Grub goes off on your expense. Figure the Chinese cook will charge one dollar eighty a day. You make six bucks a day clean. Hell, don't stand and guffaw; come along."

Only ten minutes ago Dobbs would have run after a job for two dollars a day like a hungry cat after a fat cockroach. Now he looked as though he expected an embrace of gratitude for taking the job offered.

"Come on or go to the devil," the contractor cried. "You have to come the way you are; there's no time to get your things. The ferry doesn't wait, nor the train either. And if we don't go right this minute we can't make the train."

Without waiting for a reply he grasped Dobbs by the sleeve and dragged him on the ferry.

10

Pat McCormick, the contractor, was an old-timer. Before he had come down here, he had worked in Texas fields and afterwards in Oklahoma. He had come down here before the war, before there was anything that looked like a coming boom. There wasn't a job connected with oil at which he had not tried his hand. He had been teamster, truck-driver, time-keeper, driller, tool-dresser, pumpman, storeman—anything that had come his way he had tackled. In recent years he had found out that there is more money in rigging up camps by contract—so much for the camp ready to start drilling. He had acquired an excellent eye for judging the job. He could look over a lot in the jungle and name his price for the job in such a well-calculated way that the company thought they were buying cheap when in fact he made a large profit on every contract. His trick was to get good and efficient labor cheap, cheaper than any company could get it. A company cannot hire workers with back-pattings and cajoling, making them believe they are being taken on out of pity. Pat knew how to play the good fellow, even the Bolshevik comrade, to catch his men cheap. He could curse the big capitalist companies and their unscrupulous shareholders better than a Communist speaker when he wanted to soft-soap good workers. According to him, he never came out of his contract with any profit; he always lost his good money, so hard-earned in better times, and he took contracts, he said, only because he could not see men who wanted to work suffer from unemployment and starvation. In camp he played the good fellow-worker, joking and friendly. The whole job he handled as if it were a sort of co-operative enterprise in which all joined for the general good. He told how excellent Communism is; if he had his way, the United States and all South America would become a paradise for the Communists tomorrow.

American boys he couldn't catch so easily with these ideas. Americans knew this sort of Pat too well to fall for his co-operative contracts. He took on Americans only when he could procure no others. Most welcome were the newly arrived Hunks, Czechs, Poles, Germans, Italians, fellows who had heard back home the stories of men working in the Mexican oil-fields and earning from thirty to fifty dollars a day almost without bending a finger. Having arrived in the republic, they learned during the first week that such fantastic wages were as rare as are the wages a bricklayer gets in Chicago, according to the fairy-tales circulating in Europe. After these men are here two months or so they kneel down before any contractor who offers them five dollars a day, and if he offers them eight, they worship him as they never worship the Almighty, and the contractor may do with them what he likes. After six months without a job they are ready to accept whatever is offered.

Dobbs would not have fallen for the doctrines of Pat McCormick had he tried them on him. His economic condition left him no choice. He was in his way as glad at land-ing this job as were the Hunks.

The co-operative arrangement made it obligatory for all hands to work eighteen hours out of twenty-four, every day as long as the contract lasted. There was no extra pay. Eight dollars was the pay for the working-day, and the length of the working-day was decided by Pat. There was no rest on Sunday. The Mexican hands were protected by their law. They could not be worked a minute longer than eight hours or Pat would have landed in jail and been kept there until he paid ten thousand pesos for breaking the labor law.

A sort of road had been cut out of the jungle so that in very dry weather the trucks could come right on the lot where the camp was to be rigged up. Mexican peons, having been sent a few weeks ahead by Pat, had the camp-site cleared when the rig-builders arrived.

Eight dollars a day looked like a lot of money when Dobbs had nothing in his stomach, but he learned that eight dollars a day may be meager pay for certain jobs. The heat was never less than one hundred degrees in the open, where all the work had to be done, surrounded by jungle. He was pestered by the ten thousand sorts of insects and reptiles the jungle breeds. He thought a hundred times a day that his eyes would burn away from the heat above and around him. No breeze could reach the men at work here. Carrying lumber, hoisting it high up for the derrick to be built, and hanging often for minutes like monkeys with only one hand on a beam, or holding on with one leg snake-fashion around a rope and grasping heavy boards swinging out that had to be hauled in to be riveted or bolted, he risked his life twenty times every day, and all for eight dollars.

Pat allowed no rest except for a few hours' sleep. Until eleven at night they worked by the light of gas-lanterns, and at five in the morning they were already hard at work again. "We have to use the cool morning hours, boys," Pat would say when he waked them. No sooner had they gulped down their coffee at meal-time and settled to pick their teeth leisurely than Pat would get restless and hustle them up: "Boys, sure it's hot. I know. We're in the tropics. It's hot in Texas sometimes too. Hell knows it's not my fault. I have to finish that God-damn contract. The sooner we're through, the sooner we'll be out of this hell here, and we'll go back to town and have cold drinks. Hi, Harry, get the Mexicans, those damn lazy rascals, to unload the steam-engine, and start to adjust the parts. Jump at it. And, Slick, you and Dobbs get the drum up the derrick and have it anchored. I'll see after the cabins. Hurry, hurry up and get busy."

Pat McCormick sure made a pile with these contracts. He was paid well by the companies for the rigging contracts. The companies allowed fair wages and decent working-hours for all, but the sooner Pat could finish the job, the more was left over to go into his pockets, for he had no other expenses than the wages he paid out. To drain the last ounce of work out of his men he promised them a bonus if inside of a certain number of days the job were finished. This promise of a bonus was his whip, since he knew that a real slave-driver's whip would not do with workers today. He won; he won always. He rigged up two camps in the same time other contractors would have rigged barely one.

"All right, boys, put all your bones into that job. You'll be with me again on my next contract. I've already got three almost for sure coming my way. Get going." This was another whip he used, promising his slaves future jobs provided they worked the way he wanted them to.

When the camp was rigged, the gang went back to town. The Mexican peons returned to their near-by villages.

Said Dobbs: "Now what about the pay? I haven't seen a buck yet from you, Pat."

"What's the hurry, pal? You'll get your dough all right,

don't you worry a bit. I won't run away with it. You're again on my next contract I have with the Mex Gulf. Sure you are."

"Now look here, Pat," said Dobbs, "I haven't got a cent even to buy me a new shirt. I look like the worst bum."

"Now don't you cry out for mother here," Pat tried to quiet him. "Tell you what I'll do. I'll let you have thirty per cent of your pay. That's all I can do for you. And don't you tell the others."

Dobbs learned that none of the other boys had received his wages in full. Two who were eager to be with Pat on the next contract again had asked very humbly "at least a little, please, Mr. Pat," and they were awarded five per cent, so that they could have a few meals; they had not eaten since they had returned to town.

11

Within a few days Dobbs had heard many tales about Pat McCormick. Pat was known not to pay cash to his men if he could avoid it. This was one of the reasons that he seldom had an American with him on a contract. Only foreigners and half-baked Americans fell for him. Most of them were glad to go with him any time he hollered. They had their meals because Pat paid the Chinese cook for catering as advance on the wages for the boys. And usually he paid something in cash when the boys he owed were running after him and crying that they had no money for eats and for beds.

One afternoon when Dobbs was drinking a glass of coffee at the bar of the Spanish café on the plaza, Curtin, passing by, saw him and stepped up.

"I might as well have coffee too. What you doing, Dobble?"

Curtin, who was from California, had worked for Pat with Dobbs.

"Did you get your money?" Dobbs asked.

"Forty per cent is all I've squeezed out of that bandit so far."

"I'd like to know one thing—if he has collected the pay for the contract—that's what I would like to know," Dobbs said.

"Rather difficult to find out," answered Curtin. "The companies are often a bit slow in paying the contracts. Often they are short of ready cash, since the funds they have here in the republic are all taken up for drilling-expenses or for paying out options unexpectedly acquired."

"You've got no idea, Cuts, for which company the contract was?"

"Not even a touch. Could just as well have been for an outsider, a private party that wants to try his luck in oil. What do I know?" Curtin said.

For a whole week Dobbs and Curtin had been running after Pat. He could not be found anywhere. At the Bristol Hotel, where he usually lived, the clerk knew nothing about him.

"He's hiding out somewhere to get away with the money," Curtin thought. "He knows that we can't hang around here all the time. So he waits for the moment that we take another job; then he comes out of his hole."

Dobbs, after another gulp of coffee, said: "I wouldn't be at all surprised if that guy uses our money to speculate with in some new well. He's got tips all the way to the Alamo and to the Ebano sections."

This idea made Curtin hot. "That guy's going to learn something from me. Just let me catch him."

At that very instant Pat McCormick strolled across the plaza, with a Mexican dame at his side who was flashing a new dress, elegant shoes, and a new colorful silk umbrella.

"What do you think of that?" Dobbs asked. "Rags paid for with our hard-earned money."

"Let's get him, right now," Curtin hollered, "and let's get him hard this time."

As quick as the devil Curtin was at Pat's side, and with him was Dobbs.

Curtin caught Pat by the shirt-sleeve, for he was wearing no coat.

"How are you, boys? Want **a** drink?" Pat tried to be friendly.

Then he noticed that these two men were deadly serious, so he said to the dame: "Perdóne me, shlucksy dear, mi vida, I've got some business to attend to with these two gentlemen. I'll take you over to that café. You wait there for me awhile, honey."

He steered her to the colonnades of the Light and Power building, ordered a sundae for her, patted her on the back, and said: "Just wait here, mi dulce, I won't be long, only a few minutes, no más que unos minutos, sure."

Dobbs and Curtin waited only a few feet away.

Pat came strolling down the few steps and down the street along the plaza as though he were alone. Seeing that the two fellows did not leave him, but kept close by his side, he halted before the W.U. cable office and said: "Let's have a drink, it's on me."

"Okay," Curtin gave in. "Let's have one. But you understand that's not why we're after you."

They stepped into the Madrid cantina, and Pat ordered three shots of Scotch.

"Make mine a Hennessy," Dobbs said to the bartender.

"Make it two," from Curtin.

"Scotch is still good enough for me." Pat repeated his order for himself.

When the drinks were before them Pat asked: "Now, what do you want? Sure, I take you on my next contract. Don't you worry."

"Don't play innocent; you know what we want." Dobbs came to the point.

"Look here, to make it short and plain," Curtin pulled his drink closer, "where is our money? You won't get away this time, I can tell you that. We worked harder than nigger slaves, you know that. Now we've waited three weeks for our pay. Let's have it, and right here and now and no mebbe."

The drinks were gone.

"Three habaneros," ordered Pat. "No, Chuchu, make them big, make'm schooners."

"Habaneros? Playing the miser, mister? Won't do," Dobbs sneered. But he shot in the drink just the same.

"Now, look here, boys," Pat tried his game. "Fact is I haven't got that God-damned contract paid yet myself. If I had the money, I'd pay you the first thing. You know that. I'll take you both on my next contract, you can count on that. Sure shot. It'll go through by Monday and we can set out Friday. Glad to have you boys with me again. Well, here's mud in your eyes. Shoot."

Curtin was not impressed by this soaping. He said: "Good of you, Pat, to take us with you again. But don't you get the idea you can honey-smear us with this likker and with your oiled tongue. We know those speeches of yours by heart. They don't work any more. Come across with the smackers, and no stalling either. Get me?"

"Damned son of a dog, get the money or you won't leave this joint alive! Geecries, I am sick of that swashing of yours!" Dobbs yelled, and tackled him with his two hands and bent him hard against the bar.

"Be quiet, gentlemen, quiet please, this is an orderly

place," the bartender butted in. He didn't mean it. He just
wanted to show that he had something to say and that,
should anything serious happen, he could claim that he had
tried his best to calm the men. He took up a rag and wiped
the bar clean. Then he broke in: "The same, gentlemen?"
Without waiting for their answer he filled up the good-
sized glasses with the golden habanero. Then he lighted a
cigarette, put his elbows on the bar, and read *El Mundo*.

Pat could easily have licked Dobbs, and also Curtin, one
at a time. To try to lick both of them at the same time
would have been too costly for him. Since he had a new
contract waiting for him, he couldn't afford anything beyond two black eyes and a few bruises. He could see that
Dobbs and Curtin were in a state of mind which would
make them forget to fight it out in a decent way, and that
he had every chance to land in the hospital and stay there
for weeks, while the contract would go to someone else.

Realizing that it was the cheapest way out for him to
pay them their money, he said: "Tell you, boys, what I'll
do. I gave you thirty per cent. I'll give you another thirty
now, or I reckon I can make it forty. The balance let's say
the middle of next week."

"Nothing doing next week," Curtin insisted. "Now and
here every cent you owe us, or I swear you won't go out
of here. At least not alive."

Pat drew up his lips in an ugly manner. "You are thieves
and highwaymen. I should have known this before. I
wouldn't trust you to sleep in the same cabin with me, or
I might wake up in the morning and find myself murdered
and robbed. Take you again on one of my jobs? Not on your
knees. If I saw you dying in the street, I wouldn't even
kick you to give you the last grace. Here, take your dough
and get out of my sight."

"Aw, shut up," Dobbs shouted, "we know your church

sermons. Get the money and be quick about it."

While Pat was talking he must have counted the money in his pocket very accurately because now with one jerk he brought out a bunch of dollar bills, crumpled them in his fist, and banged them upon the bar. "There is the money," he said. Then he winked at the bartender, threw a handful of pesos on the bar, and bellowed: "That's for the drinks. I don't accept drinks paid for by skunks. Keep the damn change and buy you a hotel."

With this he tipped his hat back on his neck and left.

2

"Why are you living in the Roosevelt Hotel, buddy?" Dobbs asked Curtin as they passed the Southern Hotel. "You pay at least five pesos a day there."

"Seven," Curtin answered.

"Better come bunk with me in the Oso Negro. Fifty centavos the cot."

"I couldn't stand the dirt and living among that crowd of tramps, beachcombers, and damn bums."

"All right, president, just as you like," Dobbs said. "Some beautiful day when all the pretty money is gone you'll land in that dirt, too. Bet you. Right now I could afford to stop in any swell joint for a while. But I learned my lesson. I keep my little buckies together. Who knows in which of the next four centuries another job'll come along. It's getting worse every day here. Say, four, five, or six years back you were begged to accept a job and make your price. It's different now. To me it doesn't look a bit as if it would change for the better during the next few years. Believe it or not, I'm still going to the Chink for my eats, fifty centavos each meal. I don't mind. Nobody gives me anything when I haven't got a dime."

They had reached the corner of the plaza where the great jewelry house, La Perla, had its store. In the four huge windows was a display of diamonds and gold which could hardly be equaled on Broadway. There was a diadem on

display priced at twenty-four thousand pesos. Never could
there be any occasion in this port for a lady to wear such
a costly diadem. It was not meant for wear in this town, as
whoever bought it would know. A few hundred men in this
town made such heaps of money and made it so quickly and
with so little sweat that they simply did not know what to
do with it. Luxurious cars were out, because there were no
roads for them. And the streets were mostly still in such a
condition that only the flivver could go everywhere. These
men could invest their money, and they did. But the more
they invested, the more money they made, and then they
were faced with the same question again, only this time
more urgently. What to do with that dough? The pro-
prietors of La Perla knew what they were doing when they
displayed such high-priced jewelry. Any piece that looked
pretty to a newly rich oilman and that carried a fantasti-
cally high price was rarely in the window for more than
three days. Then it was sold to a man who stepped in looking like a bum, without a coat on, soiled all over with oil.
"Wrap this up for me and be quick about it; I'm in a
hurry." And throwing the money on the counter, he would
put the elegant little case in his pants pockets as though it
were a cake of soap and leave without saying "Thank you!"
or "So long!"

Dobbs and Curtin looked at these treasures worth all together near a hundred thousand dollars, and a crowd of
thoughts sprang up in their minds. Of stealing any of these
jewels they did not think for a minute. During all the years
the boom was on, there was practically no bank hold-up, no
wholesale robbery in the port. The only bank hold-up that
occurred left not one of the bandits reaching the curbstone
alive, and the man waiting outside in a car had to be taken
to the hospital, where everything possible was done not to
let him survive. These jewels displayed behind window-

panes were as safe as inside a vault. It was not that people
were any better here than anywhere else. There were pickpockets everywhere in town, American pickpockets of
course taking the lead. But banks and jewelry were safe
from bandits. Bandits could not make a get-away, as there
were no roads on which cars could run. Only two trains
left the port daily, and these could be watched successfully
even by third-rate detectives. All ships, passengers and
freighters alike, had their guards on the gangways. The
port was protected on one side by the sea, on the other
side by river, swamps, and jungle. The three or four dirt
roads leading out of the port were watched by mounted
police. Mexicans might have kept in hiding, but they were
not smart enough to do a big job of this sort. American
bandits had no chance to hide anywhere. Since all bandits
knew from experience that no bandit if caught would ever
arrive at a police-station alive, people—yes, even mere boys
—could walk the streets with bags filled to the brim with
gold coins on their shoulders without being accompanied,
and they would bring home the money surer than in an
armored car in the United States.

So it was not the thought of robbing the store that occupied the minds of Dobbs and Curtin.

All those living and working in the port at that time were
concerned with oil and nothing else. Whatever you did had
in some way or other to do with oil. Even when eating your
dinner or drinking your coffee the smell of oil was about
you. You might see a lady well dressed, perfumed and all;
you would be sure to find somewhere about her a stain or
a spot of oil—on the elegant dress, the white shoes, the
umbrella, or the handbag—somewhere you would find traces
of oil, you bet.

Now, looking at all the gold in the window, for the first
time in months if not in years Dobbs and Curtin thought of

gold and for a minute forgot to think of oil.

Then they stood with their backs against the post-office building, looked across the plaza, and saw the masts of the ships that were in dock. Only the upper parts of the masts were visible from where they stood, and the bow of a freighter. Seeing the masts reminded them of travels in far-away countries. So they came to think of other countries in the world and other possibilities of making money. Why should it be oil all the time? Wasn't there anything else on earth? Take gold for instance, to name only one thing.

2

"Say, Curts, what's your idea?" Dobbs asked. "I mean your idea about all this here. Hanging around all the time, waiting and waiting until you land a job again for a few weeks or a few months. Then you are on the bum again, waiting and waiting for another break. Forever dependent on the good humor of a contractor who may or may not take you in, and your money getting thinner every day. After a while you are broke and you begin once more pushing gents for a dime, sleeping in freight cars or under trees or what have you. I'm sick of it. Sick of oil. That's it. Sick of oil. I want to see something different, want to hear somebody talking of something else."

"Same here, pal. Exactly the same. In fact, I'm thinking now for the third time of pulling out of here. I know perfectly well how it goes. Into a job, out of a job. Polishing the corner of the Banking Company in the Southern and waiting for some guy to step up and take you on for another few months. Why not try gold-digging for a change?"

"You said it, buddy." Dobbs nodded. "That's what I was thinking as I stood before that lay-out of gold and diamonds. Prospecting—that's the word! Come to think of it, it isn't any more risky than waiting here for another break. Did it ever occur to you, old man, that this is the country where the heaps of gold and silver are just calling for you to help them out of their misery, help them out of the ground; make them shine in coins; on the fingers and necks of swell dames? Well, my man, we're right on the spot."

"Let's sit on that bench over there," Curtin suggested. "We have to figure this out. It's a swell idea. We have to make plans. Just wait a minute. Let me think this over."

After they were seated, Curtin continued: "Tell you a secret. I didn't come to this here country for oil. Never dreamed of it. I'd had my nose full of it already in San Antonio, ol' Texas. No, I came here just for gold, and nothing but. My idea was to work for a year or two here in the camps to stow away enough dough to buy a decent outfit and then go off to the Sierra, west and more west, and there look for the real thing that counts. But, damn it all, I never got the money. When I had five hundred bucks and was all set to make another five, then there was no job for months and the money went rolling away from me just like that."

"In fact," Dobbs said, "the risk isn't so big. To wait here until you land another job is just as tough. If you're lucky you may make three hundred a month. If you're unlucky you may wait for twelve months and not get even a job carrying lumber. And what is the risk anyway? If we don't touch gold, it may be silver. If isn't silver, it may be copper or lead or precious stones. There's always something to be found that has value. Life is cheaper in the open than it is here. Our money lasts longer, and the longer it lasts, the greater is our chance of digging up something."

When it came to making more definite plans, they found that the money they had was far from sufficient to make even a try. So their enthusiasm died down.

Once more, men who had a good idea appeared to give it up as soon as they met the first obstacle. This happened to most of the men here. There was not a single man in port who had not thought several times of looking for a lost gold mine—or for a new one. All the mines in the country which produced any kind of mineral had been found and opened by men who originally went out to look for gold. Then, not finding any gold, even in small quantities, they were well satisfied with copper, lead, zinc, or even talcum.

Dobbs and Curtin would, most likely, never have thought again of looking seriously for gold after they had talked it over. It was so much easier to sit and watch two men at work in a rather dangerous position on a roof fixing telephone wires, it was so much less trouble than thinking for yourself, or standing all day long opposite the bank waiting for something to turn up all by itself. It is always more convenient to dream of what might be.

3

Curtin decided to stay one night more at the Roosevelt and the next day change over to the Oso Negro.

When Dobbs returned home he found in the same shack with him three other Americans. The rest of the cots were not yet occupied. One of the three Americans was an elderly fellow whose hair was beginning to show white.

On entering, Dobbs noted that the three fellow-guests ceased their talk. After a while they took it up again.

The old man was lying on his cot, the other two were sitting half-undressed on theirs. Dobbs started to turn in.

At first he did not catch what they were talking about. It did not take him long to understand that the old fellow was telling the two younger men his experiences as a prospector. The two young men had come to the republic to look for gold because back home the most fantastic tales about the riches of lost gold mines here in this country had stirred their ambition to make their millions down here.

"Anyway," Howard, the old fellow, said, "anyway, gold is a very devilish sort of a thing, believe me, boys. In the first place, it changes your character entirely. When you have it your soul is no longer the same as it was before. No getting away from that. You may have so much piled up that you can't carry it away; but, bet your blessed paradise, the more you have, the more you want to add, to make it just that much more. Like sitting at roulette. Just one more turn. So it goes on and on and on. You cease to distinguish between right and wrong. You can no longer see clearly what is good and what is bad. You lose your judgment. That's what it is."

"I don't see why," one of the youngsters broke in.

"Oh yes, you'll see it. When you go out, you tell yourself: I shall be satisfied with fifty thousand handsome smackers, or the worth of it, so help me, Lord, and cross my heart. Elegant resolution. After sweating the hell out of you, going short of provisions, and seeing nothing and finding nothing, you come down to forty thousand, then to thirty, and you reach five thousand, and you say to yourself: If I only could make five grand, Lord, I sure would be grateful and never want anything, anything more in all my life."

"Five thousand wouldn't be so bad, after all," the same young fellow butted in.

"Oh, be quiet," said his partner; "can't you shut up a minute when you see somebody is telling you something worth listening to, you mug?"

"It's not at all so easy as you fellers think it might be," Howard went on. "You'd be satisfied with five grand. But I tell you, if you find something then, you couldn't be dragged away; not even the threat of miserable death could stop you getting just ten thousand more. And if you reach fifty, you want to make it a hundred, to be safe for the rest of your life. When you finally have a hundred and fifty, you want two hundred, to make sure, absolutely sure, that you'll be really on the safe side, come what may."

Dobbs had become excited. To show that he had a right to be there and to listen to the wise man he said: "That wouldn't happen to me. I swear it. I'd take twenty thousand, pack up, and go. I'd do that even if there were still half a million bucks' worth lying around howling to be picked up. I wouldn't take it. It's just twenty grand that I'm after to make me perfectly happy and healthy."

Howard looked at him, scrutinizing, it seemed, every wrinkle of his face. He did so for quite a while. But he answered indirectly. As though he hadn't been interrupted he continued: "Whoever has never been out for gold doesn't know what's really going on at the spot. I know for a fact it's easier to leave a gambling-table when you're winning than to leave a rich claim after you've made your good cut. It's all spread out before you like the treasures of that Arabian mug Aladdin. It's all yours for the taking. No, sir, you can't leave it, not even with a wire in your fist that your old mother back home is dying and all alone. See, I've dug in Alaska and made a bit; I've been in the crowd in British Columbia and made there at least my fair wages. I was down in Australia, where I made the fare back home, with a few hundred left over to cure me of a stomach trouble I caught down there. I've dug in Montana and in Colorado and I don't know where else."

One of the youngsters asked: "As you say, mister, you've dug practically all over the world, then how come you're sitting here now in this dirty joint and all broke?"

"Gold, my young man, that's the gold, that's what it makes out of us. There was a time when I had a bank account of over a hundred thousand spot cash, and another hundred grand invested. One of the banks went singing the old song: that there wasn't one cent to the dollar left. Two of the investments failed and left me with the first claim on a melting company. After all was paid out, I had on hand a debt of some sixteen grand. I've made here in this port some seventy grand on a gusher. The last fifty, which I kept with the idea that I'd never touch the principal, went into a dry hole. So you see me here now in the Oso Negro, pushing old friends in the streets to get fifty centavos for a cot to sleep on. Sure, I'm an old bone by now. No doubt as to that. But don't you kids think that the spirit is gone. Not on your life. I'm all set to shoulder pick-ax and shovel again any time you say—any time somebody is willing to share the expenses. I'd like best to go all alone, all by myself. But I haven't got the funds to do that. Tell you, the best thing is going alone. Of course you must have the guts to stand loneliness. Lots of guys go nutty being alone for a long time. On the other hand, going with a partner or two is dangerous. All the time murder's lurking about. The cuts are not so good as when you're all by yourself. Worst of all, hardly a day passes without quarrels, everybody accusing everybody else of all sorts of crimes, and suspecting whatever you do or say or even look at. As long as there's no find, the noble brotherhood will last. Woe when the piles begin to grow! Then you know your men and what they are worth."

None of the three fellows interrupted the old prospector. Lying on their cots, they listened to his talk with more eagerness than they would have shown in reading a hot story. Here one of the true regulars was speaking, and such a chance might never come again. The stories told in the pulps seemed to them right now just so much rot. Who writes these stories, anyhow? Men sitting in an office in a big city. Men who have never been on the spot themselves. What do they know? The real life is quite different. Here it was, the real life, and the man who had lived the real life and had seen the world, who had been rich, very rich, and who was now so broke that he had to ask a fellow in the street for fifty centavos for a meal with the Chink.

Once started, and seeing around him three fellows who forgot their breathing while he spun his yarns, Howard gave them a story such as they never could have read in a magazine sold at street corners.

3

"Ever heard the story—I mean the real true story—of La Mina Agua Verde, the Green Water Mine? I don't think so. Well, here it is for your benefit. I got it at first hand from Harry Tilton. He was one of those who made their pile in that mine.

"It seems a company of fifteen fellows set out to trace that old mine. You couldn't say that they went absolutely unprepared. Far from it.

"In that section, right at the international line of Arizona and the Mexican state of Sonora, a rumor about a lost gold mine would never die. The tale had come down for the last four centuries if not more. The old Mexicans, the Aztecs, had worked that mine long before any European knew a thing about America. The gold was carried to old Tenochtitlan, that is today Mexico City, to be worked there into ornaments and dishes for their emperor and for their kings and nobles, and of course for their great temples.

"The Spaniards in their greed for gold tried to locate all the gold and silver mines on seeing the rich treasures of the Aztec and the Tarascan kings. By the most terrible tortures, which only Spaniards grown up under the régime of the Inquisitors could conceive, the old Mexicans and the other Indians were forced to reveal the mines where the gold had come from for the royal treasures. All the gruesome tortures were committed for the love of Christ and the Holy Virgin,

66

because there was never a torture without a monk holding out a crucifix before the victim, and the greater part of the gold was to go partly to the Spanish king and partly to the Holy Father in Rome. As the Indians were not Christians, but wretched heathen, it was no sin to get hold of their gold by robbing them.

"This mine was betrayed to monks who had come to the Indians with oiled speeches of saving their souls and shipping them off to heaven. The church took possession of the mine. Before long, however, the viceroy of New Spain— that was what Mexico was called in those times—in consideration of huge land concessions, bought the mine in the name of the king.

"It was an unbelievably rich mine. The gold lay practically open, and in thick lodes. The mine was located in a mountainous region, and near by was a little lake of crystal-clear emerald water bedded in the rocks. From this beautiful little lake the mine received its name.

"Something was certainly queer about the mine. The Spaniards who were working there as officials seldom survived for any length of time. Hardly one of them ever saw his country again, and few even returned to the capital. They were attacked by all sorts of misfortune. Some were bitten by snakes; others by venomous scorpions or tarantulas; others contracted rare skin diseases that never healed, or they caught a sickness the cause and nature of which nobody, including all their doctors, could explain. As if this was not sufficient, whoever was spared attacks from reptiles and mysterious diseases died from the different kinds of fevers that abounded.

"It was evident that the Indians had cursed the mine to revenge the tortures inflicted upon them for the possession of the mine and the outrageous robbery committed by the invaders. In those times whatever could not be explained was considered caused by witchcraft.

"Priests and even bishops were sent to bless the mine. When this was of no avail the Pope himself sent his special benediction for the mine. A hundred masses were celebrated all about the mine; every drift-way and tunnel was blessed separately; all tools, machinery, and furnaces were blessed.

"Anyway, the curse of the Indians turned out to be far stronger than all the blessings and benedictions of all the dignitaries of the Roman church. Conditions became worse. Officials lasted hardly a year; then they died or disappeared on hunting-trips.

"Men, Christians and Jews alike, are so greedy or brave where gold is at stake that, regardless how many human beings it may cost, as long as the gold itself does not give out and disappear, they will risk life, health, and mind, and face every danger and risk conceivable, to get hold of the precious metal.

"The curse, or what the invaders called the curse, took on greater dimensions, but this widening of the curse had nothing to do with mysterious doings of the Indians and of their chiefs.

"All the real work at the mine was done by Indians. At the beginning, when the monks owned the mine, labor was acquired by a clever scheme of the fathers. The Indians were baptized, and in return for having their souls saved, they had to work for the new Lord in heaven, since they were considered now His beloved children and with those Indians it was law that children had to work for their fathers whenever required. Occasionally the fathers gave them little gifts of cheap merchandise. One of the various reasons why the church so readily agreed to sell out to the government was that the labor problem had become extremely difficult. The Indians became wise to the real meaning of the tricks of the fathers and to the fact that these white men with their new

god cared less for the earthly welfare of their children than
for the riches they could accumulate. Consequently the
fathers found every day fewer men willing to work here
just for the grace of the Lord. Since the fathers were more
concerned with an easy life for themselves than with walking
on thorny and rocky roads and doing all the work in the
mine without the help of the innocent children of the earth,
it was decided that exploiting this gold mine was a sinful
operation if carried on by the church, and that it was more
virtuous before the Lord to accept the good offer of the
government to buy it. Concessions for immense tracts of
land suited the church better, for a mine may give out, while
land will last for ever. Besides, a very important point had
been that the fathers could not transport the proceeds of
the mine to the capital without the help of the government,
which furnished the soldiers to protect the transport. And
the viceroy, if asked for the convoy, never had soldiers
ready, for—this was his excuse—they were badly needed to
quell an upheaval of rebellious Indians somewhere. No gold
has any value if it cannot be transported to a place where
people need it. The pious fathers knew too well that if they
hired soldiers on their own account, these soldiers would
never reach the capital; but the transport would fall into the
hands of somebody else, very likely the viceroy himself.

2

"The government, once in possession of the mine, tried to
get out of it as much as it held in the shortest time possible.
The tricks used by the fathers to procure sufficient labor did
not work any longer. They did not work at all with the
government officials, and without native labor the mine was
worthless. For a while the government tried to work it with
convicts. But long before the transport reached the mine,

there was no convict left to work. They had all turned highwaymen, and to catch them the government had to send out whole regiments.

"Natives were lured to work with the promise of gifts, consisting of cheap jewelry, goods, and light hardware. After working for a few months they asked for their wages. But either the merchandise promised them had not arrived or the officials had traded it to other natives for necessities. So the workers found themselves cheated of their wages and they decided to leave. This was prevented by the officials through all sorts of nasty tricks and severe punishments. The natives, knowing the country, succeeded in escaping one by one or in groups.

"Now the officials, all armed, went raiding all the villages and brought in as many men as they could capture. The prisoners could not be put in chains, for there were no chains. All heavy hardware was needed for the mine, and to transport any superfluous amount of hardware on these two-thousand-mile trips when so many other things were needed more urgently would have been sheer madness. No matter how well the captured were guarded, after a few weeks not one was left to work.

"So there was nothing to do but again raid the villages. The natives had burned their own villages and had emigrated to other parts. The raiding-trips had, therefore, to be made farther away from the mine.

"To prevent desertions the Spaniards went to villages to which the deserters belonged, and here, as a warning, they caught at random a dozen women, children, and old men and hanged them as punishment for the desertion of men they could not capture.

"Such things can be done for a long time with Africans. But they never went for long with American Indians. One day, when a raiding party was away from the mine, the warriors came, killed every white found about the mine, and destroyed the whole place. This done, they waited in ambush, and as soon as the raiding party returned with their captives, the Spaniards were massacred, with the assistance of the prisoners. Not a single Spaniard survived or escaped.

"A transport from the mine to Mexico City, the capital, took, according to the season, between two and three months for the journey. When this massacre took place, a transport had just left the mine. It was not until six months had elapsed that the government received word of what had happened. An expedition was sent to recover the mine. This expedition arrived there almost a year after the massacre. The leader of the expedition sent a strange report to the capital, saying that after six weeks' tedious exploring the mine had not been located. Worse, not even the site where the mine had been could be made out with any certainty. There was no lake or any sort of cave-in that would be of help to indicate even approximately the site. It was obvious that the Indians had destroyed the mine so completely that all signs and landmarks had changed places or disappeared altogether. Not satisfied with this, the Indians might have gone so far as to plant trees and shrubs all over the place and cover certain places with rocks and patches of new soil. Since a whole year had passed by, the climate had done its part to change the aspect of the ground so much that even if there had been any officials left, they themselves would hardly be able to find the mine again.

"Four more expeditions were sent out during the next twenty years, with engineers, maps, and all sorts of instruments. It was all in vain. Well, boys, to make a long story short, the mine was never located again," Howard concluded.

One of the two youngsters broke in: "I don't believe that this mine can't be located. I feel positive it could be found even today."

"Provided," said Dobbs, "it ever was there. All we have is a tale about it, but no proof."

The other youngster said: "Right you are, mister. This happened anyhow a hundred and fifty years ago. What do we know about those ancient times? I say the same: there is no proof, and there never will be any proof."

Howard, in his slow way, spoke again: "You are all wrong, boys. There is proof, or I wouldn't have told you that story. And there is plenty of proof. The mine did exist. It is still there where it was buried by the Indians. Because it was found not so long ago."

"How? Tell us. Come on." The two youngsters became excited at once.

3

"Easy, fellows, I'll tell you the rest of the story sure enough. Because here and now is where my old pal Harry Tilton comes in.

"The massacre I was telling you about happened in 1762— a long time ago. But the mine never disappeared from the minds of those who were interested in gold and silver mines, including the lost ones.

"Scores of men have gone nuts trying to locate that mine. Fact is, the mine has never been left alone. That is to say, there have always been adventurers during all these hundred and how many years who have sacrificed their money, their health, and their lives to find the spot again.

"A particularly big start was made when Arizona was annexed to the United States. A whole hundred were once out all at the same time. Some never came back. They died on the desert or fell from the rocks. A dozen were found gone crazy with thirst by a searching party. Another dozen came home sick or entirely broken down.

"Luck is often very friendly to the uninitiated and to those who never think of chasing luck. At least so it seems, and I have quite a number of proofs of that.

"It was in the seventies when three college boys went on a long vacation trip to see the country first-hand. They roamed about Arizona. One night they came to a small town, and, not finding any other lodging, they were taken in by a father who was the priest in that town populated mainly by American-Mexicans.

"The priest liked them and asked them to stay for a few days, since there was pretty hiking-country all around.

"One day, looking about the library of the father, they discovered a number of old maps of this part of the country and part of northern Sonora. One of the maps indicated a mine which was named La Mina Agua Verde. When they asked the father about this, he told them the story of this mine. He admitted that the mine was one of the richest known, but said that it was surely cursed, whether by the ancient owners, the Indians, or by the Almighty he would not venture to say. But cursed it was. Whoever went near this mine was sure to be overtaken by misfortune. He would not advise anybody to look for it. And he himself would be the very last person to try to locate it, since his aims were not worldly.

"Next day the father had to attend a funeral. While he was away the three boys made a careful copy of the map, sure that they would be able to find the spot as easily as their college building at home.

"Having returned from their vacation, they talked about what they were after to more experienced men who had the means to capitalize the expedition and who were anxious to enter into a partnership.

"The expedition marched off, fifteen members, the three

college boys the youngest, the others ranging between twenty-two and forty.

"The map was all right. No mistake. But upon coming to the spot indicated, everything looked different from what they had expected when they studied the map at home. Three mountain peaks peculiarly formed were there as sketched on the map. Also the peak of a certain other mountain was clearly seen, the one that had to be in a right angle with the three other peaks to give the exact position of a certain site. But big trees and huge rocks necessary to make the position final were either missing or so located that they did not fit in with certain other very definite landmarks.

"They dug deep and wide, they blasted with dynamite every piece of rock which looked suspicious. In one spot they dug for a hundred feet because one of the party conceived the idea that the Indians had covered the mine with mountains of earth and that deep down on this certain spot they would find the little lake. The calculation proved wrong, as had all others.

"It cannot be said that they went about their job without plans. After they had worked for two weeks in a more general way, they changed plans again. Now five gangs were formed, each having three members. Each gang went out in a different direction, with the help of the map. After working for three days, all the gangs joined late in the afternoon and stayed together for the whole night, using this joint camp to discuss their finds and thoughts and experiences of the last three days, and by doing so to form new plans.

"Weeks passed. Provisions became short. Work was hard; the sun maddening. The whole outlook was desperate. The situation was truly heartbreaking. Nevertheless the men did not falter. Nobody gave up. Not so much because of faith in the outcome as because of fear and envy. Everyone was afraid to leave, fearing that as soon as he gave up, the others might make the lucky hit. There was nothing to do but stick it out.

4

"Then one day, late in the afternoon, those in one group were sitting around their fire waiting for supper. The coffee would not boil because a strong wind blew the flame away, so one of the boys dug another fire-hole near by, deeper and better protected against the draft.

"When he had the hole about a foot and a half down, he came upon a bone. He pulled it out and threw it away, hardly looking at it. The hole ready, fire was laid in, and soon supper was ready.

"As they were eating their meal in leisure, one of the boys happened to see that bone, picked it up, and began to scratch figures in the sand.

"Suddenly Stud said: 'Let's see what you've got there.' He examined it and remarked: 'I'll be damned if that isn't the bone of a man's arm. Where did you pick it up?'

" 'Right here where I dug the hole.'

" 'The whole skeleton ought to be there.' Stud meditated for a while and then said: 'We'd better hit the hay. It was a hard day.'

"Night had fallen. They wrapped themselves in their blankets and lay down.

"Next morning, while having breakfast, Stud said: 'This bone we found last night sets me thinking. In fact, I've thought it over all night long, how that skeleton came to be here.'

" 'Easy,' Bill answered; 'somebody kicked off here or was slain or died of hunger or thirst.'

" 'You may be right,' Stud admitted; 'many have roamed around here. But for the love of an old penny I can't quite figure why they should have been killed or died right here. There must be a reason, or let's say a certain justification. There has come into my mind the idea that, since none of the Spaniards was ever found, dead or alive, it is possible that the whole mine with all the men was covered inside of a few minutes by a sandstorm or by a mountain slide or by an earthquake. Our map is all right, so I figure the landscape has been changed by some natural disaster. Mountains may have disappeared entirely or broken in two or flattened out.'

"Brawny broke in: 'Quite so. I know something of geology. Things like this happen more frequently than most people are willing to believe.'

" 'All right,' Stud continued, 'this establishes the fact that the Spaniards who were near the mine could not have evaporated by some miracle. Their bones must still be near where the mine used to be. Of course a single bone might be carried off by a vulture or an animal, but let's see if we can find the rest of the skeleton. If we find it, then we can look for another near by. If we find two, we can assume there are more, so if we follow the skeletons we may come to the mine, or at least to the spot where it was. My idea may prove wrong but I think it's worth trying.'

"Stud was right. The whole skeleton to which the bone belonged was dug out, and, digging in a circle, soon they came upon another. Digging in the direction from the first find to the second they found more and more, and then they came upon all sorts of tools. A few yards farther on they found broken ore so rich with gold that the rock was more metal than stone.

" 'Well,' Stud said, 'I reckon we have made the hit. What now?'

" 'Let's call the whole gang together,' advised Bill.

"Brawny looked at him: 'I knew it, I knew all the time that you are just another jackass. But I would never have believed that you could be so big a damned jackass. What do you think the others would do if they had found the mine? You don't think them such fools that they would come along and invite you to the big party? I know them a lot better. They would cheat you out of it. Why, we had the idea, we had the brains, so it's only just for us to cash in. Besides, didn't this dead Spaniard just invite us to come and lift the cash? It was us he lent his arm and beckoned to. If he had wanted them to have it he would have acted otherwise. So let's shut up. We return to town with the others, and two months later we come out here and collect. Right?'

"So it was agreed.

"They picked up all the rich rocks which were laid bare and put them into their bags with the idea of selling them to buy tools and provisions for the next expedition.

"Carefully they covered all the diggings, to make rediscovery by any outsider impossible.

"Before they had finished doing this, one of the other groups unexpectedly showed up. They looked suspiciously around and one of them said: 'Hi, you guys, what's the game? Holding out on us? Is that it? Come, come, cards on the table.'

"Those accused denied having double-crossed anybody and said they had found nothing of importance.

"As though their quarrel had carried through the air, a third group came up, arriving at the scene at the precise moment that the first two groups were ready to go into partnership. Perhaps they would have taken the third group in also had not a fourth group shown up an hour later, and the arrival of this group caused the second and the third groups to forget everything about a possible agreement with the first, and the second group was now the hardest of all, accusing the first of foul play. One man was sent away to call the fifth so as to have the whole expedition together to court-martial the treacherous first group.

"The court was not long in session before sentence was passed. It agreed upon hanging Stud, Bill, and Brawny by the neck on the nearest tree. The verdict was unanimous for the simple reason that by hanging the three accused the cuts for these three former partners could be divided among the gentlemen of the jury. These gentlemen of the jury, each one of them, given the slightest chance, would have done precisely what the accused had tried to do.

5

"The mine was fully discovered and worked with all the zeal avaricious human beings could command. The gain was almost unbelievably rich and the prospectors felt sure that they had not yet come to the most valuable veins.

"But provisions ran short and new tools were needed, so five men were sent off to town to sell a quantity of nuggets and with the proceeds buy all that was needed to go on with the exploitation.

"Harry Tilton, the one who later told the story, was satisfied with what he had earned up to this time. He decided to leave with the five men and not to return. He received his proper cut and left. A bank in Arizona paid him for his load twenty-eight thousand dollars. He had promised his partners not to tell about the mine. This promise he kept. With the money he went back to his native state, Kansas, where he bought a farm and led an easy life.

"The five men ordered to get provisions bought horses, tools, clothing, and sufficient food to last for a long time. After they had their claims properly registered, they returned to the mine.

"Arriving there, they found the camp destroyed and burned down. Their partners, six in number, were dead, killed by Indians, as could be seen from the manner in which they had been slain.

"The gold and everything else was untouched.

"From the way the camp looked they knew that a fierce battle had taken place before their partners had been defeated.

"Nothing else was to be done but to bury the men and then go to work once more.

"Hardly a week had gone by when the Indians returned. They came about eighty men strong. Without any palavers or warning they attacked so quickly that the miners were killed before they had time enough to draw a gun or fetch a rifle. The massacre over, the Indians left without taking even a nail.

"One of the prospectors, who was gravely wounded and left for dead, managed to crawl away after the Indians had gone. How long he dragged himself across the desert, whether days or weeks, he could not remember when he was picked up by a farmer out hunting. The farmer was living all by himself in a lonely shack some thirty miles from the nearest town. The wounded man told his story. The farmer could not carry the man to town because he could see that his wounds were such that he would not live. A few days later the man died.

"The farmer reported the case when he was in town about five months later. Nobody, not even the sheriff, took his tale seriously. People there considered the story evidence that the farmer's mind was unbalanced—as they had suspected since the day the stranger had settled so far out in the desert.

6

"Harry Tilton of course did not know anything of what had happened after he had left. He thought his partners had

returned to their homes after having made their fortunes.
He wasn't much of a talker anyhow. He admitted that he
had made his pile in prospecting, and let it rest there.

"Then came the gold fever all over the world. In three
different corners of the earth, Australia, South Africa, and
Alaska, deposits were found. People everywhere became
mad in their desire for riches. If every tale about gold-
finds told in those days had been true, the world today would
have more gold at its command than lead. One prospector
out of ten thousand would make a hundred thousand dollars
inside of six months. In consequence of this plain fact stories
were spread and believed that every one of twenty thousand
prospectors within four weeks had picked two millions for
his own share.

"It was these exaggerated tales that brought to the mind
of adventurous men living in the same county where Harry
Tilton had his farm bits of the story Harry had told.

"An expedition was formed and Harry, much against his
will, was made leader. He did not care to go out again, for
he was satisfied with his life. But these men tired him out,
pressed him day in and day out, called him a bad citizen, a
liar, an egoistical and jealous neighbor, threated to run him
out of the county, until he saw no other way but to take
the party to the old mine.

"Almost thirty years had passed since Harry had been
there, and his memory was no longer accurate. He could
rather easily describe certain landmarks that had been near
the mine when he had worked there. He drew maps and
made sketches which seemed clear to every member of the
expedition.

"I was a member of the party," Howard concluded, "I
had staked quite a bit of money on this adventure. But I tell
you boys, and it may sound silly, we never did find the
spot. We searched and dug like madmen. Twice or oftener

each day Harry would say that it must be there; a few hours later he would say that he was mistaken, that it must be two miles yonder. He became more and more confused every day. The men thought finally that he had intentionally misled them. This, of course, was unjust. He was honest. What interest would he have had, old man that he was, in concealing the location of the mine? If he had known it, he would have shown it.

"The party became furious. One night they tortured him in the most cruel way, believing that he would tell, but he couldn't tell something which he himself didn't know. Two went so far as to suggest that he should be killed like a rat for having double-crossed them. Luckily for him, the majority of the party were still sane enough to prevent this injustice. It surely would have been a funny trick of fate had he died near the same spot where all his former partners had lost their lives.

"The second night after the party was back home again, his farm buildings were burned to the ground. He was tough, however—a real pioneer. He did not give in. Right away he began to build again. When he had nearly finished the buildings, they burned down again while he was gone to town.

"Harry had to sell out for half the money the farm was really worth, for he knew that he could no longer live there.

"He left the state. I don't know what has become of him.

"Well, and here, boys, is the end of another of the stories about the one-man mining companies. I have seen quite a number of men get rich prospecting, but I haven't yet met one who stayed so. My old friend Harry Tilton was no exception. And he sure was a man who tried very hard to keep what he had made."

4

The next morning Dobbs retold this story to Curtin while they were sitting on the plaza.

Curtin listened eagerly to the yarn. When Dobbs had finished Curtin said: "I figure this story is a true one."

"Of course it's true," Dobbs maintained. "What made you think it might be a weak magazine tale?" He was surprised that anybody could doubt the truthfulness of the story, which Dobbs thought the prettiest he had ever heard.

Yet Curtin's question with that glimpse of doubt had a strange effect upon the mind of Dobbs. Last night, when Howard had told the story in his slow, convincing tone, Dobbs had felt that he himself was living the story; he could not detect any fault in it. Everything had seemed as clear and simple as if it had been the story of a man who had made good in the shoe business. But the slight doubt of Curtin had raised the apparently plain story to that of high adventure. Dobbs had never before in his life thought that prospecting for gold necessarily must carry some sort of mystery with it. Prospecting for gold was only another way of looking for a job or working. There was no more mystery about it than about digging out a tank on a cattle ranch or working in a sand mine.

"I haven't said that the story is not true," Curtin defended his opinion. "There are a million such stories. Open any magazine and you will find them. But even if part of the story sounds like fiction, there is one incident in the old man's story which is true as sunlight. It is that incident where the three partners, after having spotted the mine, try to hold out on the rest."

"You said it." Dobbs nodded. "That's exactly what I say. It is that eternal curse on gold which changes the soul of man in a second." The moment he had said this he knew he had said something that never had been in his mind before. Never before had he had the idea that there was a curse connected with gold. Now he had the feeling that not he himself, but something inside him, the existence of which until now he had had no knowledge of, had spoken for him, using his voice. For a while he was rather uneasy, feeling that inside his mind there was a second person whom he had seen or heard for the first time.

"Curse upon gold?" Curtin seemed entirely unmoved by this suggestion. "I don't see any curse on gold. Where is it? Old women's tattle. Nothing to it. There is as much blessing on gold as there is curse. It depends upon who holds it—I mean the gold. In the end the good or the bad character of its owner determines whether gold is blessed or cursed. Give a scoundrel a bag with little stones or a bag with silver coins and he will use either to satisfy his criminal desires if he is left free to do as he pleases. And, by the way, what most people never know is the fact that gold in itself is not needed at all. Suppose I could make people believe that I have mountains of gold, then I could arrive at the same end as if I really had that gold. It isn't the gold that changes man, it is the power which gold gives to man that changes the soul of man. This power, though, is only imaginary. If not recognized by other men, it does not exist."

Dobbs, only half listening to what Curtin was saying, leaned back on the bench and looked up at the roofs of houses where men were at work putting up telephone wires.

He had watched them the day before and he watched them now, waiting for something to happen to them. They were standing there so unprotected that he wondered how they could work at all. "And all this," he said, "all this for four pesos and fifty centavos a day, with the possibility of dropping off and breaking their necks. A working-man's life is a dog's life, that's what it is. Oh hell, let's talk about something more amusing. Getting back once more to that story, I wonder would you betray your pals just to have all the gold for yourself."

Curtin did not answer right away. "I don't think that anyone can say what he would do if he had a chance to get all the cuts for himself just by a little trick or a bit of cheating. I'm sure that every man has acted differently from the way he had thought he would when face to face with a heap of money or with the opportunity to pocket a quarter of a million with only the move of one hand."

"I think I would do as Harry Tilton did," Dobbs said. "That is the safe thing. Then one wouldn't have to sweat for others and run around hungry all the time. I sure would be satisfied with a certain sum, take it and go away and settle down in a pretty little town, and let the others quarrel."

2

Returning to town in the afternoon after a swim in the river and a walk of three miles back to the city along a dusty road, to save the fifteen centavos street-car fare, the two men began to talk about prospecting again.

It was not exactly the gold alone they desired. They were tired of hanging around waiting for a new job to turn up and of chasing contractors and being forced to smile at them and laugh at their jokes to keep them friendly. A change was what they wanted most. This running after jobs could not go on forever. There must be some way out of this crazy-go-round. It was so silly to stand by the windows of the Banking Company and block the way of everybody who looked as if he might give you a job somewhere out in the fields.

Half a week went by without even the smell of a job. It looked more than ever as if the whole oil business were going to die, at least in the republic here and for sure in this section of the country.

By the end of the week Dobbs felt that for the next three months there was practically no chance of any paying job. Many companies were beginning to close up a great number of fields, and others were making preparations to withdraw from the republic altogether. Men who had worked steadily during the last five years were coming back to town and crowding the jobless. Dobbs, in a fit of desperation, said: "Everything is dying now. A lot of boys who have got the money to pay for the tickets are making off for Venezuela, where a boom seems to be on its way. So everything is at an end here now for sure. Tell you, buddy, I'm making off now for gold even if I have to go all by myself. I'm sick of this town and of this life. If I have to eat the dust, I may just as well do it among the Indians in the Sierra Madre as in this dying town. That's what I think and what I mean."

"You said it, brother," Curtin admitted, "and as for me, you may count me in; I'm ready even for stealing horses or cattle-rustling."

"That's what I like to hear. What chances are you expecting to have after, let's say, four weeks?" Dobbs asked. "Pocket-picking and the Islas Marias."

"Islas Marias? Are there new oil-fields?"

"No, you sap," Dobbs put him right; "that's the penal colony where you will go if the pocket-picking goes wrong and somebody grabs you firmly by your wrist. It isn't just a vacation to be on those islands, if you ask me. Do you know why the pictures of the Holy Virgin you see here in all churches show a knife stabbed into her breast? That knife has been thrust into the heart of the Virgin by someone who had come back alive from the Maria Islands. There are very few guards on these islands, but you can't escape by swimming or going off in a small canoe, because they are guarded by half a million ferocious man-sharks."

"Pretty place, I have to say," Curtin laughed. "And so pocket-picking and the like are out. Who wants to be guarded by sharks?"

"That's what I said. So I think we shuffle off tomorrow. The sooner we leave, the better. In this town we spend our money for nothing; when we're on our way, we're actually investing our money. I'll talk it over tonight with old man Howard."

"With him?" asked Curtin. "What for? You don't mean to take him along? He's too old. We might have to carry him on our back."

Dobbs didn't agree. "Now don't you make a mistake about that old man. He may prove tougher than both of us put together. Those old guys are like good old leather more often than not. Besides, there's another point to think of. To tell the truth, I don't know much about prospecting. Frankly, I don't know anything of what gold looks like in the sand. It may lie there right in front of you and you won't know it. You may think it's only another sort of rock or dust or clay or what have you. Then what? All your hard work and sweat is no good if you can't make out what is the real stuff and what is plain dirt. He's an old-timer at that job. He sure knows gold when he sees it, and he knows how to lift it. That's what we need. I tell you, we must have him, an experienced guy like him. Question is, will he go out with us puppies? Fact is, we should congratulate ourselves if he does."

"I never thought of it that way. I think you're right. Let's ask him right now." Curtin no longer had any objections.

3

On coming to the Oso Negro they found Howard lying on his cot reading about bandits in a pulp.

"Me?" He was right afire. "Me? What a question? Of course I'm going. Any time, any day. I was only waiting for one or two guys to go with me. Out for gold? Always at your service. I take the risk and make the investment. Let's see, how much do we have?"

He took a pencil and began scribbling on blank spaces of a newspaper ad. "I've got three hundred bucks ready cash here in the bank. Two hundred of them I'm all set to invest. It's the last money I have in the world. After this is gone, I'm finished up. Anyway, if you don't take a risk, you can't make a win."

Curtin and Dobbs also began to go over their property, which consisted of what was left from the wages made under Pat's contract. It didn't amount to very much. All their money put together did not come up to what the old man meant to invest.

"Well, I'm afraid this won't go a long way." Howard had made a list of the most essential provisions and tools needed, and he saw that even these modest expenses could not well be met with the money they had.

Dobbs took a deep breath. He remembered his lottery ticket.

"Don't you get superstitious," Curtin warned him. "I've never yet seen a person who won anything worth while in a lottery."

"It won't cost me anything to look at the list, will it?" Dobbs rose from his cot.

Curtin laughed heartily. "I'm going with you, Dobby. I wouldn't miss seeing your long face when you look for your number and don't find even the last figure of your ticket, that assures you you'll get your money back. All right, let's go and have the free circus."

There were lists everywhere. They were hanging in front of every sweet-shop and cigar-counter to make it as easy as possible for people to examine them. Most of the lists were printed on white cotton goods because they were examined so frequently and so nervously that those printed on paper did not last long, and they had to last for a year, since premiums were payable any time inside of twelve months after the drawing.

At the tobacco-stand outside of the Bristol Hotel there hung a list.

"Just came in, the list, caballeros," said the girl in charge of the stand.

"And what now? Hey? What about superstition now, you sap?" Dobbs patted the list in a caressing way. "That's the sugar papa likes. Just look at this fat rich printed number smiling at you. That's my number. That's what it is. Know how much it means in cold cash for my twentieth? One hundred pesos. A full hundred. Welcome, sweet little smackers."

"All right, you win. But this is an exception, and only the dumbs ever win; that's my idea."

"Your idea all right." Dobbs felt superior with his hundred pesos easy money. "Maybe it's the dumbs that make the money. Doesn't matter. Point is to have the dough. And besides, you have to have a good hand to buy the right ticket, see? How does a dumbhead know which is the winning number and which not? Tell me that. I picked the right number, didn't I?"

Meanwhile they had come to the agency where the tickets were paid. The ticket was carefully examined, because smart fellows could change the printed numbers of tickets so well that even experienced tellers were, at times, deceived. But the ticket was okayed and Dobbs received his money.

"Now it's my turn again to get a hundred to make our investments as even as can be." Curtin was trying to think of a way to get some money. At this moment boys were running along the street with bundles of papers under their arms.

"San Antonio *Express*! The *Express*! The *Express*, acaba de llegar, just arrived by train!" they were yelling. One stopped in front of Dobbs and Curtin and offered the paper. Curtin bought it. Hardly had he glanced at the front page when he said: "Here is the solution. That guy here, see his name? He owes me a hundred dollars and I see he is now in the big money. He's bought a corner at Commerce Street. I'll wire him. He's a square shooter. He'll ship the dough."

So they went to the Western Union cable office and with a few words Curtin told the old pal of his plight. The same night the pal from San Antonio cabled him two hundred dollars instead of the borrowed hundred.

"Didn't I tell you he's on the level, that old pal of mine over in good old S.A.? That's what you may call a friend in need." Curtin felt not less superior now than Dobbs had felt on cashing his lottery ticket in the morning.

"We'd better not wait long," Howard suggested. "Let's take off tomorrow."

They agreed. Next day they took the night train to San Luis Potosí, where they boarded the train for Aguascalientes to reach the main line going north. Four days later they were in Durango.

Here they occupied themselves for two days studying maps and trying to get information from all sorts of people who knew this part of the republic.

"Now look here, you puppies," Howard explained. "Where you see a railroad, there's no use going there. There aren't any motor-roads. So let's forget about these roads. Don't even look near dirt roads. Wherever there is a railroad or any other road, there's no use going close. Because railroad-constructors and road-builders usually examine every bit of soil near the roads while they are building them. That's only natural, and it's part of their business. So it would be waste of time to look for anything around places where engineers have been at work."

"I think I see what you're driving at." Dobbs began to understand Howard's plans.

"Not so difficult to see, boys, after I've made it clear what is virgin soil and what isn't." Howard went with a pencil over the map he had spread out before him. "We have to go where there is no trail. We have to go where we can be positive that no surveyor or anybody who knows something about mining has ever been before. The best spots are those where you feel sure that anybody who is paid for his job would be afraid to go and would not think it worth while to risk his hide for the salary he gets. Only at such spots is there a chance that we might find something. These are the regions we have to make out on this map."

He drew a few lines over small sections of the map, made a few dots here and a few dots there. For a while he looked at these vague sketches, seemingly weighing one against the other. Then, with a definite gesture, he made a little circle on the map at a certain point. "Here's where we are bound. Hereabouts." He thickened the little ring with his pencil.

"The exact site doesn't matter very much—not in detail, so to say. Let's see the spot at close range and then decide what to do. Here on this map I can't make out properly whether it's mountain, swamp, desert, or what. But that shows that the makers of the map themselves don't know for sure what there is. Once on the spot, all you have to do is to wipe your eyes and look carefully around you. I once knew a feller who, believe it or not, could smell gold if it was close, just as an ass will smell water if he is thirsty and wants to drink. And this reminds me, boys, we'll have to go out to a few villages near by to buy burros, which we need for carrying our packs and for other services at the camp."

So they spent the next three days buying burros from the Indian peasants.

5

Curtin and Dobbs learned soon that without Howard they would have been utterly helpless. Had they been alone, they would not have been able to follow even a trail. They had no idea how to keep the burros at the camp during the night, how to pack them the right way, or how to make them go over the rocky paths across the high mountains, where often the boys themselves could not get hold with their feet.

On this trip the boys had to do without such little conveniences as were always found even in the most primitive oil-camps. It took them almost a week to learn how to pitch camp under such difficult conditions as they found here every day. This was no boy scouts' hike and camp-fires were not built according to instructions in printed guides for hunting parties. Here it meant work, and nothing but hard work. Often at night when they were so tired that they could sleep like blocks they had to get up and search for the burros that had gone astray. There were many other things to attend to even more disagreeable and more wearisome and annoying.

There were many days and more nights when both of them said that if they had known beforehand what it meant to go prospecting, they would have preferred to stay in town and wait for a job to turn up.

Every day their respect for old Howard grew greater

and greater. That old fellow never complained, never whined, never felt too tired to lend here a pull and there a push. He appeared to become younger and more active with every mile that the little train made toward its goal. He climbed steep rocks like a cat and trotted for long, dreary hours across arid stretches without even mentioning a drink of water.

"Never fail to understand the reason why gold is so precious," he said occasionally when the boys were all in. "Perhaps you know now why one ounce of gold costs more than a ton of cast iron. Everything in this world has its true price. Nothing is ever given away."

The trip alone was of minor importance. The main thing was how to find the metal and how to get it after having found it. In this respect Dobbs and Curtin were still at a greater loss than in knowing how to drive a little bunch of donkeys to a certain place. When still in town, they had thought that prospecting for gold was just like picking up stones in a dry river-bed. Their idea was that you cannot make a mistake, that when you see something that glitters, it must be gold. To their amazement, they found almost every day patches of ground that were covered with glittering yellowish powder, and they found the same glittering sand in brooks and creeks. Whenever they saw this sort of sand, they were sure that it must be the right stuff or at least something that was heavily charged with gold. Howard did not laugh at them. He just said: "I'll tell you when to pick up. This here stuff wouldn't pay you a dinner for a truck-load unless you can sell it in town right in front of a house under construction."

Gold doesn't call out loud to be picked up. You have to know how to recognize it. "You have to tickle it," Howard would often say, "you have to tickle it so that it comes out laughing. You may walk over it twenty times a day and you won't see it if you don't know its call."

Old man Howard knew gold and what it looked like in the raw. He saw it even if there were only a trace of it in the vicinity. He could tell from the landscape if there might be gold around or not. He knew whether it would pay to spend a day or two at a certain place to dig and to wash and to make tests so as to be sure that to work the ground would pay enough wages for a living. Whenever he stopped to get his frying-pan from the pack and wash a few shovelfuls of dirt in a brook, the boys would know that he had made a discovery.

Five times they found gold. But the amount which could be taken by the primitive means they could afford was not sufficient to pay them a good day's wages. Once they came upon a site that was very promising, but the water necessary for washing the sand was six miles away. So they had to give up the find.

"Now, don't you kids think it's child's play to prospect for gold," Howard said to his partners, who were about to lose the last flicker of hope. "Gold means work, and very hard work at that. Just discard everything you have ever read in stories in the magazines. Forget it. It's all lies. Bunk, that's what it is. Don't believe that millions are lying around. There are very few men in the world, or in all history, who have actually made millions by digging for gold. You can't make it single-handed if you want to have the millions, believe me."

2

One morning they found themselves entirely surrounded by wild, desolate mountainous country. It looked as though they could not go on nor go back. Panting and gasping, cursing and swearing, the two boys were trying, by cutting the thick underbrush and by climbing the rocks, which seemed inaccessible, to open a trail by which they could go on and at the same time get out of the wilderness. The difficulty became so great that they lost all hope and were ready to give up the whole outfit, leave everything behind, and return to a civilized world, where there were no jobs, but also no such hardships to endure. They were at the edge of what any sane person can bear.

The old man seemed to be in his most hilarious mood. To him, with so many experiences to draw from, such complications were the regular thing when you are after gold.

"Well, tell my old gra'mother I have burdened myself with a couple of fine lodgers, two very elegant bedfellers who kick at the first drop of rain and crawl under mother's petticoat when thunder rumbles. My, my, what great prospectors a driller and a tool-dresser can make! Drilling a hole with half a hundred Mexican peons around to lend you hands and feet! I still can do that after a two days' spree, you bet. Two guys and what shit! Two guys reading in the magazines about crossing a lazy river up in Alaska and now going prospecting on their own."

"Shut your stinking trap!" Dobbs howled. He took up a rock and threatened to use it.

"Throw it, baby, throw it. Welcome. Just do it. You will never leave this wilderness without my help, if you know what is good for you. You two would die here more miserably than a sick rat."

Curtin tried to quiet Dobbs. "Leave the old man alone. Can't you see he's nuts?"

"Nuts, hey? Is that what you mean?" Howard, instead of being angry, just laughed in a satanical way. "Nuts? Now, I'll tell you somethin', you puppies. What did I say? Yes, two fine lodgers I've burdened myself with. You two are so dumb, so immensely stupid and dumb, that even a secret-service flat would stand amazed at such dumbness. And that's something."

Dobbs and Curtin began to listen to the old man. They looked at each other and they looked again at Howard. They seemed to become convinced that the old man had really gone mad, perhaps from the hardships or from senility.

"And what I was saying," Howard went on, "you two are so dumb that you don't even see the millions when treading upon them with your own feet."

The two boys opened their mouths wide. It was clear they had not understood the full sense of what Howard had said. Not yet. But after a minute they came to. Seeing Howard still grinning at them while he held, in both his hands, sand picked up from the ground, letting it run through his fingers, it dawned upon them that the old man was as sane as ever and that what he said was true.

They did not start a dance out of this joyful relief nor did they holler to clear their breasts of the anguish that had filled them during these last few days. A long breath they took and then sat down and fingered the soil, looking at it carefully.

"Don't you expect to find nuggets of molten gold." Howard was still standing upright. "It's not that rich. It's only heavy dirt. And it's not here either. Here are only traces of the stuff. It comes from somewhere farther up there." Howard pointed up to certain rocks which they had been about to cross. "There is where we have to go. And if I am not mistaken, it will be there that we will settle for a few months. Let's go."

While this stretch which they had now to cover was short, it meant harder work than any other trail they had encountered so far on the expedition. The distance was less than two miles, but it took them a whole day to reach the site indicated by Howard.

When the outfit arrived at the spot, Howard said: "We'd better not pitch camp right here where the works are. We should build the camp a mile or even a mile and a half away. Some day you may learn why this is for the best."

It had got dark, and so for this night they camped right there.

Next morning, however, Howard and Curtin went exploring for a good camp-site while Dobbs remained with the animals.

Having found a suitable place sufficiently far off the field, camp was built at the spot where it was to stay.

"Suppose somebody should accidentally come upon this camp, you two fellers understand we are just hunters, professional game-hunters for hides of commercial value. And don't you make any mistake. It may cost you dearly." Howard surely knew what he was talking about.

6

If Dobbs and Curtin had ever worked hard in their lives, they would have thought that what they were doing now was the hardest work anywhere in the world. For no employer would they have labored so grindingly as they did now for themselves. Each working-day was as long as daylight would make it. Convicts in a chain-gang in Florida or Georgia would have gone on hunger-strike, and not have minded the whippings either, had they had to work as these three men were doing to fill their own pockets.

The field which they were exploring was embedded in a crater-like little valley on the top of high rocks. The altitude of the mountains and the low pressure of the atmosphere made work still harder than it would have been under better conditions.

In daytime the heat was scorching, and the nights were bitterly cold. There were none of the conveniences which even a working-man in a civilized country—yes, even a soldier in the trenches—is used to and thinks he cannot live without.

One should not forget that though the Sierra Madre is in fact a sister to the Rocky Mountains, it is in the tropics. There is no winter, no snow and ice, and consequently all plants, shrubs, insects, and animals keep alive all the time, and very much alive at that.

There were mosquitoes biting day and night. The more
you sweat, the more they like sucking your blood. There
were tarantulas the size of a man's hand, and spiders the
same size, not very pleasant to have for permanent neighbors.
And then there was the real genuine pest, a little yellowish-
reddish scorpion the sting of which kills you within fifteen
hours.

Gold has its price. Make no mistake as to that, and forget
the stories and the blah of promoters who want to sell
worthless ground at the price of cultivated orange-groves
in the Royal Valley.

"Never have I dreamed that I would have to work like
this," Curtin growled one morning when Howard was shaking him by the collar to get him up from his cot.

"Never mind," the old man calmed him, "I've worked
this way more than once in my life and often for years.
I'm still alive, and, what is more, still without a bank account
to help me along for the rest of my life. Well, get up and
make the burros carry the water up."

As the working-field had no water, it had to be carried
on burros' backs from a brook about three hundred and fifty
feet lower than the field. When, in the beginning, they had
found that there was no water for washing the dirt, and
that the water was so far down, it was proposed that the
diggings should be carried by the burros down to the brook
to be washed there. After long deliberation it was decided
that it would be better to carry the water up to the field
than to carry the dirt down. By digging out tanks and by
using channels easily built from wood, the water once carried up to the field could be used over and over again before
it evaporated. A wheel was constructed with empty tin cans
and small wooden cases, and with the help of a burro this
could be made to draw the water from the tank, lift it with

those cans and cases up to the upper tank, from where, on opening the shutter, it would run down the channels to wash the sand.

Howard was an all-around expert. Whenever he came out with a useful idea, Dobbs and Curtin would ask themselves earnestly what they would have done in this wilderness without him. They could have met with a field rich with fifty ounces to the ton of raw dirt and not have known what to do with it, how to get it out, or how to keep alive until time to carry it home.

Howard even burned lime out of the rocks, mixed it with sand and clay, and built a tank that would lose not a drop of water except what evaporated. With the same stuff in other combinations he tightened the wooden channels and the basins so that here, too, no water was wasted.

The men had breakfast long before sunrise to start work as early as possible. Often they could not work during the noon hours, as the terrific heat made their heads hum and their limbs ache.

"Another reason why I preferred carrying the water up to carrying the dirt down is this," Howard explained; "we can hide the whole field so well that it is almost impossible for any sniper to find us. If we washed the dirt down at the brook, a native hunter might see us and get suspicious. On the other hand, if he meets one of us with the burros carrying the water up, it will be clear that the water is meant for the camp, for cooking, washing, and cleaning the hides. We'll start tomorrow to fence in the field and make it invisible. What you say, kiddies?"

"Right, daddy," Curtin answered.

Dobbs growled: "Okay by me, you know best, old rooster."

2

One day during the hot noon hours, when Dobbs and Curtin were resting on their cots and complaining of the heat and of the work, Howard, sitting on a box cutting spikes for some new invention of his, watched his two partners rolling about on their cots. "Hell and devil!" he said. "I often ask myself what you two thought it means— digging for the metal. You must have figured you just walk along and if you come near those old hills yonder, you just pick up the gold that lies around like lost grain on a wheat-field after the harvest. You put it into sacks taken along for that purpose, carry it to town, sell it, and there is another millionaire ready for the movies. You ought to know that if you could find the stuff so easily and get it home like a truck-load of timber on a paved highway, it wouldn't be worth any more than plain sand."

Dobbs was turning on his cot. "All right, all right, you win. It's hard, very hard. But what I mean to say is, I think there must be spots in the world where it is found richer and still richer, where it would not be necessary to slave like the devil to get it."

"Such spots do exist," the old man affirmed. "I've seen places where you could cut it out from the veins with your pocket-knife. And I've seen places, too, where you could pick up the nuggets like nuts under a walnut-tree in the fall. I've seen fellows making thirty, forty, sixty ounces a day; and I've seen, at exactly the same place and only a week afterwards, fellows getting mad over not finding even a grain. There is something strange about the metal. The surest way to make a good day's pay is what we do here; that is, wash dirt which carries a certain percentage of the real stuff. That usually lasts for quite some time. I mean it won't give out so soon and leaves you at the end a fairly good earning. On the other hand, take these rich veins with nuggets lying about. They sure make the first guy that steps upon it rich, and in a short time, but even that is very rare. All those who come later are losers. And what I tell you is based on more than forty years of experience."

"Well, I should say it's a rather slow way of getting rich."

"Right you are, Curty, it's a slow way. If you can stick it for five years, you may get in the neighborhood of a hundred grand. But I haven't yet seen a guy who could hold on for five years. Main trouble is the field runs out sooner than one usually expects. So there's nothing left but to go out again and try to find a virgin field. This way it goes. You may have made ten thousand in one spot. You can't be satisfied with it, you believe in your good luck, and you go out again and again until the last nickel of the ten thousand is spent just trying to find another lode somewhere in the world."

3

The outlook was anything but rosy. Dobbs and Curtin could see that. Suppose that after half a year they should have made a pile, it would have been harder earned than money made in a contract with Pat.

Blisters on their hands came and went, came again and dried up again. Washing and rinsing, catching the sand up, and washing it over and over again, this alone would have been work enough. But before it could be washed, it had to be dug out. This could not be done as in a sand mine. The ground was rocky. Shrubs held on in the soil so that the rock had to be broken to lay open the earth. Rocks had to be crushed into washable sand. Water had to be hauled and still more water, especially on very hot days, when it evaporated rapidly.

There was no Sunday—no day for rest. Their backs ached so much that after a day's work they could not stand, nor sit, nor lie down comfortably. They could hardly straighten their fingers, they had become so stiff and knotty. Neither did they shave nor take time to cut their hair. They were too tired for such doings, and, still worse, they had become utterly indifferent to their appearance. If their shirts or pants were torn or ripped, they never mended them more than was absolutely necessary to hold them together.

If for some reason one or the other had a few hours to spare, he could not make use of them for his own personal good. He had to go hunting to get a wild turkey or an antelope; or explore the surroundings to find better pastures for the burros; or go to the nearest Indian village down in the valley to buy eggs, lard, salt, corn, coffee, tobacco, brown sugar. Flour, bacon, baking powder, white sugar, good soap, canned milk, tea, and such luxuries could be had only if one made a whole day's trip to a little town far down the western slope of the Sierra. Even there these things were seldom to be had. There were no buyers for such rarities, so the grocers only occasionally carried them. If the fellow that went to get provisions brought back with him a bottle of tequila or habanero, this meant a banquet in the camp and a great day in their dreary life.

Occasionally the question was brought up as to legalizing their claim and obtaining the license necessary to mine here. It did not cost a fortune, but the government was very particular about this permit and stood ready to collect its legal share of the profits.

It was not because the fellows wanted to cheat the government of its taxes that they were reluctant to have the claim registered. Many other considerations caused them to avoid letting the government know what was going on.

The government as such was honest and trustworthy in every respect. But who could guarantee the honesty of the petty officials, of the chief of police in the nearest town, of the little mayor of the nearest village, of the general of the nearest military post? Who was to vouch for the character of the clerk in the government's office?

On filing the claim with the authorities the exact location of the field had to be given. The three men were of little consequence; even the American ambassador could give little protection should it happen that they got into trouble. It happened in this country that chiefs of police, mayors of towns, congressmen, and even generals were implicated in cases of kidnapping for ransom and in open banditry. The government, both state and federal, could at any time confiscate not only the whole field but every ounce of gold the men had mined with so much labor and pain. While the three miners were at work they would be well guarded. Only when on their way back with their hard-earned loads would they be waylaid or highjacked by a party of fake bandits acting under orders from someone who was paid by the people to protect the country from bandits. Things like that have happened even in the country to the north; why not here? It is the influence of the atmosphere of the continent.

The three partners knew both sides, and knew them well. Now their battle was only with nature. Once they had their claim registered, there was every possibility of facing a long fight with more dangerous foes. Apart from the taxes paid to the government, they might have to pay all sorts of racketeers, or, as they called them here, coyotes, and so reach port again with but a small percentage of their profit left in their pockets.

There was still another danger, which might be most serious of all. A great mining company in good standing with the government or certain officials might receive word of the filing of the claim. How long would these three miserable proletarians last after the great company started to bring before the courts claims of prior rights to this field, with some native puppet ready to swear away the blue sky for a hundred pesos.

"Here you see for yourselves, provided you have brains to think with, that, much as we want to, we can't afford to be honest with the government." Howard finished up his explanation. "I certainly don't like to cheat anybody out of a just share in my profits, not even a government. If we were on British territory I wouldn't hesitate a minute to do what is right by the law. In this case we have no alternative. Not alone our earnings but our life and health depend upon forgetting about the license. Are you guys agreed upon that?"

"We are and no mistake."

"Right. Of course, you understand that if we are found out it will mean confiscation of all we have made, of all we have here, and, very likely, a year in jail."

"I think we can take this chance, don't you?" Curtin asked Dobbs.

"Sure we take it. Not for a minute did I expect that any one of us would be silly enough even to propose any other course."

So the question of the license was settled. If you have a license, you are not protected at all against bandits or racketeers. If nobody knows what you have, you have a better chance of safety. The bush is so wide and the Sierra is so great and lonely that you disappear and nobody knows where you are or what has befallen you.

4

The discussion about the registration of their claim brought comprehension of their changed standing in life. With every ounce more of gold possessed by them they left the proletarian class and neared that of the property-holders, the well-to-do middle class. So far they had never had anything of value to protect against thieves. Since they now owned certain riches, their worries about how to protect them had started. The world no longer looked to them as it had a few weeks ago. They had become members of the minority of mankind.

Those who up to this time had been considered by them as their proletarian brethren were now enemies against whom they had to protect themselves. As long as they had owned nothing of value, they had been slaves of their hungry bellies, slaves to those who had the means to fill their bellies. All this was changed now.

They had reached the first step by which man becomes the slave of his property.

7

The three men, gathered together solely to gain riches, had never been real friends. They had in common only business relations. That they had combined their forces and brains and resources for no other reason than to make high profits was the factor which had prevented them from becoming true friends.

As it was, this proved to be to the advantage of their work. Friends, really good friends, kept together by business and forced upon each other without any contact with other people, more often than not part the bitterest of enemies.

They were not even real pals. Each was only looking for his proper share, and if a grain more seemed to be going to another partner, battle was on at once, and without quarter.

The common worries, labor, disappointments, the common hopes, made them comrades in a sort of war. More than once one had saved the life of another. Several times Dobbs had endangered his own safety to fetch either the old man or Curtin when one fell into a ravine or into a chasm or was caught in thorny underbrush on a steep rock. Help in dangerous situations had been rendered to Dobbs by the others. Still none of them ever believed that such assistance was given, or that sacrifices were made, out of pure kindness. Each of them felt that this service was rendered because, had one of them lost his life, the other two could not

have worked the field alone. Just as soldiers, personally unknown to each other but belonging to the same nationality
or to that of allied armies, will help their fellow-soldiers not
alone for patriotic reasons but for many other reasons, which
may, often, be very difficult to explain in detail.

Under such circumstances mutual service usually leads
to lasting friendship, but it did not work that way among
these three.

One day Dobbs was inside a tunnel where earth was being
extracted. While he was there, the tunnel broke down, bury-
ing him. Howard, digging on the opposite side, did not know
what had happened.

Just then Curtin returned from hauling water from the
brook below with the help of the burros. Looking at the
tunnel, he found it strange that he did not hear any movement nor see a flicker of light from the lantern Dobbs was
using. He knew then instantly that Dobbs was buried. He
did not even take time to notify Howard, as he thought it
might be too late then to bring Dobbs out alive. He went
in, although the ceiling was hanging so that it might come
down any second and bury the rescuer as well. He got
Dobbs out and then called for the old man, for Dobbs was
unconscious and had to be brought to and Howard knew
what to do in such accidents.

After Dobbs had regained his senses he realized what
Curtin had done for him and what risk he had taken to get
him out.

"Thanks, you guys," he said, grinning. "If you had waited
only to spit on your hands, it would have been all over with
me. Tell ye, I heard the harps playing sure enough."

Then they went to work again.

That same night, sitting by the fire cooking their meals,
Dobbs began to think. After they had eaten he looked at his
partners suspiciously.

"What you staring at, you mug?" Curtin asked.

"I was just thinking why the hell you fellers dragged me out of that hole? Your shares would have grown rather big if you'd left me where I was for five minutes longer." Dobbs narrowed his eyes as he spoke.

"Guess you're still hearing harps and seeing white robes." Howard tried to ridicule him.

"You can't catch me sleeping," Dobbs answered. "Don't you ever believe that. I'm not so dumb as you two guys think me. I've got ideas of my own and I stick to them. That's what. Now shake your cock with that mixture handed you, dirty-minded crooks that you are and always will be."

"Another crack like that from you and I'll sponge your face, you devil." Curtin spoke angrily.

"Who'll sponge whose face?" Dobbs jumped to his feet.

"Now, peace here, babies. No use breaking your knuckles and shins; we need them, and badly, at that." Howard's fatherly tone quieted them. He had touched the right spot. Nothing was worth more to them than their working ability. To remind them of the fact was always the best balm the old man had in store for their quarrels.

"Of course, you great-grandfather, you're too yellow to fight; you're even afraid to see a fight. You might faint if you saw a bleeding nose." Dobbs, still standing, forgot about Curtin and turned on the old man. "Playing godfather here to us. I wonder for what reason. Some day I'll find out. It sure will be a costly day for both of you."

Curtin had not moved when Dobbs had jumped to his feet. He had just looked about defensively. "Don't mind him," he now said to Howard, "don't mind him at all, that's what I say. Can't you see he's screwy?"

"Mebbe," Dobbs growled. "Mebbe screwy. All right, but believe me I know why I'm screwy and who made me so.

And I'm turning in, leaving you to discuss how to give me cold feet. But I warn you, it may turn out the other way round."

When he had gone to the tent, Howard said to Curtin: "Nothing new ever happens under the stars, it seems. I've seen this kind of thing occur so often and so needlessly that now I ask myself why it hasn't happened sooner in this outfit. You aren't so free from this disease either, Curty, as you may think. There are few who are long immune from this infection. Well, I think I'll turn in too."

2

Each night the proceeds of the day's work were carefully estimated in the presence of the three partners. This done, the shares were cut and each partner received his. This way of paying dividends was not very intelligent. Often the earnings of the day were so small that it would have taken an expert mathematician to tell exactly how to divide it justly.

It had come to be arranged this way quite accidentally almost the first day when there had been any earnings.

Curtin was the man who had suggested it one day during the second week after the gains had begun to accumulate.

"Okay with me," Howard agreed without arguing. "Better for me. Then I won't have to be the dragon to guard your pennies any longer. I haven't liked it too much, acting as your safety box."

Both his partners rose. "Who made you our banker? We never asked you yet to hold our well-earned money."

"Which means, in other words, that you wouldn't trust me?"

"That's exactly what it means in plain English." Dobbs left no doubt of how he judged his partner.

Howard smiled at them. "It's right, you never asked me. Only I thought I might be the most trustworthy among us three."

"You? How come?" Dobbs could at times be nasty.

Howard kept on smiling. He had had too many similar experiences in his life to feel offended. "Perhaps you're just waiting to ask me in what pen I grew up. Well, I've never been in any pen yet. I hope I never shall be. I can't expect you to believe this. Besides, never having been in jail doesn't mean that a feller plays straight and honest. Out here there's no sense in lying to each other. After a few weeks we'll know one another better than we ever could from a police record or a jail-warden's report. Where we are now you can't save yourself by tricks, no matter how smart you may think yourself in town. Here you may tell the truth or you may lie as much as you wish; everything will come out sooner or later. So, whatever you may think of me, of us three I'm the most trustworthy. As for being the most honest, no one can say."

Dobbs and Curtin only grinned at him for an answer.

Howard seemed not to mind. "You may laugh at what I say. It's true none the less. Why? Because here only plain facts count. We might charge you, Dobby, with taking care of the goods. Suppose I'm somewhere deep in the bush to get timber, and suppose, at the same time, Curtin is on his way to the village for provisions; wouldn't that be your big chance to pack up and leave us in the cold?"

"Only a crook like you would think me likely to do that." Dobbs felt hurt.

"It may be crooked to say what I said, but it's surely more crooked to have such thoughts and not admit them. You'd be the first guy I can imagine who wouldn't occasionally nourish the idea of robbing when given a chance. To make off with all the goods, dirty trick as it would be against your partners, would seem, out here and under these conditions, rather the natural thing to do. You think and you have thought many times of doing it; but you're too yellow to admit frankly that you've had such thoughts and that you wouldn't mind carrying them out. Right now it wouldn't pay. That's the reason why you think of it only vaguely. Some day, though, when the goods will amount to, let's say, three hundred ounces, you may get such ideas more clearly fixed in your heads. I know my fellow-men and you don't. That's the difference. If some pretty day you caught me, tied me to a tree, took all I have, and walked out on me, leaving me here in the wilderness to my fate, I wouldn't be a bit surprised, because I know what gold can do to men."

"And what about yourself, you wiseacre?" asked Curtin.

"It's different with me. I'm no longer quick enough on my feet. I couldn't do it, hard as I might try. You'd get me by the collar in no time and string me up and even forget to bark the tree. I can't escape you. I have to depend on you in more ways than one. I can't run as easily as either of you can. And so you have the plain reason why I think I'm the most trustworthy in this outfit."

"Looking at it your way, I feel sure you're right," Curtin said. "Anyway, and perhaps for your own good, Howy, it would be better to cut the proceeds every night and each partner be responsible for his own goods. That would give each of us the greatest freedom, as each could go whenever he wished to."

"Right by me," the old man agreed. "Only then everybody has to be careful that the hiding-place of his fortune is not found out by one of the others."

"Hell, what a dirty mind you must have, you old scoundrel!" Dobbs cursed at him.

"Not dirty, baby. No, not dirty. Only I know whom I am sitting here with by the fire and what sort of ideas even supposedly decent people can get into their heads when gold is at stake. Most people are only afraid of getting caught, and that makes them, not better, but only more careful and more hypocritical; makes them work their brains so that it would be difficult to catch them once they've run off. Here it's no use to be a hypocrite, no use to lie. In cities it's different. There you can afford to use all the tricks known under heaven, and your own mother won't recognize them as tricks. Here there is only one obstacle—the life of your partner. And easy as it may seem to remove this obstacle, it may, in the end, prove very costly."

"Police would find him out sooner or later—isn't that what you mean?" asked Dobbs.

"I wasn't thinking of police. Police and judges may never butt in, and most likely never would. Yet while dirty acts may never burden the conscience of a man, his mind and soul may not allow him to forget his deeds. The crime he committed may not burden him, but the memory of happenings before the crime may make his life a hell on earth and rob him of all the happiness he tried to gain by his foul act. But—well, what's the use talking about it? All right, have it your way. Every night the profits are cut and each of us hides it as best as he can. It would be hard anyway, as soon as we have made two hundred ounces, to carry it in a little bag hanging day and night from your neck."

8

Through ingenious labor the fellows had succeeded in hiding their mine. Nature had already made this place difficult to approach and to find. A wanderer passing by would never suspect that this rock lying in a little cup-like valley on the top of a high rocky mountain, was anything but a peak. Two passes led into this small valley, and it took all the strength of man to reach those passes by climbing. The rock was bare of any plants save low bushes. An Indian hunter from the village far below would never go up to this rock to look for any sort of game, for there is enough in the great valley at the base of the mountains to make it silly for a hunter to climb this mountain. The villagers have sufficient tillable land to work on near the village, so there is no need to look for new or better land on the slope of the mountains.

The passes were so well closed in by the miners with shrubs, rocks, and trunks of trees that even if by accident a man should come near, he would never think that these shrubs, so natural-looking, were pure camouflage to hide the passes. When bringing up water for the washings, the passes had to be opened, but they were closed as soon as the burros had passed.

The ground on which the men pitched the camp was left open to view to anybody that might come along. This camp was quite a distance away from the mine, and it was located lower than the mine. In the village below, the Indians knew that up here there was an American hunting, because Curtin came to the village whenever provisions were needed. Hardly any human being would come this way save an Indian from the village. This was bound to be a rare occurrence because a villager going up to this camp would have to be away from his home not only for the whole day, but for the greater part of the night, provided he did not stay overnight in the camp. None of these Indians had any business here, and to go out of pure curiosity to see what the stranger was doing would have been impolite. To be polite in their own way is unwritten law with these natives.

During all the long months the three miners had been at work here, nobody had ever come this way. The peasants below were satisfied with the explanation that the American was hunting for hides of tiger-cats, mountain lions, foxes. The owner of the general store in the village, like all the others, was an Indian, and at the same time mayor of the village and therefore the highest authority in the neighborhood. He had never had such a flourishing business in all his life as since this hunter up on the mountain had begun to patronize him. Curtin paid in cash and seldom if ever quarreled about prices. For him the price seemed ridiculously low, while the storekeeper charged him a trifle more than he would ask from his native customers. He would have lost this excellent business had he made trouble for the foreigner up there. Since this hunter molested none of the natives in any way, nobody was interested in his business. So from this side the adventurers had nothing to fear.

2

It was something else that every day became more troublesome for the partners, until they thought that it hardly could be borne any longer.

It was a miserable life they now led. The grub was the same, day in, day out. Always it was cooked and prepared hastily when everyone was so tired and worn out that he would have preferred not eating at all to cooking the meal. Yet they must eat, or at least fill their bellies. And doing so every day, treating their stomachs the way they did, it was no wonder that they began to show the effects of it.

To this was added the growing monotony of their work. It had been interesting enough during the first weeks. Now there was not the slightest variety. If once in a while a nugget were found, or now and then a few grains the size of wheat grains, so that they had something new to talk about, then they might have felt afresh that glamour of adventure which had led them out here. But nothing of that sort occurred.

Sand and dirt, dirt and sand, coupled with inhumane privations; crushing rocks from the bitter cold morning hours, through the broiling of midday, and far into the darkness of night made them feel worse than convicts. When it turned out that a huge heap of crushed rocks held, as frequently happened, hardly the day's pay of a union bricklayer in Chicago, the disappointment of the gang became so great that they could have killed each other just for the pleasure of doing something different from the daily routine.

Every night, when the day had been hard and the gains not in proportion to their labor, a hot quarrel about the uselessness of this sort of life would arise. The men would decide to keep on one more week and not a day longer. Almost every time such a decision was made, the next day or the day after the profits would rise so high that it seemed to be a sin to give up when such rich earnings could be made. So the decision was disregarded and work would go on as before.

The companionship which they had to endure had become the source of troubles they never would have thought of had they been in town. Had it not been for Howard, who, out of his long experience, could not be surprised by anything, the two youngsters would have had fights every day.

During the first weeks of work there was something new to talk about every day and always something interesting to worry about, problems to solve or to think over. These kept their minds occupied for a time, so that there was no need to look to their partners for entertainment.

Then came a time when each had heard the same jokes and stories three hundred times. Also each one, after a few weeks, knew the whole life-story of both his partners.

Dobbs, perhaps owing to an early head injury, had the habit of moving the skin of his forehead upward and so wrinkling it when speaking. Curtin had never noticed this while he knew Dobbs in the oil-fields and in town. Out here, during the first weeks, he and the old man had found this sort of frown rather jolly for the comic impression it made when used with certain phrases. Then they had come to crack jokes about it, with Dobbs good-naturedly joining in. Now came an evening when Curtin yelled at Dobbs: "You cursed dog, if you for once don't drop that nasty frown of yours, bigud, I'll smash your head with this stone. You know quite well, you pen-bird, that I'm sick of that face-making of yours, damn it to hell."

Dobbs was up in an instant, gun drawn. Curtin was saved only because he had left his gun on his cot in the tent. Otherwise Dobbs would have pulled the trigger.

"Haven't I been waiting for just that for a long time?" Dobbs bellowed. "And who is it that wants to baby-nurse me? Weren't you horsewhipped in Georgia for taking a jane across a tree-trunk? We know what brought you down here into this country. You aren't here for pleasure. One more crack about my face and I pump you up, chest and belly alike."

The fact was that Curtin did not know whether Dobbs had ever been in jail, so that he was not justified in calling him a pen-bird. Nor did Dobbs know whether Curtin had ever been in Georgia, because he had never said so and he had never mentioned that he had been out on a necking party with results not fully approved by the gal.

The old man kept quiet while this battle was on. He smoked his pipe and puffed out thick clouds to protect himself from the mosquitoes.

Finally Dobbs laid down his cannon, and Howard felt that his advice might now be welcomed.

"What's all this row about, boys? We won't make any money if we have to doctor bullet-wounds. Wait until we are back in town. Besides, we don't know yet for what better purpose we may need that ammunition you're so ready to waste, like the real boneheads you are."

Neither of the youngsters answered.

After a long silence at the fire, Dobbs took up his gun and turned in, leaving the old man and Curtin to themselves.

Soon came a morning when Curtin poked his gun in Dobbs's ribs: "Any more lip from you and I'll pull off, you rattler."

"Why don't you pull? Yellow, hey? All right, I haven't said a word. Forget it. She was only a bitch anyway. Trust me, sonny."

A new quarrel early in the morning before a hard day made Howard mad: "Why the damn hell can't you hicks behave like real guys? You act worse than a married couple on Sunday night. Bury the gun, Curty."

"You telling me, ordering us about, hey?"

"I haven't anybody to order about here." Howard, too, seemed to be the victim of that devastating disease caused

by the monotony of their life. "And I repeat, I'm not here
to give orders. I've come here to make money and not to
nurse kiddies so dumb they couldn't live out here two
weeks without being eaten alive by the coyotes and the
buzzards. Here we need one another, like him or hate him.
Gees crisp, if one is banged up by your foolishness, the
other two can go home, for two alone can't do anything
here. Not me. I want to make money, and if I want to see
a good fight, it won't be you two I'd pay to see put it on."

Curtin fingered his gun and then put it back in its holster.

"And that's not all," Howard continued. "I'm plumb sick
and dog-tired, not of the job here, but of you two guys.
I'm not willing to stay behind here with one alone after the
other has been bumped off. I'm going, that's what I'm doing.
I'm through, you can get that right now. I'm satisfied with
what I've made so far. I certainly won't take any more
chances with you."

Dobbs protested. "You may have enough, but we haven't.
Your old bones may carry you along on what we've helped
you to make, but we're still young and we have a damn
long life before us; we'll need dough, and plenty of it. You
can't run out on us like that and leave us here on the cracked
ice. We want to clean up, and not before that is done will
we give you our kind permission to walk off."

"Now come here, sweet oldy," Curtin broke in. "You
really shouldn't show your second infancy at this time. It
isn't good taste. How would you do it, anyhow? Just try.
Don't misjudge our legs, old man. Want to know what we'd
do in such a case?"

"You don't have to tell me. I know both of you so damn
well that I'm sure I'd make no mistake in guessing what
fate would be in store for me."

"Mebbe we are worse than you think." This came from
Dobbs. "We would wait until you were packed up, so as

to be sure you had your dust wrapped up. Then we'd get hold of you and tie you to a tree. With that well done, we'd go our smooth road back home, where money still counts, no matter where it comes from and how you got it. Kill? Kill you? No, it would be very nasty to do such a dirty thing to a good pal like you. You, of course, with your dirty thinking, believe we might murder you in cold blood. Nope, we aren't that bad."

"I get you, Dobby, my fine boy." Howard grinned sardonically at the two. "To tell you the truth, I had thought, really and seriously thought, that you might murder me just to get rid of me and have my dough thrown in into the bargain. But I'd never figured on anything like being left behind in the wilderness, tied to a tree, exposed to mosquitoes, scorpions, rattlers, wolves, coyotes, ants, and other pretty creatures handed us by the Lord to make life miserable. You wouldn't burden your good conscience with a merciful quick shot into my chest to deliver me from pain. Oh no, you are too good-natured for that. All right, you win. I shall stay and have my fate delivered into your soft hands."

Followed a long silence. The youngsters avoided the old man's searching face. They became restless. Dobbs surely had not meant to do such a thing; neither had Curtin. He had, or so at least Howard figured, used only the best weapon he could think of to keep him on the field, for without him they would have been lost.

Curtin couldn't stand the awkward silence any longer. "Hell, that's all bosh. Nothing back of it. We're all cracked in our heads somehow, that's what's the matter with us."

"Exactly what I was thinking myself. Don't believe a word of what I've spouted here, Howy. Cross my heart, this is all nonsense. Well, I'm shaky, sort of shaky all over.

I don't know myself what I'm saying. Forget it, oldy. Let's get to work and lift a quarter of an ounce."

Howard laughed. "Now, that's the way to talk. You're just kiddies. One day, perhaps thirty years hence, both of you will be standing in the same shoes I am in now. Then you'll know better. I didn't take you seriously, anyhow. Well, Curty, get the burros going; we haven't got water enough."

3

It had done them a great deal of good to clean their chests. After the argument they seemed to get along better for quite a while, and the work progressed more rapidly.

The last quarrel, however, had an unexpected effect. The word had been dropped that one might pack up and leave. This suggestion began to take root in their minds. Howard had said that he was satisfied with what he had made so far. He knew the value in cash of the dust they had accumulated. The boys had never sold pay-dirt, so they didn't know how much money they would have after it had been properly assayed.

Therefore it was quite natural for Curtin to bring up this question one evening: "How much do you think, Howy, we may collect on what we have so far?"

The old man was silent for a while, making calculations in his mind. Then: "I can't say in dollars and cents, but I should be very much mistaken if each of us had much less than fifteen thousand dollars. It may be fourteen, it may be sixteen. That's my figure, and I feel satisfied that I'm not very far wrong."

The partners had not expected so much. It came as a surprise to them.

"If it's that much," Dobbs said, "I move we stay here about six weeks more, work like devils, and then return to town."

Curtin assented. "Suits me perfectly."

"I've been thinking of making this proposition to you," Howard began. "Yes, that's what I was going to do. Because as far as I can figure, there will hardly be anything left after six weeks. It looks to me as if the field is getting suspiciously thin. If we should come upon a new rich layer, which I don't think will happen, then it would pay to stay on. As it is, it looks as though after six weeks there will no longer be a good day's wages in our work. So what would be the use of staying here?"

It was agreed, therefore, to put in another six or eight weeks and not one day more. Eight weeks would be the limit.

4

This decision, more than anything else, brought peace to the partners.

They fixed the day of departure from the wilderness of the Sierra Madre, and having done so, their mood underwent a great change overnight. No longer could they understand how it had been possible to fight each other as they had lately. For the first time they became confident of one another. They were on the way to becoming even real pals.

"Not so bad, the ideas that guy has," one would say to himself occasionally, and with conviction. "Why, these two mugs are almost like real brothers to me," another would think, and he would add: "I'm not so sure that a brother would act as square as these hicks do."

The reason for this change of attitude was not the decision to break camp; that in itself could not have produced such a change of mind. It was that setting a definite date for departure brought many new problems to solve. These occupied their minds to such a degree that they could no longer waste time looking for shortcomings in their neighbors. Any nation, regardless of political quarrels and fights for party supremacy, when confronted with a war or the danger of losing her most important markets, unites under her leaders. This is the reason why smart statesmen, dictators in particular, who see their power threatened from the inside try the old trick of showing the nation the arch-enemy at the gates of the country. For the genuine dictator or despot nothing is too expensive as long as it will keep him in power.

Here the same problems confronted the partners the moment the end of their adventure was in sight, and they forgot their internal fights in looking ahead.

They talked over plans for carrying the goods safely to civilization, where they would be of value. Then there were the more personal questions of what to do after collecting the cash; whether to go into business, and if so, what business; whether to invest the money in some enterprise or buy real estate or even a farm, or only to have a good time for a while. So many things in the world were waiting to be done. They began, at least in their minds, to live within civilization again. Their talk would often center on objects which had less and less to do with their present life. They discussed affairs of the town as though living there. They mentioned certain persons whom they expected to meet again; others whom they hoped would no longer be there.

The nearer the day for departure came, the friendlier the partners became. The old man and Dobbs were considering going into business together. They talked of opening a movie house in the port, Howard to be the business manager, and Dobbs the artistic director.

Curtin had his own problems. He found himself in a difficult situation. He could not even decide for himself whether he wished to stay in the republic or return to the States. Occasionally he mentioned a dame in San Antonio, Texas, whom he meant to marry some day. This idea occurred to him mostly when he felt rather lonely for a female. Since he knew her best, he naturally concentrated his special desires upon her whenever he was thinking of manly pleasures. But he was clever enough to know that, once back in town, and having met in a friendly way some easy janes, he might lose all interest in marrying the S.A. damsel. He admitted this when Howard explained to him what was really the matter and why right now he was so hot for the dame from Laredo Street.

The partners, as a rule, rarely talked of women. They knew from experience that it was not good for their health or for their work to think too frequently of things they could not have.

Anyone listening to their discussions would have been unable to imagine any of these men holding a woman in his arms. Any decent woman would have preferred to drown herself or cut her veins rather than keep company with these men. The fellows themselves, having lost all means of comparison with other people, could, of course, know nothing about the impression they would make upon an outsider who by chance should meet them. They saw only themselves, and none of them cared how he looked or how he spoke.

The gold worn around the finger of an elegant lady or as a crown on the head of a king has more often than not passed through hands of creatures who would make that king or that elegant lady shudder. There is little doubt that gold is oftener bathed in human blood than in hot suds. A noble king who wished to show his high-mindedness

could do no better than have his crown made of iron. Gold
is for thieves and swindlers. For this reason they own most
of it. The rest is owned by those who do not care where
the gold comes from or in what sort of hands it has
been.

9

I

Curtin had been to the village to buy provisions. These were meant to last until the partners were ready to leave.

"Where the devil have you been so long?" Howard asked him when Curtin arrived. "I had just decided to saddle up my ass and go to look for you. We were afraid something had happened to you. You should have been back by noon."

"Yes, sure I should." Curtin spoke wearily. Slowly he dismounted from the burro he had been riding and, helped by the old man, went about unpacking the two other animals.

Dobbs had gone to a certain look-out on the peak of the rock where he could see the whole valley below and the paths leading toward the base of the mountain range.

Only Curtin was sent out for provisions, for he knew best how to handle the burros and make them work; for the same reason he was in charge of carrying the water up to the mine. Going down to the village for buying or trading was far from being a vacation trip. It was more tiresome than working at the mine. Trading was carried on with the general storekeeper in the village merely for camouflaging the real doings at the mine. Curtin usually took down for exchange a few hides, for which he received close to nothing because the storekeeper claimed that he had no buyers for them. Most of what Curtin bought was paid for in cash.

One might have expected that whenever Curtin returned from the village he would bring back with him news from the outside world, but he did not. Nobody in this little village of very small Indian farmers ever read a newspaper. There would hardly have been found four persons in the village, including the storekeeper, who could read at all. If by any strange accident a newspaper came to the village, usually in the form of wrapping for goods received at the store, it was seldom less than ten months old. The storekeeper did not wrap up anything bought from him, because he had no paper for such a purpose. His patrons had to find for themselves a way to carry home their merchandise. This was of no concern to the storekeeper, as there was no competition, and besides, being the mayor, he was king, law, judge, and executioner all in one.

Since the papers were printed in Spanish, the three partners, not being on very easy terms with the Spanish language, would have got little out of them anyway. Of course, Curtin would speak to the storekeeper and to other men hanging around in the store, but they knew nothing beyond the affairs of their little community—an occasional murder, a wife-beating, the mysterious disappearance of a cow or a goat, the strange dryness of the present season. The burning of don Paulino's hut, a tiger breaking into the corral of the widow of don Modesto, the death of don Gonzalo's two youngest children, who had been stung by scorpions, and the paralysis of don Antonio on account of the bite of a venomous snake were the topics they discussed.

This sort of village talk was of no interest to the partners, and if Curtin mentioned it at all, it was just to tell something of what he had learned. Howard and Dobbs hardly listened. They would have been little stirred by hearing who had been nominated for president by the conventions of the Democrats and the G.O.P. Any interest in world affairs would have had a bad influence upon their work. Right now they could not afford to think of anything but how to finish up this job satisfactorily. The fact was they had no interest in anything beyond their vision, and this vision did not go farther than how to make money and, having made it, how to spend it.

2

Howard hollered for Dobbs.

Curtin opened the packs and handed out the goods he had brought. Evening was not far off, and so they decided to knock off work for the day, cook the meal, and have a long lazy chat afterwards, with pipes filled with fresh tobacco.

"What seems to be the trouble with you, Curty?" Howard asked, noticing that Curtin had not said a word for half an hour.

"I had to go a hell of a roundabout way to get back here, I tell you guys."

"How come?"

"It's like this, see. Down there in that damn Indian lay-out a guy was hanging around and he sort of blocked me. He said he was from Arizona, that mug did."

"He would be," Howard said.

Dobbs had become suspicious. "What is he after?"

"Ask me another. That's what I wanted to find out. But, hell, he kept his trap shut as to that. The natives told me that he had taken up quarters in a dirty little joint down there, a kind of a mule-drivers' lodging and boarding joint, or what they call here a fonda. He has been staying there practically a week. Doing nobody any harm. Talking quite swell Spanish. Seems to go along fine with those villagers. Doesn't drink, either. And besides he sure doesn't look like a tough gunner or as if he was chased for something he left to be settled with the D.A. No, looks rather decent, he does."

"Hell, come to the point." Dobbs was nervous.

"I wish I could. That's just the trouble, I can't see through; it's all thick. Well, fact is, he asked the natives if there might be gold or silver mines around here."

"The hell! He would ask that." Howard dropped his pipe, so startled was he by that remark.

"To this the Indians said no, there could be no gold or silver around here or they would know it, living here since the world began, and if there were any, they sure would like it, because they can hardly make their living, and if they didn't put in a heap of extra work by braiding mats and baskets and making pottery to sell in far-off towns, they would have to live like savages, with nothing to cover the nakedness of their bodies."

Dobbs looked around as if searching for something on the ground. "Do you want me to stone you, you devil of a silly talker? Say what he wants and have done."

"Okay, go down yourself and ask him for a written statement to be given to the press."

"Gosh, be quiet for once, Dobby, and let him tell his yarn in his own way. Well, Curty, go on, what's the brass tack?"

"Everything would have been fine as sunshine but for that devil of a storekeeper, whom we have actually made a millionaire. He had to brag and tell that Arizona hick that up here on this mountain ridge an American is roaming about hunting tigers and lions or weasels and what have you. That god-damn devil of a storekeeper also said that this chingando gringo is due to come down for his provisions one of these days and if that Arizona mug would stick around that long he might speak to his countryman. To this that hang-around answered that he'd like to wait and meet me."

"So you mean to tell us he actually waited for you to show

up? Is that what you mean to say?" Dobbs got more and more excited.

"You heard me, or did you sleep while I was reporting? Well, he waited for me. So the very moment I stepped into the store, he came, that hell of a brother from Arizona. He was an entire stranger to me. I'd never seen him before anywhere in this here country. 'Hello, stranger, how are ye?' and with this he bumped me. I tried to shake him off and show him an icy shoulder. I only said: 'How's y'self?' and tuned off, paying all my attention to the storekeeper. And what do you think? He didn't mind my being cold at all. He went on talking and saying that he thinks there must be truck-loads of real goods up there in the mountains. So that I might understand what he meant, he explained that he, of course, was speaking of the real stuff—that is, of yellow glittering dirt."

"Hell!" Howard blared out. "Looks tough to me, it sure does. Somehow he must have got an idea into his head when that storekeeper told him about you staying up here for so long a time without looking for other hunting-grounds."

"What did you tell him after he'd touched the right switch?" Dobbs asked.

"I said to him he shouldn't take me for a kid. Sure I've been up here for quite a while and I know the whole landscape around, and if there were a single grain of gold he could bet that I'd sure know it, and I assured him that there is nothing doing here for gold, or even copper, or I'd have seen it."

"What did he say to that door leading out?"

"He just answered with a smile showing that he was wise, and, to make everything positive and no mistake about it, he said: 'I wouldn't think you so dumb, brother. Believe me, if I only see a hill five miles away, I can tell you whether it carries an ounce or a ship-load. If you haven't found any-

thing yet, I'll come up and put your nose into it. Here in
the valley I've seen indications, lots of indications in fact,
and tracing the rocks I found that they must have come from
that ridge up there, washed down by the tropical torrents.'
'You don't say so, you mug,' I said to him, and says he: 'Yes,
believe it or not, I say so, and take this home with you.'"

Howard interrupted Curtin: "I have to say this much for
that guy, if he can tell from the landscape and from the
wash-down the load of a mountain, well, then he must be a
very great man."

"Maybe he is a geogist or what they call the guys who can
tell right from the ground if there is oil or if there is a dry
hole."

"You mean geologist, Dobby," Howard corrected him.
"Maybe he is, maybe he's just beating the brush to see if the
rabbit is coming out of it."

An idea occurred to Dobbs. "Did you ever think that he
might be a spy sent by the government or by the chieftains
of a horde of bandits, to watch for our return and rob us or
get the government to confiscate all we've made? Why, I'm
almost sure he's in touch with bandits. Even if they don't
know that we've got good pay with us, they might rob us
just for our burros and hides and, what is of more worth to
them, for our shotguns, tools, clothes. We have enough
things outside of the pay to lure any bandit to get us on our
way home."

Curtin shook his head. "I don't think so. He didn't impress
me as being a government spy or a tip-off for bandits. I'm
sure he means what he says. He is earnestly after gold. That's
what I think he is."

"How come you know what he is after?" Howard asked.

"Because he had packed up already when I left."

"What do you mean packed up? Packed up what and on
what?"

"He has two mules. One is a saddle-mule, and the other he uses for his packs."

"What sort of packs?"

"Seems to be a tent. Blankets. Frying-pans. A coffee-pot."

"No tools? I mean, no shovels and pick-axes and all that?" This from Dobbs.

The old man said: "If he's after the riches he can't very well dig up the dirt with his claws. You didn't see any shovels and such things?"

"Matter of fact, I didn't exactly search his packs."

"Of course not." Howard was thinking. Then he stared at Curtin. "He may carry the outfit wrapped up in his tent. Did the rags look as though tools might be inside of them?"

"Might. They looked bulky enough."

The fellows occupied themselves for quite a while with their own thoughts.

Curtin finally broke the silence. "I'm almost positive that he's no government spy and no crow for bandits. He impressed me as being a bit cracked up."

"Aw, let him stay, for hell's sake. I'm sick of this twaddle about that mug," Dobbs said. "We've nothing to worry about."

"I'm not so sure about that." Curtin began to explain. "I think we ought to worry. Fact is, he followed me. First he asked me right out if he might come with me to my camp. I said no, he could not. Then he just came trailing after me. For two miles I didn't mind; then I halted and let him come up. So I said to him, said I: 'Listen here, you mug, don't you make me sore. It may cost you dear. I don't butt into your racket, so you'd better not nose into mine, and we might still be friends. I can talk the other way round just as well, if you get what I mean, and believe me, you hick, I can tackle any guy your size, so you better lay off me if you know what's healthy for you. And now go to hell or heaven, what do I care?' "

"And what did he say to that?" Howard and Dobbs asked at the same time.

"He said that he didn't mean to bother me at all, and that he only wanted to be in the company of a white man for a few days because he hadn't met an American for months, and that he was about to go nuts roaming about the Sierra and seeing only Indians and never hearing a word but corrupt Spanish, and that he wanted to sit for a few nights with a white man by the fire, have a smoke together, and a damn talk, and that was all. To this I said that I didn't feel like swallowing his chatter and that I wanted to be alone. I think he doesn't know that I'm not alone up here. I think he has the idea that I'm camping single-handed."

"Where do you think he is right now?" Dobbs asked.

"Do you think he followed you?" Howard wanted to know.

"I took good care to go 'way round and look for ground that the burros couldn't easily leave stamped with their tracks. I even crawled with the animals through long stretches of brush to get the mug off my trail. But, hell, whenever I got a chance to shoot a glance back at him from a higher point of the mountains, I could see that he was coming along all right. Seems he has got a good nose. If I'd been all by myself, I could have thrown him off the trail easily, but with three burros on your hands it couldn't be done. It's only a matter of time, for if he means to find me he sure will. No way out. There's only one question to settle right now."

"What question?" Dobbs asked.

"What are we going to do with him if he shows up one of these days? We couldn't very well work the mine any longer with him around for a watch-dog."

Howard stirred the fire and said: "Hard to tell what to do. If he were an Indian from the valley or from the village below, it wouldn't matter a bit. An Indian doesn't stay. He goes back to his village, to his family. It's different with such a guy. He will smell us out. He won't be so dumb as not to ask himself why three white men are camping up here for months. We can't tell him that we're here on a vacation. We might tell him that we've committed a couple of murders and are hiding out. But suppose he's the wrong kind; he'll go back after a while and set a company of federal troops after us. If they get you, and the officer in command is in a hurry to return to his jane, he orders his soldiers to shoot you like a sick dog. They shoot you while you are trying to escape. You can't prove afterwards that they were mistaken, because they bury you right where you drop, and before that they make you dig a hole to spend your time in until the trumpets call you to check up the register of your sins."

"Tell us all this later," Dobbs broke in. "We've got other worries now. I move that we tell him to check out the minute he pops up, and say to him in a straightforward manner that if we see him around here just once more, we'll fill his belly up with plums hard enough for him to digest."

Howard was against such a measure. "That would be foolish. He'd sit around for an hour, play the innocent, and then go down to the nearest town and put the mounted police on our track. Then what? What do the police know about us? We might be escaped convicts, or rebels against the government, or bandits. The police would be here in no time if that guy told them we've got stolen treasure with us. Once the police are here, even if they didn't find anything, we couldn't stay any longer and we couldn't take home with us what we have."

"All right," Dobbs said, "then there's nothing else to do

but pull the trigger the very minute he comes. Or we might hang him. Then there'll be peace again."

"Mebbe," was all Howard had to say to that. He took the potatoes from the fire to see if they were done. Potatoes were the greatest luxury they had had since they had been here, for they were seldom to be found in the village. This time the grocer had ordered a few pounds from the town because he knew that Curtin would buy them.

Placing the pot of potatoes back on the fire, Howard began to speak: "We can't shoot him. That's out. He may be just a tramp, a guy that likes to roam about this great country without any special aim, just to thank the Lord for these beautiful mountains. We can't shoot him for that. He hasn't done us any wrong, and we don't know by a lost penny whether he means to nose into our business. Some fellows are working themselves to death in the oil-fields or in the copper mines to make a living or to pile up dough, while others prefer to go hungry sometimes rather than miss the opportunity to contemplate the wonders and the beauty of nature. It's no crime to visit these mountains with an open heart; at least it's no crime against us."

Dobbs didn't seem convinced. "How can we tell if he's that sort of a nut or if he's crooked?"

"We can't. Right you are." The old man agreed perfectly. "But we ought to give him a chance. And besides, if we shoot him, it might come to light."

"Might come to light? How come?" Dobbs could not get away from his idea of killing him. "We dig him in and leave him there. Suppose somebody has seen him coming up here, what of it? That's no evidence that we shot him. If we don't want to shoot him we can easily push him over a rock and he'll break his neck. If his body is found, everybody will accept it as a lamentable accident."

"Yes, quite easy." Howard grinned at Dobbs. "Easy. As

easy as kicking an old mule in the buttocks. And just who is going to shoot him or push him off into a ravine? You, Dobby?"

"Why not? We can flip a coin to find out who will have to do it."

"Oh, yes? And the one who did it will be forever in the hands of those who know it. Not me, brother. Count me out. That's too costly for me. No sale as far as I'm concerned."

3

During all this long discussion between Howard and Dobbs, Curtin had sat silent, drinking his coffee, poking the fire occasionally, and raising his eyes from the ground at times to let his gaze wander around the brush that fenced in the camp.

Howard suddenly noted that Curtin had not taken part in the conversation for a long time, and asked: "Are you sure he was trailing you?"

"I'm quite sure of that."

"How come?"

"Because there he is." Curtin made a tired gesture with his shoulders and shot a glance at an opening in the bushes where the path led to the camp.

Howard and Dobbs were so bewildered that for a few seconds they could not bring themselves to look in the direction Curtin had indicated.

"Where?" they asked both at the same time. They were so surprised that they forgot to fatten the question with an oath.

Curtin nodded his head toward the path.

Howard and Dobbs finally turned round and looked at the path, and there, in the deep shadows of the falling night, uncertainly lighted up by the flickering camp-fire, the stranger stood, at either side of him a mule which he held by ropes.

He looked at the three men in amazement, for he had expected to find Curtin alone.

He didn't call out a friendly "Hello," but stood silent, waiting to be called or shot at or cursed. It was difficult to tell from his attitude what he really expected to happen. He gave the impression that he was willing to submit to anything that these three rough-looking fellows should decide to do to him. At the same time he seemed too proud to beg or even to accept any sort of help for which he was not able to pay.

10

While Curtin was telling of the stranger, Howard and Dobbs had built up in their minds an idea of what he might look like. Each had pictured the stranger differently.

Dobbs had imagined him a crude tramp with the features of an old drunkard, coupled with the looks of a man who is spending his life in the tropics, living from robberies on the highway and from all sorts of tricks, and not afraid to slay any man who might resist him.

Howard, on the other hand, had pictured him as the ordinary prospector, robust, with weather-beaten, leather-like face, hands like roots of old trees, and not afraid of anything; a man using all his experience, knowledge, and brain and stubbornly trying to find a rich claim and exploit it to the limit. To Howard the stranger appeared to be an honest gold-digger of the old, sturdy sort who would never commit a crime or steal even a nail, but would stand ready to commit murder at any moment to defend his claim against anyone who tried to deprive him of what he was sure was his rightful property.

Now both Howard and Dobbs were surprised. The stranger looked entirely different from their pictures of him, and as he had appeared so unexpectedly, neither the old man nor Dobbs could utter a sound.

The stranger was still standing in the opening. Obviously he was at a loss what to do or say.

His mules sniffed at the ground, then, lifting their noses high, sniffed the air. After this they turned their heads and brayed with all their might to others of their kind in the pasture where the burros were kept. It was this earthy braying of the mules that broke the spell.

2

Dobbs rose. With long, slow strides he went across the camp toward the stranger, who did not move.

Dobbs had had it in mind to treat the intruder as rough as hell and to ask him outright what he wanted and then send him to the devil. But when he reached him he merely said indifferently: "Hello, stranger!"

"Hello, friend!" the stranger answered quietly.

Dobbs had his hands in his pants pockets. He looked at the man, moved his tongue inside of a tightly closed mouth, scratched the ground with his right foot, and said: "Okay, won't you come over and sit by the fire?"

"Thank you, friend," was all the stranger said.

He came closer to the fire, took off the packs and the saddles from his mules, coupled the forelegs of the animals with a leather thong, patted their necks in a friendly way, pushed his fist into their hams, and said: "Now, you rascals, off for your supper." This he murmured so low it could hardly be heard by the fellows at the fire.

None of the partners had given him a hand in unpacking his mules. He seemed not to have expected any assistance.

The mules shuffled off in the direction from where they had heard the call.

For a minute the new-comer looked toward the darkness which had swallowed them up. Then turning slowly about, he approached the fire.

"Good evening, all of you!" he said and sat down.

"How d'ye do?" Only Howard answered.

Curtin stirred the beans he had on the fire; Dobbs took off the pot of potatoes, shook it, and tested one with a knife to see whether they were cooked enough. Finding them to his liking, he drained off the water and set them back near the fire to keep hot. Howard was occupied with roasting meat. Dobbs rose and carried more wood to the fire. It seemed that supper was about ready. Curtin pushed the coffee-can once more on the fire.

None of the three took a look at the new-comer. Since they did not speak to each other and made themselves as busy about the cooking as could be, the stranger felt that he was not being entirely ignored, for they didn't talk among themselves and by so doing give him to understand that he didn't belong.

"I know quite well, you fellers, that I'm not wanted around here," he said when silence had become almost unbearable.

Curtin frowned and shot him a glance. "I think I made that quite clear to you when we met in the village."

"True, you did. But I can't stand it any longer among the Indians. It's all right for a while. Yet when I saw you coming along, I simply couldn't resist the desire to talk with you and try to stay a few days with a white man."

Howard uttered a short dry laugh. "If you can't stand those Indians and must have a white to talk to, why the hell don't you leave that god-forsaken region and go places where you'll find more baboons than you could bear to have around? Durango isn't so far off, nor Mazatlán. With your two strong mules and that little baggage you carry along, it wouldn't take you more than four or five days to get to where there are all the American clubs and legion posts you want."

"I'm not after that. I've got other worries."

"So have we," Dobbs broke in. "And don't you make any mistake. The biggest worry we have right now is your presence here. We have no use for you. We don't even need a cook, I should say not even a dish-washer. We are complete. No vacancy. Have I made myself clear?"

The stranger did not answer.

Dobbs continued: "If I haven't made myself clear, let me tell you that I think it would do you lots of good if you would saddle up early in the morning and go where you came from and take our blessings with you. And I'll be damned if we don't mean it that way, all of us. Get me, stranger?"

The new-comer remained silent. He watched the three partners preparing supper and dealing the meal out on the plates. He watched them without looking hungry and without expecting to be invited to partake of the supper.

Then Curtin, after having half emptied his plate, said: "Help yourself, partner. Here's a plate, and here's a spoon, knife, and fork. I hope you know how to use them. Don't use only the spoon or we might think you've broken Leavenworth. We may be the wrong sort, but we still eat as we did at the old homestead."

Dobbs watched him fill his plate. He handed him the coffee-pot. He could not do it, though, without salting the invitation: "For tonight we have something for you. Mebbe there is even a breakfast for you t'morrow morn. We're no misers and we don't let a guy starve to death. But after breakfast you'd better look out for yourself. No trespassing allowed here, you know. Dogs. You understand."

After this they ate in silence save for a few words concerned, exclusively, with details about the food before them or which they had in store.

The stranger ate very little. He appeared to eat more out of politeness than because of hunger. No word did he throw into the meager conversation of the three partners.

3

Supper over, they all washed the dishes in a bucket and laid them aside. The three partners tried to make themselves as comfortable as possible in the way they had become used to during the long months spent in the place. For a while they seemed to have forgotten the presence of the guest. They were only reminded of him when they filled their pipes and lighted them and saw the stranger returning to the fire and squatting by it. He had gone to look after his packs and get something out of them.

"Got tobacco?" Dobbs asked.

"Yes, thanks." He had no pipe. He rolled himself a cigarette rather expertly.

The partners began talking. By agreement they talked only about hunting, so as to drag the stranger off the real track. He, however, was not so dumb as to be caught that easily. They didn't know much about hunting. Therefore their talk was not very convincing to a man who knew more about it than his hosts would ever learn. Several times they caught glances from him which showed them that he knew that they were not there merely for hunting, as they wanted him to believe.

He felt sorry for them, so he finished them up with a few strokes: "This is no hunting-ground here. Excuse me for butting in. There is no game here worth going after. It wouldn't take one week for a real hunter to clean up all around for five miles in each direction."

"My, my, what a smart guy we have with us!" Dobbs sneered.

"He's right," Howard said. "There's no good hunting here. That's why we've made up our minds to leave this ground inside of a week and look for something better. You are right, stranger; this is poor ground. It took us some time to find it out."

The stranger looked at Howard with eyes partly closed. "Poor ground, you say? Depends what you call poor ground. There isn't game enough here to give you a fair living. What really is here is something else. Something better."

"And what is that, doctor, may I ask you?" Dobbs threw him a suspicious glance, and to hide his true feeling he emphasized his nasty tone.

"Gold, that's what is here." This very calmly from the stranger.

"There's no gold hereabouts," Curtin said, with a fluttering breath.

Howard smiled. "My boy, if there were one single ounce of gold here, I would sure have seen it. I know gold when I see it, believe me, stranger."

"You look like you would. And if you say you haven't found any gold here, then good night, sir; then you wouldn't be the intelligent man I thought the minute I saw you here." The stranger spoke very courteously.

None of the partners knew what to answer. They thought it wiser not to discuss this particular subject any further. Having shown no special interest in gold, they hoped that there might still be a chance to lead the stranger astray.

"Maybe," Howard nodded. "Maybe you are right. Who knows? We've never thought about it. Gives me an idea. I'll sleep over it, and so I guess I'll hit the hay. Good night, and sweet dreams of sugars in silk undies."

Dobbs and Curtin made an effort to follow up the old man in displaying indifference to the truck-loads of gold that might be lying about, according to the stranger. They knocked their pipes clean, then they rose, stretched their limbs, yawned indecently, and trudged heavily to their tent.

"Until t'morrow, stranger." Curtin nodded his head to the stranger, who was still sitting by the fire.

"You bet," he said, looking after them.

He hadn't been invited to spend the night in the tent, which was big enough to shelter three more men. He seemed not to mind.

He whistled. His riding-mule came hobbling along. He gave him a handful of corn which he had taken from the packs, patted the mule on the neck, and, with a slight kick in the hams, started it on its way back to the others. A minute later his pack-mule came and he treated it in the same way, leaving it to hobble after the first.

Again he went to his packs, brought his saddle and two blankets to the fire, arranged his bed, and, after pushing a couple of dead tree-trunks into the fire, lay down to sleep. For a few minutes he hummed a tune while rolling himself snugly in his blanket, and then he was quiet.

4

There was less quietness in the tent, which was too far away from the fire for the stranger to distinguish all that was said there, though he could hear hushed voices.

"I am still of the opinion that we must get rid of him some way," Dobbs insisted.

Howard tried to calm him: "Hush, hush! Not so hot. We don't know a damn thing about him yet. Give him a chance. To me he looks absolutely harmless. I would bet that he isn't a spy for any outside party, government or highway-men. If he were that he wouldn't come alone, and he sure wouldn't look so hungry."

"Hungry, yea? He? You make me sick," Dobbs interrupted the old man. "Did he eat? He hardly touched the food."

"Come, come. If you are as dead tired as he seemed to be you can't eat very well. I rather figure he has a guilty conscience. Guess he's running away from something or somebody. Something or somebody is after him. It may not be just murder or a hold-up. There are other things. Often worse than the cops."

Now Curtin spoke up. "Perhaps we could start a quarrel with him and make him boil over, and as soon as he draws, we could switch him off and be fully justified."

"That doesn't look so very swell to me." Howard was sitting on his cot pulling off his boots. "No, I'm against it. It's dirty—would be dirty that way. It isn't fair."

"Oh hell, fair or no fair," Dobbs howled, "we have to get rid of him. That's all there is to it. He is warned about his health, isn't he? If he doesn't take heed, it's his funeral."

Stretched on their cots, they were still talking and trying to find a solution for the problem which so unexpectedly confronted them. All were agreed that the stranger was not welcome and that he had to be disposed of. Yet they also admitted that killing him had many disadvantages and only one benefit. And even this benefit was rather doubtful.

Finally they fell asleep without having reached any definite decision.

II

1

The next morning found the three partners very early by the fire. Having had a bad night with all sorts of heavy dreams, they were in as bad humor as a girl whose new white dress has been soiled by a passing motorist just three minutes before she is to meet the boy friend.

The stranger had been busy. Fuel was heaped by the fire, which was blazing, and his own cooking-kettles, with beans and coffee, were hanging over it.

Dobbs greeted him: "Hey, you mug, where did you get the water for your stuff?"

"I just took it from the bucket."

"Oh, you did, did you? Fine. But don't get the idea into your cone that we are pulling up the water for you. We don't wait on anybody—least of all on a tramp like you."

"Excuse me, I didn't know that water was so hard to get here."

"You know it now, and no more lip from you, you son of a bitch."

"I'll get the bucket filled for you."

"Better hurry."

At this moment Curtin came to the fire: "Water-stealing, hey? And stealing our fuel? What do you think you are, anyway? Just let me catch you once more taking one thing that belongs to us. Then I'll fill your belly up, doggone it to hell."

"I thought that perhaps I was among civilized men who would not mind letting me have a drink of fresh water," he said very politely.

Dobbs was on his feet as though he had been sitting on a bomb. "You don't mean to say that we can't read or write, that we are just bandits and sons of a dozen bitches? Is that it?" And without waiting for an answer he planted his fist in the stranger's face with such force that he dropped full-length as if felled by a heavy club.

He needed time to come to. Slowly he rose and shook his head as if he wanted to find the full use of his neck again.

Then he came close to Dobbs and said: "I could easily do the same to you, and it isn't settled yet who might come out the better of us two. What good would it do me? I know you three are only waiting for the moment I draw to catch me and bump me off the landscape. I won't make it so easy for you. No fooling for me. Never mind, perhaps there will come a day when we shall have an accounting, and then we'll look at the balance. This time I took it. Thanks for your kind attention."

He went to the fire and lifted his kettles off. Just as he started to carry them away to another site, where he wanted to build his own fire, Howard approached him.

"Got something to eat, stranger?" Howard asked in a friendly voice.

"Yes, partner. I've got tea, coffee, beans, rice, dried meat, and two cans of milk."

"Never mind your own eats. Today you may eat with us. But tomorrow I'd suggest you have your own kitchen ready."

"Thanks. I certainly shall take your hint."

"Tomorrow?" Dobbs, who by his victory had steamed off his anger, spoke less harshly. "Tomorrow? Now, listen here, stranger, what do you mean? You don't mean to rent an apartment here and spend your vacation in our neighborhood? We sure wouldn't be pleased to have you for our next-door family."

"Who cares?" the stranger answered, throwing a few pinches of tea into his kettle, and without looking up from the boiling brew he added: "I mean to stay here. It's pretty around here."

Curtin with a voice louder than necessary said: "No parking here without our permission, partner."

"Bush and mountains are free, ain't they?"

"Not the way you think, friend," Howard broke in. "Free is the bush, and the desert, and the woods, and the mountain ranges for whoever likes to camp there. In that you are right. But we were the first here; we've got the first claim."

"Maybe. Maybe that's what you think. But how can you prove that you were really the first here on this spot? What if I was here long before you ever thought of coming?"

"Registered your claim?" Howard asked.

"Did you?"

"That's beyond the point. We are here right now. And suppose you have been here before, as you say you have; why didn't you stake it? Since you didn't, you haven't the slightest chance in any court if you mean to fight it out. Well, let's have breakfast."

2

Breakfast over, the partners did not know what to do. They couldn't go to work at the mine, for the stranger would find them out.

Curtin then had an idea. He said that they all might go hunting together.

The stranger looked from one to another. He was not

sure what was behind this proposal. The hunt might give the partners a great opportunity to get rid of him through an accident. Thinking this over, he concluded that if they meant to kill him they would do it anyhow, accident or no accident. They alone would be the witnesses.

So he said: "Okay with me. Today I'll go hunting with you, but tomorrow I've got other things to do, more important things."

"What?" the three partners asked almost simultaneously.

"Tomorrow I start to dig for gold here."

"You don't say so?" Howard had heard the word with a deep breath. He had become pale. So had his two partners.

"Yes, I'm going to prospect here. Right at this spot or somewhere around in the neighborhood. Here is the stuff I was looking for. If none of you have found anything here, that would only be evidence that all of you are boneheads. But I don't think you are."

"You're smart, stranger," Howard answered him. "Where would we be if it were not for you to show us the glory of heaven? My, my! What a great guy!"

"I figure you've scratched up, let's say, around fifty ounces."

"Or five hundred. Isn't that what you mean?" Howard found it hard to open his mouth, which seemed to dry out. Dobbs and Curtin were without speech.

"Or five hundred. Right, partner. But here is at least an easy million, if you ask me and my grandfather."

"A million?" Dobbs and Curtin shouted, and with this they were fully home again, color, breath, wet lips, moisture in the eyes, and all that they had lost during the last two minutes.

"Yes, a full uncut million. If you haven't found it yet, it's your fault, not the mountain's. I know you haven't got the rich pot yet, although you have been hanging around

here eight months or nine. The Indians down in the valley
told me that only one man was up here. If you had come
upon the right entrance and knocked at the door behind
which the treasure is open to view, you would have had so
much that you would have left long ago, because you
couldn't carry all that's here without arousing suspicion
and being waylaid on your road home. Or you would
have sent back just one man to get the claim legally registered and then have formed a regular mining company,
with all the machinery and a hundred men working for
you."

"That so?" Dobbs said scoffingly. "Well, you may as well
know facts. We haven't got anything, nothing. See?"

The stranger could not be talked off. "You may tell me
what you like. I don't believe a word anyhow. I don't care
what you have, how much you have, whether you have
anything at all, or what you are doing here. I'm not a baby.
If I see three men living up here for eight months, then I
know without a Bible that they are not staying for pleasure
or for an ordinary fishing-trip. You can't put this one over
on me, partners. You'd better lay the cards on the table and
then let's see who has buried away the four jacks. What's
the use playing hide-and-seek? I'm not a criminal, not a
crook, not a spy. I'm just as decent as any one of you three
fellers is. Better than you I don't want to be. It suits me all
right to be just the kind you are. We all are out here to
make money. If we were looking for pleasure, we wouldn't
select this god-forsaken region full of mosquitoes, yellow
fever, typhoidal water, scorpions, tarantulas, and even hungry tigers sniffing around the camp by night. I know quite
well you can bump me off any minute you wish. But that
could happen to me any place, even in Chicago walking
quietly down the street. You always have to risk something
if you want to make money. If you bump me off you can't

be sure but that tomorrow another guy may show up whom you'll have to give the final works. Or instead of one guy popping up, there may be a full dozen any day. Then you stop bumping off, and you are worse off than you are right now."

"All right, stranger," Howard said, "what's above your shoulders? Spit it out. We are at least willing to tune in."

3

"Let's make a clean breast," the stranger suggested.

"We might." Howard filled his cup with fresh coffee. "Now, of course we don't know who you are or what you are. You may be a spy and you may not. If you are, all that we can lose is our labor of eight months and what we have invested in cold cash. But I tell you it would be expensive for you should you squeal. We'd get you even if we had to look for you in China or on a ranch in the pampas of the Argentine. There would be no quarter. I think you have that clear."

"Yes, I have. I know I could not get away with it forever. Since I know this, I think we are now on equal terms, so I want to make it plain to you that I don't want to share in what you have so far, not a cent. I won't even work near you. We'll stake our mines and work them as we think best, each party for himself. Right?"

"Right by me. What do you think of that proposition, partners?" Howard asked.

Dobbs and Curtin waited for some time before they answered. Then Curtin said: "Would you mind, stranger, letting us three thresh this out alone among ourselves?"

"Not at all. Go ahead. I'll have to look after my mules anyway." He stood up and walked off in the direction in which his mules had gone the night before.

4

He returned after two hours.

"Found them?" Curtin asked.

"Yes, they are all right. Fine pasture you've got around here."

"Now, let's all sit down and have this over." Howard filled his pipe. Having lighted it, he said: "Yep, we've got something. Matter of fact, all taken together it's just good pay for eight months of hard work."

"That's what I thought. Now, down in the village I was not just hanging around. I looked about. I noted from sand washed down from these mountains by the heavy rains that there is quite a lot of metal up here."

Howard interrupted: "I think I know something about prospecting. Not much perhaps, not as much as you seem to know. If there were, as you say, a million here, we sure would have seen it. We haven't, and that's that."

"I'm convinced it is here." The stranger was very insistent. "It must be here. I simply couldn't be mistaken. Alone I can't do it. I need you three fellows. You've got all the tools, you've got the technical experience, and I have the better knowledge. I've studied this line, you haven't. Now the thing is to find the thick deposit, the lode. I know I could never interest a bank or a mining company in my project, because I'm working only on a hunch which would be extremely difficult to explain to a banker or to a board of directors who want to see things plain and clear. All right, my proposition is this: You keep what you have so far as your well-earned property, but all that is coming to us after we have started to work my plan is cut two fifths my way and three fifths your way."

The three partners looked at each other and then they laughed right in his face.

"Shavings we can get ourselves; for that we don't need any help from the outside," Howard said. "And fairy-tales we had forgotten long before we reached the fourth grade. What you say, partners?"

"We've got along fine without you so far and I think we can do for the rest of our stay here," Dobbs answered with a smile. "What's your opinion, Curty?" he added, turning to his partner.

"If you ask me, I'd say we haven't much to lose if we give this feller's proposition a chance, at least for a few days. Since we are here anyway, and since we have decided to make off inside of a week, we might just as well have a look at what he offers."

"Count me out," Howard said. "These are old magazine stories, nothing new about them. I'm through with this living like wild beasts. I want to have a real bed under my hams; that's what I want. I'm fully satisfied with what I've got now."

Dobbs had been stirred up by Curtin's idea. "Why, Howdy, I think Curty isn't so dumb after all. Let's stick just a week more. It may bring us something better than we have had during all the eight months of chain-gang life we've spent here."

"You guys win. I can't make the trip back to Durango all by myself. I know what I can do and what not when alone with pack-burros. So for this reason and for no other I have to stick with you for another week. All right."

"Understand, stranger," Curtin began to make clear how he meant his agreement, "we've no intention of staying long. I've got somebody waiting for me. A dame, if you must know. I need her badly, so let's say one week more. If we find inside of a week a fair trace of what you tell us

is here, then I'll be willing to hang on longer. If we don't
and it's just so much more baloney, I'm off with you, old
man," he ended, addressing Howard.

"Who agrees say: 'Ay!'" Dobbs mocked.

"Now, stranger, since we're partners, what's your name?"
Howard asked. "And if it's a secret, then tell us what you
wish to be called. We can't call you mug or stranger or
what have you all the time."

"Lacaud. Robert W. Lacaud, Phoenix, Arizona; Tech,
Pasadena."

"A rather long name for just one person. But I believe
you, don't mind the formalities." Howard laughed.

"It may not be his, after all—I mean the long name."
Curtin was grinning.

"Related to the Lacauds in Los Angeles—furniture?"
Howard asked.

"Only slightly," Lacaud answered. "I have no connections
with them any longer. Broken off entirely. Last will patch-
ers, you know."

5

"Reckon I'll have a look at the burros," Howard said.

He did not have to go, as Lacaud had, to the pasture on
the slope of the mountain to watch the animals. Near the
camp there was a good look-out from a high rock. The
partners had found that from this peak the greater part of
the slopes of the whole mountain range could be seen very
clearly, and when rain was about to come they could tell
that a speck three or five miles away was a stray horse or a
goat from the village. Coming from the camp, it took only
a few minutes to climb that peak.

Howard had hardly reached the look-out when he began
to shout: "Hell, what's this!"

"What's doing?" Dobbs called back.

"Burros gone?" Curtin hollered.

"Come up here," the old man yelled. "Come quick, hurry, I say. Hell is loose."

Curtin and Dobbs sprang to their feet and ran to the peak. Lacaud followed more slowly.

"What's this coming toward our mountain?" Howard asked his partners. "I can't make out what it is. Perhaps you can, Curty, with your eyes of a buzzard. What is it?"

Curtin looked for a half a minute. "Must be soldiers or the mounted police, or some sort of rangers, as far as I can make out."

"It's the mounted all right," Dobbs growled, his eyes on the horizon. "Yes, the mounted, and coming right up here."

The three looked at each other with faces gone pale.

Suddenly Dobbs jumped up, caught Lacaud by the throat, and bellowed: "Now, you dirty crook, son of a bitch, now we got you cached. So that's your stinking game, is it? Came out too soon, did it? All right, take what is coming to you, you skunk."

Dobbs had his gun out and pointed at Lacaud ready to shoot. "You rat, if you know a prayer, say it now and make it snappy."

Howard was quick. He was behind Dobbs, and with a hard jerk he lowered Dobbs's arm.

"Let me kill that filthy rat," Dobbs cried. "Gawd and geecries, I knew he was a pigeon, I knew it all the time, with his oily soft-soap speech."

Lacaud made no move, but said quietly: "You are wrong, partner. It means all of us, myself included."

"Means what?" Curtin asked.

"Means that I think I know who they are. They are not soldiers nor the mounted police or what they call here Rurales. They are wise to us. They are after me, and after you, Curty. They don't know yet that there is anyone else up here."

"Then they can have the know only from you," Dobbs said.

"Not from me, but from the people in the village. I think I know who they are. If I am right, then may the Lord be with us. Bandits, that's what they are. And they aren't after our money, but our guns and ammunition, since the villagers have told them about the American hunter up here who has rifles and guns and heaps of ammunition with him."

"And how come you to know?" Dobbs was still suspicious.

"May I have a look at them?" Lacaud asked.

"Wouldn't you like it, sweety, and give them signals, hey? Wouldn't you?" Dobbs sneered.

"You may stay back of me and pluck me off if you see me doing anything suspicious."

"Maybe Arizona is right," Curtin observed. "They don't look to me like police, not even like organized rangers, less like soldiers. They are just what he says, a horde of ragged and filthy bandits. Come up, Lackey, have a look. We can pluck you later."

"Wait a minute." Howard held Lacaud by the arm. "They are not after you for stealing or cattle-rustling below, are they? Better tell the truth. If they are, you are clearing out of here this very minute to take them off our track or we hand you in, dirty as I would feel; but we need protection, you know, and cattle-rustling is a dirty business, especially against such poor farmers as they are. So get this straight, we can't afford to have police sniffing about. You have to go right down and let yourself be seen to get them away from us."

"I understand, friend. But I've nothing up my sleeve. I've been for weeks in the village. Anybody could have got me if there were somebody looking for me."

"I think he's right," Curtin said thoughtfully. "He wouldn't have dared to hang around the village for so long if he'd had anything to hide. Come up and see what you can find out. I think we can trust you once more."

Lacaud climbed up to the peak and sat for a while looking carefully about.

"We'd better make no move," Lacaud suggested. "We might be seen here on this peak. Sitting quietly, we may look like part of the rock. These are no soldiers. They are no police either. They are no organized posse of deputies or Rurales, for even poor peasants organized for chasing criminals couldn't look like these men—not even in this country."

"Then we are in a god-damn hole, I can tell you," Howard said. "With soldiers or police or a posse we would at least have a chance to explain and defend ourselves and see somebody who looks like a judge and who means to judge rightly. But with bandits we've not even a Chinaman's chance in the hands of Chinese highwaymen."

Hearing this, Dobbs jerked his body around to Lacaud, saying: "Still the same crook—I think that's what you are."

Howard butted in. "Aw, leave him alone, for hell's sake. We got to work fast now."

Dobbs did not mind the old man. "Still a spy, as I thought from the first. Only not a spy for the government, but a spy for the bandits, to do the inside job. Too bad for you that we found that out before you got them here."

"Wrong again, brother. I have nothing to do with bandits either. And if you men don't stop being suspicious and accusing me of things I never thought or even imagined, you may be short one full-grown man. Within an hour or so you will need not only every man around here, but every hand and every gun, or you won't see the sun rise tomorrow morning or thereafter. Just let me have another look. Maybe I can even tell you what sort of bandits they are, because in the village I heard tales that were certainly not rumors."

Once more he climbed to the look-out, followed by Curtin and Dobbs.

"As I thought," he said after a long glance down.

"What do you think?" Curtin asked.

"Do you see among the riders a man wearing a wide-brimmed golden hat on his head that glitters in the sun?" he asked Curtin.

"No, I can't see him," Curtin answered. But after a closer look he added: "Yes, I think—well, let's see, yes, there he is. A hat like those usually worn by the Indian farmers, wide-brimmed and high. Seems to be a palm hat."

"It is a palm hat, but painted with shining gold paint, as unskilled Mexican workers paint their hats for fun whenever they are employed at a shop where there is gold or aluminum paint for painting oil-tanks and such things."

"Seems to be a sort of captain to the horde," Curtin said, still looking.

"He is the captain all right, the chief of the outfit. Now I know well who they are and why they are coming this way. Last week I was at the hacienda of don Genaro Montereal, ten miles from the village, where I stayed overnight. Señor Montereal had the papers and he read them to me, or, better, he told what was in the papers from the capital. This golden hat was mentioned in the description of the bandits. That man sure has courage not to change his hat. No doubt he is unable to read and so doesn't know that his band has been described, man by man, and horse by horse. What I couldn't gather from the papers don Genaro was reading I heard in the village from the people who had returned from town bringing the latest news with them. I will tell you the story, and then you'll understand why I said: May the Lord be with us if they come up and find us. After I've told you the story, you will no longer believe me a spy of these killers, whatever else you may think of me. I would rather help the devil fire the boilers in hell than have anything in common with these bandits."

While all four men were sitting on the peak watching every move the bandits made below in the valley, Lacaud told the story of the bandits.

12

At a little, unimportant station of the railroad which links the western states of the republic with the eastern, the passenger train stopped only long enough to take on the mail and express, if any, and to hand out mail-bags, a few chunks of ice, and a few goods ordered by the merchants. The town, a very small one, was located three miles away from the depot, and connected with it by a poor dirt road on which a rattling flivver would occasionally be seen asthmatically making its way.

Passengers boarding the train or leaving it at this station were seldom many. Half a week would pass by at times without any arrivals or departures.

The east-bound train stopped about eight in the evening, which in a tropical country is pitch-dark summer and winter alike.

Anyway, neither the station-master nor the conductor of the train was very much surprised when, one Friday night, more than twenty passengers, all mestizos, boarded the train at the depot. From their simple clothing they were sure that they were peasants and small farmers going to the Saturday market in one of the bigger towns or working-men on their way to a mine or to road work. The station-master, nevertheless, thought it a bit strange that these men did not buy tickets from him. Still, this happened frequently, particularly if there were many and if they were late. They might arrange the fare with the conductor on the train. He was glad in a way that they did not ask him for their tickets, because he was busy enough checking the express and seeing to his many duties as the only depot official.

The mestizos wore their huge palm hats pulled rather low on their foreheads, for the wind would blow their hats off when riding on the train, as they prefer to stand on the platform or sit on the steps, partly because they feel uneasy inside the train, partly owing to their fear of train-wrecks. They were clad in white, brown, or yellow cotton pants; some wore half-woolen shirts, others had on dirty-looking cotton shirts, some torn, some crudely patched. On their feet some wore low boots, others sandals; some were barefooted; a few had on one foot a boot and on the other a well-worn sandal; some had their calves covered with weather-beaten boot-hose of leather. And there were two who had a boot-hose on only one leg, while the other was covered by pants.

All had bright-colored woolen blankets tightly wrapped around their bodies, for the night was rather cool; and, as these people usually do, they wore their blankets wrapped around them so high up that their faces were covered up to the nose. With their hats pulled close to their eyes, only a very narrow strip of their faces could be seen.

Nothing was unusual or strange about the way they wore their hats and their blankets, for every Indian or mestizo farmer will do the same if he feels cold. So no one on the train, neither train-officials nor passengers nor the military convoy paid the slightest attention to these men when they got on.

They looked around for seats, or at least they pretended to. There was only standing-room in the second-class cars which the new-comers had boarded. The men distributed themselves slowly over both the second-class cars and the one first-class car.

Crowding the train far above its capacity were families with children, women traveling alone, salesmen, merchants, farmers, workers, lower officials. In the first-class car the well-to-do people were reading, talking, playing cards, or trying to sleep. Two Pullman cars occupied by tourists, high officials, and rich merchants were coupled to the first-class car at the end of the train.

In the second-class car which came after the express car the first benches were occupied by the convoy. This convoy consisted of fifty federal soldiers, among them a first lieutenant as commander, a top sergeant, and three cabos or corporals. The lieutenant had gone to the dining-car for his supper, leaving the convoy in charge of the top sergeant. Some of the soldiers had their rifles between their knees, some had laid them on the bench against their backs, and others had put theirs up in the racks.

Some of the soldiers were drowsing, others were playing games to pass the time. Most of them, however, had their first readers upon their knees and were studying the basic elements of education. Those who had reached the second grade were helping those who had just started first-grade work.

A train-employee walked along the aisles offering bottled beer, soda-water, candy, cigarettes, chewing-gum, magazines, papers, and books.

Most of the passengers made crude preparations to pass the next hours sleeping. The inside of the cars, particularly the second-class cars, made in the uncertain and not too bright light a colorful picture. Whites, mestizos, Indians, men, women, children, clean people and dirty, many women and little girls dressed gaudily in the costumes of their native state, all crowded together.

2

The train had picked up speed and was hurrying to reach the next station, which was about thirty-two minutes away.

While taking up standing-room, the mestizos saw to it that they had all the entrances to the cars well covered. No suspicion was aroused by the new-comers' standing by the doors, as it was practically the only place where enough space for them was left, the aisles being so crowded that even the conductors had difficulty in walking through to inspect the tickets.

The train was now running at full speed.

All of a sudden and without the faintest warning the mestizos opened their blankets, brought out rifles and guns, and began to fire among the crowded and huddled passengers, not minding men, women, children, or babies at the naked breasts of their mothers.

The soldiers had been cornered so perfectly that before they had time even to grasp their rifles and get them up they fell, fatally shot, from their seats and rolled about the floor. In less than fifteen seconds no soldier was left able to fight. Those who still had life enough to moan or to move received another bullet or were knifed or had their skulls crushed.

Some of the train-officials were dead, some so wounded that they staggered about or dragged their bodies along the floor.

For a few seconds all the people in the passenger cars behaved as if paralyzed. They sat stiff, with eyes wide open, looking at the killers and hearing the shots, as if they perceived something which simply could not be true, which must be a nightmare out of which they might awake any moment and find everything all right.

This strange sensation of feeling unable to move or to

cry, coupled with a ghastly silence in the face of such a catastrophic interruption of the most peaceful occupation, lasted only a few seconds.

Then came an outcry which seemed to rise in unison from all human lips present. It was the cry with which man awakes from a horrible nightmare. Men were shouting and cursing, and some were attempting to resist the killers or to escape through the windows. Whoever reached a window and lifted his body to drag himself out was shot in the back or mercilessly clubbed to death. Many tried to protect with their bodies their women and children. Others tried to crawl under the seats or into corners to hide behind baggage.

Women were hysterical, moving about as if they had been blinded. Some ran against the muzzles of the guns and held them against their breasts, begging to be shot. The killers served them all as they wished. Women were on their knees, some praying to the Holy Virgin; others took out the amulets worn around their necks and kissed them; others simply shrieked and tore their hair and mutilated their faces with their fingernails. Those with children held them up against the bandits, begging for mercy in the name of all the saints, and offering, by the eternal grace of Our Lady of Guadalupe, their own lives in exchange for those of their babies.

Not women alone, but also men were crying like little children. Without begging for mercy, they were not even attempting to hide themselves. They seemed to have lost all sense. Many of them made faint efforts to fight, with the hope of ending it sooner. Their nerves had given way.

With their war-cry: "Viva nuestro rey Cristo! Long live our king Jesus!" the bandits had started the slaughter. With the same cry the signal was given to begin plundering.

Those still alive had not waited for that signal. Most of them had piled up before the bandits all they possessed—

their watches, chains, and every cent they had. Fearing the bandits would cut off their fingers and ears to get their booty in the quickest way, the passengers stripped their fingers and ears and necks of whatever jewelry they wore, and handed it over.

Having cleared both the second-class cars, the bandits went to the first-class car. Here only a few men had been stationed to prevent the passengers from escaping or going to the assistance of the passengers in the other cars.

As they entered to repeat here what they had accomplished in the second-class cars the lieutenant returned from the dining-car. He had heard shots and was hurrying to see what was going on. As he stepped into the car, half a dozen bullets felled him.

Triumphantly the murderers shouted their "Viva nuestro rey Cristo!" on seeing the lieutenant dead at their feet.

Then the looting began here also.

For some reason they killed here only those passengers who tried to resist them, and wounded by clubbing or stabbing those who were not quick enough to hand over all they had or who tried to hold out gold pieces hidden away somewhere. It seemed that their thirst for blood had been satisfied with the killing of the poorer people. Since this car was occupied by the well-to-do, the loot was more valuable than that taken in the second-class cars. This fact may have accounted for the greater mercy shown to the victims.

One group went to the Pullman cars. The lieutenant had slammed shut the door behind him when leaving the car, and it had locked. The bandits broke the panes, opened the door from the inside, and entered the sleepers.

Passengers sitting in the dining-car were robbed first. This done, the bandits made the rounds of the other passengers. Some had already turned in; others were still sitting up.

None of them was hurt, but they were robbed of all they had about their persons, and a few suitcases were pried open to examine their contents. In none of those suitcases was anything of value found.

Perhaps the fact that the train was rapidly nearing the next town prompted the bandits to have done with the whole job.

3

Someone pulled the stop-cord, and the engineer, hearing the signal, became suspicious. He had seen the mestizos board the train and, by sheer intuition, he realized that they might have something to do with the shots he had heard faintly. So he gave the engine all the steam she could swallow, and the train took up a maddening race. The sooner she could make the next depot, the better it would be for all concerned. The engineer figured that the stop-cord might have been pulled by the bandits themselves. By instinct he felt that the worst thing he could do was to bring the train to a stop and so give the bandits their chance to get away with the loot. No life could be saved by stopping the train. It was more likely that passengers would try to escape and be shot just the same.

The bandits now returned to the second-class cars, where the passengers, still too frightened and too confused to shout, were panic-stricken on seeing the bandits returning. Their thought was that they had come to kill all those who were left. But so stricken by fear and panic were they that they no longer begged for mercy. They faced their fate with the conviction that it was their destiny and that it was no use to fight. Some prayed in low tones, others only moved their lips; others, who could not even say a prayer, stared at the bandits with glassy eyes.

The bandits did not care any longer about the passengers. They stamped through the cars, stepping on the bodies or kicking them aside.

Entering the express and baggage car, they killed the officials handling the mail and arranging the goods to be put off at the next stop.

From here six men crawled into the tender and reached the engine. The fireman jumped off the train and, while jumping, was shot.

The engineer, seeing the bandits coming, also tried to jump, but was caught and held. He was ordered to stop the train and to unhook the engine and the tender so that they might be used by the bandits to make their escape.

While this was happening, a dozen men were busy throwing all the baggage, the express goods, and the mail-bags out of the train along the track, where accomplices of the bandits were waiting to pick them up.

In the express car a few bandits had discovered half a hundred five-gallon cans filled with gas and kerosene consigned to various general stores in little towns along the road. Seeing these cans, the bandits hit upon a fiendish idea. They opened the cans and soaked the two second-class cars and their passengers with gas and kerosene and set the whole on fire. In an instant the cars were ablaze, as if by explosion.

The fire, thrown backwards by the draft of the train, quickly spread to the other cars, which in a few seconds were wrapped in flames.

Yelling, howling, crying, laughing in madness, acting no longer by reason or by instinct, the passengers tried to escape. In the meantime the men on the engine had forced the engineer to bring the train to a full stop, unhook the engine and the tender from the train, and take the bandits away from the scene.

A wide circle of darkness was lighted up by the flames

and in that ghastly brightness there ran and danced a yelling horde who only fifteen minutes before had been normal human beings peacefully traveling from one place to another. Mothers without children, children without mothers, men without their wives, wives without their husbands, all of them mad, many of them fatally burned, many of them fatally wounded by bullets or knives, none of them any longer normal.

The passengers from the first-class car and from the Pullman cars, who were but little affected, did their utmost to assist those getting out of the burning train, aiding the wounded, consoling the dying, and reasoning with the mad.

4

The engine and the tender loaded with the bandits came suddenly to a halt, as ordered, at a spot where they had decided to get off and where they had early in the afternoon left the horses now needed to get away with their booty. All the baggage thrown out from the train was left in care of the groups posted along the track; these men would join the first party later in their hide-out in the Sierra Madre mountains.

The last bandit to leave the engine shot the engineer, kicked him off the engine, and threw him down the track. There he left him for dead and joined his partners.

All this had taken less than ten minutes, and the next depot was still more than ten miles away; there was no village near by from which any help could come. The brightness of the burning train might be seen far away, but since this fire was dying down, anybody who might have seen it would have thought some shack had caught fire and have paid no further attention.

Passengers who were still sane gathered together and

went about picking up men and women who had jumped out of the windows while the train was still moving and who were now lying along the track.

The engineer, also lying on the track and left for dead, came to after a while. With the little strength still left him he crawled up the track, dragged himself on the engine, and succeeded in getting it under way and to the depot.

The station-master, seeing a lonely engine pulling in and recognizing it as that of the train long overdue, found the engineer unconscious in his cab. In a dying condition he was taken into the depot, where, with his last few words, he told what had happened.

With the help of officials, passengers, and people on the platform who had been waiting for the train, a freight at the depot was hurriedly converted into an emergency train and driven to the site of the wreck.

The train-officials, knowing with whom they would have to deal, ordered the engine of the passenger-train brought in by that brave engineer to go ahead of the emergency train to make sure that the tracks were still in condition and not broken or blocked.

On nearing the wreck, but still more than half a mile off, the engine was fired at by bandits lying in ambush or on their way home with the loot. One fireman got a shot in his leg; the other fireman serving the engine got a scratch on his skull. But in spite of all that, the engine reached the wreck safely.

The emergency train was also under fire, but the officials and a few of the volunteers who carried guns answered the fire, which made the bandits believe that this emergency train carried soldiers. So the bandits dropped their heavily loaded bags and hurried to get away with the little they could carry without interfering with their retreat. The more important booty was on the farther side of the wreck, where the train could not go, for the wreck blocked the way.

All wounded and dead that could be found were taken into the emergency train, as well as those who were unhurt, and the baggage that was lying about, and then the train returned to the depot, where by now the whole town had gathered.

At the depot a dozen official telegrams had arrived. A hospital train would be there in the morning. The chief of the federal military force of the state and of two neighboring states had, by order of the government, mobilized cavalry troops to be sent after the bandits by special trains. The mounted police of all districts in the vicinity of the attack had been ordered to hunt down the bandits and bring them in by whatever means possible, but run them in they must.

The tragedy was not ended, for twenty-four hours later, when the hospital train with all the surviving passengers arrived at the main station of the capital, where thousands had been waiting for many hours, there were no less than twenty men and women who turned insane or committed suicide at the sight of a loved one among the dead. There were three who killed themselves in the belief that their relatives had been murdered. They were so excited that when the expected person was not among the first to leave the train, they were sure that he must be dead, and shot themselves or threw themselves before other incoming trains. For the metropolitan press, with such a piece of news at its command, had turned hysterical and had done its best to excite the whole population, so that practically no individual could be found sane enough to look objectively at this disaster. Every person able to read the papers was made to identify himself with the victims.

Man can more easily endure a train-wreck or a ship-disaster or an earthquake with a loss of many hundreds of

lives than wholesale murder by criminals. Men feel sorry
about a thousand lives lost by a shipwreck; they will do all
in their power to help the victims and to avoid a similar
catastrophe. But the same men will rage like savages for
vengeance if only twenty persons have been willfully murdered by bandits for purely material reasons.

5

The government considered it its foremost duty to hunt
down these murderers who in the face of the whole civilized
world had besmirched the honor and the name of a civilized
nation just then mistrusted and detested everywhere. Roman
Catholics, ignorant or misled as to the facts, were trying to
get other governments to interfere in what they thought to
be suppression of religious liberty.

In certain countries whenever banditry occurs on such
a large scale, it is not always possible to determine who
profits by what bandits do. The bandits may get all the
booty for themselves, but often they may not know for
whom they are fighting. A man high up in politics, a general
hot after the seat of the president, a dismissed secretary of
commerce, may use these bandits, whom he calls rebels, to
destroy the reputation of the government before foreign
nations and before their own. Many attacks by bandits in
these countries can be explained in this way, as it frequently
happens that the bandits after an assault are not prosecuted
in the way the public has a right to expect. In such cases
only a few are caught, and the report is given out that they
have been executed, but sometimes it happens that they are
later found to be soldiers in the army, where they hide out.
The pursuit of the bandits cannot be followed up by the
public in general, for they know only what they read in
the papers, and what is printed may be true or it may

not. After two or three weeks no more is heard about bandits, other affairs having taken the foreground in the public mind.

The bandits in this case made it quite clear that they were fighting for their king, Jesus. Fighting on behalf of the Roman Catholic church, for religious liberty. The fact is that they had only a very vague idea as to who Cristo was. It would have been quite easy to make them believe that Bonaparte, Columbus, Cortés, and Jesus were all identical. The Roman Catholic church during its four hundred years of rule in Latin America, of which three hundred and fifty were an absolute rule, has been more interested in purely material gains for the treasuries and coffers in Rome than in educating its subjects in the true Christian spirit. Governments of modern civilized countries have quite a different opinion from the church on education, and these governments have also different opinions as to who is better suited to rule, the state or the church.

No better proof of what the Roman Catholic church in these countries has done to the people could be found than the fact that the same men who cried: "Viva nuestro rey Cristo!" killed mercilessly and robbed for their own pockets men, women, and children whom they knew were members of the same church, believing at the time that they were doing so to help their church and to please the Holy Virgin and the Pope.

Two Catholic priests had been recognized by passengers as active members of the bandit band. Later these priests were caught, and they admitted that they had been leaders, not only in this train-assault, but also in half a hundred hold-ups on highways and ranches. They considered their own actions similar to those of the Roman Catholic priests, Father Hidalgo and Father Morelos, who fought against the Spaniards for the independence of their country. They had also paid with their lives for the failure of their enterprise, because they were fighting under absolutely different conditions from Washington the Great, and these fighters for their country were condemned not only by the crown of Spain but also by the Holy Inquisition although they fought under the flag of the Holy Virgin of Guadalupe. A few years later when the Roman Catholic church became interested in separating the Latin-American countries from Spain, because Spain had started to throw off the yoke of the Roman church, the independence of the Latin-American countries was won by the help of the same church that had only ten years before helped execute patriots who did what the church now wanted done, and the beheaded bodies of these rebel priests were buried in the main cathedral.

Besides these two recognized priests, the government did not know who was leading the hordes of bandits fighting for King Cristo. To find the real boss who pulled the strings, or to show American tourists that the country was safe and that such an incident would be punished severely and swiftly, the government changed certain military chiefs in whom it had lost confidence and then went with all its might on the trail of the malefactors.

6

In pursuing bandits along the Sierra Madre it does not help you to take finger-prints from the walls of railroad cars or to file all finger-prints at headquarters. The thing is to get the bandits. When you have them, shoot them. This done, you may check up on the finger-prints. There is no other way.

In certain Latin-American countries, including Mexico, bandits, gangsters, hold-up men, highway-robbers, never see a court from the inside, never have a lawyer to speak to, never are allowed bail, never hear of a parole-board. This is the reason why there are no bandits and no gangsters who rule by their own laws. They may get away with one hold-up, perhaps with two; when very lucky, with three. Then they are no longer.

The bandits, corrupted Indians in part, mestizos mostly, are with rare exceptions small farmers, more peasants than farmers. They know every trail for miles around their homes, every mountain path, every hole in the ground where a man may hide, every crack in the rocks where a man might squeeze himself through. In such a crack a fugitive may sit for three days without food for fear of betraying his hiding-place.

Eighty out of every hundred federal soldiers are pure Indians, selected from those tribes for whom war has been the main occupation since this continent rose above the oceans. Against them no hide-out is of any use. The rest of the soldiers are mestizos who know all the tricks and can make use of them more cunningly than the bandits, for they have the advantage which every hunter has against the hunted. The officers in charge of the hunt know by long experience and by special education how to make use of their men to the best advantage.

Soldiers—all cavalry men in this case, and led by a first lieutenant or a captain—about eighteen in all, ride into a village. The officer has traced the tracks of certain horses to this village or to the vicinity. For many reasons he thinks it likely that a few of the bandits may live in this village, or have relatives here or friends.

The train had been attacked by about two hundred men, only twenty or twenty-five of them doing the actual killing and robbing, all the others being stationed along the road to take part in the fight only should it happen that the train came to a stop before the convoy was subdued. Otherwise they were to carry away the booty thrown out of the train by the robbers.

The assault over, the band breaks up in little groups. Most of them return to their villages, where they own a piece of land, have their families, and live the life of peaceful farmers. Many of them do not even tell their wives or mothers where they have been and what they have done while they were away, apparently gone to market. On coming back they hide their guns, or not, since the peasants after the revolution were allowed to have guns to fight the big hacendados, the former feudal lords, who by the revolution lost the greater part of their huge domains, which were parceled out to the peasants; so the possession of fire-arms alone is no proof that their owner is a bandit.

The officer works mainly on hunches, and he uses certain tricks which he knows that these bandits, ignorant and superstitious men with little intelligence, will inevitably fall for. Their minds are not quick enough to answer questions for any length of time without being so bewildered that they confess.

Now, the soldiers are riding into Chalchilmitesa, a village far off the roads, inhabited by Indian farmers.

In the shade before a palm hut two mestizos are squatting, smoking cigarettes they have made by rolling tobacco into corn leaves. They watch the soldiers with little interest and without making any move or trying to hide.

The soldiers pass. But thirty yards beyond the hut the officer orders them to halt. One of the mestizos rises and tries to go behind the hut. His pal, however, with a gesture of his head, tells him to stay where he is. He squats down again.

A sergeant has taken notice of the behavior of the two men and says a few words to his captain, who rides to a hut

opposite the one where the two mestizos are. He asks for a
drink of water and dismounts. Taking the earthen vessel in
which the water is offered, he drinks, and asks if they have
had much rain lately.

He meditates for a while, apparently about nothing in
particular, and walks across to where the two mestizos are.

"You are living in this pueblo?"

"No, patrón, we are not living here."

"Where are you from?"

"We have our house and our piece of land, our milpa, in
Mezquital, mi jefe."

"On a visit here? Visiting your compadre, I figure."

"Yes, coronel."

The captain calls one of his men to bring his horse. The
officer tries to mount his horse. He seems tired from the long
march over the hot country. the horse is dancing about,
and the officer has trouble getting his foot into the stir-
rup. The horse is nearly kicking the mestizos, so one of
them rises and comes close to help the officer get into the
saddle.

The captain has somehow touched the man. He sets his
foot firmly on the ground again as if waiting for the horse
to get quiet.

"What have you got in your pocket?" the officer asks the
man unexpectedly.

The mestizo looks down along his pants and fixes his eyes
on his pocket, which seems rather bulky. He turns around
as though he wants to go back to the hut. But he notes all
the soldiers coming along without having received an order
to do so. At least so it seems to him. He now tries to calm
himself by rolling another cigarette and asks his pal if he
also would like another.

The captain is still standing, seemingly absolutely unin-
terested in anything. Just as the mestizo lights his cigarette,

the captain grasps him by the shirt-collar with his left hand and at the same time thrusts his right hand in the man's pocket.

The other mestizo has risen. He shrugs his shoulders as if to say that he does not care about what is going on here. But when he wants to go behind the hut, he finds three soldiers standing in his way. He grins and tries no other move.

Now the captain looks at what he has taken from the pocket of the mestizo. It is a rather expensive leather purse.

The captain laughs, and both the mestizos laugh as if the whole thing were just a joke.

He empties the purse into his hand. A few gold pieces, silver, a few coins, and small change. Twenty-five pesos.

"That's your money?" asks the captain.

"What do you think, chief, of course, claro, it's my money."

"So much money and such a ragged and torn shirt?"

"I was just about to go to town tomorrow, coronel, and buy me another shirt."

"You suffer often from nose-bleeding?" the captain asks.

The man looks down at his shirt. "You said it, mi jefe, I certainly do."

"I thought so." The officer looks at the other things found in the purse. A railroad ticket to Torreón. First class. This mestizo never rides first class. Something more still. The ticket has the date of the day when the train was robbed.

The other mestizo is searched quickly. He has little money loose in his pocket, but he has a diamond ring and two pearl ear-rings tucked away in the watch-pocket of his pants.

"Where are your horses?"

"In the corral back of the jacal," the mestizo answers.

The captain sends one of his men to examine the hoofs. The man returns. "The hoofs fit all right, my captain."

The horses are poor beasts. The saddles are old, worn-out, and ragged.

"Where are the rifles and the guns?"

One of the mestizos answers: "In the corral where the horses were."

The captain goes to the corral. He scratches the ground with his feet and picks up a rusty revolver, an old-fashioned pistol, and a battered shotgun.

He returns to the mestizos, who are fully surrounded by the soldiers. Seeing the guns brought by two soldiers, they shrug their shoulders and smile. They know that they are lost. But what does it matter? San Antonio, their patron in heaven, did not want to protect them, so what is the use battling against destiny?

"No more guns?"

"No, jefe." Unconcerned about their fate, they smoke their cigarettes and watch the preparations of the soldiers as if they were looking at a show.

Only a dozen villagers have assembled around the soldiers. And of course quite a number of boys. A few of them are helping the soldiers to guard their horses. The great majority of the villagers remain in their huts. From there they watch everything that goes on outside. They know by long tradition that it is not wise to be seen when soldiers or mounted police are around. None has an absolutely clear conscience, or at least none feels that he has. There are hundreds of orders given by the government or by other authorities of which they may have broken many without knowing it, so it is best not to be seen by soldiers. Once seen, one might easily be accused of something, whatever it may be.

"What are your names?" the captain asks the mestizos.

They give their names, or what they think are their names.

The captain writes the names down in his notebook.

"Where is the cemetery?" he then asks a village boy standing by.

The soldiers march the two captured men off to the cemetery, guided by the boy and followed by about twenty grown-up people and almost all the boys of the little community. While marching, the captain orders a couple of boys to get two shovels from the man who usually digs the graves.

Having arrived at the cemetery, the two prisoners are handed the shovels and led to a site where there are no other graves. They need no further orders. Leisurely they begin to dig, and both, after digging deep, lie down in the graves to see if they would rest comfortably for the next hundred years. They try them three or four times until they are satisfied and then drop their shovels, indicating that they have finished.

Then there is an intermission. The two men must have a rest after so much digging under the blazing sun. They squat and start once more to roll their cigarettes. The captain, seeing this, takes out his own cigarettes and offers the prisoners the package. They look at the package and say: "Thanks, coronel, but we are no sissy smokers, we'd better smoke our own brand."

"As you wish," says the captain, and lights a cigarette for himself.

The prisoners begin to talk with a few of the soldiers and find that they have acquaintances in common, or that they know the villages where some of the soldiers were born.

Having smoked three cigarettes, the prisoners look at the captain, who responds by asking: "Listo, muchachos? Ready, boys, for the trip?"

Both answer with smiling lips: "Sí, coronel, yes, we are ready."

Without being ordered, they stand up in front of the holes, each taking good care that he is in front of the hole he has dug and tried out.

The sergeant names the two squads and has them marched up before the prisoners. The prisoners, seeing everything ready, murmur a dozen words to their saints or to the Virgin, cross themselves several times, and look at the captain.

"Listo, mi coronel, ready," they say.

Thirty seconds later they are already covered with the earth which they dug out a quarter of an hour before.

The captain and the soldiers cross themselves, salute, cross themselves once more, and then leave the cemetery, mount their horses, and march off to look for other bandits.

This murder trial, including the execution, costs the people who pay taxes three pesos and fifty centavos, the cost for cartridges. The final results are more effective than in countries where an average murder trial will cost around two hundred thousand dollars.

7

The apprehension of the bandits is not always so easy.

There was another detachment of cavalry hot on the trail of a group of bandits. On reaching the top of a hill the officer noted ten men on horseback riding three miles ahead. When these men became aware of the soldiers, they fell into a gallop and soon disappeared among the hills. The officer with his men followed the tracks. Since the country after a while turned very sandy and tracks of other horses crossed the trail, the pursuit had to be given up.

In the afternoon the soldiers approached a big hacienda where the officer had decided to spend the night with his men. The soldiers rode into the wide inner patio of the hacienda, and the officer, after greeting the hacendado, asked him if he had seen ten men on horseback coming that way. The hacendado denied having seen a single soul the whole day long and added that he should know whether or not men had passed the hacienda during the day, since he had been at home all the time.

For some reason the officer changed his mind about staying here overnight, but he told the hacendado that he had to search the hacienda, to which the hacendado answered that the officer might do as he pleased.

No sooner did the soldiers come near the main building than they received a good greeting of bullets from all directions. One fell dead and three were wounded when the soldiers in retreat reached the main gate of the hacienda.

Haciendas are often built almost like fortresses, with all the buildings inside of a very wide patio, which is surrounded by stone walls crowned at intervals by little towers.

As soon as the last soldier left, the huge gate was closed from the inside. And now a real battle began. The officer of course might go back to headquarters and ask for more men and machine-guns. But he is a true soldier and does not run away from bandits. Nor would his men like him to do so. He would lose their respect. He has to accept battle and fight until the last cartridge is gone.

Since revolutionary times both parties know that the battle will end only with the destruction of one of them, and that no quarter will be asked or given. The besieged bandits know they have nothing to lose. They are shot anyway if caught alive. The same will happen to the soldiers if they don't win the fight. If you wish to survive, you have to win the battle.

The officer ordered all the horses led behind a hill so that they would not be shot. The bandits do not waste bullets

on the horses, for they know they must save their ammunition, the more so since their arms are not all alike, so that
the same cartridges cannot be used by everyone. Besides
they also hope to win the battle, and it would be bad econ-
omy to shoot the horses which they would own if they win.

The soldiers found they were not in a good position.
The hacienda was located on a plain, and every soldier
approaching could be seen as if marching on an ice-covered
lake.

First, just to get the thing under way, the officer ordered
a general attack on all four sides of the hacienda. The
soldiers, well trained in modern warfare, scattered and
crawled along the ground, making only short forward jumps,
without waiting for the officer to whistle.

The officer took advantage of the fact that the hacienda
had two gates, one in front, one at the back. He let his men
go on, keeping up a slow fire to keep the besieged busy.
A few soldiers reached the walls, but they were too high
and could not be climbed without sacrificing every man
who tried to get over.

After two hours' fighting in this ineffectual way, the
officer sent word round to all his men to be ready for the
final attack. He gathered the greater number in front of
the main gate and by a few tricks made the bandits believe
that the attack would take place immediately, with an effort
to break in the main gate. While the bandits concentrated
all their attention on this gate, a small group of soldiers took
the back gate, which was defended by only three men. Far
less strong than the main gate, this one was easily opened by
a man who, catlike, squeezed himself through a crack in the
wall near it. The moment the bandits found the back gate
in the hands of the soldiers, they were so confused that they
all forgot about the main gate and put their whole force
against the invaders at the back. Having foreseen that this

would happen to a body undisciplined and without definite leadership, the officer now stormed the main gate with all his might. Before the bandits could think of organizing again to defend the main gate, it had been opened and the soldiers swarmed into the patio.

Here, of course, the fight became fiercest—man against man. Guns could no longer be used, and knives, stones, fists, had to take their places. The battle was finally carried inside the house, into the living-rooms and bedrooms.

Three hours after the soldiers arrived at the hacienda, the fight was over, won by the soldiers. Four of them were dead, three badly wounded, and ten had received slighter wounds. The officer had been shot twice, but he was still up and in full command.

The ten bandits had been joined by three other men who were hiding in the hacienda when the bandits arrived. The hacendado was found dead, so he could not be questioned to ascertain whether he himself was an accomplice of the bandits or whether he had been forced by them to take their side. Seven bandits were dead, two were wounded, and so was one of the three who had joined the bandits in their fight. The wounded and the sound alike were executed against the back wall half an hour later. Who would be so stupid as to take a bandit to a hospital to be cured and made fit once more to follow his trade? Not the officer and the soldiers sent after bandits to rid the country of public enemies, the pets of sob-sisters and prison-reformers. Rattlesnakes are killed whenever found near the dwellings of human beings. If man wants to follow his peaceful occupations, he cannot have a live rattlesnake in the neighborhood.

The peons of the hacienda went into hiding when the battle began. They now came out of their holes and helped the soldiers to get in the horses. The family of the hacendado were away on a visit in the capital.

In the pockets of the dead and the executed were found purses, jewelry, train-tickets, dollar bills, ladies' handbags, and other things that come into the possession of active bandits. So there was no doubt that the officer again had got the right men. And again he got them in the right way—that is to say, he killed the rats first and afterwards looked them over to find out if they carried the pest. Luckily there were no reporters or photographers around to fill the papers with stories of heroic bandits fighting and dying bravely.

In this way all the bandits were caught sooner or later and executed on the spot. The country has its sporadic spells of banditry, but banditry never has become an institution, not even when, as may occasionally happen, a general or a politician uses hordes of bandits to further his own ends.

8

"That is all I know about this train assault and about the rounding up of the bandits," Lacaud concluded his report. "Part of it I had from don Genaro, who read it to me from the papers, and part of it I heard on my way down to the village and from villagers who had been to market in town."

For a minute Lacaud was silent. Then he asked: "Now that you know these men, do you still think me a spy or an accomplice of those murderers now on their way up here? Just answer me."

"We have never said you are, and not for a minute do we think you have any connection with these women-killers," Howard said. "Well, partners, I guess the question of confidence in our new partner is now settled."

"All right with me." Dobbs stretched out his hand to Lacaud. "Shake, partner," he said.

"Welcome here." Curtin offered Lacaud his hand.

Howard suddenly took a deep breath. "Why, the hell,

then these men must be the last of the criminals the government is so hot to corner."

"I'm sure of that," Lacaud admitted. "In the papers there was something about a gang still not caught, and the leader of this group, the worst of the whole lot, was described as wearing a gold-painted palm hat."

Curtin made a face. "If that is as you say, Lak, then it sure will be no laughing matter for us." He climbed upon the rock and looked down the valley. After some time he said: "I can't see these devils any longer. They must have gone another way."

"Now, don't you be so sure, kid," Howard corrected him. "They are by now at the loop. You can't see it from here. But as you can't see them anywhere else, I'll lay you any bet that they are right on the road up here. Let's all go over to that side of the rock. There we may see them again when they have passed the loop and turned into that path crossing the naked rock. They ought to be on that path inside of a few minutes. If we don't see them, they may have given up coming here. Otherwise—well, we'll have to face the enemy."

13

They were all sitting at their second look-out watching for the bandits to come out of the loop, to make sure that they were on their way up.

"How many did you say you counted, Curty?" asked Howard.

"Fifteen or sixteen."

Howard addressed Lacaud: "According to what you told us, there could not be that many left in this part of the mountains."

"Certainly not. But they may have been joined by another stray group not yet captured."

"It looks like it," Howard said. "Well, there are hard times coming for us. The peasants down in the village, to get rid of them as quick as possible, have told them that up here there is a hunter who has guns and plenty ammunition. That's what they want, because they may need them badly. We'd better start thinking of our defense."

Howard directed the plans, while Curtin, having the best eyes, was to stay at the look-out to make sure that the bandits really were coming.

The burros were brought in from the pasture and taken into a thicket in a ravine near by, where they were tied to prevent them from running away.

Right at the base of the naked rock that formed a sort of wall for the camp, there was, almost the whole length of this rock, a narrow and not very deep ravine, which appeared to have been washed out by the rain. This ravine was like a natural trench. Howard was quick to choose this as the main bulwark in his tactics. This trench could hardly be attacked from the back, because the rock was rather high, and its form was not straight, but rounded. Anybody on the top could not shoot anybody in the trench. Only with the help of long ropes would it have been possible for a man to come down from the top to the trench, and in a fight he would never set foot in the trench alive.

The trench could not be flanked either, as rocks also prevented this. On one side the rocks had to be climbed almost from the valley up, and it had to be done just at this slope, which could be scaled only by experienced alpinists with perfect equipment. The other side was partly walled in by rocks, and the only opening could easily be covered by the gun of one man in the trench, whose duty would be to watch this opening.

The bandits had no choice but to pass the whole camp if they wished to attack the trench. The camp offered no ambush, and the defenders in the trench had only to take aim to finish any bandit who came in sight.

The buckets were filled with water and brought into the trench. The tent and all the belongings of the partners, including provisions, were also taken into this fortress.

"We have to keep them away from the mine," said Howard.

"From the mine?" Lacaud asked. "I haven't seen a mine yet."

"Now you know it, you jackass," Dobbs sneered. "The cat is out of the bag. Did you think we were up here to tell one another bedtime stories, you mug?"

"We can keep them away best by holding them here," Howard explained. "We'll make them believe that this is the only camp we have. Besides, they won't come across the mine anyway, even should they try to corner us from that side. The mine is not in their way, whatever they do to try to lure us out of our hole."

"They couldn't do anything with the mine anyhow, even if they found it." Dobbs was gathering the ammunition out of the bags.

"No," said Howard, "you are right, they could do nothing with it; I mean they could steal nothing. But—and this would be just too bad—they could destroy everything there. Still, come to think of it, it wouldn't matter so much; that would save us the labor of breaking it down ourselves when we leave."

"What about a retreat?" Lacaud suggested. "It might be better strategy not to fight at all—just to hide out and let them leave with long faces."

"I've thought of that also," Howard answered. "In the first place, there's no other road out of here but the one on which we'd have to meet them. If it comes to a fight, we are better off here than on the road or anywhere else. Of course, we can hide somewhere near; we might even try to go across the rocks, but we might break our necks in doing that. What is worse, we could take nothing along with us. We'd lose the burros and our whole outfit. The outfit we could bury or hide somehow. But do you think they would leave us alone? They would be after us whatever trail we took. In finding trails in the Sierra we can't beat these men. At that they are experts and we bad amateurs. Better not think of that any more."

"You're right, old man, as usual." Dobbs patted him on the back.

At this moment Curtin called from his look-out: "They are at the loop now and turning into the trail up here." He jumped down and came to the others, who were completing the last things to be done.

"You know the trail best, Curty," Howard said. "How long do you think it will take them to get here?"

"With their tired horses it will take them two hours at least. Of course, they may be lazy and take a rest, or have difficulty making out the trail and the shortest route. So it may be as much as four hours."

"All right." Howard jumped into the trench. "Let's say for sure two hours. Two hours in our favor. Let's make the best of it. Have our eats now, so we waste no time when the dance starts."

2

They sat down, built a fire, and cooked their meal. All this was done inside the trench.

Curtin did the cooking while the others were busy building stations and getting all the guns and ammunition at hand.

"If nobody objects, I'll take command. Right by you, partners?" Howard asked.

"No objection," was the answer.

"I'll take the left center. You, Lacaud, take the right center. Dobbs, you take your station at the left corner, and, Curtin, you take the right corner. This corner you are to hold, Curty, is important, for here is where, through that crack in the rocks, a guy may sneak in. So you watch that side well, and Lacaud may also have a look at that flank."

When the meal was ready, they sat down and had their final war-council while eating.

3

The partners were still strengthening their stations with piled-up earth, so that they could hide their heads while shooting, when the first bandits appeared on the glade.

Howard hissed to get the boys' attention. A hiss was a very good signal, invented by the old man, as it was not different from the natural sounds of the vicinity and so was noticed only by those who were meant to hear it.

Three men were standing in the narrow opening of the bush. One of them was the man with the huge gilded palm hat. They stood for a while rather bewildered, seeing the place bare and no sign of a human being near. They called back to the other men coming into the clearing. It seemed they had left their horses on a little plateau, located some hundred and fifty feet below on the road, where there was a bit of thin pasturage. Since this last part of the trail was the hardest to make with animals, they had left the horses farther down and so reached the camp earlier than the boys had figured they would.

Two minutes later all men save two who guarded the horses were on the camp-site. What they said the boys in the trench could not hear; the distance was too great.

All the men carried guns on their hips—guns of different types and calibers. Four men carried shotguns, and two had rifles. All were in rags and had not washed or shaved for weeks; for months they had had no haircuts. Most of them wore the usual sandals; a few had boots, but ripped open and with torn soles; some had on leather pants like those worn by cowboys or cattle-farmers. All carried cheap woolen blankets over their shoulders.

Two men ventured farther into the camp-site. They noted that a tent had been pitched and a fire built not long before. Then they looked around and, on seeing no other sign, returned to the other men, now squatting on the ground near the opening.

From the spot where they were sitting, it was hard to tell that there was a ravine at the opposite part of the camp.

They were smoking and talking. The boys in the trench could see from the gestures of the men that they did not know what to make of all this or what to do. A few were heard quarreling because they had made so hard a trip without the slightest gain.

Some rose and began again to walk about the place to see if there was any trace of the hunter supposed to be there. When they returned to the main group it seemed as if they had decided to leave the camp, go down the valley, and look there for further adventures.

There was a long discussion about several points. A few men went to the middle of the camp and sat down there. Now they had to talk louder so that all the men spread over a wider space could understand what was said and give their opinions. The leader seemed to have little authority, nor was there any sort of discipline among them. Each had his own opinion, and each thought his own advice should be followed by the others.

One proposed that they use this site for headquarters from which to raid the villages in the valley.

"That would be the god-damned worst thing they could do," said Dobbs to Howard in a hushed voice.

"You bet it would, but be quiet, so that we can listen in better."

"I wonder," said Curtin to Lacaud, "if it wouldn't be best to bump them all off right now; none could escape alive. Give the word to the old man and ask him what he thinks."

The word came back from Howard that he meant to wait; they might change their plans yet and go.

"Just look at these guys nearest here." Curtin spoke again to Lacaud. "A fine bunch they are; they have hanging around their necks medals and pictures of the saints and the Virgin to protect them from the devil. That's something, oh boy!"

"I told you that the papers said that the passengers had observed that all these murderers were pious Catholics."

"Here the church has sure done a great thing," Curtin said. "Our Methodists can't beat that. But, man, look, what are they about now?"

Two men began to build a fire right where the partners used to have theirs, where there were still a few half-burned sticks lying about.

"There's no doubt that they mean to stay here at least for one night," Howard said to Dobbs.

"Well, it won't be long now before we'll have a real movie here."

"They've got plenty of ammunition." Lacaud pointed to some of the men who had three cartridge-belts slung about their chests, most of them well filled.

4

Having built the fire, one of the men went exploring, for fuel or for water or for a rabbit-hole or for wild green pepper. He went straight across the camp and right up to the trench.

He did not look at the base of the rock, but glanced up the rock, thinking perhaps he might find a trace of the gringo. Perhaps there might be a cave in which he lived.

Not seeing anything, he was about to return to the fire when he looked down to the bottom of the rock, where he saw just the head of Curtin—nothing else. He seemed not quite sure whether he had seen right, so he stepped one pace closer.

"Ay, caramba, chingue tu madre," he said in a surprised voice. Then he turned round to his gang and shouted: "Ven acá, come here, all you muchachos. Here you will see a great sight. Hurry. Our little birdie is sitting on his eggs, waiting to hatch. Who ever would have thought them god-damned gringos and cabrones would use a skunk-hole for their headquarters?"

All the men rose and came hurrying toward him.

When they were half-way across the camp, Curtin shouted: "Stop or I shoot!"

The bandits immediately stopped and the man who had discovered Curtin and was only five feet away from the trench raised his arm and said: "All right, all right, bueno, muy bueno, don't get sore at me, ya me voy, I am on my way." Saying this, he retreated, walking backwards. He made no attempt to reach for his gun.

The bandits had been so taken by surprise that for a while they could not speak. They returned slowly to the opening where the trail ran into the thicket.

Here they began to talk rather rapidly. None of the boys in the trench could understand a word of what they were saying.

A few moments later the leader, the one with the golden hat, stepped forward right in the middle of the camp. He put his thumbs close together in front of his belt, wishing by doing so to indicate that he did not mean to shoot as long as the other did not draw.

"Oiga, señor, listen. We are no bandits. You are mistaken. We are the policía montada, the mounted police, you know. We are looking for the bandits, to catch them. They have robbed the train, you know."

"All right," Curtin shouted back. "If you are the police, where are your badges? Let's see them."

"Badges, to god-damned hell with badges! We have no badges. In fact, we don't need badges. I don't have to show you any stinking badges, you god-damned cabrón and ching' tu madre! Come out there from that shit-hole of yours. I have to speak to you."

"I have nothing to say to you. If you want to speak to me, you can do so just as well from where you are. You'd better not come any closer if you want to keep your health."

"We shall arrest you by order of the governor. You are hunting here without a hunter's license, nor have you any for carrying guns. We have orders to confiscate your guns and your ammunition."

"Where is your badge?" Curtin asked. "Let's see it and I might be willing to talk things over with you."

"Be reasonable, tenga razón. We are not going to arrest you. Just hand over your gun with the cartuchos, the ammunition, you know. Your shotgun you may keep for yourself. That's the sort of guys we are."

He came two steps nearer the trench. Four or five of the others started to follow their leader.

"Another step," Curtin yelled, "and I shoot, so help me!"

"No sea malo, hombre. Why, we don't want to do you any harm. No harm at all! Why can't you be just a little more polite? Or at least more sociable. We mean well. Give us your gun and we'll leave you in peace. Sure we will." He made no attempt to come nearer.

"I need my gun myself and I won't part with it."

"Throw that old iron over here and we'll pick it up and go on our way."

"Nothing doing. You better go without my gun and go quick. I might easily lose my good temper, listening to your babble." Curtin waved his gun over the rim of the trench.

The man retreated a few steps and again held council with his followers. They had to admit that Curtin held the strongest position. It would have cost the life of at least three of them had they tried to overpower him by direct attack. None of them wanted to be the victim. The price for that gun was too high.

The bandits squatted around the fire and cooked their

meager meal, consisting of tortillas, black beans, green pepper, dried meat, and tea brewed from lemon leaves.

They were fully convinced that the gringo and his gun would be in their hands soon enough; it was only a matter of a few hours. He could not escape. He would have to sleep some time.

While eating they did not talk very much. Later, however, after they had had their siesta, they were looking for some entertainment. So they began to think about the gringo —to get him alive by any means and then make him the object of their enjoyment. They would begin by putting little pieces of embers in his mouth and watching him make funny faces. After this there were more refined ways by which to obtain pleasure during the next twenty-four hours. The victim usually does not like them. He may die too soon. So every kind of precaution has to be taken to make the entertainment last as long as possible.

These men are never at a loss about what to do and how to do it. They are well trained in their churches from childhood on. Their churches are filled with paintings and statues representing every possible torture white men, Christians, inquisitors, and bishops could think of. These are the proper paintings and statues for churches in a country in which the most powerful church on earth wanted to demonstrate how deep in subjection all human beings can be kept for centuries if there exists no other aim but the enlargement of the splendor and the riches of the rulers. What meaning has the human soul to that branch of this great church? No follower of this same church in civilized countries ever seems to question the true origin of its grandeur or the way in which the riches of the church were obtained. So it is not the bandits who were to blame. They were doing and thinking only what they had been taught. Instead of being shown the beauty of this religion, they had been shown only the cruelest and the bloodiest and the most repulsive parts of it. These abhorrent parts of the religion were presented as the most important, so as to make it feared and respected not through faith or love, but through sheer terror and the most abominable superstitions. This is why these men were wearing upon their breasts a picture of the Virgin or Saint Joseph, and why they go to church and pray an hour before the statue of San Antonio whenever they are on their way to commit a wholesale murder or a train-assault or a highway hold-up, praying to the statues before and after the deed and begging the saint to protect them in their crime against the shots the victim may fire at them, and to protect them afterwards against the authorities.

5

There was now no urgent occupation for the bandits. They planned to catch the gringo and begin the fun.

Curtin and the other partners had understood what the bandits had been discussing and knew that a fresh attack was to be made. No doubt of that.

One man stood up. He pushed his gun under his ragged short leather coat so that the gringo in the trench should not see that it was ready to be fired, but Curtin, knowing gangster tricks, had seen this move.

The man came closer. All the others rose also and walked slowly to the middle of the camp.

"Listen, you." The leader with the gilded hat addressed Curtin. "Listen, we'd better come now to a quick understanding. We want to go, because our provisions have given out and we want to be at the market early tomorrow morning. Let me have your gun and the ammunition. I don't wish to have it for nothing. I want to buy it. Here I have a genuine gold watch with genuine gold chain, made in your own country. That watch with the chain is worth at least two hundred pesos. I'll exchange this watch for your gun. Good business it is for you. You'd better take it." He produced the watch and swung it on its chain around his head.

Curtin answered: "You keep your watch and I'll keep my gun. Whether you go to market or not doesn't matter to me. But you won't get my gun; of that I'm sure."

"Oh, are you? Won't we get it? You mongrel, you dirty cabrón. I'll show you." This was spoken by the man nearest the trench. He pointed his gun, still hidden under his coat, at Curtin.

A shot was heard and the man threw up his hand in which he held the gun and shouted: "Holy Mary, Mother of the Lord, estoy herido, I am hit."

The bandits looked in the direction from which the shot had come. It was not Curtin who had fired. It had come from the opposite corner of the trench, where a faint cloud of blue smoke was still to be seen.

The bandits were so surprised that they found no words to express their amazement. Going backwards, they returned to the bushes. Here they squatted and went on talking. They seemed very much confused. The information obtained in the village must have been incorrect. They had expected to meet here only one occupant of the camp. Now they became suspicious that the police might be here, or soldiers. But on the other hand soldiers would not have a gringo with them. And again, the gringo might have been kept here by the soldiers just to fool the bandits into attacking.

One of the guards by the horses had heard the shot and came up to the camp to ask what had happened. After being informed, he left for his post again. He was told to keep the horses ready for any emergency.

When the discussion had been on for half an hour, the

bandits suddenly laughed and rose.

They went once more to the center of the camp. "Hey, señor, you there, you cannot play such tricks on us. We are too smart for that. We know that you had your rifle over in this corner and that by the help of a long string you pulled the trigger from where you are. We know these tricks. We do the same when hunting ducks on the lakes. Don't try this on us."

With a rapid move all the men had their guns up aiming at Curtin. "Now, come out of your dirty hole. No stalling any longer. Come, come, vamonos, or by the Most Holy Virgin we'll drag you out like a rabbit."

"Nothing doing. No vengo, cabrones. Another pace and you are done for. Keep your distance and go farther back. I don't like you so close. Andele, and pronto!"

"All right. As you wish. Now we have to use force. We shall tear open your mouth to your ears just for the goddamned cabrones you called us. Stinking gringo bred by funking dogs, that's what you are."

All the men dropped on the ground and, guns in hand, started crawling toward the trench, taking care not to expose their bodies to the gringo, who seemed to be a very good shot.

Hardly had they advanced six feet when four shots rang out, each one coming from a different gun. Two of the bandits shouted that they had been wounded. All of the men turned round and, without getting up on their feet, crawled back to the bushes.

They no longer doubted that the trench was occupied by soldiers; perhaps by only a few, but soldiers they must be. Probably a bigger troop was already on the way to attack them from the rear.

One man was sent down to the guards by the horses to ask if they had seen soldiers marching in the valley. The guards said there were none or they would surely have seen them.

When this message reached the men, they felt better. After a long discussion they decided to take the trench at once. If the men in the trench were soldiers, they would get rid of them and so have only one front to fight against. It was more important, and actually the decisive factor, indeed, that in winning the trench they would come into possession of more guns, ammunition, provisions, and clothing than they had ever thought was in store here. For these riches they were willing to sacrifice one of their own men, because such a sacrifice would pay well. All agreed upon this decision.

6

The partners in the trench felt that they had won a breathing-space. Since the bandits had not been scared away but were discussing a new plan, the defenders knew they would be attacked again.

"If we only could guess what they are going to do next," Curtin said.

"It would help us little to know," Howard said. "We can only act according to their plans, for they show us their plans by every move they make. All we have to do is to keep awake. I think they are coming very early in the morning, hoping to find us asleep. Seldom do these mestizos and Indians fight at night if they can help it."

"I suggest that we get up and attack and not wait for them," advised Dobbs.

Lacaud said: "I don't think that would be clever. As it is, they don't know how many of us there are. They may think there are ten of us. That is greatly to our advantage. If we all step out, they will know our number. I suppose we are pretty safe here in this trench. They have no idea how many of us there are, how many guns we have, or whether we might go round and attack in their rear."

"The question is," said Curtin, "how long we can resist before we have to surrender."

"If we live very economically, we can stay here for two weeks. The only thing that might prevent that is the lack of water. Of course, in the morning there is always dew; a bit is running down the rock right into our kettles. We may also have rain very soon." Howard seemed to have thought everything over carefully.

The burros were braying in their little corral. The bandits heard them, but took no particular notice. They had no need for burros, and besides they seemed rather far away; perhaps they were burros belonging to the villagers. To get to the animals the bandits would first have to be in full possession of the trench. It would have made a deeper impression upon them if the neighing had come from horses. This would have been evidence that soldiers were in the trench, and the bandits might have been induced to leave rather than take up battle.

"Had we prayed to the Lord for a little bit of help," Howard said, "certain things couldn't have been better. We have full moon. Moonlight practically the whole night. By this excellent light we can see the whole camp before us, whereas these rascals can see nothing of us. Against the dark rock behind us they can't even see our heads rising above the rim."

"Right, old man," Curtin admitted. "We are really not so bad off as it seemed a few hours ago."

"For the night, we shouldn't keep the stations we kept during the day," Howard explained. "We stay in two groups. Dobbs and I take the left section, and you, Curty and Laky, you take the right section. As long as there is no move in sight one may have a nap and the other watch. As soon as things start, you just kick the sleeping guy in the ribs and he will be up. Better still, two of us lie down right now. I'm positive there will be no move on the other side for the next six hours. It will be different around three in the morning. All right, Dobbs and Lacaud, dismissed. You two take your sweet slumber now."

7

It was half past four in the morning when Dobbs kicked Howard and Lacaud kicked Curtin in the buttocks.

"I think they are coming," Dobbs said to Howard in a hushed voice. "I've seen them moving."

Both Howard and Curtin were up like partridges surprised by a fox.

The camp-site was flooded with moonlight, so that even a cat could not have crossed it without being seen.

Howard walked quickly to the right section to make sure that Curtin and Lacaud were awake and at their posts. He gave orders to fire the very moment four men should reach the middle of the camp and to take careful aim and, if possible, to kill. "There is no longer any other way out. It's us or them," he said. "They know no mercy."

The bandits seemed to be sure that the besieged were asleep, so they were not too careful when making their attack. On reaching the center four shots whipped simultaneously across the camp, and two men cursed and shouted for their saints, because they had caught bullets. Somehow they seemed not to mind. They could not only send out bullets but also take them like real bandits. Gangsters they were not.

Most likely they still thought that Curtin had played a trick on them in some way or other. They felt sure that only one shot could be expected when storming the trench. All lay down on the ground and crawled farther on toward Curtin. The last third of their way they meant to run and so make it impossible for Curtin to shoot more than once or twice. A few appeared not to be patient enough to go slow, for the one who had the gringo by the collar first would have his choice of the guns of the victim. They jumped up and began to run out of line. Hardly had they risen when again four shots were fired, and three men seemed to have been hit. None was dead, however, so far as the partners could see. They still seemed to be in possession of all their faculties. Anyway, the lesson they had received made them more careful. That four shots had been fired twice and that all had been well aimed upset their plans. None knew what to think of the situation. There might be two dozen soldiers in this trench. Yet when they arrived once more at the bushes and discussed new plans, they came to the conclusion that if there really were two dozen men hidden in the trench, they would have attacked from ambush just before the bandits entered the camp, where they would have had no chance to defend themselves.

8

Morning came in a hurry.

The bandits now settled down to cook their breakfast. The hurt were doctoring their wounds in a way that would have thrown a hospital interne into a coma. They spat into their wounds, rubbed dirt and chewed leaves plucked from the bushes into them to stop bleeding, and bandaged them with strips of their filthy shirts.

In the trench the partners also had their breakfast. It is a strict rule of Mexican bandits and of Mexican soldiers fighting bandits or revolutionaries that no attack be made

by either side while they have their meals. To do so would
be considered as tactless as shooting at trucks bearing the
Red Cross sign or at men waving a white flag among civilized nations at war.

"Now, don't you boys make any mistake," Howard
warned them when Curtin mentioned that they might be
left alone from now on. "You don't know them if you think
that. They will come again, likely late in the afternoon.
They need our guns and our ammunition more than they
need bread. The more we shoot, the better they know that
here is a sort of armory worth fighting for. If I judge these
killers right, they are not going to repeat the attack the
same way. They will look for a new way to get us. Every
shot we fire is a shot lost to them. They don't want us to
waste the ammunition which they feel is theirs already. I
mean to say, they are going to prevent us from shooting,
some way or other."

"I'd like to know how they think they can get us without
making us fire at them," Lacaud said.

"Let's wait and see. Don't forget all these men have been
soldiers during the last revolutions, or if not soldiers, then
fighters against the regulars. They are trained and have all
sorts of experience. I'll get a rest now."

The old man made himself comfortable on the ground.
So did Lacaud. Curtin and Dobbs were watching the camp
leisurely.

The bandits had gone down the trail, except two who
were left to keep watch. They got drowsy after half an
hour and fell asleep.

9

About the middle of the forenoon Curtin called Dobbs:
"Do you see what I see?"

"Those god-damned devils! If we could only send them all to hell!" Dobbs answered as he roused Howard and Lacaud.

"What is it?" Howard asked. "Coming again?"

"Just have a look at a fine performance; you don't have to go to the movies this afternoon to learn new tricks." Dobbs whistled through his teeth out of excitement.

Howard watched the bandits for half a minute. "I reckon they are going to trap us now. We have to think awfully fast to meet their old Indian trick. Doggone it to hell, I've got to get an idea what to do now and, hell knows, I haven't any. If none of you mugs knows anything new, and pretty quick too, then we may as well say our last prayers, if you still know some."

The bandits were busy cutting saplings, branches, and twigs. They were constructing movable barricades, Indian-fashion. Once ready, they would push these barricades before them, using them as shields while steadily moving on. All the attacked could do would be to fire against the thickly interwoven branches and foliage. The bullets might not even penetrate, and the man crawling behind could not be aimed at. The possibility of being hit was reduced tenfold. It could be reduced still more by forming two attacking lines, one closing in behind the first.

"If they use that trick at night or early before sunrise," Howard said, watching them eagerly, "then we haven't even a Bolshevik's chance. We'll be killed like rats. My gold mine for two dozen grenades or one Jack Johnson! Oh hell, I'd exchange it for an old minnie, or even for half a dozen smoke candles, my swell mine. Well, partners, to tell you the Bible's truth, this is what we may call H-hour for us. If my mother were still alive I'd ask her forgiveness for having stolen her jam and then lying about it, cross my heart."

"It looks to me," said Dobbs, "as if all we can do now is

to sell our hides for the highest price possible, and at the last minute, when they jump in here, send as many of those sons of bitches to hell as we can."

"And don't you forget one last bullet to blow your head off yourself," Curtin suggested. "I pray to all the gods in heaven that I don't fall into their hands alive. If you can't shoot yourself, try to stab yourself to death. It will still be sweeter than being peeled by them. Hell forbid they hand you over to those we wounded."

Lacaud had become very pale. He tried to grin at the jokes cracked by the other fellows, but he failed in his effort.

Howard looked at him and felt pity. He slapped him on his back and said: "Well, buddy, if you had asked me before, I'd have told you in my most straightforward manner that gold is always very expensive, no matter how you get it or where you get it."

Hearing this, Curtin had an idea: "Perhaps if we offer them our goods and the guns, they will let us off."

"No, honey dear, you still misjudge them," Howard said. "This race has lived for four hundred years under conditions in which it never paid to trust anyone, it never paid to build a good house, it never paid to take your little money to a savings bank or invest it in some decent enterprise. You can't expect them to treat you in any other way, considering how they have been treated by the church, by the Spanish authorities, and by their own authorities for four hundred years. If you offer them your gold and your guns, they will take them and promise to let you go. But they won't let you go. They'll torture you just the same, to find out if there isn't more than you offered them. Then they kill you just the same, because you might give them away. They have never known what justice is, so you can't expect them to know it now. Nobody has ever shown them loyalty, so how could they show it to you? None has ever kept any promise to them, so they can't keep any promise they may have made you. They all say an Ave Maria before killing you, and they will cross you and themselves before and after slaying you in the most cruel way. We wouldn't be any different from them if we had had to live for four hundred years under all sorts of tyrannies, superstitions, despotisms, corruptions, and perverted religions."

"I'd like to know," Curtin broke in, "why they didn't come out with that old redskin trick earlier?"

"Huh, they are lazier than an ol' mule." Dobbs really smiled. "Too lazy for that. They tried to catch us without so much work. Only when they saw they couldn't get us any other way did they come to that smart tank attack. I bet they're cursing now that they have to work so hard to catch us."

Curtin was looking up the steep rock. Howard saw him. "Yes, kiddy, I've thought of that several times. Kept me from sleeping well last night. I had my eyes on this rock most of the time, thinking and thinking about a solution—a way out over this rock. But there is no escape over this rock, and none on either side of this furrow here. Not even under the cover of night, with the thickest thunderstorm coming to your aid above you, can you get away from this trench without running straight into their arms."

The bandits were again cooking their meals.

The partners looked at them at times as if by merely watching them they might come upon an idea to help them out of the grave they already felt buried in.

Into this silence came suddenly an excited cry: "Compadre, compadre, pronto, muy pronto, quick, come here!"

"What the hell is up?"

One of the guards by the horses, who from his post could overlook and watch the trail leading to the camp, had come up and called the chief.

All the men banded together, and the partners could hear the men all talking to each other at the same time. But it was difficult to make out what it was about. Then the men hurriedly picked up all their things that lay about and went off down the trail.

Curtin started to jump out of the trench to watch them more closely. Lacaud pulled him down, saying: "Wait, pal, this may be only a trick to lure us out of here and get us without even using their barricades."

"I don't think so," Howard said. "They would have to be awfully good movie actors to play a trick like that so perfectly. Didn't you notice that guy running up here like wild with his message? There's something else behind this. I wonder what."

Curtin, not heeding Lacaud's warning, had left the trench and gone far to the left, where he climbed up to their lookout, whence the whole valley could be seen. There he sat for quite a while looking around, seeming to see something of importance.

Then he called: "Hey, partners, up here, all of you. Here is a sight, if there ever was."

The partners, forgetting all about the bandits, climbed up to where Curtin was sitting.

"Trust my eyes," Howard exclaimed. "Do I see right or do I? Hell, that's a pleasure. I should say a real relief."

It was surely a good sight for the partners: a marching squadron of federal cavalry.

There was not the slightest doubt as to what they were after. The villagers must have tipped them off that the bandits had gone up to this plateau to rob the gringo of his shotguns and provisions, for these soldiers were coming up the trail to the camp.

"I can't quite get it why these bandits left rather than wait for the soldiers up here," Dobbs wondered.

Howard laughed. His laughter was heartier than it was meant to be, for it carried all the anxiety he had felt during the last two days, all the anxiety that he now wanted to blow off. "You mustn't think them dumber than they are. They may not have as much brain as you have, Dobby sweet, but they still have something in their cones. Didn't I tell you they are old fighters, fairly well trained in all tricks of warfare? If they should wait here, they would be lost for good. In the first place, they would have us at their backs and the soldiers blocking their only way of escape. Even if they could overcome us, and I'm sure that was what they discussed so hotly, they couldn't hold out very long in this trench. The soldiers would attack them the minute they arrived, perhaps even using the same shields these rascals had fixed to catch us with. Their only way to safety, or at least to a few days more of life, is to get out of this trail before the soldiers enter. That's the reason why they are in such a devilish hurry. Their pants are wetter now than ours were an hour ago. Tell you that."

It was not a great joke, but all were laughing as they had not laughed for weeks.

Dobbs said: "For once in my life I'm actually grateful that there are still soldiers in the world. Geecries, they sure have come at a good time, that's what I say. I could kiss them soldiers wherever they would like it, those sons of sunshine. Gee, fellers, tell you the naked god-damned truth, I was already chewing earth between my teeth, and that's the damned truth, it sure is. Do I feel happy, do I?"

"You bet." Lacaud had got his color back and also his speech.

Howard laughed again. "Yeah, and these bandits, I think, have done us still another favor by leaving in such a hurry. Had they stopped here and waited for the soldiers—well, boys, I wouldn't have liked it too much to have soldiers sneaking about here. Soldiers are all to the good sometimes, but sometimes they can be a real nuisance to a decent feller. They might, if only for fun, start to grill us about what we're doing up here and they might nose around. I wouldn't have liked it so very much, would you, partners?"

"It's better this way, I figure," Dobbs said.

"Let's take in the second act of the picture." Curtin was again watching the valley eagerly.

The soldiers had taken up the trail. There could no longer be the slightest doubt. When still half a mile away from where the trail entered the base of the mountains they divided up in three sections and formed a very wide circle. They did not know precisely where the trail left the valley. This was to the advantage of the bandits, for when the bandits finally reached the valley, the soldiers were not close. So the bandits, riding in the brush along the base of the mountains, won a good headway against the soldiers.

For two hours the partners could only occasionally see a soldier, because the squadron had come close to the base. But then shots were heard roaring over the valley. The soldiers had caught sight of the bandits, and those who had come upon the fresh tracks had fired signal shots to get the whole troop on the right trail.

Now a lively race started in the valley. The soldiers were chasing the bandits, who disbanded, each trying to escape in his own way. Such were their usual tactics, a procedure which made it very difficult for the soldiers to round up all the bandits within a short time. A few always escaped. These men joined others, also escaped, and formed a new band no less ferocious than the original one. The task for the soldiers and the police was seldom an easy one. Many of them lost their lives in these battles, and still more returned to their barracks wounded, or crippled for the rest of their days.

For the partners, watching the fight of civilization against barbarism, it became more and more difficult to follow the events in the valley. The bandits were seen riding in all directions with the soldiers after them. They went farther and farther out of sight down the valley. Shots became fainter and fainter.

"I would suggest," Dobbs said, "that we now, for the first time in two days, sit down to a quiet and decent dinner and have a friendly talk about the news of the day."

"Not so bad, that idea. Let's do it right away." Howard laughed.

"If I should be asked," Curtin shouted mirthfully, "I'd say it's okay by me. What say, Laky-Shaky?"

Lacaud made a hardly visible effort to smile, which he hoped Curtin would understand and take for a perfect answer.

14

Camp was pitched once more. Having had their eats, the partners were loafing about. Sunset was still far off. Yet no one felt like working. The burros were taken from their hiding-place and led down to be watered and then left to return to pasture.

After nightfall, when they sat around the fire smoking and discussing the events of the last forty hours, they found the happenings of the last two days had so exhausted them that they had lost interest in the work which had enabled them to endure all sorts of hardships and privations for so many months. They felt almost as though they had aged overnight.

Curtin gave these feelings words. "I suppose Howard is right in what he said day before yesterday. That is, that the best thing we can do is to close the mine, pack up, and leave. Devil knows how long it will be now before we have soldiers coming up here. We might well make another grand by staying here another two weeks or three. Anyway, I am of the opinion we should be thankful for what we have and go home."

For a few minutes there was no answer. Then Dobbs said: "I had preferred to stay here a few weeks longer, you know. I said so before. Still, come to think of it, it's all right with me, brethren. Let's strike the mine and make ready to toddle off. Fact is, I no longer have the slightest ambition to hold on. It's all gone."

211

Howard nodded without saying a word.

Lacaud was smoking. He did not even remind them that they had closed a deal with him to stay for another week at least so as to assist him in trying out his ideas. He seemed to be more concerned about keeping up a good fire than anything else.

Finally Howard looked at him. "Nervous? What for? It seems to be all over now."

"Oh, I'm not nervous, partner. Not exactly. I don't know why I should be." After this he again fell silent.

Perhaps he had been thinking how to arouse their interest once more, so they would stay and help him for a few days. He didn't wish to come out directly with what he wanted, so he tried another way.

"Did you ever hear the story about the old Ciniega Mine?" He asked this rather suddenly, perhaps too suddenly, for the partners seemed to feel that he was not being straightforward.

Slightly bored, Howard said slowly: "We know so many stories about old mines that we don't know what to do about." He had been interrupted in his thoughts of how he would use the money he had earned to live a quiet life in a small town, sitting on the porch smoking and reading the papers, the comic strips, and bunk adventure stories, concerned about his health and about his meals, and going to bed early, with funds to get well soaked at least once a month.

As if he were awakening, he looked up at Lacaud. "The truth is I had forgotten all about you, Laky," he said.

Curtin laughed. "You see, Laky, we have our own thoughts, and you are not in them. We three have become so accustomed to speaking to each other that we sometimes forget you are here. No harm."

Dobbs butted in. "It's only to let you see how unimportant

you are, brother. We've eaten together, we've fought together, we've even been very close to going to hell together,
but you are still outside of the community, if you get what
we mean. We might have come to like each other. But now,
I reckon, it's too late."

"I get what you mean, Dobbs."

"That reminds me," Howard addressed him; "didn't you
say something about a plan?"

"Yes, your plan." Dobbs spoke up. "Yes, that plan of
yours. Well, you may keep it as your well-earned property.
I'm not interested a bit. I've got the same idea old man
Curtin has; to be more exact, I'd like to see a girl and see
how she looks underneath, you know, and I have the funny
desire to sit once more at a real table in a restaurant with
well-cooked food set before me."

"But can't you see? Here are tens of thousands of dollars
lying about ready to be picked up!"

Curtin yawned. "All right, sweety, pick them up and be
happy. Don't let them lie around here, somebody might
come and carry them away. Well, partners, should somebody ask me how I feel right now, I'd say: I'm going to
hit the hay in the old barn. Good night."

Howard and Dobbs rose also, stretched their limbs, yawned
with mouths wide open, and walked to the tent.

Curtin, already standing by the tent, called: "Hey, Laky,
if you want to bunk with us, the apartment we have here is
big enough to house you too. Just step in and don't slam
the door."

"If you don't mind, I prefer to sleep here by the fire. I
have to think a few schemes over, and I can do it best with
the stars above me. Thanks just the same." Lacaud carried
his packs and blankets near the fire. "Only I'd like to put
my packs in your tent, in case it should rain."

"Bring them in," Howard invited him. "Room enough;

no storage charged."

When the three partners were alone in the tent, Curtin said: "I still can't see what is wrong about that guy. Sometimes he seems perfectly all right, and then again he seems to be all nuts."

"Poor feller, he is," Howard said. "He's cracked somehow. He hasn't got all his screws tight. That much is sure. I think he is an eternal."

"An eternal? What do you mean?" Curtin was curious.

"An eternal prospector. He can stay for ten years at the same place digging and digging, convinced that he is on the right spot and that there can be no mistake about it and that all he needs is patience. He is sure that some day he will make the big hit. He is of the same family as were men in bygone centuries who spent their whole lives and all their money trying to find the formula for producing gold by mixing metals and chemicals—smelting them, cooking them, and brewing them until they themselves turned insane. He is the more modern sort. He is working day in and day out over plans and schemes just as men do who want to bust the banks in a gambling-resort."

"Tomorrow he will see our mine," Dobbs said.

"Let him. It doesn't matter, since we are leaving. We close it properly, and if he should open it again, that's his affair, not ours. I really feel sorry for that guy." Howard admitted this. "Really sorry for him. But you can't cure these fellers, and I suppose if somebody could cure them they wouldn't like it. They prefer to stay this way. It's their whole excuse for being alive."

Dobbs was not fully convinced. He said: "I'm not sure there isn't something else behind that guy. He doesn't seem to be all cracked up."

Howard waved his hands and shrugged. "Have it your way. I've met this sort before. Good night."

15

Another week of labor was put in by the partners, during which they worked up all the piles of dirt and rocks which had been ready to be washed. It proved worth while to get out of these piles all they contained. It was good pay. But nevertheless they stuck by their decision to give up. So they began breaking down the mine.

While doing so, Dobbs cut his hand and yelled angrily: "For what hellish reason of yours do we have to work like hunks in a steel-mill to level this field? Just tell me, old man."

"We decided upon that the day we started to work here," Howard answered, "didn't we?"

"Yes, we did. But I say it's a waste of time, that's what I think."

"The Lord might have said it's only a waste of time to build this earth, if it was He who actually did it. I figure we should be thankful to the mountain which has rewarded our labor so generously. So we shouldn't leave this place as careless picnic parties and dirty motorists so often do. We have wounded this mountain and I think it is our duty to close its wounds. The silent beauty of this place deserves our respect. Besides, I want to think of this place the way we found it and not as it has been while we were taking away its treasures, which this same mountain has guarded for millions of years. I couldn't sleep well thinking I had left the mountain looking like a junk-yard. I'm sorry we can't do this restoration perfectly—that we can do no better than show our good intention and our gratitude. If you two guys won't help me, I'll do it all alone, but I shall do it just the same."

Curtin laughed. "The way you talk about a mountain as a personality is funny. Anyway, count me in. I'm with you. You should sweep a cabin when leaving it after it has sheltered you for the night. All right with me. Let's tackle the job."

"I have still another reason," Howard explained, "a reason which is less sentimental, and I suppose this is a reason which will appeal to you, Dobbs, in particular. It's this. Suppose after we have left, somebody comes up, looks around, and touches the right button. What then? We'll have a dozen god-damned bandits after us inside of a few hours, to catch up with us and ease us of our lives and our income. Well, Dobbs, better level this part off and make it look like a flower-garden. Don't always think of your pay. There may be good pay in it anyhow, even if we don't see it right now."

"All right, I'll do what I can, but leave me alone; I'm no gardener." He was reconciled, Dobbs was, only he didn't want to show it for fear Curtin might poke fun at him.

2

Lunch was as usual. A kettle of tea, a leathery pancake, and a piece of dried meat which needed constant chewing. Lunch over a pipe or two, and they were at work again. Daylight had to be used from the first ray to the last. Days in the tropics, even in midsummer, are not long—only slightly longer than the nights. Breakfast had to be over when the first rays of the sun shot above the horizon, and the mine was never left before dark had fallen. Only so had it been possible for the partners to do much work, interrupted as they often were by tropical cloudbursts, when for hours the whole plateau would become a lake.

"It sure has been the hardest job I ever had," Curtin said when they were sitting by the fire smoking and reflecting on their life during the last months.

"Doubtless it was hard work," Howard admitted. "But I'm positive that none of us in all his life ever made as good wages as we have made here."

"Maybe." This from Dobbs. "Yes, maybe. Only I think it might be better—"

"Better what?" Curtin asked, afraid that Dobbs might again bring up the question of staying for a few months more.

"Oh, nothing. Forget it." Dobbs tried to shake off certain thoughts which apparently were troubling his mind.

"Yes, we've got our pay." Howard spoke as though he had not listened to what the other two had said to each other. "We've got the money. That's perfectly all right. But I figure as long as it isn't in the bank, or at least in a civilized town, we can hardly call it our own. We have a hellish long way before us and a tough job still before we have everything safely at the nearest depot. That worries me a lot."

Neither Dobbs nor Curtin said anything. They knocked their pipes out and all went back to work.

3

The derricks, stages, and wheels were finally broken and set fire to, so as to leave no trace of their machinery. Then they covered the charred timber with earth. After this was done they dug shrubs from the woods and planted them here.

Howard had a good reason for doing everything so carefully. "Suppose one of you guys gambles his earnings away or loses them some other way, he may return, and he can still make his living here. So let's hide the place as well as we can to keep it safe for any one of us who might be in need."

Within two days the partners had changed the mine so much that a few weeks later it would have been very difficult to discover that it had formerly been a working-place.

Lacaud, out during these days looking over the surroundings, came back to the camp only at night. He did not ask where the partners were working nor where the mine was. He was not interested in knowing the location. It was his idea that wherever their mine was, it must be the wrong place and not worth exploring. Because the partners had not found the lode after so many months of hard work he would not touch the mine even should he come upon it. If those fellows had not found the real mother vein near their mine, he would not try there, for to him it was proof that this was not the place he was after. He would not lose his time and labor investigating even the surroundings of their mine.

"Did you find your lode today?" Dobbs asked when he came to the camp.

"Not yet," Lacaud answered. "Somehow I have the feeling that I have never been so close to it as I was this afternoon."

"You have my blessing and don't you get tired out before you find the right spot."

"Don't you worry, I won't." Lacaud's confidence could not be shaken so easily.

"You're invited to dinner, Laky," Howard said in a very friendly tone. "Leave your cooking alone. You'll need your grub."

"Thanks, partner."

4

That night the three partners felt like factory workers on Saturday evening. Tomorrow they would plant more shrubs and saplings on the mining field and destroy the narrow path leading to the mine so that the shrubs might have time to root and grow and make the plateau appear as untouched a wilderness as it was when it was discovered.

This work would take the whole day, but it would be a joyful day like a Sunday spent working in your own garden. Then they would rest comfortably and the day after they would prepare the packs and get the whole pack-train ready so that they might leave two days later.

It was a jolly evening they spent, and for the first time they felt growing among them a bond which came very close to real friendship. So far they had never been friends or comrades, only business partners without any common interest other than their work.

During these long months they had had no papers or books to enrich their thinking or their vocabulary. Always overtired, they had shortened their speech to such a point that Lacaud sometimes failed to understand what the three partners were talking about. Pick-axes, spades, water, dirt, rocks, burros, food, gold, clothing, the parts of their primitive machinery, and all details of their work were referred to by signals, often merely single letters, which only they themselves understood. They could talk to each other for half an hour without an outsider knowing what they said. They themselves did not realize that their speech had changed to such primitiveness, for only by living in larger groups can man compare his speech with that used by others. Only when Lacaud did not grasp their talk in full and had to ask over and over again did they realize that they had acquired a lingo of their own which was incomprehensible to outsiders.

5

The mine was leveled to the satisfaction of Howard. Anybody now coming upon the mine by chance would never think that a mine had been worked here, or if at all, not during the last hundred years.

"Doesn't it give you guys a real joy to look at the place now?" Howard asked with pride in his voice.

"All right," Dobbs said, "you have it your way and you feel happy, so please, for the love of Mike's booze, leave us in peace with your feelings. Sometimes I think you must have been a preacher, only the hell of it is I can't figure what church it was you wanted to catch birds for."

That night Howard said: "Something very important is really worrying me. I've been thinking things over, and I've come to the conclusion that it won't be so damn easy to get our goods safely to town."

"Just what do you mean?" Curtin asked.

"The trip has its damn hazards."

"Oh, we know that. Tell us a better one." Dobbs was impatient at hearing what he thought was an old story.

"Don't you get nervous, Dobby. This trip will be different from the one that brought us here. Likely it will be the most difficult one you ever made in all your life. There may be bandits. There may be accidents. All sorts of accidents can happen on these dreadful trails across the Sierra. The police might pass our way and be a little bit too curious about what we're carrying in our packs. We've worked hard here, if any devils ever worked hard. But I tell you guys, as long as we haven't got the whole cinnamon safely stowed away inside the strong boxes of a good bank, it isn't ours. I just wanted to mention this to make you understand you are not rich yet."

Lacaud came to the fire. For a long while he sat staring into the fire without saying a word. Then, as if coming out of a long dream, he said: "And I'm sure it must be around here somewhere."

"Sure," Howard said smiling. "But leave your worries for another day. Help yourself to a good dinner. It's all waiting for you." Then to Dobbs: "Hey, cook, what about the coffee?"

"Yes, ma'm, coming." Dobbs pushed the coffee over to the old man.

16

I

"As I have said to you guys several times, to bring every-thing safely home and have it credited to your account isn't quite so easy as wading in clay and having water at hand to wash your feet afterwards." Howard was taking up this problem once more. It seemed that he could think of nothing else, and to him this problem had become really acute since they had decided to close the mine and leave for the port. He simply couldn't free his mind from the difficulties which he foresaw would be theirs on the march.

He went on: "Did you ever hear the story about that treasure-burdened woman, the most honorable and distin-guished doña Catalina María de Rodríguez? I'm sure you haven't, because there aren't many people in this world who have. I mean, of course, the true story. With her it was not the question of how to get the gold and silver, but how to get it home, where it would have done her the most good. Gold is of no use to anybody as long as it is not where he wants it.

"It seems that in the Villa de Guadalupe there is an image of Nuestra Señora de Guadalupe—that is, Our Lady of Guadalupe, the holy patroness of Mexico and all the Mexi-cans. The little town is a suburb of Mexico City and can be reached from that city by street-car. To the Mexicans and the Indians of Mexico this image is of great importance, because whoever is in trouble or pain undertakes a pil-

grimage to that shrine feeling sure that the Holy Virgin
will help him out of his worries, whatever they are. Our
Lady of Guadalupe has a very great heart and she under-
stands fully the depths of the human soul. She is even supposed to help a peasant to a piece of land which belongs to
his neighbor and to help a girl out of the natural conse-
quences of a wrong step. Anyway, the Mexicans know how
to use her to their benefit, and so do the holy persons who
take care of the lady and are in charge of everything, including collecting the fees."

"That's all superstition. To hell with all those people who
coin money out of the superstitions of the ignorant!" Curtin
interrupted the tale.

"I wonder," Howard said. "You have to believe, and then
it will help you. It's the same with the Lord. If you believe
in the Lord, then there is a Lord for you; if you don't believe in Him, there is no God for you—nobody who lights
up the stars for you and directs the traffic in the heavens.
Now, don't let's argue about such details; let's come to the
plain story. I'm telling you that story just as it happened."

2

At about the time of the American Revolution there lived
in the vicinity of Huacal, in northern Mexico, a well-to-do
Indian farmer, who, in fact, was chieftain of the Chiricahua
Indians. These Indians, very peaceful people, had settled in
this region hundreds and hundreds of years before and had
found more pleasure and riches in tilling the soil than the
neighboring tribes who went marauding whenever they felt
like it.

The chieftain, who was otherwise so blessed with well-
being, had a great sorrow which overshadowed his whole
life: His only son and heir was blind. In former times this

son would have been done away with right after being born.
But under the influence of the new religion even the Indians
had become more generous in such things, and the child, as
he was otherwise normal, was allowed to live. The boy was
a strong and healthy child, handsome and well formed. He
grew not only in size but in intelligence, and the nearer he
came to manhood, the more sorrowful became his father.

It so happened that a monk came that way, a holy person
who understood well how to live on the hospitality of the
Indians without giving them more in return than an occasional story about events supposed to have taken place between two and three thousand years ago, concerning people
entirely different from the Indians. Finally the monk felt
that he had to do better if he wished to stay longer without
having to plow and to sow for his living. Besides, he needed
ready cash for some purpose or other. So he began bar-
gaining with the chieftain, telling him that for a worth-
while consideration he would give him advice as to how to
win the grace of the Holy Virgin and make her do what no
doctor ever could do: give light to the eyes of the chief's
only son. The monk was expert in giving good counsel to
the suffering and afflicted. He had been trained for it.

"Of course," he explained to the chief, "this heavenly
grace of Nuestra Señora de Guadalupe is not easily gained.
You understand, my son, such a great lady cannot be treated
like an ordinary hussy. Therefore do not spare the rich
offerings, as the Holy Virgin, just to make it quite plain to
you what I mean, is always in a very receptive mood towards
money in any form and also jewelry. And so are the most
holy persons who wait upon this great lady."

For this sure remedy the monk expected his own reward
at once, as no one, regardless of how holy he may be, is expected to live on hope for the manna which once came, but
which may never come again. The monk, having received

his pay, gave the chief, his wife, and his son his blessing and went on his way to find another tribe that might be willing to support him well for telling stories about miracles.

The chieftain left his possessions in charge of his uncle, gathered together all the money and all the jewelry he had, and went on his long pilgrimage to Nuestra Señora de Guadalupe. No horse, mule, or burro was to be used on this dreary way. With his wife and son and three servants, he had to make this journey of nearly fourteen hundred miles on foot. At every church on his way he had to kneel down and say three hundred Ave Marias and to offer the church a certain number of candles, a silver eye, and money. To make this pilgrimage last as long as possible may have been of importance to the monk for reasons of his own, but since he was a loyal Christian, let us presume the journey had to be made in this way so as to be a success.

The chief reached Mexico City at last. After having made his offerings in the cathedral, confessed, and prayed there for a whole day, and with special blessings from the fathers, he went about the last part of his hard task.

It is slightly more than three miles from the cathedral to the image of Guadalupe. These three miles the chief, his wife, his son, and his three servants had to walk on their knees, and each of the pilgrims had to carry in his hands a lighted candle, which must not be permitted to go out, no matter what the weather. If a candle should burn out, it had to be replaced with a new one. Since the candles had been specially blessed in the cathedral, they were far more expensive than ordinary candles, and whenever a new one was lighted, a hundred extra Ave Marias had to be said. It should be added that the Ave Marias were practically the only prayers the chief and his family knew how to say.

So they went chanting and praying all the way, being blessed and crossed by all the faithful persons who passed by.

On the knees any trip will last long. So this journey lasted all afternoon and the whole night through. The little boy fell asleep, but was wakened again and again. He whined for water and for a tortilla to eat. But it was against the rule to eat or drink on such a pilgrimage.

Not everyone who passed by blessed them. Many shrank in horror from the little group, thinking what terrible sinners they must be to have been commanded by the church to go through such an ordeal.

Wholly exhausted, they reached the base of the Cerrito de Tepeyac. This was the hill on which, in the year of Our Lord 1531, the Holy Virgin in person had appeared to the Quauhtlatohua Indian Juan Diego and had left painted in his ayate, a sort of over-shirt, her picture. No one had taken notice of this miracle at the time it happened. Not until one hundred years later were the faithful reminded of the fact that this miracle had occurred on the 12th of December 1531. But the picture was there, and it was framed in a costly gold frame, where it can be still seen, and it has brought, and still brings, to the church more money than a successful comedy on Broadway makes for its producers and owners.

The story of the image, true or not, was of no importance to the chieftain, who was in sorrow. And the story has never been of consequence to anybody who has come faithfully to the shrine and asked the help of the Virgin.

Three days and three nights the chief, his wife, his son, and his servants prayed on their knees before the image. They did not eat, they did not drink, and they used up all their strength to avoid falling asleep. But nothing happened.

The chief had promised the church all his cattle and his whole crop for the year should it please Our Lady to light the eyes of his beloved son.

On the seventh day, as the Virgin still refused to perform the expected and paid-for miracle, the chief, urged by the clergy in attendance, offered all his worldly possessions, including his huge farm, to the Virgin, in exchange for the eyesight of his child.

Still no miracle took place, and the chieftain began earnestly to doubt the power of the Virgin. His own gods had done better under similar circumstances.

The boy had meanwhile become so weakened by the long fast, the constant praying, and the attempts of his parents to keep him awake during these days that his mother finally asserted herself, took her son out of the church, and, Virgin or no Virgin, devoted all her time to the boy, saying: "I prefer my boy alive, even if blind, to a boy dead who could see once."

The chieftain, being desperate, said now quite openly to the priests that he did not believe any longer in the Virgin and that he would rather go home and have the medicine-men of his tribe treat his son's eyes once more. The fathers accused him of blasphemy and warned him furthermore that were he not an ignorant Indian, they would take him before the court of the Holy Inquisition and torture him into swearing away his heathen gods and then fine him for his blasphemy until he and all his relatives had nothing left and he would be grateful that he was spared the fate of so many other unbelievers who were burnt alive at the stake on the Alameda. Eager not to lose the whole tribe of which he was the chief, the fathers explained why the Holy Virgin had refused him help. Perhaps he had not said three hundred Ave Marias in each church on his way; it might have happened that he had said only two hundred and eighty in some places, and he might even have skipped a few churches, being in a hurry to reach the shrine. The Virgin knows such things and he could not cheat her as he perhaps had done with his own gods, who could not see farther than to the top of the nearest mountain. Possibly he had drunk water in the morning before crossing himself and saying his prayer. Perhaps he had made mistakes with the candles on the last stretch of his pilgrimage.

The chieftain finally had to admit that it was possible that he had not always said the full number of Ave Marias, but this was not his fault, because he was not used to such high figures and he might have skipped a few. And he remembered now that he had drunk water hastily without first crossing himself, because it had been very hot and he was thirsty, as he had given all the water they carried in pumpkin bottles to his wife and his son, who were dying in the heat. So the fathers said that under such circumstances he should not blame the Virgin, who is stainless and blameless for ever and ever, but should blame only himself, because he was a great sinner and not an asset to Christendom, and he had better go back home and repeat the pilgrimage after six months, when the Virgin surely would grant him what he asked in good faith and as a true believer in the church.

The chief, however, had lost faith in the power of the goddess, for he was an Indian who belonged to a tribe that always received the rain its medicine-men prayed and danced and chanted for. A goddess that cannot or will not help men when in need and pain is no good for an Indian.

He took his family and returned to Mexico City, ate and drank heartily, and was happy once more. He even took his young wife again into his arms, as he had not done since they had left their home, for the monk had told him that if he committed such a sin, he would lose the grace of the Holy Virgin.

While in Mexico City, he was looking about for a doctor whom he might consult. He was given the name of don Manuel Rodríguez, a famous Spanish doctor who had become prominent on account of an eye operation performed on the wife of the prefect of the city. Before this successful operation he had been but a quack. Having made a careful examination of the boy's eyes, he told the chief that he was sure that he could cure the boy—that the boy might regain the full use of his eyes. "The main question," he added, "is what you can pay me."

The chief, clad like all his kind, did not look like one who could pay as much as the prefect had. He said that he owned a good farm and cattle. "That is not cash," don Manuel said. "What I need and what I want is cash—money, you know—heaps of it. I wish to go back to Spain, to a civilized country. I cannot live in this god-forsaken country here. And when I return to Spain I wish to return rich, and when I say rich, I mean, of course, very rich. Your farm and your cattle don't interest me. Gold is what I want."

To this the chief answered that he could make don Manuel the richest man in New Spain, as Mexico was called in those times, if the doctor would make his son see like other human beings. How could he do that? the doctor asked. The chief said that he knew a very rich gold and silver mine and that he would show it to him on the day they reached his home and the boy had his eyesight.

Don Manuel was not easily convinced, so they made a cruel contract stipulating that don Manuel should have the right without being prosecuted to destroy the boy's sight again if the mine which was to be his did not exist or belonged to somebody else or was exhausted.

Don Manuel worked as he never had worked before. He operated on the boy and treated him for two months, with so much care and attention that he neglected all his other patients, including even men high in office. The fact was that he had become professionally interested in this case, although he did not forget for one hour the reward awaiting him for his labor. When ten weeks had passed, don Manuel called the chief and said that he might come and get his boy.

The joy of the father was unbounded when he found that his son could see like a young eagle and was told by don Manuel that the cure would be permanent. This was true.

With the gratitude only an Indian can feel, the chief said to don Manuel: "Now I shall prove to you that my word is as good as yours. The mine I am going to show you and which is now yours is the property of my family. When the Spaniards came to our region my ancestors buried the mine, for they hated the Spaniards who had committed so many cruelties against our race in this country which our gods had given to us. The whites loved gold and silver more than they loved their own God. The Spaniards learned from tortured members of our tribe of the existence of this mine. They came and tore out the tongues of all the members of our family whom they could lay hands on and, piece by piece, burned them to death to learn the place of the mine. But my ancestors laughed in their faces, even under severe pain. There was no torture cruel enough to make my ancestors reveal the mine. The more the conquerors tortured, the more did my forefathers hate them, and it was their ardent hate that made them bear all cruelties rather than tell. The word that has come down to us from my ancestors is this: If your family or your tribe has been rendered a great service which neither the feather-crowned god of our race nor the blood-crowned god of the whites had been able or willing to render, then you shall give the treasure of the mine to that man who served you so well. By your deed, don Manuel, this word has now been fulfilled. You, don Manuel, have given eyes to my son and heir, who after me will be chieftain of our tribe. You did what the Mother of the god of the whites could not do or would not do in spite of all my sufferings and prayers and humiliations. This mine is now rightfully yours. Three months hence follow me on the road I shall describe to you, but speak to no one of what you know. And, as I have promised you, I will make you the richest man in all New Spain."

3

Don Manuel, having liquidated his affairs in Mexico City, went after three months on his long and laborious way to Huacal to take possession of his property. He brought with him his wife, doña María, who had refused to stay behind and live quietly while her husband was on such an adventurous journey. The women of Spanish pioneers were no less brave and courageous than were the women of American pioneers.

Don Manuel found the chief and was welcomed by him like a brother. Not alone the family of the chief, but everyone else in the tribe had only gratitude and admiration for the great doctor, who was treated as a guest of honor.

"While on my way up here," don Manuel said to the chief, "I came to think that it is rather strange that you, Aguila Bravo, did not exploit the mine yourself. You could easily have earned a hundred thousand gold florins, with which you could have paid me in full for my work, and I would have been satisfied."

The chief laughed. "I do not need gold nor do I want silver. I have plenty to eat always. I have a young and beautiful wife, whom I love dearly and who loves and honors me. I have also a strong and healthy boy, who now, thanks to your skill, can see and so is perfect in every way. I have my acres and fields, and I have my fine cattle. I am chief and judge, and I may say I am a true and honest friend of my tribe, which respects me and obeys my orders, which they know are for their own good. The soil bears rich fruit every year. The cattle bring forth year in, year out. I have a golden sun above me, at night a silver moon, and there is peace in the land. So what could gold mean to me? Gold and silver do not carry any blessing. Does it bring you any blessing? You whites, you kill and rob and cheat and betray for gold. You hate each other for gold, while you never can buy love with gold. Nothing but hatred and envy. You whites spoil the beauty of life for the possession of gold. Gold is pretty and it stays pretty, and therefore we use it to adorn our gods and our women. It is a feast for our eyes to look at rings and necklaces and bracelets made out of it. But we always were the masters of our gold, never its slaves. We look at it and enjoy it. Since we cannot eat it, gold is of no real value to us. Our people have fought wars, but never for the possession of gold. We fought for land, for rivers, for salt deposits, for lakes, and mostly to defend ourselves against savage tribes who tried to rob us of our land and its products. If I am hungry or my wife is hungry, what can gold do, if there is no corn or no water? I cannot swallow gold to satisfy my hunger, can I? Gold is beautiful, like a flower, or it is poetic, like the singing of a bird in the woods. But if I eat the flower, it is no longer beautiful, and if I put the singing bird into a frying-pan, I can no more enjoy his sweet song."

"All this may be how you feel, but as far as I am concerned," don Manuel said jocularly, "I won't put my gold into my stomach, I can assure you that, Aguila Bravo. I know what I shall use the gold for, don't you worry."

"I suppose you know, and you must know best. I won't advise you what to do. You see, my dear friend, I can serve for my acres, but I cannot and I would not serve for gold, because then I would have no corn to eat, and my wife and my son and my old father and all my servants, who all depend on me, would go hungry. This I could not bear. Anyway, my friend, I think you don't know what I am talking about, and how I mean it; and I feel that I cannot quite understand what you mean. Your heart is different from mine, and your soul is not like mine. God has made us this way. Yet whatever may happen, I shall always be your friend."

4

Six long days did the chief, accompanied by the doctor and by two of the chief's men, crawl through the under-brush looking for the mine. They dug and scratched here and there. Don Manuel was inclined to misjudge the doings of the chief. He thought that the chief was only trying to get out of the agreement some way or other, and that no mine existed at all. Yet when he saw how carefully the chief searched, how logically he worked along a certain line, how he watched the shadows of the sun and compared them with peaks of hills and rocks, he became convinced that the chief knew precisely what he was doing and that he was sure to find what he was after.

"It is not quite so easy as you may think," the chief said to don Manuel one evening when they were seated by the camp-fire for supper. "You must understand, my friend, there have been earthquakes, torrential rains, landslides, changes in the course of rivers; brooks have disappeared and others have come anew; small trees have grown to giants, and big trees have died. All such things have been marks to locate the mine, and these marks do not exist any longer, and so I have to look for other marks. It may still be a full week before we find the mine. Have patience, my friend. The mine cannot run away like a deer."

The search lasted far longer than a week. Then there came an evening when the chief said: "Tomorrow, my dear friend, I shall give you the mine, for tomorrow my eyes will have reached it."

Don Manuel wanted to know why they could not get to the place immediately to make sure. He was restless.

"We might go right now, my friend," the chief answered, "but it would not help us much. You see, all these days the sun was not throwing his shadow where I had to have it. Tomorrow the sun will point exactly to the mark. I have known the location for several days now, and tomorrow I will find the mine."

So it was. Next day the mine was located in a ravine. "You see," the chief explained, "there a hill has broken off and buried all the ground near by. You can easily see that. That is the reason it was so difficult for me to find the exact place. Too many changes have occurred during the last two hundred years. There is the mine, and it is now rightfully yours. And here we part. Now I beg of you to leave my house and my land."

"Why?" don Manuel asked.

"My house would no longer be good enough for you. You now own the rich mine, and no longer will happiness be yours." The chief stretched out his hand to shake.

"Wait," don Manuel said, "I should like to ask you something."

"Yes, my friend."

"Suppose I had asked one hundred thousand gold florins to cure your son; wouldn't you have opened the mine to get it?"

"I certainly would. Because I wanted my son to see, and I would not have him blind if I could help it. But after I had taken the necessary gold out of the mine, I would have closed it again, for gold makes no one happy. Besides, it might have happened that the people that rule—the Spaniards, I mean—would have heard of it, and they would have murdered me and all my family to get the mine. Whichever way you look at it, there is no happiness in it. And all that counts in life is happiness, or what else do we live for? Take my advice, my dear friend, take care that you are not murdered just for this mine as soon as your own people have word that you own it. If your people know that you own nothing but your bread, tortillas, and beans, nobody will murder you.— I have to go now. I shall always remain your friend as long as I live, but we must part now."

5

Don Manuel began at once to build a camp. Aguila Bravo returned to his home, which was about one day's distance from the mine.

Before don Manuel had left the city he had secured from the authorities all necessary papers giving him permission to prospect for metals and making him the sole owner of mines he should discover. Taxes he would have to pay on the shipments to the city.

He returned to the town where he had left his wife. Here he bought tools and such machinery as he needed, and also blasting-powder. He hired labor and bought pack-beasts. Taking his wife with him, he returned to the mine and started to open it.

The mine proved so rich in silver ore that its production beat that of all the other mines. The main product was silver. But it carried a good amount of gold as by-product.

Experiences of other mine-owners had taught him to say little about his find. Bandits were less to be feared than high officials and the high dignitaries of the church. These lofty persons understood well how to deprive plain citizens of their property when the property was worth the trouble. The owner would disappear suddenly and nobody would find a trace of him. No last will would be found and so the mine would be declared church property or property of the crown. Furthermore, in Latin-American countries the Inquisition lasted far longer than in Spain, and its unholy power was nowhere exercised more rigorously than in this unhappy land.

Against such power what could a plain citizen do? A bishop or a cardinal only needed to get word that a certain citizen was in possession of a very rich mine and it would not be long before witnesses would appear and swear that the mine-owner had doubted the purity or the virginity of the Lord's Mother or that he doubted the miracles of Nuestra Señora de Guadalupe or uttered blasphemous speeches or said that Luther had been just as right as the Pope. If he denied the charges, he was tortured until he not only admitted that the witnesses had told the truth, but added anything else that he was asked to admit. He was found guilty, and was happy if he was granted the great mercy of being strangled before he was burned, because they might have burned him alive by a very slow fire. According to the special rules of the Holy Inquisition, all the property of a condemned man, all the property of his wife, his children, his parents, and most of his relatives, was confiscated by the church. A small percentage, according to the same rules, had to be given to the denouncers and witnesses.

Don Manuel was too clever to be caught so easily. He made only very poor shipments to Mexico City, shipments that looked so cheap that he was pitied by everybody because he had to work so hard for such small winnings. He shipped only what he needed to buy better tools, provisions, and money for wages.

At the mine, however, he began to accumulate and to pile up the rich outputs, hiding them away and waiting for the day when he would make a great last shipment and then leave the mine to whoever wanted what was left.

Although the mine gave him great riches, he treated his

Indian laborers worse than slaves. He hardly paid them
enough to keep them alive, and he made them work so hard
that often they broke down. Day and night he was after
them, whip in hand, and using his gun whenever he thought
it necessary. Indians, particularly those of the North American continent, cannot be treated in this way for long. No
wonder that one day there was rebellion in the mine of don
Manuel. His wife escaped, but don Manuel was slain and the
mine destroyed. The Indian laborers left for their homes.

Doña María then received word that the mine was abandoned and that it seemed to be safe once more. She came
back and found all the treasures untouched, in the same
hiding-places where they had been left. She buried her husband and then thought of working the mine again.

She should have been easily satisfied for the rest of her
life with the silver and the gold that had been piled up during the last years, under the management of don Manuel.
On seeing this bullion before her, however, she was seized
by a mania of grandeur. Hailing from a poor family in a
provincial town of Spain, she suddenly imagined herself
returning to her native country the richest woman in the
world. She was still young and agreeable to look upon. Coming home with unheard-of riches at her command, she could
buy the most ancient and beautiful castles in Spain, and she
could select for her husband a member of some noble family, perhaps even a duke. She might become a member of
the court of the mighty King of Spain, or even lady-in-
waiting to Her Majesty the Queen. She could show the
folks at home what a poor girl from a poor family such as
hers could achieve in life if possessed of intelligence. Why,
the daughters of Spanish grandees had married princes of the
Aztecs, of the Tarascans, of the Peruvians. Then why should
not she, being of pure Spanish blood, marry a Spanish
marquis?

From the moment when that idea took possession of her, she became a changed woman. A dormant business instinct in her awakened and made her do things she would never before have dreamed of doing. She began to consider how much half a dozen castles in Spain might cost; how much a duke might spend during his lifetime; how much it would cost to keep up all these castles, including an army of servants, the best horses, elegant carriages, life at court, journeys to France and Italy, and all that was essential for a really great noblewoman married to a pauperized duke or marquis. It reached a fantastic sum. She included the taxes and the special donations to the church she would have to make to be left in peace by that mighty institution. Included in these donations also was a cathedral to be built near the mine and the resting-place of her husband. After she had summed up the whole amount, she decided to double it so as to be on the safe side and to cover any mistake she might have made in her calculations. It came to a figure which, when written down, was almost a foot long. Yet she was not afraid of this figure, for she was convinced that she could have it inside a certain length of time, because the mine seemed to contain unlimited riches.

6

There followed truly hard years in which she had to live and battle for the goal she had set for herself. Far from civilization, far from even the smallest comfort, she was at her post day and night. She knew no rest or fatigue. Whenever she felt as though she would break down, she only had to think of the duke and of the castles in Spain, and back came all her strength.

Doubtless she faced the conditions confronting her far better than her husband ever was able to do. She got along with the laborers without paying them much higher wages than had her husband. She was robust in her way, tenacious, and even hypnotic when dealing with men. If with force she could not make men do what she wanted them to do, then she tried all sorts of diplomacy, and always won them over to her will. She could laugh like a jolly drunken coach-driver; she could weep heart-rendingly when it seemed expedient; and she could swear like a highwayman. If nothing else would do, she could pray and preach so convincingly that begging monks would have given her their last highly treasured gold pieces.

She paid her men just enough so that they had always a little more than they needed, and for that they stayed on.

It was not alone the problems concerning the workingmen that she had to solve day in, day out. The mine was forever in danger of being robbed by gangs of bandits composed of escaped convicts, murderers at large, deserters from the army, and all sorts of soldiers of fortune and adventurers. Hordes of criminals such as the world has not seen since, and of the scum of the towns, swarmed the country—mestizos, Indians, and white outlaws and outcasts. It was the time when, owing to the American and the French revolutions, the power of Spain on the American continents began to totter, and in consequence of that all sound economic conditions began to break up, for rebirth of political and economic conditions was in sight.

From these hordes of outlaws doña María was never secure, and she had to use all kinds of tricks and camouflage to keep them from finding the treasure. When they came upon the mine, as happened at times, she had to pretend to be the poorest of human beings under heaven, working like a slave, not for her own profit, but to atone for a horrible sin she had committed against the church, to conciliate which she had to labor hard to build a cathedral.

Finally there came a time when doña María was overcome by such a longing for her native land, for a clean house, for a pretty kitchen, for a beautiful bedroom and a soft bed with a male companion in it, and for surroundings free from mosquitoes, fever, polluted water, snakes, and other horrors that she knew she could stand this life no longer. She felt she had to leave now or she would go insane. She wanted to see the faces of Christians again instead of Indians, of whom she now frequently became really afraid, as a man quite suddenly may become afraid of his great Dane for no particular reason whatever. She was longing to speak to decent persons of her own race in an uncorrupted language; she wanted to be caressed by someone she loved; she wanted to dress like the women she was thinking of who still lived in cities.

All this came over her so suddenly and unexpectedly that she had no time to collect her thoughts or to analyze her feelings as she had done formerly. She found she no longer had the strength to conquer these desires. She knew she had to go or she would do something foolish—perhaps give herself to one of the Indians or kill herself or kill all the men or take out all the bullion and scatter it about.

She made a final balance of her treasure and found that it would be enough for whatever life she wanted to lead in Spain. She could not even wait a week more so as to plan the homeward trip carefully.

7

Lately doña María had hired two Spanish soldiers who had come this way and who either had deserted or had been discharged. With the help of these two men she formed a special guard composed of mestizos and of Indians and fairly well armed. This guard had become necessary owing to the increase in the number of bandits roaming the country.

One of the Spanish soldiers was made captain of the day, the other captain of the night. This guard proved valuable now that doña María had decided to break camp, pack up, and take her riches to Mexico City and from there to good old Spain. The transport would have been practically impossible without an armed convoy.

The metal, of which about one sixth was gold, the rest silver, had been properly smelted and was in bars. In this form it was packed away in crates and boxes and even in baskets made by the Indians. The value of the treasure may be figured from the fact that about one hundred and thirty strong mules were needed to carry the metal alone.

8

The pack-train, accompanied by thirty-five men, of whom twenty were well armed, got under way. They had to march nearly fourteen hundred miles from the mine to the capital, through deserts, across rivers and ravines, and up ten thousand feet across the high passes of the Sierra Madre. They had to hew their way through jungles and virgin forests. They passed through the Tierra Caliente—that is, the tropical districts of the lower regions of the country. They climbed over the stormy and ice-cold ridges of the highest ranges of the Sierra and down again to the tropics. The transport was threatened by heavy tropical rains and cloudbursts; and while traversing long stretches of deserts and rocky lowlands, the beasts almost died of thirst.

The transport in itself was lively enough. Doña María was never short of excitement. Mules with their packs broke away and had to be caught; others fell and were killed, and at times their packs had to be hauled up from the depths of a ravine. Other beasts were drowned, and their packs had to be fished out of the torrents of a river. There was never a day without its own peculiar adventure.

An evening came when doña María found the camp stirred up. She investigated and saw that one of the Spanish captains was making trouble.

He strode up to doña María. "Now, listen here," he said, "and listen well, lady. Will you marry me or not? And no perhaps, if you know what is good for you."

"I marry you? You? A stinking highwayman? I marry such a god-damned son of a bitch? Marry you?"

"All right, hussy," the man said; "I can easily get a greater beauty. I can take it all very well without you being thrown in like a dry bone."

"What can you, cabrón and son of a dog, take without me, you stinking coyote?"

"I mean, of course," the Spaniard explained, "I can take, without marrying you, all that is in the packs."

"Oh, can you? Is that so? Well, you've made yourself clear. Thanks for the notice."

The Spaniard grinned at her. He waved his right hand and drew doña María's attention to where the men were camped. "Look at that, fine lady. Perhaps now you are ready to go to church with me and after that to bed. Or before, just as you say, dear. I'll give you just one hour to find out that you are really in love with me. I don't need you, see? But I'll take you just for your own sake."

"Why wait an hour? I am not used to waiting." Doña María had not lost her bearings. "Fine work you have done, you skunk; I admit that and I admire your courage. I like that type of yours."

She looked toward the camp and saw the other captain tied to a tree, and all the Indians bound with ropes and lying helpless on the ground. The mestizos alone were standing up. It was these mestizos whom the Spaniard had won over to his side by promising a rich cut of the booty.

"Yes," doña María repeated, "yes, fine work indeed! You've done a very good job."

"And that means you will come to reason, my fine lady," the Spaniard suggested. "I hope you won't delay any longer."

"Right you are, you god-damned devil. I won't delay any longer." Doña María said this very quietly. She stepped close to one of the many saddles lying on the ground and with a quick move she gripped one of the heavy mule-whips. Before the Spaniard realized what she was doing, she lashed him such a terrific blow across his face that he staggered back and fell, covering his eyes and moaning. With the speed of lightning she gave his face half a dozen lashes so mercilessly that he rolled over as if blind and crawled away, covering his head and his face with one arm, using the other to help him up and out of the blows.

This was only the beginning. The mestizos were so stunned by what they had just seen that they did not try to run away. Before they had time to come to their senses, the whip swept across their faces. Those who did not drop to the ground ran away, hiding their heads in their arms. Not for an instant did they think of attacking the raging woman. By the time they felt safe enough to go back, doña María had cut the bonds of the Spaniard who was tied to the tree and had handed him a knife to free all the Indians that had been faithful to their mistress.

The Indians lost no time getting their horses and lassoing the mestizos trying to escape.

Doña María lined them up with the treacherous captain in front.

"Hey, you dirty cabrón, chingue tu matrícula y abuela," she yelled at him. "What did you say? Didn't you propose to marry me? And didn't I tell you that you will be in hell

before I would even think of taking you? Hang that god-
damned funking cabrón and make a good job of it. Let me
see how he sticks out his blasphemous tongue. Up with
him!"

While he was swinging from the tree, doña María shouted
at the mutinous mestizos: "And you, you funking pus-
covered dogs of swine, it surely would do my sore eyes
good to see you all dangling from the branches, too. What
the hell shall I do with you? Peel off your stinking leather
by tying you to the tails of horses and letting the Indians ride
them, and after that hang you, hang all of you? I'll get a
reward from the crown for doing the job for the hangman
you escaped. All right, you stinking scoundrels, I'll show
you mercy, as I surely hope to receive mercy from the Most
Holy Virgin on my last day. I shall leave a hole by which
you may escape. Sooner or later you will run straight into
the hangman's noose anyhow, no worry about that. I won't
spoil his earnings; maybe has a big family to feed. But make
no mistake, if I ever catch any one of you again playing
your nasty damned tricks against me, I tell you that you will
rather wish you had been tortured by the Holy Inquisition
instead of by me, you sons of lousy—well, you know your
mothers better than I can imagine them. And that's that.
Get to work. Hey, wait a minute. You don't have to stay
here with me. I can do without you. But there will be no
wages if you leave. If you wish to stay on I will give each
one of you the horse he has been riding, and you may each
keep the pistol received from me, and the saddles. And,
maybe—I say maybe—a bonus in cash, outside your wages.
Now to work! Saddles mended and the mules doctored!
Hustle up!"

The men went off quietly.

"Don't you dare to cut down that hanging devil," she
yelled after two of the gang who wanted to let the corpse

down from the tree. "Leave his carcass to the buzzards. His soul is already in hell."

When the mestizos were all busy about the packs, mending broken saddles, curing the sore backs of the mules, stuffing with grass the pads of the pack-saddles, and cooking their meals, doña María called the Spaniard who had been faithful. Whether he would still be loyal to her tomorrow or next week she did not know. He might get it into his head to try it next time for himself, avoiding the mistakes the other had made. He was hardly better than the hanged captain. He had only missed his chance this time.

Doña María's firm handling of the mutiny had doubtless made a strong impression upon him. But doña María was a woman and he might, just because of that fact, try the same trick again and come out better, knowing her tricks. After all, he had the Indians on his side.

Doña María understood the situation very well. She knew that she could not trust him. She had good reasons for trying to conciliate the mestizos by making them gifts they had never expected. It was now the strong point in her diplomacy to create two parties, each hating the other. In this way she could always have one party on her side, playing it against the other. She considered which of the mestizos she would make captain of his group so as to have it under better command. The troop that was on duty during the night guarding the camp against bandits or rebellious Indians could easily overpower her and all the rest of the men, kill them all and make off with the goods. Under such conditions it took the brains of a great leader to bring the transport to its destination.

She called for the captain. "What is your name, hombre?"

"Ruego Padilla, doña María, Ruego Padilla, su muy humilde servidor. I am your humble servant, doña María, at your very kind command."

"Bien, don Ruego." Doña María laid a slight stress on the "don." Ruego was taken in. He and his hanged partner had heretofore never been addressed by doña María in any other way than "Hombre, hey!" or "Tú, ven acá!" He felt like a soldier decorated in front of his fellows, who would never amount to anything.

"Very well, don Ruego," doña María spoke up. "I have not been blind to your great abilities. You behaved like a real nobleman, a brave caballero and a true and honest protector of a defenseless woman. I admire you for what you have done and the way you did it." She gave him a smile.

The fact was, of course, that he had done nothing in particular. He had been taken by surprise by the other captain, and with the help of a couple of mestizos had been tied to the tree, kicked in the ribs, and left to look at what was going to happen in the camp. Had it not been for the courage of doña María, he would now have to serve his former partner or hang from a tree.

Doña María knew this very well, but she ignored the truth and made him believe that she thought he had fought like a lion to protect her. This flattered him immensely.

Yet doña María had only begun to play her game to make sure of her safety for the rest of the march.

"Yes, as I said, don Ruego, you behaved like a true Spanish nobleman. When we are in the capital I shall reward you as you deserve. I shall give you—" she was about to say the mule with the whole pack on its back, but she recovered in time from this exaggerated generosity and continued: "I shall give you the right pack of that mule over there, and the Indians of your troop shall divide among themselves the left pack of that same mule. Those damned robbers, those funking mestizos, if they behave well from now on, shall each receive a bonus of one fourth of what the faithful Indians shall have. Of course, don Ruego, the horse you are riding, and the pistol and the rifle you carry, shall be yours as a token from me; and the Indians shall have their ponies and their pistols."

"Muchas gracias, doña María, I kiss your feet," Ruego said, kissing her hand, and then added: "May I, with your very kind permission, now go to look after the work?"

"You are handsome, Ruego. Do you know that? I never noticed that before." She said this with a true feminine smile, looking at him with narrowed eyes. "Yes, you are handsome and very strong. Strange that I never noted you before, Ruego." She gave him another smile. "Let's talk this over, Ruego, when we are in the capital. You know this is no time nor place to talk of such things."

Ruego snaked his body from his feet up as if he wished to wind himself into the form of a corkscrew; had he been covered with feathers one might have thought him a turkey at coupling-time.

"Look after the men and see that they are doing their work properly, don Ruego. You are now the mayordomo here and in charge of everything, the only man I can perfectly rely on."

"Yes, doña María, por la Santísima you can, by the Holiest Virgin you surely can, and once more, mil gracias for your kindness."

Doña María turned round and went to her little tent. "What brains a man has!" she said to herself.

9

The mutiny was quashed. There was no other similar incident the rest of the way. Ruego did his part as doña María expected him to. Any new uneasiness among the men could now, with the help of Ruego, be quelled at its first sign.

Doña María had, in fact, never thought of any sort of rebellion in her own camp. There were other problems which she had taken into account. The nearer she came to more populated regions of the country, the less safe became the roads. Hordes of bandits, footpads, deserters from the army and from ships, escaped convicts, were practically everywhere. The power of the Spanish rule in Latin America was inevitably breaking to pieces. Since this rule had been nothing short of dictatorship and tyranny, conditions were as they always and everywhere are when a dictatorship is nearing its inglorious end. Dictatorships do not and cannot allow people to think politically or economically for themselves, and so when a dictatorship is tumbling, people are in no way prepared to meet the changed conditions, and chaos is the result. Here authorities were so hard pressed from all sides and from all quarters that they no longer could cope with the growing unrest all over the country.

Day and night doña María lived in constant fear of being attacked, robbed, and murdered. Every mule and every pack on the backs of the animals had to be guarded. There were days when the whole train made hardly ten miles, and even these ten miles under difficulties which seemed impossible to overcome.

During this journey doña María lived through a period still more trying than that at the mine. There she could not remember any day when she had felt happy and safe. She had never felt sure of her treasures. Always in fear, always worrying, and at night plagued by nightmares and terrible dreams. She could not recall a night of sound and refreshing sleep. And during the daytime she was hunted by worries and fears even worse.

What had kept her spirits up during these years was the thought of the future. In imagination she could see herself walking by the side of her duke to the throne of the king

and there curtsying and having the honor of kissing the
heavy ring on the finger of His Most Holy Majesty.

10

The great moment finally arrived. The transport reached
Mexico City without a single bar of the precious metal lost.

Hardly had she reached her destination when the fame of
her riches spread all over the city. The news of the arrival
of the richest woman in the Spanish empire came even to the
ears of the viceroy, the most powerful person in New Spain.
Doña María was honored with an invitation to a private
audience with the viceroy which lasted, as the whole city
noted with amazement, more than an hour.

Her gratitude knew no limits when this high personage
promised that her treasures would be well taken care of in
the vaults of the king's own treasury, the safest place in
New Spain, safer than the vaults of the Bank of England in
those times. Guarded by the whole Spanish colonial army
garrisoned in the city and under the personal guarantee of
the viceroy himself. In these vaults her treasures could rest
until they were transported under the vigilance of special
troops of the king to the port of Veracruz to be shipped
from there to Spain. Doña María, overwhelmed by such
generosity, promised the viceroy a gift in cash which even
a viceroy of New Spain could verily call most princely.

Doña María paid off her men in full, giving them even
more than she had promised for faithful service, and discharged them honorably. This done, she went to the best
hotel in the city to take up quarters fit for a queen.

Now, at last, she could sit down to a decent meal for the
first time in many years. After so many hardships and sorrows she could at last eat peacefully and with gusto.

Then, after a most enjoyable supper, she lay down in the

finest and softest bed to the sweetest slumber she had had in long, dreary years. Upon awakening she could think of finer, sweeter, more womanly things, and of a handsome duke, perhaps a marqués.

But now something happened that doña María in all her calculations had never foreseen.

Her treasures did not disappear, they were not stolen from the vaults of the king's treasury. Something else disappeared and was never seen again or heard of.

And this was: doña María herself. She lay down in her queenly bed, but since she did so, no one has ever seen her or heard of her. She disappeared mysteriously, and nobody knew what had become of her.

But while no one knew anything about doña María, everyone in New Spain knew that the riches of doña María had not disappeared, but were safely in the possession of one supposed to know better what to do with them than a foolish woman who thought that nobility stands for honesty.

11

When Howard had ended his story, he added: "I wanted to tell you this tale to show you that to find gold and lift it out of the earth is not the whole thing. The gold has to be shipped. And shipping it is more precarious than digging and washing it. You may have a heap of it right before you and still not know if you can buy a cup of coffee and a hamburger."

"Isn't there any chance to find out where the mine was?" Curtin asked. "That woman surely didn't take out all that was in it."

"No, she didn't." Howard made a face at Curtin. "There is much left, even today, only you are late as always, Curty. The mine is worked by an American company, and it has yielded ten times more than doña María ever succeeded in taking out of it. You can easily find the mine, and it seems to be inexhaustible. Its name is the Doña María Mine, and it is located near Huacal. If you wish, you may go up and ask for a job. Maybe you can land one. If you are lucky, they may pay you forty a week. Just try."

12

For a good while the men sat in silence by the fire. Then they stood up, stretched their legs, yawned, and made ready to check in.

"That story is more than a hundred years old." Lacaud suddenly broke the silence.

"Has anybody around here said it isn't?" Dobbs sneered.

"Certainly not," Lacaud answered. "But I know a good story about a rich gold mine which is only two years old, and just as good or better."

"Tell it to your grandmother," Dobbs said. "We don't want any of your good stories, even if they're only a week old. They're stale already when you open your mouth. Better not say a word. What is it you are? Oh, yes, an eterner, isn't it?"

"A what?" Lacaud looked at him with wide-open eyes.

"Aw, nothing, baloney. Leave me in peace."

"Don't listen to him, Laky." Howard tried to calm Lacaud. "You mustn't take that Dobby guy seriously. Can't you see that he was born crosswise? He's still suffering from it. That's the trouble with him. If you hand him a double cut of apple pie with sweet cream he'll scoff at you and ask why you didn't give him pumpkin pie. That's him."

"Oh, you mugs, you make me sick, all of you." Dobbs made a rather dirty gesture and went to the tent, leaving the others by the fire.

17

The next day, the last the partners meant to spend here, found them so excited that they hardly could eat their breakfast. Everything was ready for the homeward trip.

They crawled into their special hiding-places and brought forth their earnings to be packed up. The goods looked poor enough in their present state. Small grains, dirty-looking sand, gray dust, wrapped in old rags and tied up with string. Each of the partners had quite a number of these bundles. The problem was to pack them well away between the dried hides so that any examination of the packs by authorities or by bandits would not reveal them. By doing this the partners hoped that they could bring it all safely to town. The main thing was to have the packs at the nearest depot where they could take the train back to the port. Once on the train, there would be little danger.

When the packs were ready, Dobbs and Curtin went hunting to get sufficient meat for the trip. Howard stayed in the camp to make pack-saddles and overhaul the straps and ropes so as to avoid breakage and delays on the road.

Lacaud had, as usual, gone his own way. He was roaming over the mountain, crawling through underbrush, scratching the ground, and examining it with a lens. He carried also a little bottle with acid in it with which he frequently made tests of the soil he dug out from under rocks. At times he went with a bagful of sand down to the brook to wash it.

Curtin thought better of Lacaud than did Dobbs, who, whenever he thought it opportune, ridiculed him. Howard rather liked him. One day he said to Curtin: "He knows what he wants, that guy does. Anyhow, I don't think he will ever find anything worth while around here."

"Suppose he does." Curtin wanted to know what they would do if this should happen.

"Even if he should bring me a piece big as a walnut, I wouldn't stay on," Howard answered. "I'm through here."

"Believe me, brother, me too," Curtin responded. "I wouldn't stay on for a pound pure. I only wonder what Dobbs would do."

"I suppose he would throw his lot in with that Arizona guy. He's a bit too greedy, Dobby is. That's his only fault. Otherwise he's a regular guy."

This talk had taken place two days before. Howard was just thinking about it when Dobbs and Curtin returned with two wild turkeys and a good-sized wild pig.

The old man smiled approvingly. "Well, boys, this will last us the whole trip. You know man can live for a long time on nothing but meat and be just as healthy as a well-fed elephant. I think we can even leave part of our provisions for this Lacaud mug."

2

That evening as they sat by the fire roasting the pig, Curtin said to Lacaud: "I presume you mean to stay here, Laky?"

"I certainly do. I'm not through yet."

"Have you found anything yet?" Dobbs asked.

"Nothing of much value so far. But I'm hopeful."

"That's fine. Stay that way." Dobbs seemed to be pleased that Lacaud had again searched in vain. "Fine, I say. Being hopeful is always a fine thing. Smells after paradise. You know that's also hope, all hope. Count me out, brother."

"I didn't mean to count you in."

"Don't you get fresh around here. We're still here, and as long as we're around, you are still a guest, and not so very welcome either. Get that straight, pal of mine."

"Dobby, what the hell is up with you?" Howard watched him with curiosity. "I've never seen you this way. You behave like a little child."

"I don't like to be bossed, that's all. Never liked it."

"But, man on earth," Howard spoke in his fatherly way, "nobody is bossing you. You must be feeling ants running wild on your skin."

This was their last night in the camp.

3

Before sunrise the three partners were ready to march. Lacaud was cooking his breakfast.

Howard went over to him, shook hands, and said: "Well, comrade in the wars, we're on our way. Now, look here; we've left you coffee, some tea, quite a bit of salt and pepper, sugar, and here is a huge piece of a fat pig we got yesterday. You may need it. We don't want to carry more than we'll need on our way. The burros have quite a load, and part of the packs we have to carry on our own backs, which will be hard enough on us when we're making the steep trails."

"Thanks a lot. You've been awfully good to me all the time, Mr. Howard. Well, again, thanks for everything. And all the luck on your way back home!"

"Over there you'll find a good piece of canvas. You're welcome to it. I see that you have only a little scout's tent;

that's rather uncomfortable, especially during the heavy rains."

"Hey, old man," Dobbs was yelling, "are you coming or are you coming? Just tell us. Hell of an old woman's chatter; why the devil don't you marry him and be happy ever after?"

"Coming," Howard shouted. Then, lowering his voice, he said to Lacaud: "I hope you find what you are looking for."

"Thanks for wishing me luck. I sure will; I mean I sure shall find the right thing. I know I am on the right track. Of course, it may be a week longer, or two weeks, but trust me, friend, I'm on the right track, and no mistake about it."

At this moment Dobbs and Curtin returned, leaving the burros at the entrance to the path.

"Sorry," Curtin said to Lacaud, shaking his hand, "I forgot to say good-by. I didn't see you, it was too dark. Excuse me, old feller. But see, I was busy and really quite a bit excited. Want some tobacco? Take more, I have plenty. We'll soon be at the depot or passing through a village where we can buy as much as we want."

Dobbs slapped Lacaud on the back. "Lonely, that's what you're going to be. By the way, I noticed you use the same cartridges for your shotgun that I do. Have a dozen. I can spare them. Well, to make it a round sum, take ten more. We won't do much hunting on our way, so we won't miss them at all. I hate to carry them on my back. Well, good-by and forget what I've said. I didn't mean it, anyhow. It was just for fun, you know that. I sure hope you make that million here which we didn't make. Some guys have all the luck. By-by, old boy."

Then they had to hurry after the burros, as they had wandered off already.

Lacaud, left alone, stood for a while and watched the partners leave the camp and disappear into the bushes.

For a good while he heard them calling from far off, trying to get the burros properly on their way. The voices then faded slowly out. A heavy stillness settled upon the camp.

Lacaud became aware of it. He turned toward the fire, pushed a few sticks into it with his boots, and said aloud: "A pity!"

The first rays of the sun gilded the heads of the rocks as Lacaud heard the last forlorn cry from one of the partners driving on the burros.

18

1

The partners went a long way round the village where Curtin used to buy provisions. It was better to let the villagers believe him still up in the mountains. Whenever it could be done, they avoided villages, traveling, wherever possible, isolated trails. The less they were seen, the less apt they were to be molested.

They had very little cash about them. Upon reaching the station they would sell the burros, the tools, and even the hides, which would give them more than sufficient money to buy second-class railroad tickets to the port.

Most of the trails led naturally into villages, and so it frequently happened that they found themselves unexpectedly at the first houses of a village which they had not been able to see before, owing to the woods, hills, or curves. Turning back when in sight of the houses would have aroused suspicion, so they had to go on into the heart of the village, where one of them usually went into the general store and bought something—cigarettes, a box of matches, a can of sardines, sugar, or salt. Here he spoke a few words to the storekeeper and to bystanders, so as to let everybody know that the three had no cause to hide their faces.

2

On the third day they found themselves, about noon, in

a village which they would have avoided had it been a matter of their own choice. On reaching the plaza they saw four Mexicans standing in front of an adobe house. Three of them carried guns, yet they did not look like bandits.

"Now we're caught," Dobbs said to Howard. "That's police."

"Seems so."

Dobbs stopped the burros as if to try to lead them through the village some other way. Curtin marched behind the last animal.

"You'd better not make any foolish move," Howard warned Dobbs. "If we arouse suspicion now, we're in for it. Let's go straight on. All they can do is search us and hold us for taxes and for dodging the permit."

"Exactly! And that may cost us everything we have, even the burros."

Curtin came up with the last pair of beasts. "What is this man doing there—I mean the man with specs and no gun?"

This bespectacled man was standing in the portico of the humble house, discussing something with a few residents gathered around him. There was a very small table set up in the portico. Spread on this table was a white cotton cloth, none too clean.

"I figure," Howard said, "this guy is a special commissioner of the gov'ment—the federal government, I mean. Hell, I can't quite make out what he wants."

"Looks to me as if he's questioning the villagers," Dobbs said. "I hope he isn't asking them any questions about us."

"What of it? It's too late now, anyhow." Curtin kicked a burro nibbling at the grass of the plaza.

"All right, let's pretend we don't mind." Howard lighted his pipe to cover his nervousness.

The Mexican officials, occupied with the little crowd of villagers at the house, had taken no notice of the pack-train.

Pack-trains of burros or mules passing through the villages on the slopes of the Sierra Madre are no novelty. The three partners reached the center of the square before any of the officials noticed them. Then one said a few words to his companions, and all of them looked at the partners, who went on their way. As they neared the opposite end of the plaza, one of the officials stepped out of the portico, walked a few strides toward the passing train, and called: " 'ello there, caballeros, un momento, por favor!"

"Good night, now we are finished," Dobbs said, and swore.

"Wait here," Howard ordered. "I'll go over alone first and see what they want. You stay here with the burros. Maybe I can square things with them better alone. I can make them think I'm a Baptist preacher from an abandoned mining town."

"He's right as always, the old man is," Curtin admitted. "That's why I'd never try to play poker with him. Okay, go over and give them a good look at your honest face and tell them the story of Jonah in the whale or maybe Elijah flying a plane up to heaven."

Howard crossed the plaza and walked over to the officials. "Buenas días, señores. What can I do for you? Qué puedo ofrecerle?"

"Lots you can, señor," one of them answered. "You come from the mountains, señores?"

"Yes, we do. And it's a god-damned hard journey. We've been on a hunting-trip. Got quite a few hides, and we hope to get a good price in San Luis Potosí."

"Are you all vaccinated?"

"Are we what?"

"I mean have you got with you your certificado de vacunación, your vaccination certificate? It's the law that everybody in the republic has to have been vaccinated inside of the last five years to prevent smallpox epidemics."

"Oh, caballeros, we were vaccinated back home when still kids. But, of course, we don't carry our vaccination papers with us."

"Of course not, gentlemen, and who does? Not even I do." The officer laughed. So did all the other officials. "You see, we are the Federal Health Commission, sent out by the government to vaccinate everyone, especially the Indians, who suffer most from the smallpox. It's a hard task for us. They run away from us whenever we come to a village. They are afraid. We'd have to bring along a whole regiment of soldiers to catch them. They hide in the mountains and in the bush and don't go back to their homes until we have left the district."

"Yes," said another official, "look here at my face, all scratched up by women who defended their babies whom we wanted to vaccinate. But you know our country. Look at the thousands who have lost their eyesight on account of the ravages caused by smallpox epidemics. Look at the thousands and hundreds of thousands of pretty girls and women whose faces are scarred."

"And when we come to these people to help them," another of the officials broke in, "they fight us and even stone us as if we were their greatest enemies and not, as we really are, their best friends. They don't have to pay a cent. Everything is done without any charge. The government only wishes to save them."

Now the man with the eyeglasses spoke up. "See here, my good friend, I know you and your compañeros over there are all vaccinated. But we would like you to do us a great favor. Let your friends come over here voluntarily and get vaccinated once more, please. What we need is to show all these ignorant people that you, white men, are not afraid of what we are doing and that you come to get the scratch as if you were going to a dance. In all those huts behind the saplings there are families watching us. We have been here four days, offering vaccination for nothing and persuading people to come and take it. What makes things worse for us, the church is set against vaccination because it was not ordered by the Lord, just as this same church is against educating the children, because they might read books written against the church and write sinful love-letters. Well, you know all this without my telling you more about it. Now, won't you, please, help us?"

"Why not? Of course," Howard replied. "We are pleased to help you and the government."

"I thought so when I saw you coming," the doctor said. He laid before Howard his book with blanks. "Now, just write your name and your age on this line. After the vaccination you receive this slip, which is good for the next five years. If officials at a railroad station or in a town bother you about vaccination, all you have to do is just show them this slip. All right, let's have your left arm and clean first with alcohol. Okay, friend, there are the few scratches."

"Gracias, doctor." Howard meant his thanks in more than one way.

"Now, please, tell your friends when they come over here to roll up the sleeve of their left arm while crossing the plaza so that the people watching from their huts can see what they are doing and that they are not a bit afraid of the medicine. We'll put this table farther out in the open to make it a great show. To have you three white men, Americans, coming here of your own free will to get the scratch, or the medicine, as these Indians call it, is a great help to us. They'll see that we don't mean to poison them, and they'll have more confidence in our work. So, please, let your friends put on a great show for the benefit of the villagers. Thank you, and have a pleasant trip home."

"Gee, I got scared," Dobbs said when Howard returned

to the waiting train. "Seeing that feller take out a book and make you scribble in it, I was sure everything was lost. Huh, of course we'll make them a great circus. Just watch me, how I handle a big show."

So Dobbs and Curtin rolled up their sleeves and shouted in Spanish from where they were: "Sí, doctor, what a pleasure to get that sweet vacuna in our arms! We've been waiting for it for ten years and couldn't get it. In town the doctors charged us fifteen pesos for each little scratch, and you give it away for nothing. Yes, we are coming."

As the officials had expected, the plan worked fine. The villagers, first mostly men and the bigger boys, came out and stood in the opening of their huts, watching the show Curtin and Dobbs were offering them. When Dobbs held his arm toward the doctor, he laughed out loud. Curtin whistled a jolly tune. Men and boys came closer to see the procedure. The doctor smiled and the officers persuaded one of the men standing nearest to come and have the same thing done to him. Curtin pushed him closer jokingly, as the man was still frightened. But after he had the few scratches and felt nothing, he pushed his two boys forward and ordered them to hold still and have it over. When the partners finally left the plaza, the officers were so busy that they had to line up the people waiting for their turn, and among them now there were already women offering the arms of their babies to the officers.

After passing the last hut of the village, Dobbs said with a laugh. "Hey, Curty, you're a funny mug."

"What the hell is so funny about me?"

"You see ghosts like an old woman. If you see a guy with a rusty gat on his hip, right away you think the goods are gone. Anyone could have told you that these guys didn't want anything from us. You could have seen that the guy with the specs was a doc. Couldn't you see that right away from the table with a white sheet spread out on it? What else could a table with a white sheet on it serve for?"

"You're telling me, wise mug!" Curtin grinned. "Anyhow, joke or no joke, I like it better this way."

"So do I," Howard threw in.

19

I

That night the partners pitched camp not far away from the village of Amapuli. An Indian meeting them on the trail had assured them that the next water was too far off to be reached before nightfall, so they decided to pass the night there by a brook, although it was still early in the afternoon.

While sitting by the fire cooking their supper, they were surprised to see four Indians on horseback coming into their camp. The visitors greeted them courteously and asked permission to sit down by the fire and rest a little.

"Ay, como no?" Howard answered. "Why not? It's a pleasure to have your company. No, no bother at all, caballeros. Feel quite at home, es su casa. Want to have some hot coffee with us?"

The coffee was accepted, and the four natives helped themselves, all drinking out of the same cup, which Curtin offered them. Dobbs offered his tobacco-pouch, which the men also accepted. They each took a pinch of tobacco and rolled it in corn leaves which they carried with them. In return they offered the partners tobacco of their own.

Silently they watched Howard and Dobbs roast their pork and cook their rice. Curtin was taking care of the burros.

Then, after a long wait, one of the Indians seemed ready at last to come to the point of their visit. It is not considered polite among them to make their wishes clear during the first half-hour.

"I presume," the speaker began, "you caballeros come from a far-away country, and I trust you will travel a long way from here. I think, and my compañeros think the same, that you are very clever, very intelligent, and highly educated men."

"Fairly." Howard took up their way of talking. "We can read books and also papers with all the news, and we can write letters and also count with written figures."

"Figures?"

"Yep, figures," Howard repeated. "To say it more plainly, ten, five, twenty—those are figures."

"But," said the Indian, "that would be only half of it. You can't say ten or twenty. You have to add what ten you mean, ten goats, or ten centavos, or ten horses. Ten alone means nothing."

"Tal vez, maybe you're right." Howard had never looked at figures this way.

For a quarter of an hour more the Indians watched the partners preparing their food.

Then the man spoke again: "You see, caballeros, it is like this. My boy fell into the water today. We fished him out soon enough. I do not think he is dead. I think he is not dead at all. But he simply won't come to, see? He can't move and he doesn't know it. He doesn't wake up. That's the whole trouble with him. Now, I understand you have read many books in which much is said about all the wisdom of doctors and medicine. And so I came with my dear friends here to find out if perhaps one of you, having read all the clever books written by great men, might know what is the matter with my boy who fell into the river, not very wide, but right now very deep."

"When did your son fall into the water? Was it yesterday?" Howard asked.

"No, señor, he fell into the water only today—this afternoon. But he does not wake up. When he did not come to and we no longer knew what to do, along came don Filberto, my friend here and neighbor. He is the man, you will remember, who met you today in the bush and whom you asked how far away the next water might be. So we thought that you might know what we can do to bring my son back to life."

Howard looked at the four Indians. Then he looked at the supper, now almost ready. And he said: "I will go with you, friends, and have a look at the boy. I don't know if I can do anything. But I'll do my best to help you."

The Indians stood up, politely took leave of the two remaining partners, and with Howard in their midst went to their little village. Howard had been given a horse, while the owner of the horse took his seat behind the saddle of one of the others.

It was a poor adobe house which they entered. A petate, a palm mat, was spread over the only table in the house, and on this mat the boy lay.

Howard examined him carefully. He lifted the boy's eyelids and held a lighted match before the eyes. Then he pressed his right ear against his heart. He put his hand against the upper part of the skull to see if it was still warm. Then he pressed the fingers and the toes of the youngster, watching to see if the pressed nails reddened quickly.

All the people assembled in the house seemed to expect that the American would now perform a great miracle such as raising the dead by sheer command. Howard stood for minutes silent, hesitating what treatment if any he should try first. "I will see if I can bring him back this way," he finally said.

There was little water coming from the body. The old man tried artificial respiration, something these Indians had never seen before. This treatment made a deep impression and added to the belief that Howard was a great medicine-man, even a magician. They looked at each other approvingly, and once more became convinced that those goddamned gringos could do things they had thought only God Himself could do.

Howard, examining the boy again after fifteen minutes of this work, was sure that he showed slight signs of life. He asked for a little mirror, and when he held it to the boy's mouth, he thought he could see a trace of mist on the glass. He had the women bring him all the hot water that was in the house and in the neighborhood and boil as much more as could be had. He got towels and made hot compresses to put on the boy's belly, and when they were in place he rubbed and slapped the patient's hands and feet. Then he forced his mouth open, pulled the tongue out as far as he could, and poured a teaspoonful of tequila into the mouth. Next he began to massage the heart. When he listened again with his ear close to the breast, the heart had begun to pump feebly. Howard could hear it very distinctly. And just then the boy began to cough.

Half of all this procedure, Howard knew, was unnecessary. He had gone through it merely to impress the Indians with his great wisdom, for he noted that the Indians were watching every move he made. He admitted to himself that the boy if left entirely alone might, perhaps, have come to just as well. Why he put on this show he could not explain. He had the feeling that the more he acted, the more these people would respect and admire him; though why, again, he should yearn for the admiration and respect of these poor folk he would not have been able to explain, even to himself.

All the people present considered that he had performed a miracle. Even now, when the boy opened his eyes and began to recognize his surroundings and his father and mother, the onlookers acted as if under a spell. They did not utter a word, but simply looked at the awakening boy and at Howard in awe.

When Howard had made sure that the boy was all right and that there would be no bad reaction he took his hat and said: "Buenas noches! Good night!" and went to the door. The father of the boy followed, shook hands, and muttered: "Muchas, muchas, mil gracias, señor, thousand thanks!" Then he returned to the table, where the boy was trying to sit up.

2

It was now pitch-dark. Howard had some difficulty in finding his way back to camp. No one accompanied him, but the faint light of the camp-fire flickering in the distance guided him.

"Well, what did the great doctor achieve?" Dobbs asked when the old man came near.

"It wasn't anything to speak of. Artificial respiration and some boy-scout tricks and he came along fine. I think it was more shock than drowning. He hadn't swallowed much water, as far as I could tell. Perhaps he was stunned when diving. Now what about my part of the supper? Any meat left?"

"Plenty. Don't you worry," Curtin laughed and heaped his plate.

3

Dawn saw the partners already on their march again. They wished to reach the village of Tominil, where they would try to cross the high passes of the Sierra.Madre.

At noon they stopped to give themselves and the animals a rest, as the sun was mercilessly hot.

They were just ready to pack up again when Curtin exclaimed: "Now what the devil is coming? Looks as if we have something on our heels."

"Where?" Dobbs asked. At the same moment he had caught sight of a group of Indians on horseback.

It was not long before they reached the partners, who recognized four of the men as the same who last night had come to their camp to ask for help. Two others Howard knew had been in the house when he had treated the boy.

The Indians greeted the travelers, and one of the men asked: "Señores, why did you leave our neighborhood so soon?"

Howard laughed. "We weren't running away, señores. The fact is we have to go to Durango, to attend to our business, which is very important."

"Business?" the father of the rescued boy questioned. "What is business, after all? Just hustle and worry. Business can wait. There is no business in this world which is urgent, señores. Urgent business is nothing but sheer imagination. Death finishes the most important and the most urgent business in a second. So what? There are more days coming, as long as there is a sun in the heavens. Every new day you can use to do business. Why just today? There is always a mañana, always a tomorrow, which is just as good as today. What's the difference between today and tomorrow? It's only imaginary. And so I say, señores, you cannot go. You cannot leave me like that. No, señor. You cannot leave me in debt to you. I invite you to stay with me. You rescued my boy from certain death. For having done this great service I should be damned and burn in hell for all eternity if I allowed you to go without first showing you my deep gratitude. What is more, all the people in the village would believe me a sinner and a devil if I did not reward you properly for what you have done for me and my family."

Dobbs pushed Curtin in the ribs and said in a low voice: "Seems to me a similar story to that told us by the old man the other day about the doctor who cured the eyes of the son of an Indian chief, and this time it's us that gets the benefit. Sure, that guy knows a lost gold mine he's going to offer us. I bet you."

"Keep quiet and let's listen first," Curtin said.

The Indian continued his speech. "You see, señores, the only way I can show you my gratitude is by inviting you to be my guests for at least two weeks."

Dobbs looked sour.

"No, señores, let's make it six weeks; that would be better. I have good milpas, very fine acres. Lots of corn. I have many goats and quite a number of sheep. I am not so poor as I may look. Each day I shall have a turkey roasted for you, and as many eggs and as much goat's milk and roast kid as you can eat. I have already ordered my wife to make you at least three times a week the very best tamales she can make. In fact, she has been hard at work since long before sunrise to prepare a great feast for you. You cannot well leave her now with all the good food cooked. She would die of shame, thinking you believe her a bad cook. She isn't; my wife is a great cook. I think she is the best cook for miles around."

"I thank you for your kindness, for your very great kindness indeed," Howard responded, falling in with the elaborate speech his would-be host had used. "To tell you the truth, I'm very sorry we can't stay on. We have to go to Durango. Unless I am in Durango inside of a week, I'll lose all my business."

"In this you are mistaken, my friend. You won't lose your business. And if you should, why, pick up another one. There is so much business in the world just waiting to be picked up. No use to hurry. All I can say is that you cannot

go like this. I have to pay you for your medicine. I haven't
any money. All I can offer is my house and my most sincere
hospitality. Sorry, my friend, I'm afraid I shall have to insist
that you stay with me at least six weeks. You will get a
good horse to ride on. You may go hunting and get more
hides. You haven't so many. We have the best game around
here. I will see the musicians tomorrow, and every Saturday
night we will have a dance. The prettiest girls will come
and be pleased to dance with you. I will make them, because
you are my guest. Why worry about your business? There
is only one business on earth, and that is to live and be
happy. What greater thing can you gain from life than
happiness?"

"I am extremely sorry, señor, but I cannot stay." Howard
had no means and no words with which to explain to these
simple men that business is the only real thing in life, that
it is heaven and paradise and all the happiness of a good
Rotarian. These Indians were still living in a semi-civilized
state, with little hope of improvement within the next hundred years. "No, honestly," he added, "I can't accept your
hospitality, much as I'd like to."

"Understand, caballeros," Dobbs cut in, "we can't stay
here. We can't, I say, we simply can't, and that's that;
there's no other way out."

"You'd better not try to come into our deal, young man,"
said the Indian, who took little notice of Dobbs and his
opinion. He again addressed Howard: "I don't accept re-
fusal, caballero. We have taken your help without question
and we accepted what you offered us. You cannot back out
now and refuse what we wish to offer you in return for
your service."

To get angry would not help. The partners felt that
there was no escape. Here were six mounted Indians with
a firm and unshakable idea of what they wanted. They were

determined to show their gratitude in their own way, and show it they would if it meant taking the partners to the village as prisoners.

At this stage of deadlock Curtin said: "Oiga, listen, friends, we want to talk this thing over among ourselves, if you don't mind. Will you please leave us alone for a minute?"

When they had stepped aside, Dobbs spoke up: "Look here, Howy, I don't think we can get out of this. They will take us along by force if we don't go. Now, the thing is, they want only you, you alone, not us two. That much is clear."

"Looks like."

"Okay. So I propose that you stay a few days and we go on. You may follow up later, meeting us in Durango."

"What about my packs?"

"You take them along with you," Curtin suggested.

Dobbs was against it. "That wouldn't be wise. They might, out of pure curiosity, search the packs, and if they discover what is in them they will rob you, perhaps kill you. You can never trust an Indian. No road would be safe for you traveling alone. You know that, old feller, don't you?"

"All right. What can I do? Spill it."

"I suggest we take it along with us, and, as I said, we would wait for you in Durango City. Or if you should stay longer, we might take the whole lot with us to the port and deposit it in your name in a bank there, in the Banking Company or in the Banco Nacional, just as you say."

After some further discussion they decided that this was the best suggestion, in fact the only one to consider under the circumstances which confronted them.

Curtin wrote out a receipt for so many bags of dust of approximately so much weight. He signed the receipt and so did Dobbs.

"I don't think it necessary for us to exchange receipts,"

Curtin explained, "yet something might befall one of us. On such a trip one isn't always sure of reaching his destination. If we can't wait for you in port, this receipt will give you the right to claim your portion, which we'll deposit with the Banking Company—you know that bank on the ground floor of the Southern? We will tell the manager that you hold the receipt. We'll leave with him our signatures to identify this receipt. Okay?"

"I guess that's really the best we can do. Agreed," Howard said. "You take, of course, all the burros along with you. These fellers will surely let me have a horse to ride to Durango. If lucky, I may catch up with you sooner than you expect."

"That would be fine. I hate to be separated from you like this." Curtin reached out his hand to shake. "Good luck. And hurry up to join us."

"I sure will."

"Good-by, old rascal." Dobbs shook hands with Howard. "Make it snappy. I'm feeling sort of lonely leaving you behind. I'll sure miss your preaching, and more so your hot-mamma stories. Well, as a dried-up hussy once told me in Sunday school, sometimes, in this sad life, we have to swallow disappointments. Nobody can help that. Have all the luck, old man!"

"And here is some good advice that might come in handy, Howy," Curtin said, laughing. "Don't you get mixed up with some of those Indian dames. They are often really smart, and also awfully pretty. Lots of them are. You know that, you old rider. And don't you come some day and tell me you've actually married a squaw. You know, quite a number of guys do it, and like it a lot. But don't tell me later I didn't warn you if anything goes wrong, you old bucker." Curtin slapped him on the back till the old man coughed.

Still coughing, he said: "Maybe, I will get me such a bronze-colored hot dame myself. I'm not so sure. They've got class, real class, if you know what I mean. And there's no hustling and worrying about them. They are easy to feed and easy to entertain. No taking them every night to the god-damned pictures and bridge-parties where they lose your hard-earned money, god-damn it. And no nagging either. I'll think it over, Curty. Maybe I am going to change my outlook on life. Well, have an easy trip, partners."

The burros had become restless. Dobbs and Curtin went after them, and the train was on its way.

Howard watched his two partners go down the trail. When he turned to the Indians, patiently waiting for him, his eyes looked watery.

He was given a horse to ride.

Shouting joyfully, they all rode off. Howard was led in triumph into the village, where all the people, old and young, were awaiting him and cheering him as though he had returned from some victory in foreign lands for the glory of this little village.

20

Curtin and Dobbs were not in good humor. The pass across the highest mountain range was still far off, and the trail leading to this high pass had become so difficult that the two partners became near senseless from desperation.

They no longer spoke to each other in the usual manner. They bellowed at each other, howled like wild beasts, and cursed themselves and the rest of the world for the hard job they had undertaken. And most bitterly of all they cursed the absent Howard. While they had to drive his burros, to load and unload his packs, and to take care of all his belongings, he was most probably now enjoying himself, with a pretty Indian hussy sitting on his knees and another brown wench hanging on his neck and before him a swell meal of roast turkey and a bottle of tequila. And here his two partners had to slave for him and die for him on that god-damned hell of a funking trail, put there by the Lord for no other reason than to make you suffer for all the dirty sins fifty generations of your forefathers committed.

"Why the hell did we offer to take along the packs of that son of a skunk? As if he couldn't take them by himself, or with the help of those god-damned Indians, who, of all the people in the world, had to come to get that god-damned boy of theirs out of hell, where he was already being well cared for and where he properly belonged!"

"And isn't it always his burros that, god-damn it, won't

march in line, and stray off and smash their packs against the trees, trying to get them off their funking backs?"

"He knew, that god-damned story-teller did, why he wanted us to take along his packs. They are the heaviest of all and the most carelessly packed. Gawd knows, his burros are the laziest that were ever born anywhere under heaven, and the most stubborn. Hell, how I wish they would break off the trail and drop down the three thousand feet of the gorge and crash their bones! What would I care? To hell with him and all he has!"

It was lucky for them that heaven was too high above to hear them and lay half a hundred broken trees across the trail and soak the narrow path with so much water that the burros would sink into the mud up to the saddles, so that for once they would learn what a really tough trail on the Sierra Madre is like when hell and heaven are against the traveler. What they encountered was in fact nothing, if you would ask a hard-boiled arriero whose business it is to bring pack-trains of mules across the Sierra Madre at any time of year.

Of course, it would have meant much to have one more man at hand on trails like this one. A pack which has come off the animal's back can only be properly replaced by two men, and while these two are loading, another man is needed to look after the rest of the pack-burros, so that they will not break loose and stray off and enter dead trails.

No sooner did the two realize that it was ridiculous to curse the old man than they started quarreling, and yelling and shouting at each other.

The burros did not mind, because they had more sense and besides had been raised on a better philosophical system.

All of a sudden Dobbs halted, wiped the sweat from his face with an angry gesture, and said: "I stop here for the night. If you want to go on, it's okay by me. Only leave my packs and my burros here. I am no god-damned nigger slave. Get me?"

"It's only three o'clock. We might still make four miles more." Curtin saw no reason for camping so early.

"No one has ordered you to camp here. If you want to march twenty miles more, what the hell do I care?" Dobbs stood before Curtin as if he were ready to spring at him.

"Ordered? You?" Curtin asked. "You don't mean to say you are the boss of this outfit?"

"Perhaps you are. Just say it. I'm waiting." Dobbs's face became redder.

"All right, if you can't do any more—"

"Can't do any more? What do you mean by that crack?" Dobbs seemed to go mad. "Don't make me laugh. I can do four times as much as a mug like you and kick half a dozen of your size both sides of your pants. Can't do any more? And how is your grandmother? It's simple; I don't want any more, if you must know, mug."

"What's the good of hollering?" Curtin stayed calm enough. "We've started; now we have to stick it out, like it or not. All right, then, let's camp here."

"That's what I said long ago. Here is water, and very good water. It's a good place for camping, isn't it?"

"Right you are. Not likely we'd find any water during the next three hours."

"So what's the arguing about?" Dobbs began to unload the burro standing next to him. Curtin came close and gave him a hand at the job.

The burros unloaded, quarreling started again. Who was to cook, who was to look for fuel, who was to care for the burros, who repair the pack-saddles? There had never been any disputing about these jobs as long as Howard had been with them. Now it seemed as if they had lost the capacity for sound and simple reasoning. They were overtired, their nerves quivering like telegraph wires in the open country. They couldn't agree any longer on who had to do this job and who that. When the meal was finally cooked and ready, Curtin found that he had done most of the work—three times his share. He didn't mind, and said nothing. He put up with Dobbs's bad humor. Something during the march today, the climate, the growing altitude, a fall, the hot sun, a sting from a reptile, a bite of an insect, a scratch of a poisonous thorn, whatever it was, must, so it appeared to Curtin, be responsible for Dobbs's strange behavior.

2

Eating usually conciliates people. So also here in the loneliness of the Sierra the meal Curtin and Dobbs had together softened their feelings toward each other. It calmed their nerves. They came to speak with less yelling and with more sense than they had done during the last six hours.

"I wonder what the old man is doing now," Curtin said.

"I'm sure he's having a swell time with these Indians," Dobbs replied. "His meal will be better than ours, sure."

At mention of the old man, Dobbs looked casually at Howard's packs, which lay close to where Dobbs was sitting and filling his pipe. For a minute his looks were fixed on these packs, and in his mind he tried to figure out how much they might be worth in dollars and cents.

Curtin misjudged Dobbs's expression, for he said: "Oh, I think we can manage his packs all right. This was the first day we had to handle everything without his help. Tomorrow it will be lots easier, once we get the real go of it and are used to being one hand short."

"How far from the railroad do you think we are now?" Dobbs asked.

"As the crow flies, it wouldn't be so far. Since we aren't

crows, it will take us quite some time. Days, perhaps a week more. These mountain trails make the way ten times longer, winding round and round and going up and down as if they would never end; and if in the evening you look behind, it seems as if you can almost spit at the place you left in the morning. The worst isn't over yet. One of the guys we met near the village told me we'll have stretches where we will hardly make six miles during the whole day, loading and unloading a dozen times when the animals can't take the steep ravines. I figure we can make the high pass in two days more. Then three or four days more to go before we actually reach the railroad. But it may be more still. Any sort of difficulties may come our way any time."

To this Dobbs said nothing. He stared into the fire. Then he filled his pipe once more and lighted it. It was as though he could not take his eyes off the packs; his glance wandered from the fire to them and back again very often.

Yet Curtin took no notice of it.

3

Unexpectedly Dobbs pushed Curtin in the ribs and laughed in a curious way.

Curtin felt uneasy. Something was wrong with Dobbs. He was not himself any longer. To cover his growing anxiety Curtin tried to laugh, his eyes resting on Dobbs's face.

As if keyed up by Curtin's nervous laugh, Dobbs broke out into bellowing laughter which made him almost lose his breath. Curtin became still more confused. He did not know what to make of it. "What's the joke? Won't you let me in on it, Dobby?"

"In on it? I should say I will." He roared with laughter and had to hold his belly.

"Well, spill it."

"Oh, sonny, my boy, isn't that too funny for words?" He had to stop for breath, for his laughter became hysterical.

"What's so funny?" Curtin's face was turning gray with anxiety. Dobbs acted no longer sane.

Dobbs said: "This old jackass of a boneheaded mug hands over all his pay to us and lets us go off with it like that." He snapped his fingers.

"I don't quite understand."

"But, man, can't you see? It's all ours now. We drag it off and where can he look for us? We don't go back to the port at all. Sabe? We go straight up north and leave that ass flat. Let him marry an Indian hussy. What do we care?"

Curtin was now all seriousness. "I simply can't get you, Dobby. What the hell are you talking about? You must be dreaming."

"Aw, don't be such a sap. Where did you grow up? Under the canvas of a revival show or what? Well, to make it plain to a dumbhead like you, we take the load and go off. What is there so very special about that? Nothing new to you, I should say."

"I begin to see through it now."

"Long distance, was it?" Dobbs giggled.

Curtin rose. He moved around as if to get his bearings. He could not believe his ears. There must be something wrong.

He came back to the fire, but did not squat down. He looked around, gazed up at the clear sky, and then said: "Now, get this straight, Dobby; if you mean to lift the goods of the old man, count me out. And what is more, I won't let you do it."

"And who else? Just come and tell pop."

"As I said, as long as I am around and on my feet, you won't take a single grain from the old man's pay. I think

I've made myself clear enough, or have I?"

Dobbs grinned. "Yes, you have, sweety. Sure you have. I can see very plainly what you mean. You want to take it all for yourself and cut me off. That's the meaning."

"No, that is not the meaning. I'm on the level with the old man exactly as I would be on the level with you if you weren't here."

Taking up his pouch, Dobbs filled another pipe. "Mebbe I don't need you at all. I can take it alone. I don't need no outside help, buddy." He laughed while lighting his pipe.

Curtin, still standing, looked Dobbs over from head to foot. "I signed that receipt."

"So did I. And what of it? I've signed many receipts in my life."

"Doubtless. I've signed lots of things too, which I forgot about as soon as the ink was dry. This case I think is different. The old man hasn't stolen the goods. They're his honestly earned property. That we know only too well. He didn't get that money by a lousy cowardly stick-up, or from the races, or by blackmailing, or by the help of loaded bones. He's worked like a slave, the old man has. And for him, old as he is, it was a harder task than for us, believe me. I may not respect many things in life, but I do respect most sincerely the money somebody has worked and slaved for honestly. And that's on the level."

"Hell, can your Bolshevik ideas. A soap-box always makes me sick. And to have to hear it even out here in the wilderness is the god-damned limit."

"No Bolshevik ideas at all, and you know that. Perhaps it's the aim of the Bolsheviks to see that a worker gets the full value of what he produces, and that no one tries to cheat a worker out of what is honestly coming to him. Anyway, put that out of the discussion. It's none of my business. And, Bolshevik or no Bolshevik, get this straight, partner:

I'm on the level, and as long as I'm around you don't even touch the inside of the old man's packs. That's that, and it's final."

Having said this, Curtin squatted down by the fire, took out his pipe, filled it, and puffed lustily. He soon looked as if he had forgotten the whole affair—as if it had been only another of the many silly talks they had had during the long months when there was never anything new to talk about and they talked only for the sake of talking.

Dobbs watched him for many minutes. Then he chuckled. "Uh-huh! You are a fine guy. I've always had my suspicions about you. Now I know that I've been right, brother. You can't befuddle me. Not me, smarty."

"What suspicions are you talking about?"

"Easy, my boy, hold it! Get this and weep. You can't hide anything from me, brother. I know that for some time you've had it in mind to bump me off at your earliest convenience and bury me somewhere out here in the bush like a dog, so that you can make off not only with the old man's stuff, but with mine into the bargain. Then having reached the port safely, you'll laugh like the devil to think how dumb the old man and I were not to have seen through your hellish schemes. I've known for a long time what was brewing. I'm wise to you, honey."

4

The pipe dropped out of Curtin's fingers. His eyes had widened as Dobbs talked. He couldn't think straight. His head ached and he felt dizzy in a strange way. When, after a while, he succeeded in getting command of his thoughts again, he saw for the first time a great opportunity to enrich himself as Dobbs had suggested. This struck him as alien because never before had he had any idea of the kind. He was in no way scrupulous in life. Far from being that, he could take without remorse anything that was easy to pick up. He knew how the big oil-magnates, the big financiers, the presidents of great corporations, and in particular the politicians, stole and robbed wherever there was an opportunity. Why should he, the little feller, the ordinary citizen, be honest if the big ones knew no scruples and no honesty, either in their business or in the affairs of the nation. And these great robbers sitting in easy chairs before huge mahogany tables, and those highwaymen speaking from the platforms of the conventions of the ruling parties, were the same people who in success stories and in the papers were praised as valuable citizens, the builders of the nation, the staunch upholders of our civilization and of our culture. What were decency and honesty after all? Everybody around him had a different opinion of what they meant.

Yet, from whatever angle he looked at the accusation Dobbs had made against him, he found it the dirtiest he could think of. There was no excuse for such a thing as Dobbs had proposed.

This brought him a new thought. If Dobbs could accuse his partner of such intentions, it was proof of Dobbs's shabby character, now revealed in full for the first time. If Dobbs had such thoughts, then Curtin must look out for his own safety. Dobbs would not hesitate to try to get for himself all that he accused Curtin of trying to get.

Curtin could now see that in the future he would have to fight constantly not only for his property, but for his very life. Realization of this dulled Curtin's eyes as he stared at the fire. He saw danger lurking, and he knew he could not elude it.

He was helpless, Curtin was. He had no means of protecting himself against Dobbs. For four or five, perhaps even six or seven days, they would still be alone together here in the mountains, wild, desolate, and forsaken as few other mountain regions in the world are. The two might meet somebody on the trails, but that would not mean security for Curtin. For a few pesos Dobbs could easily persuade anyone to take his side. If they met no one, so much the better for Dobbs. Curtin might pass one night on guard against Dobbs, but during the next night he would surely fall asleep and sleep harder than ever. Then Dobbs would not even need to waste a bullet on him. He could bind him tight or knock him cold and then dig him in. He need not even trouble to crush his head; he could just bury him alive if he wished.

5

There was only one way out of this danger. Curtin had to do to Dobbs what Dobbs had in mind against Curtin. There was no other way of escape.

"I don't want to have his dirt," Curtin thought; "his dirt may rot in the bush for all I care. My life is worth just as much to me as his is to him."

He looked for his pipe, which had dropped on the ground. His right hand rested on his right knee as he bent down to pick up his pipe. With a slow gesture he moved his right hand toward his body and let it slide toward his hip. But before his hand reached the holster, Dobbs had his own gun out.

"Another move, brother, and I pull the trig."

Curtin kept his hands where they were.

"Stick 'em up! Up, up!" Dobbs shouted.

Curtin raised his hands to his head.

"Higher, please, or I'll pluck you off like a shot from hell."

Dobbs smiled, satisfied, and nodded his head. "Was I right

or was I? Didn't I judge you right, son of a stinking dog? Talking big, hi? Talking Bolshevik Sunday school. You can't smoke me, brother, with sweet love-songs. Nope, not me. Protecting other people's goods. You!" Dobbs changed his tone and yelled: "Stand up, you skunk, and take it like a man."

Curtin rose slowly to his feet, and, with his hands still up in the air, turned round. Dobbs reached for Curtin's gun. And as Dobbs grabbed the gun, his own gun went off, because he had had the trigger rather loose. For a fraction of a second Dobbs was surprised, and Curtin, feeling by instinct that Dobbs was off his guard for a quarter of a second, jerked about and landed Dobbs a good hook on the jaw, knocking him to the ground. He threw himself upon Dobbs quickly and disarmed him. Then he sprang up and stepped a few paces back with two guns pointed at the rising Dobbs.

"Cards are now dealt the other way, Dobby," Curtin said, and laughed.

"So I see." Dobbs was on his feet. He knew Curtin would not shoot him when he had no gun in his hand. It gave him a curious taste in his mouth to realize that Curtin would play fair, whereas he knew that he himself would not give the other a chance. He wanted to win, no matter how. To admit, even to himself, that Curtin had nobler feelings than he only made Dobbs hate him the more.

"Now look here, Dobby," Curtin said in a calm and conciliating voice, "you are all wrong. Not for a moment did I ever mean to rob you or to harm you. I would fight for you and your stuff just as I shall for the old man."

"Yes, I know. Fine. If you really mean what you say, then hand over my cannon."

Curtin laughed out loud. "I'd better not. Little boys shouldn't play with matches and scissors. Mother spank."

"I understand," Dobbs said shortly. He went over to the fire and squatted down.

Curtin emptied Dobbs's gun, weighed it in his hand, threw it up in the air and caught it cowboy-fashion, and then held it toward Dobbs, hesitated for a second, looked Dobbs in the face, and then put the gun in his own pocket on his left hip. He squatted down by the fire, taking care not to get too close to Dobbs. He took out his pipe, filled and lighted it. After he had taken a few puffs he looked at his pipe as though examining it and said in a casual way: "And that was another day."

6

Curtin knew he was not any better off than half an hour before. He could not watch Dobbs day and night for the next five or six days. He would fall asleep sooner or later and Dobbs would get the better of him. Dobbs would show no mercy—now less than before.

Only one of them could survive this trip. He who fell asleep would be the victim of him who kept awake. There would come a night when one of the two would kill the other for no other reason than to gain one night of sleep.

"Wouldn't it be better under these circumstances," Curtin finally began, "yes, as I said, wouldn't it be better, the way it stands, to separate tomorrow, or right now this very night? I earnestly believe that would be the best way of solving this tough problem."

"Of course it would be the best. I see the whole thing. That would suit you fine."

"Why suit me more than you?" Curtin asked, rather perplexed.

"So that you could fall on me from behind. Stab me or shoot me in the back. Or perhaps tip off bandits and send them after me. You're a great pal. My pal! Shit!"

"If you think that, then I can't see any way out of this fix we are in." Curtin shrugged. "There seems nothing to do but tie you up every night, and during the daytime too."

"Yes, agreed upon. I think you must, brother of mine," Dobbs sneered, and stretched his arms as if to show his strength. "Come on, you lousy yellow skunk, come on and tie me up. I'm waiting. Waiting I say; hear me?"

Curtin realized that it would not be easy to tie up Dobbs. He realized also that the only chance he had to overpower Dobbs was now, and that this chance most likely would never come again. But he was afraid to take what he knew was the only road to save himself. In situations like this, Dobbs was the stronger, because he would act upon his impulse and think afterwards.

21

I

A night of horror began for Curtin. Not so for Dobbs. Dobbs had discovered Curtin's weak spot. Now he felt absolutely safe. He could play hide-and-seek with Curtin.

Curtin had lain down where he could watch Dobbs, and yet far enough away to have sufficient room and time should Dobbs try one of his tricks.

It was difficult for Curtin to stay awake. The march during the day, all on foot, climbing up the steep trails, wading in mud, driving the burros, reloading packs that came loose, and helping the animals over the barrancas, would make the strongest man weary.

When sleep almost overcame him he got up and walked around. He found that this made him still more sleepy. So he tried sitting up. Then he thought it might be better to roll himself in his blanket and keep still, and so give his body a rest. He might make Dobbs believe that he was still watchful while he got a few winks of sleep.

An hour later, when Curtin had not moved for a long time, Dobbs rose and started to crawl over to him. Curtin, however, had seen Dobbs's move and at once drew his gun and yelled across the flickering fire: "Not another foot toward me or I pull the trigger."

Dobbs laughed. "Excellent night-watchman. I have to hand it to you. You should try a bank for a job."

Shortly after midnight Dobbs was wakened by the bray-

288

ing of one of the burros that seemed to smell a tiger around the camp. Dobbs again began to crawl, but again Curtin had the gun up and shouted his warning.

Dobbs knew now that he could not win this night, and so he enjoyed a good sleep. These two little tricks he had played on Curtin were not meant to overpower him. He had used them only to keep Curtin awake, so that the next night he would be asleep the moment he lay down.

2

The following day Curtin ordered Dobbs to lead the train so that he could have him in sight most of the time.

Late in the afternoon camp. Evening. And then night once more.

Shortly after ten Dobbs rose, went over to where Curtin slept like a bear in winter, and relieved him of his gun.

After he got the gun, he kicked Curtin hard in the ribs. "Up with you, you lousy rat. Cards are dealt once more in another way. This time for the last time. No more shuffling."

"What cards do you mean? Oh hell, I am so tired!" Curtin tried to rise.

"Keep seated," Dobbs said, and sat near him. "Let's have a last talk before I ship you to hell. Your funeral has come. Because I can't stand living in constant fear of you. It gets on my nerves, and on my stomach too. So it must be finished up now between you and me. No other way. I won't be your watchman as you were mine for the last twenty-four hours. No more orders from you such as I had to swallow today. Get me?"

"In other words: murder. Is that what it means?" Curtin asked drowsily. He was far too sleepy to comprehend the full meaning of what was going on about him. All he wanted was sleep.

Dobbs kicked him again to arouse him. "No, brother, no murder. Your mistake. I don't mean murder. I only want to free myself from you and from your intention to kill me whenever I may not be looking."

Curtin tried to shake off his drowsiness. "Oh yes, I know you mean to bump me off right here and now. But don't think it will be that easy. The old man will look after this. Just wait and see."

"Yeah? Will he? And who else? I've had the answer for that ready for a long time. You want to know what I'll tell him? You tied me to a tree and made your get-away with all the goods, yours, mine, and the old man's. Then he'll be looking for you, never for me. You are the criminal, not me." Dobbs laughed as if at the best joke he had heard.

Curtin fought hard to keep awake and get a clear understanding of what Dobbs said. He moved his shoulders jerkily to shake his sleepiness out of his system. In this he failed.

Dobbs pushed him violently in the chest and yelled: "Up now, and march where I tell you. Today I had to march to your music, now you have to march to mine. Go on!"

"Where to?" Curtin asked, his eyes now wide open. "Where to?"

"To your funeral. Or did you think I'd take you to a wild party with booze and hussies undressing to please ye? Want to say your prayers? I might let you. It won't help you much anyhow. You are going to hell." Dobbs paused, watching his victim's movements.

In his mind Curtin had the sensation that he was dreaming. And it came to him that once somebody had said to him, or that he had read somewhere, that in a dream one might see revealed the true character of a person more clearly than when awake. And he decided, in what he thought to be a dream, to be more careful against Dobbs in the future and to warn Howard against Dobbs also.

While he was trying harder and harder to get out of this haze and drowsiness, Dobbs lost patience, grabbed him brutally by the collar, and yelled: "Now stand on your feet, god-damn it, and have it over!"

"Oh, why can't you let me sit here for a while and have just another hour of sleep? I'm all in. I can't march now. Let the poor beasts have an hour more rest too. They are all overworked, and their backs are sore."

"Get up, damn it! You'll have time enough to sleep in a minute. Come, come, and I don't mean maybe!"

Curtin felt Dobbs's harsh commands in his brain like piercing stabs, and he thought he would go mad if he could not stop his yelling. It hurt him all over. He stood up heavily and staggered off in the direction Dobbs indicated as if acting in a dream. He obeyed merely in the hope that Dobbs's yelling would cease if he did as ordered.

Dobbs kept close behind him, pushing and kicking him forward. He drove him some hundred and fifty feet into the bush, then shot him down without saying another word.

Curtin dropped like a felled tree. Once on the ground, he made no other move.

Dobbs bent down and listened for a few seconds. When he heard no breath, no moan, no sigh, he rose with a satisfied gesture, put the gun back into its holster, and returned to the glowing fire.

There he sat for half an hour, thinking what to do next. But no thoughts would form in his mind and take definite shape. He stared into the flames, shoved more sticks in, and watched them catch fire. He thought for a moment that he saw a huge red face in the fire that ate and swallowed the flames. Then he filled his pipe and lighted it with a burning twig.

3

He puffed for a few moments.

"Maybe," he was thinking, "I didn't bump him off at all. Perhaps he only staggered and dropped to the ground without being hit. Let's figure that out. How was it?"

He turned his face around toward the woods where Curtin lay. For a good while he stared into the darkness as though he expected Curtin to appear at any moment.

He felt that he sat uncomfortably, so he rose, walked several times around the fire, and looked again toward the dense bush which hid Curtin. He stood for a while staring into the fire, pushed with his feet more sticks into the flames, and then squatted down.

After a quarter of an hour he knocked out his pipe, rolled himself in his blanket, and stretched himself full length near the fire. He hoped to fall asleep instantly by taking a long, deep breath. But in the middle of this long breath he stopped. He was sure that he had not hit Curtin, and that Curtin would appear before him the next minute, gun in hand. This idea kept him from falling asleep.

He now became restless. Throwing off his blanket, he crawled close to the fire and scratched his arms, his legs, his back, his chest. He felt chilly. Again he turned his face toward the bush.

With a nervous gesture he pulled a thick piece of burning wood out of the fire to use as a torch. He blew it into bright flames and hurried into the bush.

Curtin was lying motionless in the same spot where Dobbs had left him. Dobbs wanted to kneel down and press his hand against the breast of his victim. But, feeling uneasy, he jerked up, and then bent down, carefully listening for any sign of breath.

There was no sigh, no moan, not even the slightest movement of the fingers. Dobbs held the burning stick close to Curtin's face, almost scorching his nose, and moved the stick back and forth close to the eyes. There was not even a flicker of the eyelashes. The shirt on Curtin's breast was wet with blood.

Satisfied with his investigation, Dobbs straightened up and started to return to the fire. Before he had gone ten feet he pulled out the gun, turned around, and let Curtin have another shot, to make absolutely sure. He dropped the torch, which by now had died down. For a moment he hesitated. Then he pulled out the gun once more and threw it toward where Curtin lay. "It's his, anyhow," Dobbs muttered, "and it looks better this way."

He came back to the fire. Once more he rolled himself in his blanket. Yet, as he felt more chilly than ever, he sat upright, staring into the fire.

"Damn it," he said in a full voice, "damn it all! Who the hell would have thought that conscience might trouble me? Me? Well, it seemed about to, but now I'm quiet." He laughed. But his laughter sounded like barking.

The word "conscience," spoken by him in a full voice, got hold of him somehow. It seemed to penetrate his mind in a curious way. From this moment on, the word "conscience" sprang to the fore and dominated his thoughts, without any clear and definite meaning of what the word really stands for. Had he been asked what conscience was, he would not have been able to define it correctly or even to make it clear by comparison.

He debated with himself: "I want to see if conscience can play tricks on me. Murder is the worst man can do. According to books and sermons from the pulpit, conscience ought to show up now. But it doesn't. As a matter of fact, I've never heard of a hangman bothered by his conscience. He moves a lever, and bang! a trap springs and the poor devil is hanging by his neck in mid air. Or the warden presses a button or puts forward a switch, and the mug sitting tight in the chair gets the shock and meets the devil at the gate with a brass band waiting for him. Not me, brother.

"Didn't I kill quite a number of Heinies in the big parade? Did I? Hell, how they jumped! There was no conscience giving me nightmares or taking away my appetite. Not me.

"So why should I whine now and feel sour in the stomach for that rat kicked off the platform. I only hope he is really finished. Otherwise conscience might—it might—pop up and scratch my spine.

"Yep, of course, there is conscience, and lots of it. And you sure feel it all right if they catch you, and you sure may get twenty years up the river. Not so good. And, of course, conscience will make it rather uneasy for you waiting for a certain week when the Lord may have the mercy on your soul which was asked for in court by the judge in his sentence.

"Haven't I heard that the guy kicked off may appear before you at midnight and make you shiver all down your spine? What time is it? Uh! Only half past eleven. Still half an hour to go. Somewhere in the world it is midnight already. All the time it is midnight somewhere, so the ghosts have to travel fast to be on time where they want to be. Come to think of it, I might pack up and leave. But, hell, I couldn't make out the trail at night, dark as it is. I might go to jail for it. And if I get out, let's say after a couple of years, the ghost won't bother me any more, because I will have paid for him by having done my stretch.

"I wonder if I could make out the trail at night. I might try. If only I could get away from here! I think the climate must change farther down the trail. It's rather chilly here. Well, I'd better stay by the fire and not lose myself in that god-damned Sierra. Damn the fire, it doesn't give any real light. Why the hell didn't I bring in more sticks before dark? No, I won't go now and get them in the bush.

"Wonder how much it will make all together, mine, his, and the old man's lift. It may bring in the neighborhood of fifty grand. I'm sure they won't find him, but I'd better dig him in first thing in the morning, and leave no trace. Funny that now I've got the whole load for myself. Won't the old man get mad if he comes to the port and steps into the bank with a bright face and then finds himself without any funds! Wouldn't I like to see his sour face and hear him calling them sons of I don't know what!" He barked out a suppressed laugh.

Suddenly he stopped. He was sure he heard laughter behind him in the deep darkness of the bush. He turned round as if expecting somebody to stride out of the darkness. He crawled round the fire so that without turning his head he could watch the bush where he thought he had heard the laughter. He blew into the fire and made it blaze up, lighting up the whole surroundings. While the fire was at its brightest he tried to penetrate with his eyes into the deep shadows of the dense foliage around him. He imagined he saw human forms, and then he was sure he saw faces. Then he realized that the shadows from the fire had befuddled him.

"Conscience," he began again reflecting on this word and speaking to himself, "conscience! What a thing! If you believe that there is such a thing as conscience, it will pester you and blast hell out of you, but, on the other hand, if you don't believe in the existence of conscience, what can it do to you? And I don't believe in it any more than I believe in hell. Makes me sick, so much thinking and fussing about nonsense. Let's hit the hay."

He stretched himself by the fire, rolled in his blanket, and slept undisturbed until the sun began to rise.

4

It was late. Usually they were on their way long before sunrise. Hurriedly he drank the coffee left over from last night's supper and ate the cold rice.

He was in such a hurry that he did not give corn to the burros as they usually did since they had hit this hard road.

Not until he began to load the burros did he remember Curtin, whose absence he considered now as something as inevitable as fate. Not for a moment did he feel a grain of pity or repentance. Curtin was no more, and that gave him great satisfaction and quietness of mind. He no longer had to worry about being attacked from behind.

But suppose Howard should trace him? What was he to answer about Curtin and the goods? The story he had in mind to tell might not go over well with the old man. Perhaps it might be better to change the whole story altogether. Easy that. Bandits got them on the way and killed Curtin and robbed them, while he himself, Dobbs, had a chance to get away with two of his burros and his own goods. It would be only natural that he would look first after his own. The smartest guy under heaven couldn't find anything wrong with that story. The country was full of bandits and highwaymen, wasn't it? Everybody knows that.

22

The burros, with their loads on their backs, waited patiently for Dobbs to kick them as a signal that it was time to shuffle off. Now and then they turned their heads toward Dobbs, hoping to get the few handfuls of corn they had become used to since leaving the mine. Surely they were wondering why Dobbs didn't shout to them to be on their way, for they were accustomed to march the moment they felt that the packs were well tied to the saddle.

Dobbs had had more trouble loading them than he had expected. It was not easy to pack burros properly without the help of another man. One man alone cannot pack two sides at the same time, at least not easily. With many oaths and kicks Dobbs finally succeeded in his task, but much time had been lost and it was now near noon.

At the very moment he was just ready to march, he thought of Curtin. He had, of course, thought of Curtin scores of times during the morning, though not as a person dead and gone for good. They had been together for such a long time that he thought of him as gone hunting or to the village to buy provisions. But now for the first time during the morning he realized fully that Curtin was dead. It came to him suddenly, as a shock. Had he not been alone with his thoughts, he might have completely forgotten Curtin in a few hours. Being alone in such a wilderness, however, he

297

continually thought he heard Curtin's voice and a sneering laugh.

He hesitated, then decided it might be better to leave the body where it was. Even should Indians come up this trail, the body was hidden so deep in the dense bush that it seemed most unlikely it would be discovered.

Another thought sneaked into his troubled mind. Suppose he buried the body and it should be found by dogs or by coal-burners. Should this happen, it would be taken for evidence that the story he intended to tell could not be true.

So he concluded to leave the body unburied, as that would look more as if Curtin had been killed by bandits or had shot himself. Besides, if he left the body exposed, lions, tigers, wild pigs, buzzards, worms, and ants would do away with it so quickly that in a month it would be impossible to tell whose bones were bleaching in the bush. But then the rags of clothing and things Curtin carried in his pockets might tell more than the body would.

Suddenly Dobbs noted that everything about him was silent. He had never taken any notice of the fact that nature in the tropics, as noon approaches, becomes drowsy and falls asleep. Birds cease to sing and no longer fly about, insects become quiet and hide away under leaves and in other shady places, squirrels are no longer seen, and greater animals seem to vanish as if chased away. Even the wind goes to sleep; the leaves no longer whisper.

Dobbs felt this growing silence like something strange happening in the whole world. It seemed to him as though trees and leaves became petrified. Their color turned from green to a dull dustlike gray. The air felt strangely heavy, and the atmosphere appeared to have turned into gaseous lava.

Dobbs could see little of the sky because of the dense foliage above him, and the air seemed so thick that he could scarcely breathe. The mass of underbrush and the trunks of the trees seemed to close in on him and swallow up the last bit of air. Wherever he looked, all around him had turned gloomy, as though in a dream.

Thick sweat broke out all over his body. He had the sensation that if he did not move that very second, he also might become petrified, like everything else around him. Fright came upon him.

The burros were standing as though turned to stone. Trained to follow commands, they were waiting for their orders. With their large dark eyes they stared at Dobbs without blinking.

Dobbs, realizing that the eyes of the burros were resting unceasingly upon his face, became afraid of the animals. For a second the idea struck him that these burros might be charmed human beings, knowing and understanding fully what he had done and ready to accuse him, spring at him, and kill him. He shook off this idea and tried to grin at it, but he could not.

He stepped over to the burros and worked about their packs, tying a rope here, fixing a twisted strap there, and pulled at the packs and saddles to see that they were tight for the trip. He pushed the animals around and pressed his fists into their flesh to assure himself that they were alive. After that he felt easier.

But this feeling of relief did not last long. When he caught one burro staring at him again with its large eyes, he thought that perhaps Curtin might glare at him with eyes exactly like those of the animals.

"Anyway, I think it's safer by all means to bury him. But I can't look at his eyes. I might never forget him. Yet I never bothered about the staring eyes of the dead Heinies. How was that? Well, no other way out; I have to dig him in. It's better to do that."

He pulled a spade out of one of the packs. When he had it in his hands, he again became undecided. Should he dig that carcass in or would it be a waste of time? Hadn't he better hurry and get the burros going and try to reach the railroad station as soon as possible?

He pushed the spade back into the pack, and as he did so, he became suddenly curious to see if the buzzards had already started to feast upon the body. To know this before he left the place would give him a welcome feeling of security. So he pulled out the spade once more, threw it over his shoulder, and went resolutely into the bush.

2

He walked straight to the spot where Curtin's body lay. He could have found the spot with both eyes closed. He was sure he would be able to find it as easily fifty years hence.

But when he got there, the place was empty.

He knew then that he had erred in the direction. The darkness of the night and the uncertain flicker of the campfire and of the burning torch in his hand had confused him.

Nervously he began to look for the body. He crawled through the underbrush, pushing hastily through the branches of shrubs, spreading open the foliage, glancing left and right, and becoming more nervous every second. He feared that he might come upon the body unexpectedly and that it would give him a shock which would break him.

So he decided not to search any longer, but to hurry back to the burros and march off as quickly as possible.

Half-way back he realized that he would never find peace if he left without seeing the corpse and making sure that the job had been done well.

Again he began to search. He ran about this way and that

in the bush. The more he ran, the more confused he became. He hurried back a dozen times to where the camp had been last night, to take up the direction afresh. But now he could not recall precisely the direction into which he had driven Curtin. It was all in vain. He could not find the body. For a minute he rested to get his head clear and to concentrate on the direction.

His nervousness made him tremble. The sun was now straight above him in the sky, and its heat penetrated the crowns of the trees. He felt the sun scorching his brain. He panted and cursed himself. He was bathed in sweat. Down he went on his knees by the little brook near the camp and lapped up the water like a thirsty dog. Then, kneeling there for a few seconds, he felt that his thoughts were going to run amuck.

Searching again through the brush and crawling along the ground covered with low prickly plants, he turned his head nervously from side to side. He tried to convince himself that it was not fear that tortured him, that it was nothing but the heat and exhaustion. Without forming words he babbled to himself that he was not afraid, that he was afraid of nothing, that he was only excited by the aimless running about and the vain search.

"Hell, he must be here. He couldn't have flown away," he cried out breathlessly. In the deep silence of the bush he heard his own voice as if it were the voice of somebody hidden behind the foliage. And his voice frightened him as no man's voice had ever frightened him in his life.

3

The burros showed an increasing restlessness. The leader started to march off. Soon the whole train was under way, following him. Perhaps they smelled a good pasture ahead.

With an oath Dobbs sprang after the burros. This confused and frightened them. They began to run. He had to run faster and faster to overtake the lead and stop the train.

Panting and nearly breaking down, he drove the animals back to the camp. They stood quiet for a while, nibbling at the sparse grass.

Then two of the burros looked at him with their great black eyes without moving their heads and Dobbs felt as if they were trying to search his mind. This frightened him more than ever. For a second he thought he would blindfold them to be safe from these terrifying looks. But his thoughts wandered away from this intention before he had taken a step toward the burros.

"Geecries! Where the hell is that damned guy?" he gasped, and wiped his face with his sleeve.

Once more he began to search the bush. He was for the hundredth time convinced that he must be on the very spot where he had shot Curtin. He noticed a piece of the charred torch with which he had lighted up the place the night before when he went back to give his victim another shot. This charred piece of wood left no doubt any longer that this was the place where he had shot Curtin. The ground was disturbed, but that might easily have been caused by his running about. There was no trace of blood.

"Where under heaven is the body?" he asked himself. Perhaps a tiger or wild pigs had dragged it to where they could eat it in peace.

He stood thinking. "Nothing better than that could have happened," he said aloud, looking at the ground. "Very soon not even a bone will be left to tell the tale. Done as if by order. It's almost too perfect to believe."

With a satisfied feeling Dobbs walked slowly back to the camp. The burros, the packs still on their backs, had lain down on the ground. Dobbs was so quiet that he now could take out his pipe, fill it, and have a smoke.

He thought seriously about getting started. When he was ready to make off, he again felt slight shivers running up and down his back. The sweat on his body seemed to turn to ice. He buttoned up his shirt almost to the neck.

He shook himself as if to pull himself together resolutely. He shouted at the burros to get up. The train was once more on its way.

Dobbs found the march more difficult than he had expected. If he marched ahead, the burros in the rear strayed off looking for food. He had to stop the train, go back, and bring up the rear. If he marched behind the last animal, the leader either stopped or went off the trail, or lay down. He had to run up and down the train like a dog keeping a flock of sheep together. He tried tying a rope around the neck of each burro and fastening it to the saddle of the burro ahead. The animals could only march single file, as the trail was not wide enough to let them go side by side. Leading them by ropes did not help much. If a burro at the rear stopped, he would pull so hard at the rope that the burro ahead of him would also stop and so the whole train would come to a standstill.

Dobbs tried again without ropes, leaving the burros free to march as best they could. He found that this worked best. Once they were well on their way, all Dobbs had to do was to call occasionally to let them know that he was still there ready to whip them should they lag.

He took out his pipe and had another smoke. He walked now leisurely behind the train.

This leisure, though, made his mind wander again.

"I should have looked around more carefully. And, hell, come to think of it, I didn't see his gun I threw upon him after the last shot." He touched his hip. "I've got my own gun all right, but not his. How is that? Perhaps he was not

dead at all, only badly hurt. He may have come to. Perhaps
he is crawling through the bush farther and farther away.
If he should reach an Indian village, he might get help.
What then? What would I do then?" He turned round,
stopped, and listened. He thought that the Indians had
found Curtin and were already after him on horseback.

"Whatever he did and whichever way he went, he can't
be in a village yet. The nearest one must be at least ten
miles from that place. He couldn't make that in one day,
hurt as he is. I'd better go back and find him, cost what it
may. I simply have to find him; otherwise I may get twenty
years on the Maria Islands. It's a hell of a place, they say.
Not so good."

He concluded that there was no way out but to go back
and look once more, this time more thoroughly. He remembered that there was one direction he had failed to cover
completely. It might be just there where he would find
Curtin, dead or still alive. He was sure that he would find
him there.

4

It was almost dark when Dobbs got back to the camp.
He did not bother to unload the burros just then. He could
do that after nightfall. He had to use the last light of the
day for his search. So he went straight at his task.

Although he had made up his mind, while marching
back, to look less hastily than he had in the forenoon, he
began to search just as nervously as before. He could not
force himself into a disciplined, calm exploration.

Night fell quickly, too quickly for Dobbs. He had to
return to the camp-site. There he unloaded the burros and
lighted a fire.

He was too weary to cook much food. All he had was

coffee and a few tortillas that were about to turn musty.

Thinking things over, he decided that he could not waste one hour more on the search for the body. Next morning he would leave at the first glimpse of light. He would try his utmost to reach Durango inside of two or three days. There he would sell the burros, the tools, and the hides for any price offered, just to get cash. Then he would take the train and, instead of going to the port, he would take the shortest route north and cross the international line before Howard could hear what had happened and wire a description of him to the border stations.

Dobbs remembered now that he was already on the eastern slope of the Sierra Madre and that yesterday he and Curtin, standing on a high bare rock, had seen the smoke of a passing train far away.

23

Before sunrise next morning Dobbs was on his way. Once started, the pack-train traveled fairly well. The burros were more willing than they had been yesterday, as they had not been forced to wait so long after being loaded and Dobbs had given them their ration of corn, which made them more lively.

Then one burro became frightened, for some unknown reason, and ran against trees and rocks breaking the straps, ropes, and girth which held packs and pack-saddle. Free of this, he ran away like mad. Dobbs was unable to catch up with him and had to let him go. So he divided the packs and loaded them on the other animals. He was sure the burro would later follow up and come to camp at night looking for his pals.

Now Dobbs could see the railroad at almost every turn the trail made, because the trail led, from now on, down the mountains straight into the valley. He could have reached one of the smaller stations along the railroad this very day, but he thought it better not to board a train at one of the small depots, where he might easily arouse suspicion, appearing alone with so many loaded burros. Then, too, he could not expect to sell his burros and tools in a small village. Dobbs needed cash to pay for his ticket and the freight charges. So he must go to Durango, the nearest city.

Durango was still two long days off, if not three. The

trail became easier and apparently safer on nearing town. Dobbs began to feel fine. He whistled. Getting along so easily, he could dream about his future, what he would do with his riches, where and how he was going to live. He contemplated a trip to Europe, to France, and to England and Scotland, where he could have for once a plate of real haggis of the kind his mother had talked about when he was a boy.

"If I only could know for sure that he's dead and that he's been eaten by a tiger or something." He spoke so loud that the burro in front of him turned his head, thinking perhaps Dobbs had given him an order.

2

That night when Dobbs pitched camp he felt easier than on the two previous nights. He knew his conscience would not trouble him here. Such things only happened in the mountains, where trees seemed to speak and foliage to frame strange faces. Here, in full view of the plain, he found real tranquillity. He sang and whistled as he cooked his meal.

The burro that had broken away during the day now came walking into the camp.

"That means good luck," Dobbs said, "getting something back which seemed lost for good. I like that. Besides, it means fifteen bucks more cash in my pocket. Hello, old pal, how are ye!" he greeted the returned member of the family, and patted him on the back.

That night Dobbs slept well. Not once did he wake up thinking he had heard voices or footsteps as he had the two preceding nights.

At noon next day while crossing a hill, he caught sight of Durango in the distance, bated in golden sunshine and nestled beside one of the wonders of the world—El Cerro del Mercado—a mountain which consists of more than six hundred million tons of pure iron. What a lovely city, with its balmy air and its beautiful surroundings!

Evening saw Dobbs for the last time cooking his meal in a camp and living like a savage. Next day he would be in the city, sleeping in a good bed in a hotel, sitting at a real table with well-cooked food before him, served by a bowing waiter. Two days later he would be riding in a train which would take him in two or three days to the good old home country.

He was all jubilation. He sang and whistled and danced. He was now safe. He could see the flares of the oil-fed engine sweeping along the railroad tracks, could hear the trains rolling by and the coughing and bellowing of the engine.

These sounds gave him a great feeling of security. They were the sounds of civilization. He longed for civilization, for law, for justice, which would protect his property and his person with a police force. Within this civilization he could face Howard without fear, and even Curtin, should he ever show up again. There he could sneer at them and ridicule them. There they would have to use civilized means to prove their accusations. If those bums should go too far, he could easily accuse them of blackmailing him. He would then be a fine citizen, well dressed, able to afford the best lawyers. "What a fine thing civilization is!" he thought; and he felt happy that no such nonsense as Bolshevism could take away his property and his easy life.

Again an engine barked through the night. To Dobbs it was sweet music, the music of law, protection, and safety.

"Strange," he said, suddenly waking from his dreams, "really strange, I should say! He didn't cry, that guy didn't, when I slugged him. He did not whine or make a sound. Just dropped like a felled tree. The blood that trickled from his breast and soaked his shirt was the only thing that moved. When I came with that burning stick and looked at him once more, his face was white. I thought I might have the quivers, but, hell, I didn't. And why should I? I could have laughed. That's what I could. Laughed right out. He looked so funny the way his legs and arms were twisted about. Almost like a coiled snake. It sure was funny." Dobbs laughed. "Just a slug and finished a whole guy that cared so much about his life and work. Funny, things are. Really funny. All things are funny."

He smoked and watched the little clouds before his face. "If I only had the slightest notion where that body can be! I simply can't figure it out. Carried off by a lion? Likely. Lots of mountain lions about. Found by an Indian and taken to his village? No, I don't think so. Anyway, suppose the body was carried away by a tiger or a cougar; I would have seen the tracks where he was dragged over the ground. The trouble is I didn't look for tracks, I looked just for him. That was the mistake I made. Hell, I should have looked more carefully for tracks of wild beasts. Now, let's see. Yes, I think that tiger, or what it was, took him up in his jaws and carried him off without leaving any tracks. That's it. Hell, tigers are strong. Musta been a big tiger, a tigre real, a royal tiger. Those big tigers are awfully strong and can easily carry away a whole cow, jumping with her over a fence. They are really big and strong."

Dobbs felt satisfied with the explanation he had given himself.

"Perhaps he isn't dead at all. Aw, nonsense. He's dead all right. I slugged him fine. Didn't I see the blood, and his white face, and his twisted body, and his closed eyes, which didn't quiver, not a bit, when I touched them with the burning stick? He was as dead as that stone here. He sure was."

Dobbs grew uneasy. He began to shiver. He stirred the

fire and pushed in a few more logs. He looked down across the plains, hoping to see flickers of light from the huts where small farmers lived. He turned his head toward the brush, sure that he heard someone coming.

At last he could sit no longer. He had to stand up and walk about the fire. He told himself he did so only because he felt cold and had to walk to get warm. But the truth was that he wanted to look around freely. He would have felt better had he had a high brick wall against his back, to be sure that no one could be behind him.

As he stood quietly for a moment, he thought he felt somebody behind him, so close that he had the sensation of breath on his neck. He imagined he felt the point of a knife in his back. He sprang forward, drew his gun, and, turning, aimed at—nothing. No one was threatening him. He saw nothing but the dark shadows of the burros grazing peacefully near the camp. Dobbs looked at them and thought for a second how happy animals are because they cannot think, as human beings can.

He told himself that he was not nervous at all; that in the wilderness one must be always on guard. To be always on the alert is the mark of a true woodman, and it has nothing whatever to do with what people call conscience. That's sheer nonsense. Alone and so far from civilization and with valuable goods, one cannot be too careful. Anybody might sneak up from behind and try to get the better of him and then make off with the booty. "Not me," Dobbs said half aloud, "no one can get me that easy. I know how to protect my hide. I'm not a yellow sissy like that Laky guy or that Cu—well, he had no guts. I'm tough, I sure am. No sneaking up behind me. No, sir."

He made an effort to chuckle and sat down by the fire and tried to concentrate his thoughts on the job of cleaning his pipe.

3

Next morning Dobbs could not leave as early as he had planned. Several of the burros had strayed. He had been careless last night in hobbling them, and they had gone looking for better pasture. He lost hours in rounding them up.

The trail soon ran into a wide dirt road covered with fine dust and sand that made traveling on it a torture.

Dobbs figured he would be in Durango about three in the afternoon. Had it not been for the loss of so many valuable hours in the morning, he would have been at the first houses of the town by now.

The road was tiresome to travel. One side of it lay along cultivated fields, now dried up for months. The rich soil was at present like powder. The other side of the road was partly walled in by a long hill of soft earth, a sort of clay of a yellowish, brownish color. Thorny bushes and magueys and nopales and organos growing along the road and partly fencing in the fields were thickly covered with white dust.

When a breeze rose, huge clouds of dust swept over the fields and made the road ahead almost invisible, as if wrapped in a heavy fog. Often Dobbs could not see farther ahead than ten feet. But this was not the real trouble, because he and the animals could find their way. It was the heavy dust sweeping in from all directions, which made breathing a real pain. The fine sand, which was like powdered glass, nearly blinded Dobbs, reddening his eyes and making it painful to open or close them. Above was a merciless sun, the pitiless sun of midday in the tropics. For months the earth had waited for rain, and not a drop had fallen in this section. The heat broke upon man and beast until they were numb in mind and body, so that they closed their eyes and staggered along not wishing anything from life but an end of this painful march.

The burros no longer strayed and nibbled at dry leaves of grass by the road. They plodded on like automatons. They hardly moved even their heads. From former experience they knew that a town means rest, protection against heat and dust, and water and food. So they hurried on toward this town, which to them, as to Dobbs, under these circumstances was the promised land.

Then, through his almost closed eyes Dobbs noted a few trees growing near the road. They were low, but they had thick, very wide crowns and offered a most welcome shade. Here he could sit down for a while and lean his tired body against a tree, have a drink of water and a smoke, and after that make the rest of the way refreshed. Even the burros would welcome the opportunity to stand in the shade for a few minutes.

The first shacks of the town were hardly five miles away.

4

Dobbs hurried ahead to turn the leading burro about. The animals came willingly to the trees. They panted, shook their heads to free them from horse-flies, and then moved slowly about in the cooling shade.

Dobbs went to one of the burros, took the water-bag from the saddle, rinsed his mouth of the dust which was grinding between his teeth, and then drank. He poured some water into his hands and wet his face and neck.

As he returned the water-bag to the saddle, he heard somebody say: "Tiene un cigarro, hombre? Have you got a cigarette?"

Dobbs started. This was the first human voice he had

heard for days, and it came to his ears with a shock.

Although the words were spoken in Spanish, Dobbs thought first of Howard and Curtin, realizing at the same moment that they would not speak to him in this way.

Turning his head in the direction the voice had come from, he saw three ragged tramps lying in a hollow under one of the trees farthest away toward the field. They were mestizos, unwashed, uncombed, with ugly faces, types that are frequently met on the roads in the vicinity of cities, where they can sleep free of charge and wait for any opportunities the road may offer. Their look alone gave evidence that they had not worked for months and had reached the state where they no longer cared about finding a job, having tried in vain a thousand times. They were the human sweepings of the cities, left on the dumps of civilization, possibly escaped convicts, outlaws, fugitives from justice. They were the garbage of civilization with their headquarters near all the other garbage and junk a modern city spits out unceasingly day and night.

Seeing these three empty tin cans of modern civilization, Dobbs, once in his life having been one of them himself, knew immediately that he was in one of the toughest situations he would ever have to face. He realized that he had made a mistake in leaving the open road and turning to the trees. The road was only about fifty feet away, but screened by these trees many things could happen. And, of course, out on the road he might not have been much safer.

Dobbs had no plan. He could only try to gain time in the hope that someone might pass by whom he might hail. He might convince the thieves that he had no money and nothing of value, but this would not be easy; his packs and his burros were enough to induce them to commit any crime to get possession of them.

"I haven't got a cigarette," he answered, trying to be

nonchalant. "In fact, I haven't had a cigarette myself for more than ten months."

He thought he had said something clever. He would show them that he was so poor that he could not even buy himself a package of cigarettes. He added: "But I've got a few pinches of tobacco, if that will do."

"And paper to roll it in?" one of the men asked. "Or a few corn leaves?"

The three thieves were still lying on the ground, their faces turned toward Dobbs. They were so well shielded by the trees that they could not be seen from the road. Had Dobbs seen them, he would not have turned off the road, but would have driven the burros hard to escape. "It's too late now," Dobbs thought, with regret.

"I've got a bit of newspaper, if it will do." He pulled out his pouch and produced a piece of paper, wet with the sweat from his body. He handed this to the man nearest him.

The three men divided the piece of paper, took the pouch, and rolled their cigarettes.

"Cerillos? Matches?" one asked, as if ordering Dobbs to wait on him. Dobbs ignored the insolence and handed them the box of matches. They lighted their cigarettes and returned the box.

"Going to Durango?" one asked.

"Yes, that's my intention. I'm going to sell the burros. I need money. I haven't got a red cent." Dobbs thought this answer clever again.

"Money? Exactly what we need. Don't we, partners?" one said.

"Do we need it?" another answered, and broke into laughter.

Dobbs leaned against a tree so that he could keep them in view. He filled his pipe and lighted it. He took his time, for he wanted to impress on these men that he was in no way worried or, worse, afraid. He was no longer tired. "I might hire them as drivers," he reflected. "That would not look so suspicious as if I came into town alone with so many pack-burros. They might like to earn a peso or two without hard work. Then they'd have a good meal and a drink coming their way." It was an excellent idea, he was sure.

"I could use a good mule-driver—even two or three."

"Could you?" One of the men was laughing.

"Yes, I sure could. These burros make me trouble enough."

"How much is the pay?"

"One peso."

"One peso for us three?"

"No. Of course not. One peso for each one of you. Naturally I can't pay in advance. I'll pay when we get to town and I've got some cash."

"Naturally," one said.

Another asked: "Are you alone?"

Dobbs hesitated, but not wishing to give the impression that he had no answer ready, he said: "Oh no, I'm not alone. How could I be? Two of my friends are coming on horseback; they'll be here any minute now."

"That's strange, don't you think so, Miguel?" one of the men said to another, who was watching Dobbs with glittering eyes, while his mouth was an open slit in which the point of his tongue could just be seen.

"Yes, that's strange, very strange, very," Miguel answered, licking his lips. "Strange indeed. This man is all by himself on a dangerous road and with a long train and his friends are coming behind on horseback, pleasure-riding. Strange, I should say, muy raro."

"Do you see the friends on horseback coming, Pablo?" asked the one who seemed the laziest of all.

Pablo rose slowly, went over to the road and looked toward the mountains, came back indolently, and said with a grin on his thick lips: "Naw, these two friends are still far behind. Far back, an hour or more. I can't even see a pinch of dust swirling up from their horses."

"So you lied to us. Well, well!" Miguel said, his tongue playing about his lips. "Well, well! And what is it you have in the packs, pal? Let's have a look at the goods." He rose heavily, as if it were too much work to get up from the ground, walked over to one of the burros, and with his fist pushed and poked the packs. "Seems to me like hides."

"It is hides, you are right." Dobbs felt more uneasy every minute and was anxious to get away as quickly as possible.

"Tigre real, royal tiger?"

"Yes, tiger and a few lions."

"Bring quite a little bit of dough."

"I hope so." Dobbs said it casually to hide his growing uneasiness. He went to one of the burros and tightened the straps. Then he walked over to another and rattled the packs to see if they were still holding fast. Then he tightened his own belt and pulled his pants higher up, indicating that he was ready to make off.

"Well, boys, I figure I'll have to beat it now. Only stopped for a bit of cool breeze under these trees anyway. Have to be in town long before evening." He knocked his pipe against the heel of his left high boot. "Now, which of you is willing to come along with me and help handle the bestias —the burros, I mean?" He glanced at the three men, at the same time circling the donkeys so as to keep them together.

None of the three answered. They merely looked at each other.

Dobbs caught one of these glances. He understood, and his breath stopped for a second. It flashed through his mind that he had seen many a movie in which the hero was trapped in a situation like this. But he realized at the same time that he could not remember one single picture in which the producer had not done his utmost to help the trapped hero out again to save the girl from the clutches of a bunch of villains. Before he could think of any of the tricks he had seen in the pictures by which the hero finally escaped, he felt, with a strange bitterness in his mouth, that this situation here was real. And whatever is real is different. No smart film-producer was on hand to open the trap with a good trick.

Dobbs kicked the nearest burro in its hams until it took the lead and set out on its way toward town. Another followed slowly. The rest continued to nibble at the meager grass growing under the trees. Dobbs rounded them up and tried to get them all started on their way.

5

The three tramps stood up and, as if they meant to tease a bit, edged in among the burros that still lingered behind. The animals, used to marching with the rest of the pack-train, became restless and tried to break past the men and reach their fellows.

At this the three men endeavored openly to prevent the remaining burros from following the others. They grasped the ropes and held on to the saddles to keep the burros from moving on.

Dobbs, ten feet away, shouted: "Get away from my burros!"

"Who? And just what?" Miguel sneered. "We can sell those burros as well as you can. They won't be any worse if we sell them. What do you think, muchachos?" he asked his companions.

"Away from those burros I tell you!" Dobbs yelled, his

face red with fury. He jumped farther back and drew his gun.

Miguel, seeing this move, failed to show either fear or surprise, as Dobbs had expected.

"With that chingando iron of yours you can't frighten even a sick louse," he chuckled sarcastically. "Not us, you dirty funking cabrón. You can only shoot one. And whoever you bump off won't mind much, because the Federals are after him anyway, and if they catch him he won't live another half-hour. So what with your gat? We take that chance."

Once more Dobbs yelled at the top of his voice: "Get back there from my burros!" Without waiting for the men to move, he aimed at the one nearest him. It was Miguel. But the gun clicked cold. Twice, three times, five times the gun clicked without making even the pfish of a toy gun.

Dobbs stared at his gun in amazement. So did the three thieves. They were so surprised at the failure of that gun that they forgot to laugh or to sneer or to say a single word or utter an exclamation.

One of them bent slowly down and picked up a heavy stone.

A short second followed, filled with such tension that Dobbs thought the whole world would explode. And in this second Dobbs remembered as clearly as if he were living it over once more why it came about that his gun would not fire. Curtin had disarmed Dobbs to prevent being killed. Curtin had unloaded the gun and put it in his own belt for safe keeping. When Dobbs the following night disarmed Curtin, he had shot him with Curtin's gun. Then he had taken his own gun back, but in the excitement in which he had lived during the last few days, he had forgotten to reload his gun, and he had thrown Curtin's gun, after he had shot him for the second time, upon the body to let the discoverer of the body figure out what had happened and how.

Still before this same second came to an end, Dobbs's mind worked intensely to think of another means of defense. His glance fell upon a machete tied to the saddle of the nearest burro. This weapon-like tool was for use in cutting a new trail when fallen trees blocked the way or the underbrush had grown too dense for the burros to pass. He grasped the haft of this machete, but before he could pull it out of its sheath, the stone one of the thieves had taken up crashed against his forehead. He fell. Before he could rise to his feet, Miguel, who had noted Dobbs's move toward the machete, jumped close up. With the sure grip of an expert he had the machete out in an instant. Tiger-like he sprang at the fallen Dobbs, and with a short powerful stroke he cut off Dobbs's head. A mighty gush of blood rushed forth from the body.

More startled than frightened, the three men looked at the body, which was still quivering. The head lay only an inch from the neck. The eyelids blinked two or three times rapidly and then became fixed, but only partly closed. Several times the hands spread wide open and then cramped into fists, finally closing more gently as life fled away and the nerves stiffened.

"You did that, Miguel," Pablo said in a low voice, coming nearer.

"Aw, shut up, you damned yellow dog! Why didn't you do it? Afraid of that funking son of a bitch by a stinking gringo, hey? I know who did it and bumped him. And I tell ye, get away from me, both of you chingando cabrones and que chinguen los cabrones a las matriculas. Do I need your stinking advice, you puppies? Out of my way, you make me sick looking at you, you dirty rats."

He stared at the machete. There was not much blood on it. He wondered why. But the stroke had been that of a master hand. He did not realize how good he was, how great an expert. He stepped to the nearest tree, rubbed the machete clean against the bark, then, wetting his fingers with his tongue, tested the edge and, satisfied with his inspection, pushed the machete back into its scabbard.

24

I

Dogs often show a real interest in what men do, even when the men in question are not their masters. Dogs even like to meddle in the affairs of men. Burros are less interested in men's personal doings; they mind their own business. That's the reason why donkeys are thought to have a definite leaning toward philosophy.

So it came about that the burros, paying no heed to what was happening, marched off, taking the way to town.

In their excitement the thieves forgot the burros while they were busily stripping the body of Dobbs and eagerly searching the pockets for money. Without any hesitation, while the clothing was still warm and wet from the dead man's sweat, they put it on after they had thrown away their own rags. Dobbs's boots and his other clothes had been in daily use for the last ten months and were badly worn. To these tramps they were still luxuries.

Only the shirt found no claimant, although the shirts they wore were in tatters.

"Why don't you want to put on the shirt, Nacho?" Miguel asked. "You would look like a dude, like a fine caballero, with such a shirt on your stinking carcass." He kicked at the body on the ground, naked except for the well-worn khaki shirt. Everything else had found a new owner.

"It isn't worth very much," Nacho answered, shrugging his shoulders.

"You've got a swell reason to say so, you filthy dog." Miguel looked at him, drawing one corner of his mouth down almost to the chin. "Compared with yours, it's a gent's silk shirt. No decency and no feeling for good things in you, that's the trouble with a pig like you."

Nacho turned away. "I'm not hot for it, that's all. Besides, it's too close to the neck. Why don't you take it yourself? Your own isn't so grand, either."

"Me?" Miguel frowned as if he had heard an insult. "Me wear a shirt still warm from such a dirty son of a gringo dog! Not me. I still have some pride left."

The truth was that for Miguel, also, the shirt was too close to the neck of the dead man. It had only a few red spots near the collar, because Dobbs had worn it open, to get all the air he could. While it looked better than any of the shirts the thieves had on, all refused to have it. It was not superstition, it was only an uneasy feeling that made them anxious not to have it on their own body.

"I am sure that cabrón has more shirts in the packs," Pablo remarked.

"You wait until I've examined these packs, and then we'll see," Miguel replied.

"You mean to tell us that you are the boss here?" Nacho's eyes narrowed and he stepped nearer to Miguel. He was still furious that he had got only Dobbs's pants, while Miguel had the boots, which he himself wanted.

"Boss? Who's asking me? A fly like you?" Miguel roared. "Boss or no boss, I'll tell what's what here. What have you done so far, hey?"

"Wasn't it me that stoned him? Without me stoning him first, you would never have dared to go near him, you yellow skunk. That's what you are, yellow, and a filthy son of a stinking cabrón.

"Huh! Don't make me laugh right out. You with your

little stone. It was just like a toothpick. A stone? Who ever heard of using a stone for bumping off a guy? Only cowards do that, únicamente cobardes y cabrones. Which of you rats would have come out and given him the final works? You are just low-down thieves and swindlers and liars. And don't you forget for one minute I can use this machete a second time. And a third time as well. I won't come and ask your permission if I no longer need you. I can do all the work alone and be better off, get me?" Miguel turned to examine the packs.

"Be cursed and damned in hell! Where the devil are these malditos burros, los chingados bestias? Gone to hell!" He was so surprised that he forgot to roar.

2

The burros were well on their way to town.

"Now, hustle up, you bandits," Miguel commanded. "We must get these burros back here, all of them. If even one of them reaches town without a driver, the cops will get busy and smell a dead rat in the parlor. Then they come out here and we'll be in a hell of a mess. Hurry and get them. Rustle your bones."

He himself started after the burros, followed by the other two. The animals were half-way to town already. As there was no roadside grass for them to nibble, they had traveled rather livelily to get to town, where experience told them they would get water, food, and a much needed rest. What was more, in the vicinity of the town lay the ranch where they had been brought up.

It took the men over an hour to get the animals all back under the trees once more.

"We'd better get busy and bury this carcass before the buzzards find it. Someone coming this way may investigate to see what the vultures are after, and then somebody else will be after us." Miguel tied the burros to the trees to prevent them from walking off again.

It was hard work to break the ground and bury the body. And work was not what these men wanted.

Nacho came up with his idea. "Why bury that heathen? He isn't even a Christian, only a godless and god-damned Protestant. If he is found, what then? He can't tell who plugged him."

"Wise guys!" Miguel sneered at the two. "If this carcass is found here and the burros and the packs are found with us, then there won't be any court proceedings, you know that. We'll be shot the very hour they get us."

"Aw, hell, shut up! We don't need your bedtime stories," Pablo said, with lips twisted into an ugly grin.

Miguel was the real boss. No doubt about that. The little brain he could afford he used. "You're a smart guy, too smart to be a dirty rat. That's what you think. But let me tell you something. Por Jesucristo y la Madre Santísima, can't the hell you mugs see that if they find the burros with us, but not the body, they can do nothing? They have to prove first that the gringo has been killed. As long as they haven't found his carcass, they can't even prove that he's dead. We bought the burros from him, and we are not his guardians, to watch out for his safety. Well, I won't listen to any more argument from you two guys. Get to work, and be quick about it. Someone might come this way any time now and take a look at this outfit. Get at it and get it done."

The men pulled a spade from a saddle and began to dig a hole. It was the same spade which Dobbs, only a few days ago, had taken from the same saddle one morning and thrown across his shoulder when he went into the thicket to bury Curtin.

The body was buried in no time. The thieves did not bother to make a good job of it. The undertakers of nature would come and do the rest. Why worry?

Right after this they started the train back toward the Sierra. Believing that Dobbs might have told the truth and that two partners of his were coming this way, they turned off the trail Dobbs had followed and went back into the mountains by another trail.

3

When they reached the bush at the base of the Sierra, their curiosity could no longer be restrained. They were eager to know how big the booty was and how much each of them could expect for his share.

It was dark, and the woods made the night still darker, but they did not light a fire. If soldiers or the Rurales were after them, it would be wise to have no fire to guide their pursuers.

They got busy. The burros were unloaded and then the packs were opened. A pickpocket could not have been more excited to learn the contents of a pocketbook or a lady's handbag than these men were while untying the bundles.

There were more pants, but they were none too good. The few shirts they found were practically rags—hardly better than the ones they had on. There were two pairs of light shoes, which belonged to Howard and Curtin. There were pans and dishes, and two aluminum pots for coffee and tea. Nothing was good enough to sell, even to the poor, as everything was battered and covered with a thick crust of greasy, hardened soot.

"Looks like that scoundrel really spoke the truth," Nacho said disappointedly. "Not a cent, save the few pennies he carried in his pants. Seventy-four centavos! All the money we get out of it."

Pablo was inspecting other things. "The hides are not of the best sort. Very poor. All shot to pieces. A lot of holes make them of hardly any value. Funny sort of a hunter he must have been. Careless in shooting, and he had no idea what to shoot or how to get good hides. Worst of all, they are badly dried up. They are stinking and full of maggots. All the hair is coming off already. We're lucky if we get twenty pesos for the whole lot. And we won't get the twenty with a smile either. Maybe no one will take them even as a present."

Miguel was working about a pack he had opened. He held in his hands a few little bags made of rags and old sackcloth. "I can't figure what in hell that guy had these funny little bags for."

He poured the contents into his open hand. "Sand. Nothing but plain sand. Now, what did he carry this sand for?"

The darkness in the bush, lighted slightly by the new moon, made it difficult for the men to examine the sand more closely and recognize what it really was. Even had they known something about gold dust they would not have thought this particular sand of real value, not at this moment, when all their thoughts were occupied in other directions. They were looking for money and for things they could sell easily. As they examined the packs in darkness, trusting to the feel of their fingers and so missing even the faint glitter this dust sometimes shows, it is not strange that they failed to discern its value.

Miguel, the most experienced of the three, had worked in the mines for a few years. He brought forth an explanation: "I see through it all now. He was a sort of mining engineer, that rascal was. He was working for some mining company. Claro, he went exploring for that company and was bringing back with him these samples of dust, sand, ground rocks, and all that, to be examined later by the chemists of his company. If they find something in these samples, then they buy the land and open a mine. Such sand has no value for us. If we took it to a company, we'd have to tell where it was found. What is still worse, it would make them suspicious and they might investigate how we got it. See?"

"Then it's no good?" Nacho asked.

"Can't you understand plain Spanish, you mug?" Pablo shouted at him. "Miguel knows. He has worked in mines. He knows more than all these gringo engineers. And you heard what he said. It might easily give us away. Throw it away as quick as you can. It's hot, too hot for us. My bags are already cleared of that dirt. What's more, the packs will be less heavy, and so we can get away easier. Get rid of it."

Nacho offered another explanation. "Miguel, I thought you were so smart, but you aren't. And I can prove it. You may have worked in mines, but this mug here was the real American fraud and bluffer, a real American cheater, if you ask me. You wonder why these little bags of sand were so well hidden inside the wrapped hides. It's all clear to me. No riddle any longer. He knew that the hides are sold by their weight, and he was such a dirty cheat that he put these little bags between the hides to make them weigh more. He wanted to sell the hides in bundles, perhaps late at night, somewhere on the plaza. And in the morning when the buyer opened his hides and found out the fraud, my good gringo would be a long way off with the train, saying: 'Now, come and catch me.' Well, I think we've spoiled his dirty business and saved a poor tanner's hard-earned money."

Pablo crouched about his packs, digging into them for better finds. "Who ever thought that these gringos would be such dirty skunks, cheating even a poor Mexican tanner?" he asked himself with a loud voice. "I don't feel a bit sorry we finished him up and sent him straight to hell."

Miguel admitted that he might have made a mistake in thinking that the bags contained samples for geological examinations. He found Nacho's idea more to his liking and accepted it as the best explanation.

Then came the night breeze which carried all the sand, strewn about the ground, far and wide in all directions.

4

It was still dark when the three thieves packed up and went on their way farther back into the mountains. They wished to be as far away from civilization as possible and to stay away for the next ten weeks if they could.

Next day they reached a little Indian village high up in the Sierra Madre. Seeing a man in the street, Pablo went up to him and asked if he knew anyone who might want to buy a few burros which were no longer needed.

The Indian nodded and said: "Might be that I take them." He walked around the burros, inspected the brands, looked at the packs, and then, as if casually, looked at the high boots Miguel wore, which were quite a bit too large for his feet. With the same curious look the Indian stared at the pants Nacho had donned. He looked at everything as if he meant to buy the whole outfit, including the clothes the drivers were wearing.

When he was through with his inspection he said: "I can't buy any burros now for myself, because I haven't the cash. But my uncle may buy a few, perhaps all of them, if you mean to sell them all and the price is reasonable. He has got the money, my uncle has, to buy as many bestias as he wants."

This was good news to the three rascals and they smiled at each other. They had not thought it would be that easy to sell the animals for cash. They had expected that they might have to visit a dozen Indian villages before finding buyers who were ready to buy burros and pay real money. Cash was a rare thing among these Indian farmers living on the slopes of the Sierra and owning only poor ranches.

Five minutes later the thieves were at the house of the uncle who was to buy the burros. Like all the other houses in the village, it was of adobe and faced the plaza, a big square which was formed on all the four sides by rows of similarly built houses. In the midst of the row which was opposite the house of the uncle, there was the modest school-house, built by the Indian villagers themselves. In the center of the plaza a little pavilion was set up. The pavilion served many purposes. Most of them had something to do with celebrations of Independence Day and other national holidays, when the school-teacher or some other citizen would make a speech, and at night there would be an orchestra composed of villagers to play the national tunes and after that play for the assembled crowd to dance and make merry. Here also the Health Commissioners sent by the federal government to educate the people in matters of hygiene and general health, commissioners of the Secretary of Agriculture, and others would make speeches about how to improve agrarian conditions. No village in the republic is complete without such a pavilion in the center of the plaza. It is taken as an evidence that the village, be it ever so small or ever so poor and populated by Indians only, is a recognized part of the republic and under an organized local government. The existence of this pavilion should have warned the three thieves to be very careful hereabouts, because such a pavilion indicates that wherever it is seen, there are men near whose business it is to see that the law is respected and obeyed.

The man who had led them to this house went inside to speak to his uncle. It was not long before the uncle stepped out and greeted the strangers, who had squatted in the shade of a few trees in front of the house.

The uncle was an elderly man with graying hair, tall and apparently strong. His face was open and frank and bronzed, indicating his pure Indian race. His dark eyes sparkled like those of a boy. His hair, though rather long at the neck, was well trimmed and combed. His clothing did not differ from that worn by all the other men of his village. And like all of them he was a small farmer.

He approached the three strangers with dignity. Without looking too closely at the three men, he went over to the burros and examined them with the utmost care, as experienced farmers do when buying animals. His eyes, however, gave no indication of his thoughts.

Miguel rose and said appraisingly: "Very fine burros, señor, bestias de carga muy excelentes. I can assure you, señor, you cannot buy better at the market in Durango."

"True, true, es la verdad, por Dios," the Indian answered. "These are in fact very good burros. Of course, they are overworked and very tired. Their backs must be sore, also."

"Not so much, señor. Slightly, yes, one cannot avoid that on these hard mountain trails, climbing over the rocks."

"Yes, yes, I can see that. You have had a long trip, I presume?"

"Oh no, not so far," Nacho broke in without being asked.

Miguel pushed him in the ribs and said: "It is not quite as my partner here says. Right now we've been traveling only two days—that is, since we had our last resting-day, but we've been on the road for a few weeks."

"How many weeks?" the uncle asked.

"Oh—oh—" Miguel was looking for the right answer. "Well, as I said before, quite a number of weeks."

The Indian seemed not to notice the vagueness of this answer. "In that case it is no wonder that the animals are slightly overworked. I shall have them all right in no time with the rich pasture they will find around here and with good care." While speaking, he looked again at the three men, noting carefully their attire and observing that the shirts and pants and boots they wore could not very well be their own, as they did not fit. He did not let them feel his scrutiny, making it appear as if he were thinking about the price he meant to pay.

"How much are you asking for the burros?"

Miguel smiled craftily and narrowed his eyes, twisting his neck like a curious turtle and trying to give the impression that he was a sly old trader in horses, well acquainted with all the tricks. "Well, how much shall I say? Among brothers I figure a price of twelve duros should not be considered too high. What do you think, hombre?"

"Twelve pesos for the lot?" the uncle asked innocently.

Miguel laughed as though he had heard a good joke. "Of course not for the lot. What I meant is twelve pesos for each."

"That's very high," the uncle said in a business-like tone. "If I were willing to pay that much, I wouldn't have to buy them here. For that price I can get them in Durango at the market, better fed and without sore backs."

"I wouldn't say so, señor. I know the prices. In Durango burros like these, trained for hard work, will bring as much as eighteen pesos, even twenty. And then you will have to drive them up here."

"Right," the Indian admitted, "but then I can have them carry merchandise for my general store here, for my tienda, and so the burros would earn part of what they cost me."

Miguel drew his lips down. "I see I have to deal with a very clever business man who knows good animals when he sees them. All right, I'll meet you half-way and I won't insist upon the price. So my last, my very last word, and may heaven forgive me for being a bad trader, nine pesos each. I know you are not a rich man and have to work hard to make both ends meet, and this year we have had a long drought. All right, all right, I'm coming along; so that we may part friends and do more business some day, well, eight pesos each." He looked around at his partners, waiting for their appreciation of his ability as a great merchant and smart trader.

"Eight pesos is still too much for me," the uncle said dryly, "demasiado mucho. Where do you think I get my money? I cannot steal my money. I have to work for my living, trabajando duro."

"Make it five, amigo mio, my dear friend, and the burros are yours; and to make it a real bargain, with the saddles thrown in. What say?" Miguel stuck his hands in his pants pockets and swayed his body nonchalantly, as if he already had the money in his possession.

"Four pesos is my offer," the Indian said curtly, without the slightest expression on his face.

"Señor, you are robbing me! Seriously speaking, and no offense meant, you are pulling my hide over my ears, you flay me, you leave me naked." Miguel looked at the uncle sadly, and from him to the nephew and the few other villagers watching the deal, and finally at his own partners, as if he were praying for their forgiveness for robbing them of their inheritance. His partners nodded their heads mournfully, as though he had given away their last shirt.

The uncle also nodded, looking as if he had already known last night that today he would buy burros for four pesos apiece. He approached the burros as though he meant to test them for the last time. Without looking at Miguel he asked: "Do you mean to carry the packs on your own backs?"

"Oh yes, the packs." Miguel was startled. He glanced at his accomplices, hoping to find a satisfactory answer in their faces. He had lost his feeling of superiority and was looking for help from his men.

Nacho seemed to understand the glance. "The packs we want to sell also, because we intend to travel by rail."

"That's right." Miguel caught his breath. He was grateful to Nacho. "Yes, we meant to sell the packs also. But, of course, first we had to sell the animals."

"Usually it is the other way round," the uncle said casually. "What have you got inside the packs?"

"Hides. Mostly hides of all sorts. And, of course, our cooking outfit. Also tools. The shotgun, you will understand, we can't sell. You wouldn't have the money to buy it."

"Of course not. Furthermore, I'm not interested in that shotgun. I have all the shotguns we need around here. What sort of tools are these? Any use for us?"

"I think so," Miguel said. He was now himself once more. "There are spades, pick-axes, shovels, crow-bars, and such things."

The Indian nodded, meaning that there was nothing strange about it. He gave the packs another look of inspection. "How do you come to carry such tools across the mountains?"

Miguel became suspicious. He glanced around at his partners, squatting on the ground and smoking cigarettes rolled in common paper, seemingly not worrying about anything. "Oh, these tools—if you mean these tools—well—these tools, you see—"

Nacho came to his rescue. "We've been working for quite some time with an American mining company here in the state of Durango."

"Yes, that's right," Miguel blurted out, relieved of a choking burden upon his breast.

"You mean to tell me, then, that you have stolen these tools from the American mining company you worked for?" The Indian, for the first time, changed the tone of his voice.

Miguel did not understand fully the meaning of this hard, cold tone. He winked one eye at the uncle as if he wanted to make him his accomplice. Then he grinned, showing all his teeth. "I wouldn't say stolen, señor," he said. "That is a harsh word, and it can easily be misunderstood by the wrong people. Fact is, the tools are not exactly stolen. We are no thieves. We are honest traders in burros, in pigs, in cattle, and also, if opportunity favors us, in second-hand goods and remnants of merchandise, you know. We haven't stolen these tools. It was simply this way: we didn't return them when we resigned from our work. We weren't paid well, and so we considered these tools sort of back pay owed us by the rich company. It's a gringo company anyhow, so what does it matter? All right, you may buy these tools for two pesos. All of them for two duros. I think that isn't too much to ask. They are very good and useful tools. We're selling them only because we don't want to carry them to the depot. It's a long way down."

5

The uncle stroked his hair back with his hand. He rumpled his face, obviously thinking hard. Looking around, he seemed to count the villagers standing near by. He glanced at his nephew and at a few other men and nodded as if he had come to a decision.

Then he spoke very slowly, almost drawling: "I can't buy all the burros. I don't need that many. I shall call together all the people of this village. Each has some money.

I can promise you that you will be relieved of the burros, as well as of anything else you have, and when I say anything else, I really mean everything you have. I shall do my best to make it a perfect deal. Won't you sit down?" Having said this, he turned round and called back to the house: "Zeferina, bring the caballeros cool water and a package of cigarettes, marca Argentinas, and matches. Make yourselves comfortable," he added, addressing the three men; "it won't be long until I have called together the village."

He looked as though he had still forgotten something. "Oh yes, Angel, you will do these caballeros the honor to keep them company so that they won't feel lonely." Angel was his nephew, who had seated himself near the strangers, a friendly smile on his lips.

The uncle also smiled at the strangers when he left them.

In less than half an hour the villagers had assembled near the uncle's adobe house. They came singly and in groups of two or three. Some carried their machetes in a holster, others in their hands. Some of them carried no weapon at all. They came chatting about ordinary affairs as if they were going to market.

On arriving at the house, they went inside, spoke a few words to the uncle, came out, and went straight over to the burros, looking at them carefully and appraising their value. They seemed to be satisfied with the animals. Casually they looked at the strangers squatting in the shade of the trees.

After a while the women of the village began to appear, some with babies in their arms or bound on their backs, some with their children by their side. The older children were already playing about the plaza.

There was no doubt that the whole village was present to witness the sale of the burros.

25

When the uncle came out of his house followed by a number of men, the villagers gathered in a wide circle in front of the house. Some remained near the burros, bending down and testing their legs, opening their mouths, and feeling the soundness of their flesh.

The three thieves had been diverted by Angel, who told them stories and made them relate their adventures with women. Now, looking up casually, they saw that they were entirely surrounded, so that there was no way of escape. Not yet did they realize that this had been ordered by the uncle on purpose, for the men near the burros looked and acted as if they were buyers in dead earnest. Their first idea was that of all thieves and bandits: that they were to be robbed or double-crossed or even killed. This fear, however, was dispelled by the words the uncle spoke to the men of the village.

He said: "Friends, amigos y ciudadanos, here are tres forasteros, three strangers, who have come from the valley wishing to sell their burros."

The strangers, so introduced, rose and greeted the villagers: "Buenas tardes, señores!"

"Buenas tardes a ustedes, señores!" came the answer.

The uncle then resumed: "The price for the burros is not high. The community could use them, or might rent them out to the poorer citizens for a little money, which, after the

336

burros are paid for, would be of help for our school, since the kids in school need books and pencils."

The speaker paused and then continued in a different tone: "The price is not high. We only wonder how it is possible that you men," addressing the strangers, "can sell burros of this good quality for so little money."

Miguel grinned. "Now, see here, señor, it is like this, we need ready cash, that's all, and since we can't make you pay more we will have to accept what you offer us."

"Do the burros have a brand?"

"Naturally," Miguel answered quickly. "They all have brands." He looked round at the burros to read the brand, but found that the men had covered them all up.

"What is the brand?" the uncle asked quietly.

This question upset Miguel considerably. He looked round and noticed that his partners were also trying to get a look at the brands. He had to answer this uncomfortable question which had been hurled at him so unexpectedly. "The brand —well—the brand is—oh, you know that, it is a circle with a bar beneath it."

"Is that the correct brand?" the uncle called to the men near the burros.

"No, compadre."

"Right, I was mistaken, excuse me, it must be the heat, and I'm sure tired." Miguel became rather foggy. He thought his knees would give way. "Now, strike me, how could I ever forget it? Of course the brand is a cross with a circle around it."

"Is that correct, amigos?" the uncle asked his men.

"No, compadre. It is a C and a—"

"I know now," Miguel interrupted in great haste; "it is a C and an R, that's what it is." He breathed in relief.

"What do you say over there, hermanitos?" the uncle asked, undisturbed.

"I was mistaken, compadre," one of them answered; "perdone, on looking closer I find it was not a C at all, and the second is not an R, not even the third seems to be either a C or an R. It can't be even a bad B. Excuse me, compadre."

All the villagers laughed. It was a great show. A few shouted: "Hey, compadre, you'd better go to school again to learn what a C is when you see a Z."

The uncle, after the merriment had died down, asked in a loud voice: "Listen, all you ciudadanos de nuestro pueblo, all you citizens of this community, have you ever met in all your life with a man who wanted to sell you burros which he claimed were his and who didn't even know their correct brands? Tell me of a single case if you can. Come on."

The only answer was hearty laughter.

When the people were quiet again, the uncle went on: "I know where the burros came from and to whom they belong."

Miguel looked round at his partners. They knew what he meant; they also were looking for a hole by which to escape.

"The burros were bred by doña Rafaela Motilinia in Avino, the widow of the late don Pedro León. I know his ranch and I know his brand. His brand is an L and a P. The P is set with its back against the L. Así correcto, hombres? Is that right, you men?" the uncle asked.

And the men standing by the burros shouted back: "Sí, don Joaquín, that is the brand."

2

The uncle turned his head as if he wanted to find a certain individual. When he saw him he called: "Don Chuncho, come here!"

An Indian, simply dressed like all the other men and wearing only sandals on his feet, strode up, a shotgun in his hands and a cheap gun in a holster on his hip. He took his place near the uncle.

The uncle turned to the three rascals. "My name is Joaquín Escalona, constitutionally elected alcalde or mayor of this community, elected by all the citizens of this place and its vicinity, and legally recognized by the state legislature. This man here at my side is my police commissioner and his name is don Asunción Macedo."

The three thieves on hearing this official statement knew why it was spoken so solemnly and what it meant when voiced on such an occasion. It was their last chance now to run away. No longer were they eager to take along their burros and their packs. They were willing to sell the whole lot for one peso, had anybody offered that much, and permission to leave the village. But they found now the men were closing in on them.

Miguel reached back to his holster to pull his gun, the one that had once been Dobbs's, intending to try to shoot his way out.

To his surprise, he found the holster empty and his gun already in the hands of don Chuncho, who handed it to his deputy.

"What the hell do you want of us?" Miguel raged.

"Until now nothing," don Joaquín, the uncle, answered, his voice calm. "We are most astonished that you want to leave us in such a hurry, without taking your burros and your packs with you. Why, friends? We haven't harmed you. We are here to trade for your burros."

Miguel, who understood the cold irony of the mayor, shouted: "We may do what we like with our burros. We may take them with us or leave them here and give them away for one peso if we want to."

Don Joaquín smiled at Miguel. "With *your* burros you

may, of course, do as you like. But these are not your burros. I know the whole story of these animals. Doña Rafaela sold them some ten or eleven months ago to three Americans who went into the Sierra to hunt big game."

Miguel detected a hole by which he hoped to get out. He grinned and said: "That's right, quite right, señor alcalde. Those are the three Americans we bought the burros from."

"At what price, may I ask?"

"Twelve pesos apiece."

"And you are so rich that you want to sacrifice these animals for four pesos apiece?"

The villagers broke into roaring laughter.

Don Joaquín went on with his cross-examination with all the shrewdness of an intelligent Mexican farmer. He proved that the citizens of the community were wise when they elected him for their alcalde.

"You told me only a half-hour ago that you have owned these animals for a long time. Isn't that so?"

"Sure, señor."

"How long would you say?"

Miguel thought for a few seconds, then blurted out: "Four months, I would say." He remembered that not so long ago he had said that they had worked in a mine and that since then they had made a long journey.

Dryly the alcalde spoke. "Four months? Huh! This is certainly a very strange story. I might say it is even almost a sort of miracle. The Americans crossed the Sierra only a few days ago. Farmers out hunting and others working in their milpas saw them and reported them to me. When they were seen only a few days ago, they still had all the burros with them—the same burros you bought from them four months ago."

Miguel tried his smart confidential smile again. "To tell

you the truth, por el alma de mi madre, and cross my heart, señor alcalde, we bought the burros only two days ago from those Americanos."

"That looks better."

Miguel shot his partners a triumphant glance. They ought to be proud to have such a great leader.

Don Joaquín, however, did not let him get out of his net. "But there cannot have been three Americans, because I know that one of them is staying in a village on the opposite slope of the Sierra. He is a great doctor and medicine-man."

"The fact is, señor alcalde, we bought the burros from one American only." Miguel scratched his head and looked at his partners for assistance.

"Where did you buy the burros?"

"In Durango, señor, in a fonda where the American stopped for the night."

"That seems rather unbelievable. The American could hardly have been in Durango when you were there to buy the burros. Not with these heavy packs and not plodding up the steep trails back up here, as you had to do. You can't very well have met him in Durango and then already reached here again."

"We marched the whole night through, señor. Didn't we, compañeros?"

His two partners vehemently admitted this.

"What I cannot understand," the alcalde said, searching the faces of the three, "is that this American should have sold you his burros while he was in Durango, where he could find enough buyers and could wait a few days until he could get the price he expected. In Durango he would not have had to sell such good animals for twelve pesos."

Nacho, who wanted to show his cleverness and perhaps even to outsmart Miguel, came close to the mayor. "How do we know the reason why that god-damned gringo sold us the burros and didn't want to trade with anybody else?"

Said Miguel: "Yes, how can we know? Gringos are funny that way, they sure are. They don't act at all as we do. They are often cracked in their brains, see?"

"All right. If the American sold you the burros, where is the bill of sale? You must have it with the brands of the animals written in, the sex, the color, and the name they are called by, if any. If you have no bill of sale doña Rafaela may at any time claim the burros as her own, since they carry the registered brand of her ranch."

To this Nacho answered: "He didn't write out a bill of sale because he didn't want to pay for the stamps on the document, as required by the government."

"That's right," Miguel said, and Pablo nodded his head.

"In that case you would have paid the few centavos for the stamps yourself, just to avoid any complications. What are a few centavos compared with the many pesos you paid for the burros?"

"Well, we hadn't the centavos to buy the stamps in the public tax office."

"You mean to tell me you could buy the burros and pay, let's say, in the neighborhood of about ninety pesos, and that you hadn't the one peso and eighty centavos left to pay for the stamps? You mean to tell me this?"

Miguel, realizing that the net in which he and his partners were caught was tightening, flew into a rage. He yelled like mad: "Damn it to hell and chinganse sus madres and I don't know what else! This is going too far. What do you want of us?" He swung both his fists and looked at the men around him as if he were threatening them all. "We are walking peacefully on our way, pass this place quietly, and you people come up, surround us as if we were funking bandits, and keep us by force from going on our way. What does this mean? We'll send in our complaints to the state governor and make him dismiss you from office for abusing your authority, that's what we're going to do."

"Well, this is beyond my comprehension." The alcalde smiled at the villagers, then turned again to the three thieves: "You come here to our village without having been invited and offer us burros for sale. We are willing to buy the burros and we are agreed upon the price. Don't you think we have the right to investigate your ownership of these animals? If we did not and should buy them and they should later prove to be stolen, we might have the federal soldiers here in no time and they would shoot every man found to possess one of these burros as a just punishment for rustling and banditry. We might even be accused of having killed the former owner of the animals. What then?"

Miguel gave his partners a quick glance. "We don't want to sell the burros at all. Not even for ten pesos each. We want to be on our way."

"You might sell us the hides and the tools?" the alcalde suggested cunningly.

Miguel hesitated. He was not sure that another trap was not being laid for him. Then he remembered that the hides and the tools carried no brand. "All right, señores, if you wish to buy the hides and the tools. What do you say, compañeros?" he asked his partners, hoping to shift attention from himself.

"We might," they answered.

"They belong to you?" the alcalde asked.

"Of course, what do you think?" Miguel replied.

"Why didn't the American sell the hides in Durango? Why did you bring them up here to sell? Do you also carry water to the river?"

"The prices were not so good in Durango."

"So you thought they might be better up here in the

mountains, where we can get them without paying for them in money?"

Miguel was trying to think of an answer, but before he succeeded the alcalde said curtly: "Did the American go to the depot naked?"

"What do you mean by that crack?" Miguel's face paled until it was a dirty gray.

"Don't you have on your feet the American's boots? And isn't this man by your side wearing his pants? Why is no one wearing the American's shirt, which was fairly good, as I know from the reports? It was far better than any of yours."

None of the three rascals spoke.

"Why didn't one of you three take his shirt? Well, I can tell you why."

The thieves did not wait for the next sentence. With one jump they broke through the circle formed by the villagers and escaped down the main street of the village.

The alcalde gave a signal and in half a minute a group of villagers were after them, not even waiting to saddle their horses. The thieves did not get far. Their pursuers caught them before they passed the last huts and marched them back to the plaza in front of the house of the mayor. Here they were allowed to squat under the trees, lashed together and guarded by five Indians sitting close, with their machetes on their laps.

The alcalde came out, leading his horse, which had been saddled in the meanwhile. Before mounting he spoke to the thieves. "We shall go now and look for the American and ask him at what price he sold you the burros, and why he stripped himself to give you his boots and his pants. We shall bring with us his shirt and find out why none of you wanted that. Make yourselves comfortable here; we won't be gone long. We won't have to go to Durango."

The men who were to form the posse had gone for their horses. They put some tortillas and cooked beans wrapped in corn leaves in their little bags, made of bast, hung the bags on their saddles, mounted, and went on their way.

3

The posse did not follow the trail by which the thieves had come. They looked for the one Dobbs had used when he had passed by this village at a distance. Soon the posse found the trail of the American. The tracks left by the hoofs of the burros could still be seen, as there had been no rain.

Since the men were riding animals used to these hard trails, they soon reached the place where Dobbs had rested under the trees. Here they noted that not all the burros had strayed down the road to town. It was plain that the burros had been led back to the trees and from there had returned to the mountains.

The Indians realized that at this place something must have happened to prevent Dobbs from keeping his burros together. The tracks left by Dobbs's boots going from the trees half a mile toward town were found to be different from those on the road coming from the mountains and ending near the trees. The boots could not well leave the same imprint as before, because the feet inside them were shorter.

The alcalde decided that the boots had been changed near the trees. He sent a man to look for footprints on the road to town—Dobbs's footprints. They would be of naked feet, for he no longer had his boots. There were no such prints.

"Then the body must be near here somewhere," the alcalde said.

"They may have taken the body along and hidden it in the woods at the base of the mountains."

"I don't think, don Chuncho, that they would have dared do that. Many people travel over this road, small merchants and peasants going to market or coming from there. It would be dangerous to carry the body on this road. Let's look around here. It must be here. If not, we may still follow the whole trail of these thieves. Somewhere along this trail we'll have to look again for the body. Anyway, let's try here first, since we are here. I am positive we'll find him here."

So the men went searching about the place.

No sign of any digging was found under the trees or near them. The men circled the place, going farther and farther. There was a cornfield near by, where the ground was soft. They had looked about this field hardly fifteen minutes when one of the men shouted: "I've got it, don Joaquín. Here he is."

The body was taken out. It was still fresh and the features could easily be recognized.

"It's the Americano all right," the alcalde said. "He was the stockiest of the three, the fair-haired one. Get his shirt off. We'll take it along for evidence."

The body was carried back near the trees. The alcalde ordered his men to dig a grave for the dead man some twenty feet away from the trees, yet not in the field. With their machetès the men dug a deep hole and lowered the body into it. All the men took off their huge hats and knelt at the open grave. The mayor said a dozen Ave Marias for the soul of the slain. Then he cut off a twig and made a little cross held together by a few threads, kissed it and blessed it, and laid it on the naked body. Thereupon the grave was covered and the ground leveled, so that the place should not reveal a grave. But the mayor made now another cross slightly bigger than the first one, blessed it and kissed it, put it into the ground where the head lay, knelt down again, prayed, made the sign of the cross over the grave and three times over his own face and heart, and said: "Let's go now. The Holy Virgin in heaven will protect him and bless his eternal soul!"

4

The men returned to their village early next morning.

They went right to the thieves. The alcalde showed them the shirt and said: "We found it."

"So I see," Miguel answered. He shrugged his shoulders lazily and rolled himself another cigarette. His two partners grinned. Miguel chuckled as if all this were a joke on him and he meant to take it without offense. He had known long before that one can do nothing against his fate; one can't even marry the right girl, or get rich, or make a fair living by decent work, if fate does not decree it. Why worry?

The alcalde had already sent word the day before to the nearest military post, and during the forenoon twelve federal soldiers led by a captain came to take charge of the prisoners.

The captain on seeing Miguel said: "We know him. We've been looking for him and his two amigos. Last week on a lonely ranch he killed a farmer and his wife. All he could get was about seven pesos, because there was no more in the house. These two birds were with him."

The captain gave orders to his sergeant. Then he turned again to the mayor: "What are you going to do with the burros and the packs, señor alcalde?"

"I know the rightful owners of these donkeys and of the packs they carry," the mayor replied. "One of those Americans is a great doctor, just now on the other slope of the mountains staying with my brother-in-law, that is my hermano político, whose son he has awakened from the dead. They don't want to let him go yet because he can perform miracles of all sorts. I'll take the burros and the packs over to him, for I've wanted, anyhow, for a long time, to pay a visit to my sister, who has her Santo next week."

"Right," said the captain. "Then I have nothing to do with the goods. We'll shuffle off now. I want to be back at the post by midnight. My woman is always a bit scared if I stay away too long."

The soldiers took their prisoners without binding them and marched them off.

5

The trail the soldiers followed was hard, and they cursed having to guard the prisoners as if they were virgins.

Night fell while the little troop was still five miles from the post.

"Let's rest here," commanded the captain. "We need a good deep breath after these god-damned steep trails."

The soldiers settled down and had a smoke.

"Sergeant De La Barra!" the captain called.

"A sus ordenes, mi capitán!" The sergeant stood before his captain waiting for orders.

"Take three men and get the prisoners over to those bushes for a few minutes. But I warn you, sergeant, don't let them escape. I make you responsible. If they escape, I shall have you put into the guardhouse for three months, on tortillas and water. If they try to make their get-away, shoot to kill and don't come back telling me that you missed. You have your orders. Repeat them, sergeant!"

The sergeant repeated the order and then selected his men.

The captain lighted a cigarette and called a private who carried a guitarro to sing him the "Adelita."

The sergeant ordered the prisoners up: "Get your bowels emptied, you rascals. No, not here; over there in those bushes. We don't want to have that stink around here among decent soldiers. March off!"

The prisoners could hardly have reached the bush when half a dozen shots were heard.

The captain took his cigarette out of his mouth and said: "Now, what the hell can this be? I hope the prisoners didn't try to escape. That would be too bad."

A minute later the sergeant stood before his captain.

"Speak up, Sergeant De La Barra, what happened?"

"The prisoners, the minute we were at the bushes, tried to get away. They pushed Private Cabrera aside and grasped his rifle, so he fired and then we shot them. Private Saldivar and Private Narvaez also had to shoot, or the prisoners would have run away. Mi capitán, I have to report the death of the prisoners."

"Thank you, Sergeant De La Barra. You should have saved the life of our prisoners. They should have had a trial in court. They are citizens and are entitled to a fair trial as the Constitution demands. Of course, if they attacked you, tried to kill you and then make their escape, it was only your duty to shoot them, sergeant. I shall recommend you to the colonel for your quick action."

"Gracias, mi capitán!"

"Get your men and bury the prisoners, sergeant. You will bury them with your caps off, and cross them."

"Yes, mi capitán!"

26

Howard was a busy man indeed, wanted everywhere and for everything. He had hoped to find tranquillity in the village so that he might give his old bones a well-deserved rest after the hard work at the mine. But he found none. He was the famous medicine-man and the great doctor who could perform many miracles—in fact, any miracle ever heard of since the Bible was first written.

The Indians living on the Sierra Madre, like all those living in the mountains of this continent, are a healthy lot. They reach ages which make old man Methuselah a poor runner-up. But they are practically defenseless against diseases which do not originate on this continent. Simple-minded people, living a natural life, they suffer, as most people on earth do, more from imagined illnesses than from real ones. The acknowledged greatness of Howard as a doctor was based, as he alone knew, on his ability to distinguish between imagined, self-suggested sicknesses and true maladies. Another thing added to his fame: He had always a good answer ready for his patients, and it was always an answer which satisfied his patients fully.

A woman came to Howard to ask why she had lice when her neighbor had none. Nothing is easier to get rid of than lice. But with Indians and mestizos lice are as much a matter of course as fleas on dogs. They actually seem not to want to lose their lice. If the Health Department of the federal government goes after them too hard, owing to the fact that lice, like fleas, are transmitters of many diseases, the Indians are liable to rise up in arms against the government; they have often done so for similar reasons.

Howard knew the country and had lived there long enough to know the people. As a great medicine-man he had to make use of his knowledge. He could have easily told the woman what to do about her lice, but he didn't wish to lose his reputation as a great doctor. And as a great doctor he knew that he must not tell his patients the truth about themselves and their ailments or he might, as has happened to many an honest doctor, have to work in a coal mine to earn his living.

Howard said to the woman: "You have lice because you have good, healthy blood, which lice prefer to suck. Your neighbor has bad blood, so she has no lice. Lice are a clever lot and shun bad blood as your husband shuns bad tequila."

The woman was satisfied and decided to love and honor her lice as the best sign that she was a healthy woman. But five minutes later the other woman came, asking the doctor for medicine to improve her blood, which must be bad, for she had no lice. Howard did as all other doctors do. He prescribed a medicine, which, to make business still better, he himself manufactured by cooking up grass, leaves, herbs, roots which he was certain would not harm even a baby. The woman was so grateful that she would have given him a hundred silver pesos had she possessed them. Howard had to be content with ten centavos, all she could afford.

Howard's stock medicine was hot water administered inside and outside the body, the quantities being changed according to carefully specified prescriptions. He had an astounding aptness for making so many variations of the same medicine that he could afford to cure each sickness and each individual in a different way.

All the Indians of the region swore by Howard and his miracles. They would have made him president of the republic had they had the power to do so.

Sick men and women came telling him that they knew death was upon them, saying that they could actually feel at what place death had chosen to sneak treacherously into them. Howard, never short of remedies, never saying he was sorry that he could do nothing, ordered hot towels laid upon the skin where it pained, upon the stomach, or the calves, or the soles of their feet, or the neck, or the back— in short, wherever there was room for placing a hot towel. Some patients were healed within three days, others within two weeks; and others died. Howard explained the deaths by saying that the patient had come to him too late, because death was already well settled inside, or that the deceased was too noble in soul to live on this cruel earth and that the Holy Virgin had decided to take him up to heaven, to have him at her side. And if the patient had been known to everybody as a rascal, Howard explained his death as God's desire to save his soul by sending it to purgatory before he had committed so many sins that there could have been no hope for saving his soul.

With bone-setting Howard was not bothered. The Indians believed firmly that their old men and women, who had done these jobs satisfactorily for thousands of years, could not be beaten by a gringo who told of trains running under rivers and of trains flying through the heavens with a tremendous noise. They agreed, however, that such a great doctor had the unquestionable right to lie sometimes for his own entertainment.

Howard could have lived here until the end of his days and been worshipped and fed and treated like a high priest. Everything was at his disposal, for he was intelligent enough to live by the approved doctrine—that is, by doing what the people wanted him to do and expected him to do, never trying to reform anybody or change the conditions of life about him, never telling other people that they were all wrong and he alone right. And so everybody liked him and was happy to have him among them.

Yet he would not have been a true American had he not longed for a change, whether for better or worse.

Daily he was thinking of leaving. Suspicion of his two partners troubled him. They might take his goods and disappear. He consoled himself with the thought that, whatever might have happened to them, there was nothing he could do. He had to trust them and hope for the best.

2

One pleasant morning he was swinging leisurely in a hammock when an Indian from a distant village rode up on a pony and stopped to ask where the great doctor lived. He spoke to the owner of the house, who took him to where Howard was resting from the work of eating a whole roast chicken.

"This is the great doctor," the host said.

"Cómo estas, amigo, how do you do?" Howard greeted the Indian.

Before the Indian could answer, the host began to explain: "See here, señor doctor, this man is from a village far over the mountains. He has come to tell you a story which he thinks you might like to hear."

The visitor sat down near the hammock and began his tale.

"Lazaro, who is my compadre and who lives with me in the same village, was in the bush to burn charcoal, which he sells for a good price in Durango. He is a coal-burner by profession, you know, my compadre is. It was very early in the morning. Coal-burners have to be up early. The sun was just out. He was deep in the bush. He had just built up the wood-stack and was covering it with earth to keep the flames well inside, when he saw something crawl along the ground in the thicket. It was still dark in the woods, so he could not see clearly what it was.

"First he thought it might be a tiger, and he was very much afraid. He reached for his machete to kill it. On looking closer he saw that it was a man crawling on the ground like an animal, and that he was a white, un hombre blanco. He was in rags, el hombre blanco was, covered with blood all over and entirely exhausted. He had many bullet-wounds. He would have died right there at the wood-stack.

"Lazaro, who is a very good man, gave the stranger water to drink and washed the blood off his face. He left his wood-pile, which, anyhow, needed little further care just then, and loaded the white man upon his burro and brought him to our village. There he took him into his own house. When he had laid him down upon the petate, the bast mat, you know, he saw that the white man was dead.

"Neighbors came in to see the stranger; also the medicine-man, our native bone-setter, a very good old man with much experience, who looked carefully at the white man and said: 'That man is not dead. He is only very sick and very weak from loss of blood and the struggle to crawl through the woods.' That's what he said.

"Then he called for Filomeno, who has a good horse, and who should ride over to this village here and call for the white doctor who is here, because our medicine-man thinks that the white doctor might know better how to cure his own kind.

"Now, I am Filomeno, see, and so I took my horse, saddled it, and rode over here like the devil to fetch you, señor

doctor, and make you look at your brother. We all think
that you can cure him, for he is not dead, he is only very
weak, and you may know a white man's nature better than
we do. You can save him if you will come with me right
now."

"What does the white man look like, Filomeno?" Howard
asked.

Filomeno described him so well that you could imagine
the man was standing before you. Howard knew that it was
Curtin, and he felt sure that Curtin and Dobbs had been
waylaid by bandits.

Howard was offered the best horse his host had, and his
host and three villagers accompanied him to the little pueblo.
It was a long way off, and the trail was difficult, as all trails
are in the Sierra Madre.

3

When Howard and his friends arrived at the village,
Curtin had already slightly recovered. The women of the
house where he was staying had been more practical than
their men. They had washed his wounds with hot water
and poured into them mescal, a very strong native brandy.
Then they had dressed the wounds as well as they could.
One of the women had killed a chicken and made a good
broth with half a dozen different herbs boiled in it, which
had a very stimulating effect upon the wounded man.

Curtin had come to and had told the villagers what had
happened to him. He said robbers had shot him from ambush.
He did not mention Dobbs, for he didn't want Dobbs to be
pursued, on account of the packs, which might get lost
some way or other. He knew that with the help of the old
man he would get that scoundrel soon enough without any
outside assistance.

When he had given Howard a true account, he asked: "What do you think, Howy, of that deal he gave me? Would you ever have expected anything like that from a pal? He bumped me off in cold blood without even giving me a dirty dog's chance."

"But I can't see why!"

"Quite simple. I didn't want to join him in robbing you and making off with your goods. He played the old racket, pretending he had to shoot in self-defense, that rascal did. Well, I could have agreed to his plans until we reached the port, and there I could have said that the deal was off. But there was one thing I thought of: you might have come sooner than we expected and have believed that I wanted to betray you. It would have been difficult for me to explain things as they really were. He might have bumped me off anyway, to make sure that he would get the whole load."

"That's a pal, a great pal!"

"You're telling me! He slugged me in my left breast and left me lying in the woods. But now I can't quite figure one thing. I've got another wound I can't account for. I almost think that the beastly rascal came again in the middle of night and slugged me another one to make sure of the job."

"How did you get out?"

"During the night I came to, and thinking he would come in the morning to see if I still had a flicker of life, I crawled away. As I inched along the ground, I came upon my gun, which he seems to have thrown beside me to make it look like suicide or a decent fight. There were four empty shells in it, so I think that dirty rat slugged me with my own gat."

"Now keep quiet and don't get overexcited or it won't be so good for your lungs," Howard warned.

"Don't you worry about me. I'll be all right, if only to get that stinking funker. Well, to finish up. I staggered along in the opposite direction from the place where he camped.

Early in the morning I came upon an Indian coal-burner. When he first saw me he wanted to cut me into pieces with his machete. Then he tried to run away. I had quite a bit of trouble convincing him, weak as I was, that I was as harmless as a snail and that he should help me out and take me with him to his home. But then, on realizing that I was in terrible need, he was the finest guy you can think of, whiter than plenty of our own mugs. Without his help I certainly would have died a most miserable death, worse than a rat in a gutter."

"So it appears that our fine Mr. Dobbs has made off with the whole train, leaving us cold."

"Apparently, old man."

Howard meditated for a while; then he said: "Come to think of it, you can't blame him."

"Meaning what?" Curtin asked, as though he had not heard right.

"Meaning that I think he's not a real killer and robber, as killers go. It's rather difficult to explain it to you, with the slugs in you. You see, I think at bottom he's as honest as you and me. The mistake was that you two were left alone in the depths of the wilderness with almost fifty thousand clean cash between you two. That is a god-damned temptation, believe me, partner. Being day and night on lonely trails without ever meeting a human soul—that gets on your mind, brother. That eats you up. I know it. Perhaps you felt it, too. Don't deny it. You may have only forgotten how you felt at certain times. The wilderness, the desolate mountains, cry day and night in your ears: 'We don't talk. It will never come out. Do it. Do it right now. At that winding of the trail do it. Here's the chance of your lifetime. Don't miss it. You have only to grasp it and it is yours. No one will ever know. No one can ever find out. Take it, it's yours for the taking. Don't mind a life, the world is crowded with mugs like him.' If you ask me, partner, I'd like to know the man on earth who could resist trying it without nearly going mad. If I were still young and I had been alone with you or with him, to tell you the truth, Curty, I might have been tempted too. And I wonder, if you search your mind very carefully, if you won't find that you had similar ideas on this lonely march. That you didn't act on them doesn't mean that you felt no temptation. You may have got hold of yourself just before the most dangerous moment."

"But he had no scruples, no conscience, I know. I knew it long before."

"He had as much conscience as we would have had under similar circumstances. Where there is no prosecutor, there is no defendant. Don't forget that.— All we have to do now is to find that cheat and get our money back."

4

Howard wanted to go after Dobbs at once so as to overtake him in Durango or at least in the port and so prevent him from crossing the border. Curtin was to stay in the village until fully recovered, when he would join Howard in port at the Southern Hotel.

When Howard told his Indian friends that he had to go to look after his property, as Curtin was sick, the Indians agreed, though they were sorry to have him go.

Next morning Howard was on his way to Durango on a good horse. His brown friends did not allow him to go alone. They insisted on going with him to protect him against any accident of the sort Curtin had encountered.

They had passed the next village when they met on the trail the alcalde don Joaquín, who, accompanied by six of his men, were bringing Howard his burros and the packs.

Howard, seeing his train complete, asked the alcalde: "Well, amigo mío, where is the American who was with the train? I don't see him. His name is Dobbs."

"He was slain by bandits not far from Durango," the alcalde answered. "We buried him with prayers and with a cross. He is resting in a blessed grave."

"Did they get the bandits?"

"Yes, señor doctor, we caught them in our village, where they wanted to sell the burros. They were taken away yesterday by the Federales and will be shot for banditry."

Howard looked at the packs and found them smaller than he remembered them.

He dismounted in a hurry, ran to the nearest pack, and opened it with nervous haste. The hides were there, but no little bags. He ran to another pack and opened it with trembling fingers. No bags were inside.

"Friends," he shouted, "we must overtake the bandidos. I must ask them something. I want to know what they've done with a number of little bags made of rags and sackcloth which were in these packs. They contained sand and dust which we meant to take to town to be tested by learned men so as to find what sort of minerals the soil holds."

"It may take us two days to reach the soldiers who are marching the bandits to the military post. They must be at the post by now. We will have to take a different direction and be quick, for once these bandoleros have arrived at the post, it will be only two hours before they are court-martialed, and after two hours more they will be shot," the alcalde explained. "Then it will be too late to ask them anything."

He gave orders to four of his men to take the train to his brother-in-law's house in the pueblo where Howard was living, telling them that he and the white doctor would come a few days later as they were going after the soldiers.

When they were ready to start, one of the Indians who had come with the mayor said to Howard: "Oiga, señor doctor, listen, is it only about these little bags you want to ask the bandoleros?"

"Precisely, that's it, amigo, nothing else. I only want to know what they've done with these little bags."

"I can tell you, maybe, señor doctor, and then perhaps we won't have to go after the soldiers."

"Yes, go on, tell me, digale," Howard urged.

"Mire, señor doctor, look here. I was one of the men that were ordered by our alcalde to guard the bandits while our alcalde and our head of police went to look for the body of your good compañero who was murdered. Well, we were sitting there and talking in a friendly way. We even played cards with the bandoleros, because we didn't know what to do all the time. We gambled for cigarettes for fun. And of course we talked a lot. The bandits told us about their life, where they had worked and in how many jails they had been and how many times they had escaped and all the nasty things they had done. They wanted to show us what great guys they really were."

"Yes?" Howard knew that he must not press these people when they are telling stories. If they are interrupted, they become easily confused. He just listened with eager attention, even to those details which were of no interest to him. He knew the story-teller would finally come to the point. It was the same with his patients, who in explaining their sicknesses, usually began by telling how many sheep their grandfathers had owned.

"So they talked and we listened. Then they said that there were more thieves and bandits in the world than themselves, and that some of them look like honest, decent men. Pardon me, señor doctor, if I say this, I feel sorry to tell you, but by these ugly words he meant you and especially the American whose head they had cut off with a machete. They said that this man was as big and dirty a thief—excuse me again, señor doctor, for saying that about your good friend—yes, they said that this American was as dirty and stinking a thief as they were themselves. He was even worse. He had put among all the hides little bags filled with sand and dirt so as to cheat the poor man in Durango who was going to buy the hides late in the evening when he could not see well. The hides would not be opened; the buyer, trusting the American, would just look at the outside of them. Inside the hides there were hidden the little heavy bags with sand to increase the weight of the hides, which would be sold by weight, not separately. So when the bandits came to the woods, they opened the packs to see how much they had made, and when they saw that in these little bags there was only sand and dirt to cheat the honest tanners in Durango, they emptied the bags and scattered the sand all over the ground. I don't know where this was done, and the wind will have carried the sand away anyhow. It lessened the weight of the packs, and so the burros, with less to carry, could get up here in the Sierra, where they hoped to sell the burros, more quickly. Now you know, señor doctor, what became of the bags, and perhaps there is no reason to follow the soldiers to ask the bandits about it, since the sand cannot be found—not even the place in the woods where it was poured out of the bags, for it was dark, and they had left the trail, for fear of meeting people."

"Thank you, my friend, for your story," Howard said, with a very sour face. "No, there is no longer any reason to go after them. They didn't carry any of these little bags with them when they were arrested?"

"Not one," the Indian replied. "They had only the boots of the man they had killed and his pants and a few centavos.

It wasn't much. And a pocket-knife. Everything else is still in the packs. They didn't sell anything on their way up here to our village, for they met no one who could buy. So there is only very little lost, señor doctor. Everything is in the packs just as you packed it. Only the sand is gone, of course."

"Yes, of course, only the sand is gone." Howard meditated for a few seconds as though he wanted to get the whole affair well fixed in his mind. Then he let out such a roar of Homeric laughter that his companions thought him crazy.

"Well, amigos finos, don't mind my laughing. This is the biggest and best joke I ever heard in all my life." And he laughed again until his belly ached. The Indians, supposing he was overjoyed about something, fell in with him, laughing as heartily as he did, without knowing what it all was about.

5

"So we have worked and labored and suffered like galley-slaves for the pleasure of it," Howard said to Curtin when he finished his story. "Anyway, I think it's a very good joke—a good one played on us and on the bandits by the Lord or by fate or by nature, whichever you prefer. And whoever or whatever played it certainly had a good sense of humor. The gold has gone back where we got it?"

Curtin, however, was not so philosophical as Howard. He was in a bad mood. All their hard work and privations had been for nothing.

"The whole output of our mine could be had for a bag of tobacco, had we met the bandits in time and asked them for that sand." Howard again burst out laughing.

"You make me sick with your foolish laughter," Curtin yelled at him in anger. "I can't understand how anybody in his right mind can laugh at such a silly thing!"

"If you can't laugh at that, my boy, then I don't know what humor is. This joke alone is worth ten months of labor and trouble." He laughed until the tears rolled down his cheeks.

"Since I was robbed, I've been made into a great performer of miracles, a doctor whose fame is spreading all over the Sierra Madre. I have more successful cures to my credit than the best-paid doc in Los An. You've been killed twice and you are still alive, and will be, I hope, for sixty years to come. Dobbs has lost his head so completely that he can't use it any longer. And all this for a certain amount of gold which no one can locate and which could have been bought for three packages of cigarettes, worth thirty centavos." Howard couldn't help it, he had to laugh again and again.

At last, Curtin also began to see the joke and broke out laughing. When Howard saw this he jumped up and pressed his hand over Curtin's mouth. "Not you, old boy, don't you try to imitate me, or you'll burst your lungs. Better be careful about them, they aren't yet entirely healed. We need your lungs to return to the port—to return as men who have owned and lost a million."

Curtin became thoughtful. "I was just wondering what we can do in the port. We'll have to look for a living some way."

"I've been thinking the same thing since I knew that the sand was gone. I might try to settle here for good as a medicine-man. I shall never run short of patrons, that's one thing I know. We might run this business together. I could make you my junior partner. In fact, I need a good assistant. Often I don't know where to go first, and, you know, one man can't very well be in two different places at the same time."

6

The partnership was never formed, for the simple reason that when Howard opened all packs, he found two bags still filled with sand. They had either been overlooked by the thieves or those rascals had been too lazy to open all the packs.

Howard held these two bags up to appraise their value.

"How much do you think they might be worth?" Curtin asked. "Do you think it might be enough to run a movie house in the port?"

"I'm afraid not. A movie house would cost us slightly more. What I was thinking is what about a grocery store, one of the better sort?"

"Where? In that port?"

"Where else did you figure? With that oil boom on, man, there's always business."

"Oil boom. Don't make me laugh. There's no boom any longer." Curtin disapproved of this plan and explained why. "During the month before we left, I remember that four of the largest and best-stocked grocery stores in the port went broke and were closed. Don't you remember that, you smart promoter?"

"Yep, I admit it might be risky. You're right, the boom is over. But it's now more than ten months since that, and many things may have happened meantime to change the whole situation. What about giving luck a chance?"

"After all, your medicine business might be still better, old man. We'll stay here for another two months. Here we always have three square meals a day, even five if we want them; we have a roof over our heads and frequently

even a hearty drink, and there will be a dance Saturday
night with other possibilities of avoiding loneliness. It's a
question whether we should have that much if we opened
a grocery store."

"You said it, Curty. And just take into consideration the
plain fact that any damned fool may become a grocer, but
not win fame among the Indians as a great doctor and be
more highly respected than the president himself. To be a
good medicine-man is not so easy as you might think. You
can't learn that profession in a university. A good medicine-
man is born, not made. I'm a born medicine-man, I can tell
you that. Just come over to the village where I have my
headquarters. Yes, my boy, even you will take off your hat
when you see how much respected I am there. Only the day
before yesterday they wanted to make me their legislature—
the whole legislature. I don't know what they mean by that,
but I figure it must be the greatest honor they can bestow."

At this moment his host stepped into the hut where
Curtin and Howard were talking.

"Señor doctor," the host said, "I am sorry to ask you to
leave your dear friend who is so sick. He will recover all
right, don't worry, for he has had your good medicine. We
shall look after him and take the best of care of him. But I
have to take you with me, señor doctor, back to our pueblo.
A man on horseback who has just arrived from there says
that so many people have come to our village to see the doctor that all our folks are anxious. They are not used to such
crowds. So I beg you to hurry and go back home, so that
the visitors may see you, get their medicine, and leave our
village peacefully."

"There you see, partner," Howard said to Curtin, "what
an important person I am, and I want you to respect me
properly."

"I certainly will, señor doctor." Curtin laughed mockingly and shook hands with Howard.

"And hurry up, old boy, and get well."

"I'm feeling fine already. I'm sure I will be okay inside of three days. As soon as I can sit in a saddle, I shall come over to your village to see the great doctor performing his miracles."

Howard had no time to answer, for the Indians snatched him away from his pal, dragged him out, and lifted him on his horse. No sooner was he seated in the saddle than the Indians shouted, whipped their ponies into action, and hurried back home.

Printed in Poland
by Amazon Fulfillment
Poland Sp. z o.o., Wrocław

58606751R00217